her Husband's back before wrapping around him. Always strong, the feel of his back, makes Lauren pull herself tight against him. He shifts in his half-sleep, reaching back to grip her leg before falling limp in dreams again. She kisses the back of his neck gently, palm flat on his chest, wishing she didn't have to get up, that she could stay here forever. She considers the time she doesn't have and what her manager said would happen if she were late again. She reluctantly climbs out of bed.

Gary wakes at her absence. 'What are you doing?'

Lauren takes her time pulling a clean towel from the wardrobe, naked apart from her no-longer-brilliant-white knickers. The air is cold outside of the covers and her skin pimples all over. Lauren doesn't care though; with Gary watching her, she glows. Lauren loves how she can affect him, that he wants her. She takes care of herself; watches what she eats and enjoys her running, swimming. She's no supermodel but she can turn heads if she wants to with her genuine blonde hair and athletic frame. 'I'm going in the shower.' And with that she leaves him to himself.

After a hot shower Lauren dresses and is greeted downstairs by wholemeal toast and a small glass of orange juice. Gary is checking the news on his phone, leaning against the kitchen counter; an old T-shirt is fitted around his arms and chest. Even after three years of marriage the sight of him still makes her breath catch. His dark hair, tucked behind his ears artistically, his piercing eyes that command obedience make Lauren want him all the more. Lauren squeezes her Husband thank-you for the breakfast and checks her phone again. 'There's more on *The Prince*, Gary. Have you seen?'

'Yeah, I'm reading it now.' His face is stern but as his eyes go back and forth across the screen his lips turn up into his confident smoulder. 'Nothing new. Police are still chasing clues.'

Lauren scans the article for more but sees the time. *Damn it!* 'Hon', I have to go. Do you think you'll finish it today?' Lauren means his latest piece in the garage. Not everyone understands Gary's art but he is years ahead of his time.

Gary chews his cheek. 'Maybe, I'll see what inspiration strikes.' A lust enters his eyes. She knows he is close to completing his masterpiece. 'You're wearing those earrings?' He notes Lauren's white gold earrings with the blue stones in the centre, the ones he bought her after selling some of his catalogue to a collector in Europe.

Lauren leans in and pecks his lips. 'I love these earrings. Don't finish it without me, OK?' Lauren's eyes shine and Gary smirks back.

'Bye, love.' He squeezes her hips, thumb tracing the little tattoo of a spider hidden beneath her waist band.

Lauren whips up her bag and takes off for work. The morning has warmed up; she doesn't need to hug the blazer around her arms as she waits for the bus. The coach is almost full when it arrives; the only seat available is next to a middle-aged man with wispy hair and a duffel coat wrapped around him. Beside the man, Lauren checks her phone again but it is so she doesn't have to look uncomfortable. She can tell the man is staring at her legs, naked from the knee down beneath her pencil skirt. She shuffles away as far as the seat will let her and tries to pull her skirt longer. Lauren's stop is next, and she hastily gets off, glad to be away. The man in the duffel gets off too. Her office is a ten-minute walk from the stop but an alley cuts the walk in half. The alley sports bins as a year-round fashion and some diabolical smell as perfume but the short-cut is worth it. And she can't be late again.

'Spare som' change?' A rough and broken voice asks from beside one of the enormous bins, making Lauren start.

Lauren catches herself, hand on heart. 'No... sorry.' She quickly moves on up the alley. She glances behind and the man in the duffel coat watches her from the mouth of the alley. He hasn't moved a step, just tracks her every move. Without trying to look like it, she hurriedly half-walk-half-runs around the corner where her office is in sight. Lauren checks behind but the curve of the alley hides the other end from sight.

'Lauren! I thought you were going to be late again.' Casey tuts, her curly red hair bounces about her head, hooks her elbow and walks her to the front doors of *Cavendish & Son's*. The building is all white plaster and floor-to-ceiling glass; fourteen floors of office space. Lauren has worked at the firm for a little over a year and Casey is a friendly face in a sea of strangers. They were friends in school but parted when Lauren went to college. When she started at Cavendish it was like they had never been apart. Maybe not a friend she can share everything with but Casey is colour in a boring job. Casey lets Laurens arm go as they push through the thick glass doors. Inside, career people mill around, meeting their first clients or to sign in at the front desk to go upstairs. Everyone is in smart attire; shirts ironed and spotless shoes, you don't work at Cavendish with scrubby clothes. They join the line to sign in.

'No, I won't get distracted anymore.' Lauren lies, shaking off the shadow of the creepy guy from the bus. Gary in his white T blossoms in her mind and she wonders at how close she was from staying in bed with him.

Casey catches Lauren's far off look. 'You can't lie to me, *Mrs* Lauren Tanner. All you do is hump that hubby o' yours. His cock must taste like caramel.'

'Shh!' Lauren pulls Casey close, looking over her shoulder in case anyone is eavesdropping. 'Don't be crude!' She whispers. 'And you can talk, at least the only man I hump is *my* Husband.' Lauren pinches Casey's arm.

'Ouch.' Casey winks, mocking harm. 'I'm sure I don't know what you mean.'

'You free for lunch later?' Lauren asks as they reach the front desk.

'Should be. I'll drop by.' Casey straightens her skirt and brushes imagined dust off her front, making sure her bust is working for her. 'Hey Jerry.' She leans on the counter, resting forward so Jerry has little choice in looking.

'Hey Casey. How you doing this morning?' Jerry smiles upon seeing what she has on show. Jerry has beautiful dark skin with close-cropped kinked black hair. He's a big man, not all of it muscle, as security guards tend to be. He's friendly, if a little naïve.

'I'm good. Thinking of going down to O'Reilly's again tonight. You comin'?' She holds his eyes as if she is the only thing in his world.

Jerry doesn't mind though, his face would crack if he could grin any wider. 'I'll see what I can do, maybe just one this time, yeah?' He winks clumsily.

'You know me, Jerry.' She winks back and signs in. 'See you later.'

'Yeah, later Casey.' He shamelessly checks her behind as she steps through the turnstile before realising Lauren is there. 'Oh, hey Lauren. How's your morning?'

The man in the duffel coat flashes through Lauren's mind and she shuffles her bag higher on her shoulder, banishing the thought. 'Morning Jerry, yeah I'm good. You?' She asks, signing in.

'Never better.' He obviously wants to look after Casey but he resists.

Lauren can't help but look at his silver wedding ring, bright against his dark skin. She pushes through the entry bars and jumps in the elevator with Casey.

'So does it?' She asks.

'Does what?' Lauren asks, confused. The elevator fills with people going up.

Casey leans in but her voice is the loudest sound in the crowded space. 'Taste like caramel?' She grins widely.

Lauren nudges her away playfully. She gets off on Fourth before her friend, waves her goodbye until dinner. A pile of paperwork is already waiting on Lauren's desk. She grabs a coffee from the machine and gets to it. After an hour, there is barely a dent made in the stack. She pulls her phone out and turns giddy as she sees a message from Gary. It's a picture message showing Gary in the garage, hammer in hand, next to his current piece. The light is dim in the garage but his shape is perfectly outlined. His smirks but that familiar hunger is in his eyes, the embers within fanned from Laurens cold departure from their bed. He leans against the sculpture in the selfie; the piece that may yet be his best work. Unfinished, it is already a thing of beauty. He sells every piece and makes more from one sale than Lauren would in five years at Cavendish. Though he has his own audience, commissioning and biting at his heels for more, there are many who don't appreciate his talents. Like Lauren's parents. They say his work is disgusting. They never approved of Gary. They don't understand what he is trying to do. Lauren does. She sees the genius in her Husband's work and is proud that he is all hers.

Another text from Gary comes through.

HURRY HOME AFTER WORK, L.

DON'T MAKE ME WAIT.

G.

Lauren fantasises over the possibilities and forces her phone away to jump back into her work. After a few more hours Casey pulls her away for lunch. They talk but Lauren isn't really listening, her thoughts caught up in getting home.

After lunch, Lauren tries to focus but the pile of work seems to grow, not whither. Finally, mercifully, she finishes for the day. Lauren signs out and waves her goodbyes to Casey and Jerry in the lobby. She excitedly marches to the bus stop, glad the workday is done. The Sun is starting to set with a beautiful pink horizon. The view only sets the mood in her mind and she wishes she could just fly home.

The alleyway stops her dead and she thinks twice about taking the shortcut. She checks the time on her phone. *If I take the shortcut I can make the next bus...* Throwing caution to the wind, she sets her destination in mind and, gripping her bag tight, strides down the alley. The smell of the bins hit her, making her nose wrinkle. The dipping Sun disappears from view and the buildings on each side stretch up, blanketing the dank alley in shadow. The sound of foot traffic and bustle echo from the shops and restaurants on the other side of the buildings; distant chinks can be heard as kitchens gather momentum for the evening. The bins are overflowing, the paint on the fire escape doors is flaking, as the evening light fades the shortcut seems less of a good idea. Small two-door cars are parked close to the wall; store managers and staff who risk the bin men instead of paying to park up across the street. Lauren lets herself breathe as the alley opens up and she sees the main road, not realising she was holding it. *Silly. I've made this walk a hundred times.*

The last sliver of sunlight glints from her white gold earrings, matching the wedding bands on her finger. Ahead, she hears the robust sound of the bus as it nears. Lauren leaps into a jog to make the stop but an arm wraps around her waist, scooping her off her feet and throwing her against an estate car. She lands face first over the bonnet, her bag flies from grasp. Before she can scream, her hair is taken roughly in a fist and slams her head into the bonnet. Lauren slumps, vaguely aware of the cold tarmac beneath her, back against the tyre. The rings are pulled from her finger. The alley spins. Lauren can't make out her assailant but glimpses her engagement ring as it is tossed aside. The figure shoves a bag over her head and bangs her skull against the car again for good measure.

2. Inspector Roy Harvey

The splash of water from the precinct toilet sink does little to ease the itching his new stubble has caused. Usually clean-shaven, Roy sighs at the state of the man in his reflection. He would give anything to be back home again with his Wife.

The paper-towel dispenser is empty and Roy sighs again, too tired for any of it. He pulls toilet tissue from one of the stalls and pat-dries his face. Graffiti on the inside wall crudely suggests the Chief-Superintendent has an oral fetish but Roy wonders if anybody has ever let themselves in for such a tongue-lashing. Throwing the towel in the bin, Roy ignores the shadow of a man in the mirror and heads to his office.

The wall looks like the clichéd madman-walls you see in the movies. Pictures of the eleven missing women are pinned to the map of Berry covering the bulk of the wall; where they were seen last. Photos and evidence, 'clues', all connected together with different coloured string in an elaborate web of conspiracy. All relevant and irrelevant information grouped together to create an answer as to where these women could be. The women are between twenty and forty years of age, are different colours and creeds, from different backgrounds, live in different areas of Berry and have seemingly nothing in common bar the obvious fact that they are all female, married and unaccounted for. There may well be more, others missing linked to *The Prince*, after all not every missing person is reported as missing.

Roy doesn't even know for sure that these women are really connected. *But all of these had their engagement ring left behind. This one wants us to know he has them.* He scratches at the stubble on his jaw, irritated he hasn't been able to shave in the last week. He checks his phone, knowing damn well Emma hasn't called but still sighs when there is nothing from her. His Wife is missing also, he supposes. Except that she isn't. Roy told her about the affair, if you can call one ten-minute lapse in judgement an affair. Shockingly, Emma kicked him out, told him never to come back, to 'go back to your whore and die', were the exact words. She is physically fine as far as Roy knows but she is missing from his life.

'Nothing?' Nora asks, handing Roy a coffee from the mouldy machine down the hall. Her concern is genuine, but Roy knows it is half-hearted and that half born of guilt.

Roy pockets his phone and shakes his head, taking the cup. Nora Murphy is his partner, a young Inspector only two years in. Although small in stature, unaided by the flats she favours over other female Inspectors who wear kitten heels, she is a quick mind and Roy has no doubt will have a long and successful career. She is pretty, in a mousey kind of way, with big eyes and a petite nose. She is also the other culprit in his ten-minute lapse of judgement that got him living in his car, unable to shave and apart from his Wife. She offered for him to stay with her until he can sort things but that would hardly help his situation. His best friend, Carl, let him shower and wash his clothes but his partner, Shay, is Emma's best friend and wouldn't have Roy in the house overnight, or in the house for too long. Carl was ready to put his foot down but Roy couldn't bear putting another marriage in jeopardy over the same stupid mistake and has made do without since.

Nora evaluates the wall of facts, statistics, and outright guesswork, much like they have every day for the last few months since it became obvious they were looking at a serial-offender. There is just no connection to link these women together. 'We're missing something. Every month, Roy. Each one and we haven't been able to stop him. Assuming it's the *same* creep who is taking these girls there has to be something that ties them all together, it can't be random.'

It can, but I pray it isn't. If this sicko has no method of choosing then it's possible we never catch him. 'The longer I look the more obvious it is we're missing something.' Roy sips his coffee, wishing he hadn't. Every day that goes by lowers the odds of these girls being alive. There's not a doubt in Roy's mind that Sam Somersby, the first reported missing on their list, is already dead. He pulls her picture from the maze on the wall; white, thirty-three years old, worked at a deli across town, married, one child, last seen leaving work nearly twelve months ago, no known enemies, no reason for her to just disappear. Miracles happen but in Roy's decade as a missing person's Inspector he has never seen one that delivers back a year-old missing body, not breathing. He scratches his jaw again and pinches between his eyes.

'We're going to find her Roy, all of them.' She squeezes his arm to reassure him but he pulls away, not wanting them to have even this small amount of affection, like Emma is watching and waiting for him to slip up again.

Damn, I'm tired... Roy slumps into the nearest chair. What he wouldn't give to be back in his bed, Emma beside him. He always took pride in his car. It's his baby. Porsche, an old classic but kitted out with all the trimmings. Sleek, sporty, a car to make heads turn as he powers up the road but damn it was not designed for a good night's sleep. He and Emma don't have children, tried for years but it just didn't happen for them. He bought the sporty two-seater like putting in the final nail of the coffin on them not having kids. Emma has her paintings and Roy has his car; each their own to love and enjoy. But now all he can think of his gorgeous Porsche is that it is too small no matter how he tries to sleep in it.

'You're exhausted, Roy.' She watches him over the rim of her cup, like a nervous girlfriend. Roy knows what she is going to say before she starts. 'Why don't you stay at mine, eh? I've a spare room, no funny business.'

'No, I don't think so, Nora.' His response is automatic but Roy considers it. The thought of another night stuck at an angle in his passenger seat doubles his fatigue. He would have a mattress, and a duvet. And a proper toilet instead of sneaking back into the office to use the one down the corridor. But something *would* happen. As much as he loves Emma, as much as he would give anything to go back and stop what he and Nora did, to be back in his own bed, Roy would crumble if Nora made another move. He hates himself for his weakness, hates that his armour does nothing against the innocent yet effective weapon that is Nora. It's not even her. She didn't seduce him or trick him into bed, she didn't entice him with something new and exciting, they simply fell into each other and then it was done. Like the only two pieces in a puzzle finally slotting together to complete itself. It just happened. They both felt terrible, is why Roy told Emma as soon as he did. Nora feels guilty for her part but the look in her green eyes, how close she stands; Roy knows it wouldn't stop her again. Roy won't accept her offer because he can't be sure he would stop either.

'You're no good to these women if you can't think Roy, they need you on your game.' She considers before going on. 'Just get a good night's sleep and a shave, one night in a bed will do you a world of good. And your scratching is driving me up the wall.' She smirks.

Roy absently rubs his rough cheek and pins the picture of Mrs Somersby back on the wall. 'I don't know Nora. I think its best if I don't-'

'Inspector's?!' Joey, one of the hard-hats assigned to them for months now, shouts from outside.

'In here.' Roy signals but something in Joey's voice makes his insides tighten.

Joey all but skids through the door. He still wears his tac vest despite being told he doesn't have to while assigned to Roy. 'Just came in, there's another one.'

'Damn it.' Nora drains her cup and gathers up her coat.

Roy looks at the crazy-wall and swears. 'Let's go.'

***

'And what time is she usually home?' Nora is calm and empathetic as she talks over the details with Gary Tanner, Husband of reported missing twenty-seven-year-old Lauren Tanner. Gary is bolt upright in a living room chair with Nora opposite on the matching sofa. His Wife didn't come home this evening. After hours of trying to call Lauren and her work colleagues, after hours of panic, he finally called the police.

Roy, unfortunately, has heard it all before. *'She's never late.' 'It's not like her.' 'I don't know where she could be.'* Two thirds of the time a missing person has intentionally wanted it that way; leaving their spouse after a fight, running from debt, or simply moving on and not telling someone they should have. To find a missing person Roy's department needs to begin the search as soon as possible. The sooner the search starts the better the chances of finding them. But of course, nobody knows somebody is missing until they are. If missing persons were reported every time somebody was caught in traffic or their phone died then Roy and Nora would waste their time throwing unnecessary files in the bin.

Gary Tanner is slightly older than his Wife but not by much, thirty at most, Roy guesses without checking the man's ID. He's in good shape, tall, a fine-looking chap. His eyes dart to Roy and Joey every few seconds, fists tight in his lap, as if waiting for one of us to start something.

Roy paces around the Tanner's living room while Nora goes over the ABC's of Lauren's schedule and habits. The room is spotless. The chest of drawers has pictures of Gary and Lauren on holiday and at a party, one shows their wedding and another wrapped up in hats and gloves while out in the snow. The dining table at the other end of the room is polished wood; not a speck of dust is on its surface, as if it had been wiped clean only seconds ago. The carpet in here is fluffy and flawless like no foot ever set foot on it. Roy has seen the like before, some people keep a nice room, for when guests visit but this room doesn't add up. There's two things; one is Gary himself, he is as tight as a drum like he's expecting us to ask to see his internet history in front of his Mother. The other is the painting on the chimney breast; it depicts a man with four arms, making love, *if that's what you call that*, to a terror-stricken woman. The man grins like a devil. He holds an ankle or wrist in each hand, holding the woman down on her back while wings of gushing blood erupt from his back to envelop them both. It is one of the most disturbing things Roy has ever seen, and he once stood in on an autopsy after a girl was pulled from the river. Nora did well to cover her reaction but she has her questions to focus on, Roy can't help but glance at the painting every time he turns.

'Alright, Mr Tanner, we've got people at her office now but we're heading over to ask our own questions. Here is my card, Inspector Harvey's details are on the back. If you think of anything that might be useful, don't hesitate to call us.' Nora shakes Mr Tanner's hand and makes to leave.

Roy hangs back. 'Excuse me Mr Tanner, I understand you're an artist?'

Gary shifts his weight as if expecting to have a debate. 'That's right.'

'Is that one of yours?' Roy nods at the painting above the fireplace.

'It is. I did it for Lauren when we got married.' Gary Tanner softens at the sight, perhaps remembering a happier day but then he turns back, rigid as stone. 'I've had interest in it, a Swedish collector offered me 150,000 but it means too much to us. It was for Lauren.'

'You're... very talented.' Roy is at a loss as to what else to say. 'We'll be in touch.'

***

In the car, driving over to Cavendish and Son's, Lauren Tanner's office, Nora shudders when Roy asks her about the painting above the fireplace. 'I took one look and that was enough. Took every effort not to look back when I was speaking with him. And as a wedding gift? What do you think something like that is supposed to symbolise, for your new bride?'

'I haven't a clue.' Roy checks the database on his phone for any priors on Gary Tanner. The moment they met an uneasy feeling settled in his gut.

'He's telling the truth about the offers though.' Joey chimes in from the back of Nora's Ford, on his own phone, scrolling the search results from Gary Tanner's name. 'Says here he sold a piece for half a mil'. And others over the last few years.'

'What the hell are they doing living on Regent Avenue then? It's a nice place, sure, but it's hardly a mansion.' Nora asks as she pulls up by an alley across from Lauren Tanner's office. The headlights turn the alley into bright white before turning dark again as she shuts off the engine.

'Yeah, even my house is bigger than...' Roy starts but remembers he is currently kicked out of his house, that he hasn't spoken to Emma in a week. '...never mind.'

'Maybe you should take some time off, Roy.' Nora glances at Roy's barren phone with her lips in a tight line of pity, then gets out of the car.

Roy sighs and stuffs the phone back into his pocket. Outside, the night air is clear and bitter, his next sigh swirls in front of his face. The office across the street is dark and deserted apart from the lights in the lobby and several cars parked close, two unmarked and two in iconic yellow and blue.

'A few days could do you good. Emma would know you're away from me and you guys could... ya know, talk.' She pointedly doesn't look at Roy as they walk over to the office. She sounds concerned enough but cannot bring herself to show the lie of the matter in her eyes. Joey conspicuously hangs back, giving them privacy.

Roy pulls his coat tighter bout him, annoyed, not at Joey for giving them a minute but because if he is aware of their situation then others could be too. 'These missing women need all the help they can get, Nora. You said so yourself. I can't just take personal days. Besides, I'll only be sat in my car. She just needs time.' How would he feel if the roles were reversed after all? If Emma had slept with somebody else would he get over it in a week? *I'd take a few choice pieces of kit from the station and break the bastard's legs.* Roy scowls at the thought of Emma with another man.

'Roy?' Nora asks.

Roy had stopped without realising, Joey all caught up beside him. 'She just needs time. Now drop it.' He orders, sharper than he meant to. Nora looks like she is about to argue but lets it go. Roy changes the subject. 'What do you think of Mr Tanner?' He doesn't expect her to answer after being barked at, but she does.

'Uptight. Every time somebody moved in that living room it was like it was all he could do not to jump out of his skin. A bit creepy.' She explains, brow furrowed the way it does when she's trying to figure something out.

'Yeah, there's something not right there. Anybody that thinks something like that painting is a romantic gift ain't right, if you ask me.' Gary's body language was not typical of somebody who feared for his Wife either, or somebody who was comfortable talking to police. It's natural to be paranoid of being blamed for something but when it's somebody that has called them for help they are usually more open. 'It will be worth looking into. Lauren Tanner worth anything, we know?'

Nora recites the initial research she did on Lauren Tanner on the way over to the Tanner place. 'Not really. Her folks still work, nearly retired, no big money. If anything, she married up. Maybe she had an aff…' She trails off, tripping on the elephant in the room.

'It's OK, Nora, you can say the word affair. And it's worth asking. But not yet, let's find out for sure that she definitely *is* missing before we start exposing anything that can be left alone.' Roy leads them to the entrance of Cavendish and Son's where a flat-foot hails them. A bulky security guard opens the door for them.

'Thank you. You're...?' Roy asks.

'Jerry Akoum. I'm the security guard here.' Jerry is in civilian dress, having been called in from home.

'Inspector Roy Harvey. This is Inspector Murphy. Thank you for coming down. You know Lauren Tanner?' Roy asks.

Jerry scratches at the back of his head, disbelief draws his expression out. 'Yeah, a year or so now. I can't believe she's missing. I only saw her this afternoon. You think she could be in some sort of trouble?'

'We don't know anything yet. That's why we're here.' Nora explains. 'Do you keep an attendance log, or do employees sign-in to their computer?'

'Errrm... both. I got the sign-in book right here.' Jerry leads the Inspectors to the main desk and pulls a wide ledger from behind the desk. 'Lauren came in around 9 as normal... here.' He flicks through the pages and finds Mrs Tanner's entry. '...8:58.'

'What time did she leave?' Roy leans over the ledger. 'Five?'

'On the dot, yeah.' Jerry confirms. 'I hope she's OK, Lauren is nice ya know?'

'I'm sure she is just with a friend or something, you'd be surprised how often it happens.' Nora explains.

'Lauren usually take the bus right? Do you know which way she would usually go?' Roy asks.

'Eerrm... not really. Seen her go down the alley across the street before.' Jerry points outside but it is pitch black.

'Alright, thank you, Jerry. We'll be back. No need to worry just yet.' Roy shakes his hand and signals to Joey. 'We're going to run the missing person's route home. Take a final statement from Mr Akoum and we'll cover it in the morning.'

'Yes, boss.' Joey asks Mr Akoum to show him where Lauren Tanner works.

'Come on.' Roy gestures outside to Nora. 'Let's take a look.'

They head back over to the car across the street. The alley is total darkness with little light from the streetlamps reaching into it. By the smell there are bins overflowing down the length of the back street.

'You think she'd go this way? Or round through town?' Nora tries to see through the black of the alley.

'In this light? Common sense says take the long way. At 5 o'clock though? Maybe she'd take the alley.' Roy speculates.

'Well, we know she left work, so Lauren Tanner has disappeared somewhere on her route home.' Nora makes to investigate the alley.

'Yeah.' Roy asks, phone halfway out of his pocket. 'Where are you going?'

'Taking a look.' Nora paces into the alley, hand wedged inside her coat for the spray she keeps there.

'Be careful.' Roy calls back to the station and organises some more bodies to come down to do the information capture. He almost thumbs in the number for Forensics but there is nothing to photograph yet, nothing to examine. *Hopefully there won't be.*

The wind picks up and Roy follows Nora into the entrance of the alley but she's nowhere to be seen. Once in the shadows, Roy pauses to let his eyes adjust and in a moment he can make out the bins and fire escapes, the drains, and the air conditioning units higher up the walls. 'Nora?'

Grey steam filters from a vent a few meters in, the most visible thing in the whole alley. The dank passage turns so the rest is out of view. *Where the hell are you?* 'Nora?' Roy asks the night, louder this time.

Nora appears from around the corner. 'Roy, I found something.' She leads him around to the other end of the alley. Several cars are parked, and distant music and bustle can be heard through the wall from the restaurant on the other side. 'Here.' Nora drops onto her haunches and pokes the petite band of an engagement ring with her pen; bright, even in the shadow of the alley. 'You think this could be hers, Lauren's?'

Roy sighs, remembering the ring on Lauren Tanner's finger from the pictures in her home. He scans the alley for some other explanation but he knows there is only one. 'It's likely. Let's find out for sure.' Roy calls Forensics after all.

3. Lauren Tanner

'…think she's waking up…'

'…Hey, you hear me…?'

'…Hey Blondie! You awake?'

Lauren reaches to her throbbing head. She can't see. Her arms are heavy and pins-and-needles assault her limbs. Her wrists are tied. No, manacled. There is a slack chain about her, binding her to something. Panic fills her and she tries to pull away. The room is dark, she can't tell where she is. She is half naked, left only in her button up work shirt and knickers. Wherever she is, it stinks. She screams. 'Help!'

'Hey!' Someone shouts from somewhere.

'What the?! Where am I?' Lauren cries, pulling at the chain so hard her wrists could pop. She kicks against the padded wall beside her and pulls with all her might, but the chain doesn't so much as creak. 'Help! Somebody help!'

'Hey! New girl!' The stranger's voice shouts again.

Lauren spins around and flattens her back against the cushioned wall, the chain coils at her side. Her vision improves a little and she can make out the thick chain reaching from each wrist to a loop above her on the wall. A bucket is at arm's length in front of her. The smell of the room infects her nostrils; old sweat and waste. Two women sit against the adjacent walls. 'Where am I? Who the hell are you?!' Lauren rages. She heaves breath after breath in, panic making her chest tight, but the heavy stench makes her retch.

'Just calm down. We won't hurt you.' The woman tries to soothe but it does little to slow Lauren's beating pulse.

Lauren tries to breathe, forcing her blood to slow and second by second, her eyes adjust to the gloom. The room is large, longer than it is wide with cushioned panels covering every surface, walls, ground and ceiling. Old wooden stairs lead up to a door on her left, with a low-yield bulb above it; the only source of light in the whole room. A plastic lunch box sits within arm-reach half-full of water, like a dog bowl. The bucket in the centre of the room is the main cause for the smell; Lauren can't be sure but fears it to be a toilet. A pack of wet wipes is next to the bucket. On the opposite wall is a woman in the same state as her but filthy, her hair erratic and greasy. She is older than Lauren by at least a few years, but the muck caked across her skin could add twenty. She would be attractive without the squalor. On the wall to her right is an Indian girl of maybe twenty that Lauren, even with the grubby appearance and low light, can tell is a beauty. Her hair is so black it sucks light in, and her big eyes examine Lauren with pity. They are imprisoned just like she is, their chains locked to loops above.

'Where am I? What the fuck is going on?!' Panic rises in Lauren and she tugs at the chain again. 'Help! Help!'

'No one can hear you!' The older woman explains impatiently. 'It's soundproofed. See.' And elbows the wall behind her.

Lauren lets go of the chain and traces the padded wall with her fingers. The fabric is tacky and worn like an old leather sofa left damp in a warm room. She brushes her legs as if she is freezing but it isn't cold in here at all. 'Where are my clothes?'

'He takes them.' The younger girl says.

'*He*? *He* who?' Lauren's heart jumps in her chest. She remembers walking to her bus stop and was knocked down. She tentatively rubs the bump on her head.

'The *Bull*.' The younger girl whispers.

'What do you mean 'the Bull'? What are you talking about?!' Lauren spits, desperation lends strength to her paper-thin rage.

'Calm down.' The other woman instructs. 'What's your name?'

For some reason Lauren doesn't want to tell them anything. Her fear and paranoia guard her against all. She doesn't know who these women are or what the hell is going on here. But they look as pathetic as anyone could and wait for her to answer. She needs to find out what is happening, and these women could help her. 'Lauren.'

'Dhanni.' The Indian girl introduces herself flatly, like she could be nameless and it would matter as much.

'I'm Angie.' She smiles half-heartedly. Angie shuffles forward as far as her chain will let her. 'I've been here… I don't know actually. I was here before Dhanni but after Jo. What date was it when-'

'Who's Jo?' Lauren interrupts.

'She was where you are now. Before she…' Angie trails off, glancing at Dhanni as if she might upset the girl.

'What happened to her?' Lauren asks, almost afraid to ask.

Angie looks at Dhanni again. The younger woman just rolls over onto her side, facing the wall. Angie grimaces sympathetically. 'She died.'

Lauren's mind races. *Died? What is going on here? Where the fuck am I?! I can't be here, I have to get back to Gary!* 'Look, I don't know what's going on. Where are we?' Her voice shakes like the buzzing of a fly caught in a jar.

Angie looks at Lauren with pity again. 'We belong to the Bull now.'

'Who the fuck is the Bull? Tell me what's going on!' Lauren screams to be heard over the pounding of her heart.

A shrill scrape shrieks from the top of the stairs as a deadbolt is pulled free, making Lauren jump out of her skin. Dhanni hugs herself tighter but doesn't turn as if what is coming is an unwelcome non-surprise. Angie sits back against the soft wall and watches as the door swings open, resigned to the arrival of the stranger. Lauren sits open-mouthed as a thing from legend ducks through the doorway. Its body is that of a muscular man, with a thick chest and dark oiled skin that reflects the low light. He is topless but for a pair of black braces running over his broad shoulders, holding up loose fitting joggers. His head is that of a bull. Curved horns reach up from the head making him look like a monster from an ancient hell. The black eyes at the base of the snout glisten like black glass. The maw is closed but Lauren can hear the beasts breathing. He carries a tray. The light from beyond the doorway makes Lauren's eyes scream but she can't look away. This is the Bull.

Its shadow stretches across the floor as his terrifying form blocks the light and the entire room, this basement, their prison is eclipsed in darkness. Lauren cringes back against the wall, as far as she can go. As he descends into their pit the ears of the beast catch what little light survives, sparkling; rings, sewn into the Bull's ears like earrings, decorate the flesh in identical rows. He takes a bowl of food from the tray and lays it at Angie's feet.

'Thank you.' She says quietly.

The Bull doesn't respond, he moves passed and places a bowl in front of Dhanni. Finally, it is Lauren's turn and without a word he sets a bowl at her feet. A hot mush steams inside it. A small plastic fork is dipped into it but rounded and fat, like what a toddler would eat with.

Lauren is stunned and confused, can't believe what her eyes are showing her. She has been kidnapped and locked up by this monster. *Why is this happening to me? What does he want with us?* Gary's face dominates her mind and all she wants to do is get home to him. Her desperation overcomes her terror. 'Hey! Just let me go, OK? I won't tell anyone, just let me go home!'

The Bull shows no sign he heard her and climbs the stairs from their prison.

'Hey!' Lauren screams at his back. 'Hey! You hear me, you bastard?! Let me go!' But she may as well empty her lungs into the wall. The Bull ducks through the door and then the cage is complete again; the bolt slides home like a shrieking full stop on her pleas. Lauren erupts. 'What is going on?!' She rages at the other two. Without waiting for an answer she bellows at the top of her lungs. 'Help! Help!'

'No one can hear. Trust me, I've tried.' Angie shrugs and starts tucking into her bowl. She runs the meat around her mouth for a second as if checking the taste.

Dhanni is still on her side, facing away, like what just happened was as mundane as a local cat wandering passed her house. Except that every muscle in Dhanni is rigid. The girl is beyond terrified but the fact she didn't turn to face her captor shows she believes there is nothing she can do, no fight to be made. She has given up.

Lauren's heart beats like a drum. Her eyes dart up to the door and back to the women in front of her. 'What are we doing here? What does he want?!'

Angie seems absurdly calm, spooning food into her mouth and chewing away as if she is sat on a blanket at a picnic. 'You.'

'What do you mean?' Lauren asks shakily, but she understands. She doesn't want to hear it, won't say it, doesn't want to think it; her state of undress, Dhanni's reaction, it all screams one word. *Rapist*. The word whispers at the back of Lauren's mind, scratches at her thoughts and frost slides down her spine. *He won't have me, I'll choke him with this chain if he tries. I'm Gary's and no one else's.*

'He'll come in and have you in front of us. Any one of us, whichever he wants. Sometimes he'll take us upstairs and do it there. Best to eat, keep your strength up.' Angie motions to the steaming bowl of Bolognese at Lauren's feet.

Lauren's mind is a hurricane of disbelief and questions. Worry, panic, and anger swirl through her like a gale over the deadly sea of her fear. But now she thinks of it, she is hungry. It occurs to her she has no idea how long she was unconscious for and probably should eat. She picks up the bowl in a shaky hand and slowly takes a bite. Dhanni slumps and pulls herself up to her own meal.

The food is good. Of the thousand questions pin-cushioning their way into Lauren's head, one stands out. 'Angie, right? You said Jo died?'

Angie nods, finishing her bowl. 'Uh-huh.'

'What happened?' Lauren swallows, fearing this Jo girl was murdered.

Dhanni clears her throat after clearing her first mouthful. 'He puts something in the food. Paralyses you from the nose down so you can't fight back. Eventually, she stopped eating.'

Lauren stops chewing. 'What?' *Paralyses? The other woman starved, so that he couldn't...?* She throws her bowl across the room as if it is a coiling snake. She wretches, sticks her fingers down her throat to bring up the food. The half empty plastic bowl bounces off the opposite wall not far from Angie and sends meat and sauce flying in every direction. 'Why didn't you tell me?!' She screams at Angie and Dhanni.

Angie shrugs, flicking a shred of mincemeat off her lap. 'Better you just get through it. The sooner you accept you're here the easier it'll be. On all of us.'

'What the fuck?! You bitch, what is wrong with you, why would I accept this?' Lauren is out of her mind with panic. *I don't want him, don't want to be here! If I'm paralysed then I'll be helpless. What will Gary do if he finds out? If another man has me? He won't love me anymore. I need to get out of here!*

Angie's face hardens. 'Have you ever seen someone starve to death? Huh? Ever seen them sink into their own bones? I don't want to watch that twice in a lifetime so fuck you! Eat, if that means you get fucked like the rest of us then whatever. It's better than the alternative, trust me.'

'I can't believe what I'm hearing! We have to get out of here!' Lauren pulls at her chains again, bracing her legs against the wall and pulling until the manacles bite into her wrists, but they don't budge. Her throat is raw from screaming. She eyes the water bowl like it's a bloody knife pointed right at her.

'I don't think he puts anything in the water.' Angie shrugs, answering Lauren's thoughts but a smile plays at the corner of her mouth.

'Fuck you. I am not drinking that. What is wrong with you?' Lauren spits.

'I ain't starving and *we* ain't getting out o' here. So, I hope your fella' is above average-' Angie points at Laurens left hand, where her wedding ring used to be. '-coz the Bull is a *big* man. Get what I mean, bitch?'

Lauren sits back, dumbstruck with terror and helplessness, at the sheer gall of this woman. Her fist is tight around the chain, ready to pull again but she lets it drop instead and stares hard at Angie, like this whole thing is her fault. Angie stares back until after what seems like an age she shrugs and rolls over.

Dhanni eats her food like it is rotten, barely a few spoons and then pushes it away. Her eyes, Lauren now sees, are a rare blue. She really is beautiful. 'I misspoke before. You won't be paralysed. You'll feel everything but you won't be able to move.'

Lauren's breath comes in short rasps, she rubs her wedding finger, feeling more vulnerable for its absence. She is having a panic attack. Dhanni blinks an apology, a look of pity from such beautiful eyes fills Lauren with despair but the young woman offers nothing more, only rolls over again, leaving her more adrift than ever. Lauren looks at the bowl of food splattered across the wall and floor. Her fingers feel numb. As tears overwhelm her she drags her knees up to her chin and hugs her legs. With her face hidden from the gloom of the Bull's prison, Lauren sobs. She tries to hold it in but it is useless, she screams every ounce of terror she has into her thighs, screams until her throat feels like it has split to release it. But it doesn't leave her. She is as trapped by it as much as the chain holds her here. The numbness moves up her arms and she prays it is from pulling against the chain and not from the mouthfuls she swallowed.

4. Inspector Roy Harvey

The drive over to the Morecombe place is quiet. Lauren's parents own a small house on Wilmore Street on the other side of town. There are a hundred things Roy and Nora need to discuss before they arrive; info they have on the parents, the strategy they'll take while talking to them, how to approach the difficult subjects like Lauren's possible enemies and of course, to actually inform them their daughter is now officially considered missing. Either one of the flat-foots or Mr Tanner himself will have phoned Lauren's parents so at least the shock from the news will have smouldered down. But Nora keeps her silence while she drives and Roy, wishing she would say something, does the same.

After another few hours in his car and a rushed 10 minutes in the station bathroom to tidy himself up it was still apparent Roy had not been back home, at least not for the night. He had driven by his house when he couldn't sleep, back and bum sore from the passenger seat of his car, but the place was as dark as it should be in the early hours. Nora is mad at how stubborn Roy is being, no doubt. But what can he do? Staying at her place would hardly balm his Wife's current boiling hatred of him. He could *not* tell Emma if he stayed with Nora throughout this, lie, but he'd tell her eventually and then it would be worse. The ironic thing is Emma only knows about the mistake with Nora because Roy was honest about it. They were both discreet, only letting their needs overcome them when they were safely behind Nora's front door. Emma would have no idea anything was going on if Roy just didn't say anything. Aside from the infidelity Roy is a very honest guy and it is his honesty which has got him living in his car and brushing his teeth in the station's toilet sinks.

Forensics didn't confirm the wedding band they found in the alley belonged to Lauren Tanner; Gary Tanner did. He tightened, as if ready to explode into action, when shown Lauren's ring in a small evidence bag, but then he turned cold again. As if the heat within was turned down so his rage was simmering beneath the surface. Not a natural response, for sure. Something about Gary Tanner just isn't sitting right with Roy. Everything about him is off; his body language, his response to Lauren going missing, his art. Gary Tanner has something going on but Roy doesn't know what, yet. Maybe Lauren's parents, Bruce and Jill Morecombe, will help pin down Roy's suspicion of Gary Tanner. It might even be that Lauren is with them after she and Mr Tanner had a fight.

They spent the better part of the morning confirming Lauren didn't make it onto her bus, checking with the bus service and inspecting the bad quality video recording from above the driver's seat. Nearby CCTV has no coverage of the alley where Lauren's ring was found. Lauren is seen leaving work and walking in the direction of the alley. There are significant gaps in the camera's fields; it could be she followed a handful of routes to wherever and not be caught once on camera. Not for the first time in his career Roy seethes at the wasted time, spent confirming what they already knew. Every hour counts and now they are behind with nothing gained. *And the engagement ring means The Prince.* Roy sighs; *another picture goes on the wall.*

Wilmore Street is lined with semi-detached houses, cars parked bumper to bumper all the way down. One street-light is still glowing amber even though it is the middle of the morning. The Morecombe place is halfway down. They pull onto the driveway behind a two-door wheelbarrow with rust around the wheel arches but it is only big enough for their one car; the back end of Roy's Porsche hangs out onto the pavement. The house is pebble-dashed, and a shaped voile is visible in the window. Through a slat-wood gate a small back garden grows free, mostly taken up by a rotten looking shed.

'Ready?' Nora asks.

Roy never likes talking to the parents. They blame you for not doing enough, or from not preventing it in the first place. Expected, but unfair. 'Yeah.'

Nora knocks on the door, taking the lead, and Roy fingers his ID wallet, ready to show. A moment later an average sized man with half a head of grey hair opens the door. 'Bruce Morecombe?' The man nods, a question forming on his lips already. 'I'm Inspector Murphy and this is Inspector Harvey. We'd like to speak to you about your daughter, Lauren Tanner?'

Mr Morecombe has the expected reaction of worry but then he surprises Roy. 'Has that degenerate Husband of hers hurt her?'

Nora glances at me and then gestures inside. 'May we come in?'

Mr Morecombe immediately ushers us in and calls for his Wife. He wears toe-capped boots and streaks of dirt up and down his jumper. Roy guesses he was doing work in the garden. 'Jill?'

'Mr Tanner hasn't phoned you?' Roy asks, usually family break the bad news.

Mr Morcombe tuts and shakes his head. 'We don't have anything to do with that animal. It's because of him that Lauren doesn't have anything to do with us. He's a pervert. What has he done to Lauren?'

'What makes you think Mr Tanner has hurt your daughter, Mr Morecombe?' Nora asks.

Jill Morecombe shuffles through from the living room, some game show is on too loud in the background. She is wrapped up in a cream cardigan with her dark greying hair in a bun. Well-used flat slippers skid and flap across the floor under her feet. 'What is it?'

'This is Murphy and Harvey, was it? They say that animal has hurt Lauren.' Mr Morecombe rants.

'Mr Morecombe, we said nothing of the sort. Let's sit down and I can explain why we are here.' Nora offers the couple into their own living room.

Mrs Morecombe immediately scrambles for the TV remote and turns it off, hands shaking with worry. Mr Morecombe paces up and down the living room, barely controlling himself. Nora sits with Mrs Morecombe and asks for him to sit down too. He does but after a moment.

Roy perches on the end of the sofa. 'Mr and Mrs Morecombe, your daughter Lauren Tanner was reported missing last night.'

Bruce Morecombe's eyes flare up again and he looks at his Wife like she is a plague upon his house. Jill Morecombe cycles through the textbook reactions; denial, humour, this must be a joke, to panic and concern, wondering how this could have happened, and finally fear. 'What? Where could she have gone?'

'We don't know. We were hoping you might be able to help us with some answers.' Nora explains, her voice as smooth as honey, little notepad open in her hand. 'She left her office but never made it to her usual bus home. Do you know of anyone that would wish her harm? Might she have left on purpose, without telling anyone?'

Mr Morecombe's temper simmers over. 'That *Husband* of hers will have something to do with it. Mark my words-'

Mrs Morecombe drops a hand onto her Husband's knee, cutting him off. 'She wouldn't just leave, not without telling Gary. He is her world.' Her lip quivers gently from the shock of the news.

'Mr Morecombe, what makes you think Gary Tanner is involved?' Roy leans forward, curious. His gut-feeling about the man ever since they met has hung around his neck, maybe Lauren's Father can give it some substance.

'He's got something wrong in the head, that boy. Had a hold of Lauren ever since they met. She always picked the bad ones, in school and then that college boy. But with Gary it was different, like he was the air she needed to breathe! And all that "*art*" is beyond me.' He shakes his head to dislodge the notion from thought. 'Disgusting, it is. How does a man come up with things like that-?'

'Alright Mr Morecombe, we understand that this is a shock. We will do everything we can to find Lauren as soon as possible. But nothing points towards Mr Tanner, as of yet. Is there anything you can tell us, has she mentioned anybody following her, anything strange?' Roy digs.

Bruce Morecombe's jaw sets harder than concrete. 'No. We don't know.'

Nora doesn't miss a beat. 'Mrs Morecombe, is there anybody she might visit, friends, family, anywhere she might go? It's possible this is a misunderstanding, Lauren safe and well. You'd be surprised how often it happens.'

Jill Morecombe looks at her Husband sadly, rings her hands with worry. 'She hasn't really seen us since she got married. I don't know where she might go.'

Mr Morecombe wraps an arm tight around his Wife and pulls her close. Jill instantly breaks down, worry and fear taking hold of her. Roy, unfortunately, has seen it a hundred times before. The shock of hearing that your child is missing is exactly that, shocking. Then it settles on you that they are *missing*, that nobody knows where your baby is. That nobody knows if they are hurt or even alive. Roy can't imagine what it must be like. Mrs Morecombe sniffles and calms herself. 'I saw her at the supermarket a few weeks ago. She didn't talk long, wanted to get going.' She sniffles and looks at her Husband as if to say *where did we go wrong?* 'She was with Casey, on their dinner break, I think. They've been friends since school, maybe she knows where she is? Have you spoken to her yet?'

Roy checks his own pad and the list of names from Jerry Akoum and Gary Tanner; Casey Williams was mentioned by both. 'We're seeing her next. I want to assure you that we will do everything we can to find you daughter.'

Nora stands to leave. 'We're sorry to bring you this kind of news. If you think of anything don't hesitate to call. Day or night. Anything could be helpful.' She hands over a card.

In Roy's experience it is better to make the first visit brief, the family of the reported missing will never be much help in the first five minutes. Roy plans to call back tomorrow if Lauren hasn't been picked up by then. After a few cups of tea or, heaven forbid, a night's restless sleep, parents are usually more helpful once the shock has worn off somewhat.

Jill Morecombe jolts back to herself, cheeks still wet from crying into her Husband's arms. 'You don't think this has anything to do with those other missing girls do you? The Prince, from the news?'

Shit. 'There is no need to think so.' Roy explains, hoping neither of them asks further about the case. 'It could be Lauren and Gary had a fight and she is staying with Miss Williams. It happens.'

Mrs Morecombe seems to take heart in the possibility but Mr Morecombe just scowls all the more at the mention of Gary Tanner. They lean together again and support each other.

'We'll show ourselves out but please call if you think of anything. No detail is too small. We'll be in touch.' Outside, Roy blows out a hard breath as they head back to his car. The curtain directly opposite falls back into place as he catches the neighbour looking. 'We should have been told the parents weren't notified. Let's speak with Casey Williams. If she doesn't give us anything we better hope Lauren Tanner falls into our lap.'

Nora and Roy strap on their belts but Nora is looking passed the world in front of the windscreen. 'He is moving them somewhere, right?' She thinks out loud. 'There's nothing to suggest he kills or otherwise badly injures them when he takes them. No blood on the scene or anything, nobody hears any screams.'

'You're assuming it is a guy?' Roy teases. Nine times out of ten it *is* a male that kidnaps women. It happens, of course, but it is almost never a woman. 'We've tried to trace a vehicle before. Each spot of abduction is out of shot, no CCTV. We've no vehicle to ID. There are dozens of tyre marks but none that match from each site, and without a visual we've nothing to link them to.' Roy sighs, pinching the bridge of his nose. Saying it all out loud makes it seem hopeless.

'Let's talk with Casey Williams, and then we'll worry about being back at square one.' Nora is as frustrated as Roy is. She has been on two previous serial cases with Roy, both of which they caught the sick sonovabitch responsible. They have worked dozens of cases together but neither of them counts the cases where the missing person disappeared without foul play; if the missing person ran away, for example. Where there is a kidnapping or a murder, then it's a *case*. The Prince is the first case for Nora to go on so long though. So long that the media is up our ass and setting up tents. Nora's first case with Roy, Daniel Funder, kidnapped two girls and molested them. Funder liked to bite and leave his marks. They rescued both girls, alive but neither were the same after. The second case was harder on Nora. Matthew Garner, twenty-two years old, at university studying history, and infatuated with this girl, Vicki Allen. Believed they had a life together, were meant to be together. Roy told her it happens all the time, if not to such an extreme extent. Matthew Garner kidnapped a friend of Vicki's, Tanya Melrose, thinking she was responsible for keeping him and Vicki apart. He strung her up by the wrists with chicken wire in a utility room beneath the university. It was Nora that saw Matthew watching Vicki on the university security feed and made the link that his Uncle used to work there as a cleaner. Matthew stole a spare set of keys from his Uncle and made the poor girl pay for what he thought she was doing to his *relationship*. Tanya died, from dehydration and her injuries. Matthew Garner killed himself in custody. Roy praised Nora for who knows who Matthew Garner would have worked into his fantasy and blamed next. But Nora could only think they should have been faster, a day, an hour, and they would have brought her home alive.

Nora sighs and starts the engine.

'You're thinking about the Garner case.' Roy states, knowing she is.

'I try not to.' Nora sighs again. 'But we need something Roy, anything to go on. As soon as I saw the look on Garner's face, I knew. Everything fell into place after that. With Lauren Tanner, assuming she is another one of the Prince, like Joanne Hannah, like Penny Wainright, like Dhanni Sandhu, and all the others, there got to be something. But I can't see it yet!'

The eleven women, twelve now including Lauren Tanner, have been missing a lot longer than any Nora has worked on. The oldest reported missing a little under twelve months ago. Similar circumstances surround each suspected kidnapping. No CCTV footage. No witnesses. And the victim's engagement ring left behind. It could be the jewellery were lost, dropped as they went on their way. Roy doesn't think so. It's too much of a coincidence. The rings were left to prove *he* has them. 'You should prepare yourself Nora. Twelve months is a long time. We won't get all these girls back. We may not catch this guy at all.'

Roy warns. As much as it grates on him it is an all too painful fact that sometimes the bastards get away.

Nora would turn to look at Roy as if he's gone mad but she can't take her eyes off the road. 'What? Where the hell has that come from? Don't you give up on these women, Roy. We're all they've got.'

Roy slumps back into his seat, ignoring the familiar ache in his back from trying to sleep here, wishing he hadn't spoken. 'I'm not giving up. We'll get him, I'm sure. But this one is careful. We should be realistic, is all I'm saying.'

'I'm not an idiot, Roy! I know the likelihood of getting them all back. But that doesn't mean we slow down. Something will lead us to him. And we'll save as many as we can.' Nora keeps her eyes forward and Roy is glad of it for the disgust in her eyes.

Good. A spiteful voice in his head shouts. Maybe he can get back into his own house if Nora is mad at him. But then he softens and almost wishes they were both back at Nora's place. He shakes his head clear but is suddenly aware that he didn't flinch at Nora driving his car when he used to make so much fuss when Emma got behind the wheel. 'You're right. We'll find something. Let's see what Casey Williams has to say. Then start from the beginning. We're missing something but we'll find it.'

Nora finally glances at Roy and that dangerous look is in her eye. Not anger or disgust, she believes what Roy preaches; she believes in him. It's the look that got Roy in trouble in the first place.

5. Lauren Tanner

Lauren hasn't slept a moment. The only sound in here comes from the three of them; shallow snores, movement on the worn cushioned panels. The absence of any other sound, of the rest of the world, is like a weight around her neck. The looming threat of that bolt shrieking free and that monster coming back has widened her senses to their extreme. Her sight, her hearing, she screams for clues of his approach, for something that can help her. But there is nothing, just the rancid smell and throbbing in her wrists. The other woman, Angie, is crazy. *How can she say things like that, think like that?* Lauren hates her, blames her for this whole thing. Deep down she knows it's not her fault but she can't help but stare daggers into the woman's back all the same.

After a few hours she stops burning holes into Angie and focuses on finding a way out. Dhanni and Angie both sleep as if this is a camping trip. Lauren spies every inch of the basement. The chain about to her wrists will only let her reach a few feet but now her eyesight has adjusted to the gloom she can see the rest of the room. Every inch of the walls and ceiling is padded in the same cushioned panels. The chain loops are bolted directly through them. The only thing that isn't padded is the door and the stairs, but they are at least ten feet away and far out of reach. With no immediate way of escape she pulls at her chain again but the strain on her chaffed and cut skin is agony. She can't pull her way free. She isn't strong enough, and she's hungry.

Lauren eye's the mush splattered across the wall and floor from her bowl of food. She licks her lips, remembering how good it tasted but then thrashes against the wall at the helplessness of her situation. *I can't eat. I won't.* She is Gary's and no other. She won't let that animal have her.

There are no windows to tell if it is day or night, her phone was in her bag; Lauren has no idea how to measure time. Not knowing how long she has been here is almost as frustrating as not being able to leave. She imagines how worried Gary must be and how cruel it is that the world can just keep on turning when she is stuck in this pit. Her stomach groans like a creaking ship so she guesses it must have been a day. Angie stirs in her sleep, facing the wall still. *What the hell is her problem anyway?*

As if hearing her thoughts, Angie stretches, arcing her back and pointing her toes like a cat. She lets out a deep yawn and rolls over. 'Oh hey, good morning.'

Lauren scowls back.

'Well, maybe not morning but-' Angie looks up and around and shrugs. 'You didn't sleep? Don't worry, I didn't the first few nights either.' She yawns again and sits up, playing with the chain between her fingers.

'How can you be OK with this? You don't want to get out?' Lauren snaps.

'Show me how and I'm game.' Angie rattles her chain to point out the obvious. Lauren scowls, grips her own chain to pull free but lets it drop. 'Listen honey, I wasn't the first girl in here and you won't be the last. Just ride the wave. You'll be happier.' Angie is so blasé about this nightmare that Lauren is dumbstruck. How can a woman accept this treatment, this attack on her life?

'And what happened to the others?!' Lauren fears, suspecting the obvious.

Angie is silent for a moment, chewing her words. 'He took them away.'

'What?' Lauren jumps on the topic of being somewhere other than here, that maybe somebody made it out. 'Took them where?'

'I dunno. Sometimes he takes us upstairs when he wants us. Sometimes he washes us, stops us getting too dirty, shaves our legs.' She explains as if this is perfectly fucking normal, like it's a treat. 'The others, they didn't come back. Reckon he gets tired of us and lets us go after a while?' Angie snorts at her own suggestion, like she's telling a bad joke.

Lauren sits back. Fear eats her anger away and creeps into her belly again, the thought of somebody else having her makes her insides crawl. Moreover, that she could never see her home again, her Gary. Does the Bull kill his victims if they don't play along, when he gets bored? Her next question opens a chasm in her already empty belly. 'How long have you been here?'

Angie considers and shrugs. 'I was shopping, last thing I remember. That was September-'

'September? Last year?!' Lauren's stomach twists into a knot.

'Was it? Fuck. You here that, Dhanni? I think I broke Jo's record.' Angie barks a dry laugh over at the other girl. 'Dhanni?'

Dhanni doesn't respond, she must be asleep.

'Hey Dhanni, don't be rude. We have a guest ha-ha.' Angie shuffles down the wall as far as her manacles will allow. 'Dhanni…? Oh. I guess it's you today.'

Lauren stares hard into Dhanni's back, as if she can look right through her to the heart of the matter. 'What's going on? Is she OK?' But Lauren sees the truth.

'She'll be fine. After.' Angie settles back, something close to sympathy saddens her eyes but then her cocky mask is back in place.

'Wh-what? We need to do something! Dhanni, right? Can you hear me?' Lauren cranes over but can't see the girls face. A barely audible mumble emits from the girl. Dhanni is trying to talk but her lips won't move right. 'Hey! Move!'

'It's no good. She'll be like it for hours. He'll be down soon I expect.' Angie nods to the door.

Lauren lurches away from the wall making the chain whip tight, desperate to get to Dhanni, to help her somehow. 'No, there has to be something we can do!'

'Be my guest.' Angie offers up her own hands, rattling her chain again.

'But-' The bolt is pulled free, flooding their prison with its shrill shriek. Lauren flattens herself back against the wall as if she can avoid being seen, eyes so wide her face aches. The door swings open and the Bull steps through, ducking so his horns don't catch the lintel. He slips the joggers from bottom half and stands completely naked apart from the mask, watching them through glassy, black eyes. The animal's fur drinks in the light whereas the man's body glistens as if he has stepped from a bath of oil. He thuds down the stairs with definite purpose. His manhood swings between his legs, not quite erect but the closer he gets the more ready he seems to be. As the Bull steps between them Lauren presses herself into the wall, wanting to sink into it and disappear. She needn't bother though; his intention is on Dhanni. Lauren and Angie could be invisible for all he sees them. The room is wide enough for him to march passed freely even if both Lauren and Angie stretched forward as far as their chains would let them, but neither of them do. Even if Lauren wasn't frozen stiff she couldn't get to Dhanni or in this monsters way.

Still Dhanni doesn't move. Angie looks on as if watching a re-run seen a hundred times before. Lauren would snap the chains from the wall, tear away up the stairs and leap into Gary's arms. But she can't. The manacles hold her as securely as before, refusing to let her go as this animal descends on his prey.

The Bull discards his bottoms and drops to his knees. Barely controlled grunts of anticipation escape the beast. He hoists the chain up, along with Dhanni's limp form like she weighs no more than a doll. He holds the chain up so that Dhanni hangs painfully forward, knees on the ground but arms pulled disgustingly upright behind her. The pressure on Dhanni's wrists and shoulders must be immense. She is helpless, cannot stop him. Her head is dead weight, hair across her face as the Bull manipulates her body to where he wants her.

Lauren can do nothing but look on, plastered against the wall. A part of her wants to help the poor girl but a much larger, stronger part of her just wants this animal to leave. Their jailer, this dark fiend is now fully erect, and Lauren can't help but stare at it like it is a knife at her eye. Angie was right; he is a big man, but it doesn't excite or impress. She is terrified and wants to go home.

The Bull takes his erection, the tip a foot in front of his hips and guides it into Dhanni from behind. She was trying to talk before, but Lauren could barely here her. They have no trouble hearing her now, a desperate half-scream emits from Dhanni's numb throat. A low growl of pleasure comes from the Bull. Lauren cringes back as tears race down her face. Her mouth is contorted in horror as the Bull ruts back and forth, his strong arms and back pulling Dhanni's limp form into him over and over.

Dhanni is trapped in her own head and there is nothing she can do as this animal fucks her from behind. *Rape.* The word is written in oil through her mind and the Bull is a blow torch. The sight of it ignites the true horror of the word and it is all Lauren can do not to pull her arms off as she heaves on the chain, desperation giving her body new strength. Hearing about the disgusting crimes that rapists do on the news is a far cry from seeing it right in front of you.

It goes on forever. The Bull's barks of pleasure get louder and louder until finally he slows and pulls out of Dhanni. He lets her drop onto her face, butt in the air and awkward as he holds one of her hips steady so he can finish on the small of her back, splashing and soiling her dirty blouse. After a moment of catching his breath he lets her sink down, almost lifeless. He strokes the hair out of her eyes and mouth, like a Father checking his child in their sleep. The Bull leaves her there, wet and defiled, and turns to Lauren.

The Bull's eyes bore into her. The diamond rings threaded into the ears dance with reflected light. Her nails dig into the panel behind so hard she could rip them. Out of the corner of her eye she sees Angie watching this beast; that stole them from their lives, has locked them up, who rapes them, and she who has been captive here for months lets an amused smile play at the edge of her mouth. Lauren can't look away, can't get away, can't even breathe as the Bull climbs to his feet, every muscle now loose but powerful all the same and steps toward her, and he leaves. The door slams shut and the bolt screeches home.

Lauren's lungs remember how to contract and she heave great relieved breaths. Lauren looks at Angie in shock and then at Dhanni, the Indian beauties eyes wide and helpless, limbs heavier than a tonne of bricks, and back again.

'It's not so bad, Blondie.' Angie stretches and leans back on an elbow. 'He's probably the best you'll ever have, ha-ha.'

Lauren is speechless. What can she say after what she just witnessed, what just happened to Dhanni. 'My Husband is the only one I want!' Lauren cries.

'*Want* has nothing to do with this, it'll be your turn soon enough.' Angie sneers.

'What the fuck is wrong with you? I don't understand! How you can be like this?' Lauren can't believe this woman. This is a living nightmare and she's acting like it is as normal as waiting for a bus.

'And what is the alternative? Huh? Freak out, panic, like you?' Angie looks Lauren up and down; her still-smooth legs and work shirt not yet dirtied by this place. There is a look of longing in her gaze, fleeting, and she smoothers it straight away. Remembering when she was clean perhaps, maybe a Husband of her own? 'I did my freaking out, more than my share. Ain't going to get us out now is it? Better you just accept it.'

Lauren sulks. There is no way that will happen. No way she can let what she just witnessed happen to her. There must be something she can do.

A gentle whimper comes from Dhanni, and Lauren instinctively edges towards the girl. Her eyes are wide open but the rest of her body is still paralysed. 'Is she OK?' Lauren asks, not knowing what to do.

'She'll be fine in a bit. You might get pins-and-needles, I always do, but other than the fucking, he doesn't hurt us.' Angie looks at Dhanni like a Mother sitting patiently while their child is examined by the doctor, wanting to lean out and hold her hand to comfort her.

'Doesn't hurt..? Look at us! We are in a fucking dungeon! *He* is a rapist!' Lauren screams. Angie's calm demeanour in the face of this situation is kindling in the furnace of Lauren's emotions.

'You know what?' Angie climbs to the balls of her feet, pulling her knickers to her ankles and the nearby bucket between her legs. A deep sound of rushing water echoes as Angie relieves herself. Lauren wrinkles her nose and looks away, not knowing what to do. 'Get it all out o' your system. Call me a bitch, scream at us, at him, scream as much as you like! I don't care. Just leave the attitude. You won't think you're better than us after he's had you.'

Lauren would punch Angie in the face but her words are a kick to the gut. 'I don't think-'

'Oh please, you're still thinking you can stop this from happening. Maybe planning how you'll fight him or free yourself. But really you're just panicking because you don't want to end up like us.' Angie finishes on the bucket and wipes herself, pulls her underwear back up, and drops the bucket as far away as she can and still have it in reach. 'We're here, like it or not. Don't you fuckin' dare pity us. Dhanni, right now, helpless as she is, is stronger than you've ever been. Don't you fuckin' dare.' She seethes with more venom than Lauren has ever heard from a person. With that she scoops up the pack of wet-wipes and tosses them next to Dhanni. She must really care for the young woman.

Lauren wants to rage and scream but she slumps. *What am I going to do?*

6. Inspector Roy Harvey

Casey Williams is distraught. Her shoulders shudder with each sob, shaking Roy as he tries to comfort the woman. Casey clings to Roy as if she would collapse without him to lean on. Miss Williams' home is clean but she keeps a 'lived-in' house, unlike the Tanner house where everything was ready for examination; a clothes-horse stands with drying clothes scattered on it, the sink has cutlery in it with two wine glasses, stained red from wine and lipstick, as many magazines as cushions cover her sofa. Casey's perfume is overpowering as each curl of her fiery hair fights to climb up Roy's nose. Roy half hugs the woman, awkwardly perched on the end of the sofa with Miss Williams leant in so close she may as well be sat on his lap.

Nora is on the other side of Casey, one eyebrow so far up her forehead it might pluck itself off and shoot into the ceiling. She stares burning holes into Miss Williams' back but their host is oblivious as she heaves great sobs into Roy's chest. Roy tries to apologise with his eyes, not wanting to say anything and make this more inappropriate than it already is. He instantly angers himself, feeling like he needs to explain something like this to Nora, like he owes her something in respect, to keep her happy. Even if they were together, which they certainly are not, he wouldn't have to justify this. Annoyed, Roy peels Miss Williams from around him, serious now. 'Miss Williams, we understand this is a difficult time but we need to ask you some more questions.' He is abrupt but it seems to be a balm to her sorrow.

Casey sniffles. Her sobs ebb away and she slumps back into the sofa, magazines crinkling underneath her, drying her eyes with a tissue from a box. 'Of-of-of-course.' She blows her nose, louder than Roy would have thought possible from such a tiny nose.

Nora doesn't show any of the usual sympathy she affects when dealing with those nearest and dearest to the missing, instead she bulls right ahead. 'When was the last time you saw Lauren Tanner?'

She's jealous. Roy's brow comes together at the thought. Both Roy and Nora agreed what happened between them was a one-time thing, no attachments, and better for both of them not to complicate their work. Roy has gotten in enough trouble at home without the Superintendent throwing it in his face too.

'We-we... left work...' Casey takes another almighty blow of her nose. '...she w-went to get her-her-her... bus.' She fiddles with the damp tissue in her hand, her bottom lip quivering and threatening to morph her face into grief again. 'I should have walked with her, seen her on to her bus! B-but I was too busy, talking to Jerry!' She spits the security guards name and throws the dirty tissue across the room to land beside a tiny bin by the door.

Nora looks to pounce on the information like a wolf but Roy slows her with a look. 'You and Mr Akoum *were* an item?' She asks instead, guessing at Casey's sudden animosity.

Miss Williams draws another tissue from the box but only fiddles with it on her lap. 'Not really. Used to meet up sometimes, ya know? Since you lot have been around the office, he hasn't wanted to. Probably thinks you'll rat him out to his Wife.' She glances up but won't look either of us in the eye.

I can hardly judge. Roy fidgets, seems everything brings him back around to his own situation. 'Miss Williams, did anything seem off on the day, anything out of the ordinary? Was Lauren acting strangely?'

'She was Lauren.' She shrugs. 'Always half listening, all loved up with Gary. But that's the way she is. She's just Lauren.' Casey smiles but it warps as a fresh tear runs down her face. 'She wouldn't just leave. Not without a word to Gary. He's her world. I hope she's OK. She could be hurt…'

Another wave of sobbing threatens to erupt but Roy needs her to concentrate. 'Miss Williams, I know this is hard but we need you to focus. We will find Lauren but the sooner we have all the facts, the sooner we can bring her home.'

Casey stifles her sniffles, forcing her hands still on her lap and finally looking up with puffy eyes. 'O-K.'

'Does Lauren have any enemies, that would mean her harm?' Nora finally turns on her soft voice, the one that makes you want to help. 'Anyone from Cavendish, or outside of work?'

Casey's response is immediate. 'No. Lauren doesn't go out much… never comes out with us from work, not even for her birthday. She only really talks to me as far as I know. Gary is everything to her, they both are very private.'

Nora is writing in her pad but Roy knows it is just for show. Logging the information that Miss Williams tells us will make her feel like she's helped even though she has just revealed that Lauren Tanner has no enemies, doesn't go out and hardly speaks to anyone. *This is a waste of time.*

'Alright, Miss Williams, you've been a great help. Here's our information, if anything else occurs to you, just call.' Nora hands over a card but Miss Williams barely pays her any mind.

She shoots up to her feet and throws her arms around Roy. 'Just find her, OK? I know you can Inspector Harvey.'

'We'll do everything we can.' Roy awkwardly pulls himself out of Casey Williams' grip. He can feel the burn of Nora's stare as he leads the way out.

Outside, the Sun is low but rising in the morning sky as they approach his car on the other side of the street. 'She seemed keen.' Nora comments coldly.

'She's only human.' Roy regrets the joke as soon as he lets it loose.

'I've another name for her type.' Nora says cattily. 'And you didn't seem to mind all that much.'

'Don't be immature.' Roy says like a disappointed Father. Nora's face drops but the evil glare is still there. 'You're jealous? I was all over her, was I?'

Nora tuts and climbs into the car.

Roy's patience is suddenly paper thin and it rips right down the middle. He's ready to wrench the car door off but instead he climbs in. 'You don't get to be jealous Nora! This-' Roy points to each of them rapidly. '-isn't anything. We are partners; we work together. Nothing more. *We* are nothing more.' He huffs and angrily adjusts his seat after Nora repositioned for driving. Stabbing the key in the ignition he realises too late he is being unfair. He slumps, knowing Nora didn't deserve his outburst. 'Nora, look…-'

'It doesn't matter. Let's go.' Her face is stone.

Sigh. 'I want to go over the locations of abduction again. We've missed something.' Despite what he told Nora before about not giving up, without any new leads, they are running out of time. If they don't turn anything up soon Roy doesn't know how they are going to find the Prince and the missing twelve.

'Fine.' Nora agrees but by her tone Roy could have just slapped her in the face.

***

There must be a connection. Roy has all twelve engagement rings, bagged and tagged from evidence, arrayed across his desk in order of date of when the owner went missing. Every few seconds he glances at the spider web of notes, photos and maps pinned together on the wall as if suddenly a bolt of inspiration will strike him between the eyes and a vital clue will reveal itself. A file for each of the twelve is stacked beside him. He knows them all by heart. A few years ago Roy had a case that ran a similar length of time to this one, another soul-destroying hunt with little trace of the guy responsible. But Roy cracked it, and the case before that. It was that one where they pulled the poor girl from the river. He saw the vital connection, eventually, and saved a few people, has been able to for high profile cases each time. It's why Nora sometimes looks at him with starry-eyes and listens to him the way she does. It's why he has this small team in Nora, Joey and why he was given this case. But he just can't make it happen anymore. Roy just can't see how the Prince is choosing the women, or what he's doing with them. Maybe he has spent his career getting lucky.

Nora is out, following up on statements taken from employees at Cavendish & Son's by Joey and the others. It's an obvious excuse for her to be out of the office but Roy is glad of it. He's trying to get passed this mistake, for him and Emma to put it behind them so they can get on with their lives together. Getting feelings mixed up with Nora is not going to help anyone. The sooner she understands that the better it will be for everyone involved.

Roy pinches the bridge of his nose until it hurts. *There must be something...* He picks up the nearest evidence bag and examines it like he has a hundred times already, it has become a meaningless chore to him, something he does as maintenance without achieving anything. Each bag contains the engagement ring left by the Prince. A simple band belonging to Sam Somersby, a deep gold piece belonging to Dhanni Sandhu, a white gold band with diamond stud belonging to Joanne Hannah, another of delicate gold, belonging to Edyta

Durak… and so on and so on until finally Lauren Tanner's piece of white gold with an enormous stone. Roy examines Lauren Tanner's evidence bag. *How are you choosing them?* There must be a connecting factor. If not, and this guy is just picking women at random, with no method or other connection, then this is going to get a lot worse before it gets better. Short of the Mayor issuing Martial Law on married females… Roy dumps the little bag on the table and sighs in frustration. The crazy-wall draws Roy in and he wanders over to it, dissecting it in his mind. The locations and photos slide away from each other and group themselves as if drawn to counterpart information. Roy was a young detective, favoured and promoted because of his mind, his previous Super held him in fair regard. He was able to see the options in a case, able to separate clearly in his head what was missing and shape it into clues as if the answer was there all along. His talent has slowed as he got older but now he feels the familiar rabbit hole in his thoughts open as he takes in the pictures darted across the wall. *We've never seen the abductions… there's always a CCTV blind spot. Does he know where we can't see…?* Colour floods the street map on the wall at the places of abduction like water filling pipes. A dozen sections fill up leaving blank areas where they have camera footage...

'Roy?' Joey asks from the doorway.

Roy is startled and the wall is as still as it ever was, the colours gone. He tries to see the groups and the gaps on the map that began to form but the method, the rhythm in his brain is thrown; like a violin screeching a note through the final crescendo. *Sigh.* 'What is it Joey?'

Joey looks sympathetic and Roy already knows what he is going to say. '*The Viper* wants to see you.'

***

Chief Superintendent Lesley Piper is Roy's immediate superior and second only to the Commissioner. Her authority is absolute with Commissioner Harris' time spent in political banter with the Mayor while playing golf. Piper runs the division, the precinct, and Berry's police; and she knows it. In her late thirties, she has risen quickly and for all she has done for Berry's finest, she is a thorn in Roy's arse. Her dark hair is scraped back into a small bun behind her head, giving her skull a sleek look. Her flat nose and wide mouth give her the faint resemblance to a snake. Coupled with a tongue sharper than a shiv, she landed the nickname *Piper the Viper*. Not even the Commissioner would dare utter the name in her hearing though.

Roy waits patiently while the Chief Superintendent finishes signing whatever papers are on top of her pile. He hasn't been offered a chair and knows better than to drag a spare one from the side of her office uninvited. The glare alone would be worse than having to stand here, awkward. Unmarried, single, so far as anyone knows, and wholly dedicated to her job, Piper is an ice queen to stand against. Her office is completely devoid of anything personal, bar the single photo frame on her desk; one would think she had moved into the room that morning. The pens on her desk are arranged in size order and the black coat on the hanger by the door is without a crease. Piper signs off her document with a flourish and pushes the stack neatly to the side.

'How are things with your Wife?' She asks. Her face is thirty-nine but her voice is sixty, hoarse but still vital.

Roy tenses. *How does she know what happened?* His thought must show.

'I have my own eyes and ears about this circus you know. You've been sleeping in your car. I assume things at home aren't all roses and riding bareback.' She splices her fingers together and rests her chin on top.

Roy always forgets how direct she can be. *But she hasn't mentioned Nora. All she knows is that I'm not sleeping at home, or is she playing me?* 'We had a disagreement. Or an agreement, if I'm honest, seeing how the whole thing *is* my fault. We'll be OK.' Roy hopes. These last few weeks have been the longest he and Emma have ever spent apart. It wouldn't be so bad but not knowing when or if he will get her back is wearing him down. Not to mention his house, his things, have disappeared with her. It's like waking up with a leg missing.

'I've been your superior for three years Roy, you know how I work.' She lithely sits back into her chair. 'I don't care if your marriage explodes or if you tattoo the Prime Minister's face across your backside. I care if you do those things, and it affects your job.'

Roy inwardly breathes a sigh of relief; certain she doesn't know what happened between he and Nora. It would mean an investigation into the department and probably cost both their jobs, not least time for the missing women while new bodies are brought up to speed on the case. Roy can't let that happen.

'Is it affecting your job?' Piper's eyes contract, examining him, like she is peeling away a mask she thinks Roy's real face might be hiding behind.

'No.' Roy knows the correction is coming but he doesn't care. He has more important things to be doing than keeping professional etiquette alive.

The Viper's eyes harden. Despite being a couple of years older than Piper, she can make Roy feel like a child being scolded by his Mother. She makes him feel like he falls short in whatever he is doing, as if solving each case is fine but never soon enough. As if the Viper could have any maternal tendencies, even disappointment. 'No what?'

Sigh. 'No Ma'am.'

'Then tell me you've got something to go on,' She pulls a copy of the Berry Telegraph from her desk drawer and shows the headline *Police Cannot Protect From The Prince*. 'Because this is a disaster.'

'I've been going over the items left by our ghost, the locations too. There's something there, I know it.' Roy knows it is a hunch but there is a vital gap in the information they have, they just need to find it. 'I want to question the Husband of the latest abduction. Gary Tanner, I've got a feeling he might-'

'*A feeling? Might?* So, you've got nothing?' Piper locks her serious, dead stare into Roy, and it takes every ounce of will he has not to punch her in the face or walk out. 'Fifty weeks and now twelve missing, and you have nothing?'

'He's careful.' Roy states flatly, an explanation fit for a simpleton but they both know how difficult it can be if it isn't a Hollywood villain leaving them clues.

'*He?*' The Viper cocks her head, watching him like he is a mouse for her dinner.

'We both know it's a *he*.' Roy spits defensively. '*He* never picks a place with CCTV coverage, there's never been any witnesses to the kidnapping. He knows when the women are going to be alone and when they won't be seen. He's careful. I haven't got much to go on because there isn't anything to go on. Yet.'

The Chief Superintendent tuts and leans back into her chair. 'The Mayor has asked the Commissioner to wrap this up or heads will roll. Free, married women unable to walk the streets without disappearing is not popular among the voters I imagine.' She stares out of the large pane window, disappointed at how the system works. 'I want you to find this bastard, Roy. You got a hunch? Follow it through. You need more men? You got it. Whatever it takes. Bring these girls home alive, some, at least.' With that she drags her paperwork back into the centre of her desk and continues signing, the meeting apparently over.

'Yes, Ma'am.' Roy gets to the door when the Viper halts him.

'Roy?'

'Chief?'

'Get some proper sleep. You look like shit.' She doesn't even look up.

'Yes, Ma'am.' He says, wishing he could disagree.

7. Lauren Tanner

Dhanni groans as her limbs return to her control, sluggish and heavy. Lauren wonders how long the girl was limp. Hours, it feels like. It is impossible to track the time down here and Lauren curses herself for not keeping some sort of count. Lauren asks if Dhanni is alright and bites her tongue as soon as she utters the words. Dhanni can't answer yet, but how can she be? She takes the wet wipes and cleans between her legs and her back where she was soiled.

Silence becomes the dominant cell-mate of this prison. Lauren's mind races. A thousand questions burn in her mind, but she can't get the words out. The horror of what happened to Dhanni, of what might happen to her is too real.

The screech as the bolt slides free makes Lauren jolt. She freezes up, scrunches her eyes shut before she can stop herself, hating herself for the fear that holds such a tight grip on her. The Bull is dressed again in loose shorts and trainer socks, but his chest is bare. The black eyes of the Bull stare at everything and nothing. He calmly carries a tray with three steaming bowls of food, like before, with rounded cutlery sitting in them.

Lauren watches as the Bull descends and takes in the mess across the wall and the upturned bowl on the floor. It was just as much of a mess when he came in before… Lauren tries not to think of those excruciating moments, watching as he took Dhanni, but it has been all that's been replaying in her mind. As if he can read the rooms history he seems to know exactly what happened with the bowl. He places the three new bowls on the floor, just in reach of them and collects the empty bowls from Dhanni and Angie. He stays far enough away that should Angie lurch up she would fall short of wrapping the chain around his neck. Lauren gauges the distance in her head and knows it is on purpose; he knows exactly how much room his captives have. He picks up Lauren's bowl from against the wall and leaves, no word, no sign he recognises Lauren is there. She allows herself a breath as the Bull climbs the stairs and disappears. He is back before she takes another with a bin bag and a fresh pack of wet wipes. He dumps them at Angie's feet and stands back.

Angie shoots Lauren a dirty look and Lauren finds this time she can't match her. Angie tuts and starts scrubbing, tosses the soiled wipes into the bin bag when they are filthy with old food. She scrubs the wall and floor panels. The clumps and stains are crusty and thick; Angie really puts her back into it to remove as much mess as she can. She sleeps there after all. Guilt hangs around Lauren's neck like a tonne weight. After a dozen wipes are turned brown, Angie sits back, flicking the last into the bag, wiping her brow with the back of her hand.

The Bull is as still as a statue, admiring her work. Or is it her? He sees Angie, taking in every line and curve of her as she wipes the sweat from her neck. Suddenly he grabs Laurens bowl from the floor, making her jump, and swaps it with Angie's. Then he leaves. Angie snatches up her bowl and starts eating straight away, staring daggers at Lauren.

Lauren chews her lip. 'Sorry.'

'Eh?' She cups an ear like a football field is between them. 'Didn't hear you.'

'I said sorry!' Lauren sulks.

Angie cocks an eyebrow as if to say *you should be* but then relents, shrugging. 'Don't worry about it. Like I said, we all did our freaking out in the beginning.'

Dhanni crawls forward as far as her chain will let her and drags her bowl back to sit against her wall. She spoons the tiniest bit into her mouth and then sets the bowl back down as if every limb is weighed down. She could be chewing raw sewage or her favourite dish for all her face shows. How many times has this happened, and to others before them? Now that Lauren thinks about it, Dhanni does look familiar from the pictures on the news. A new wave of nauseous fear washes over Lauren as the name whispers through her mind… *The Prince.* A deep well of sadness opens inside her at the thought that this has been going on for a year. She was reading about it on her phone each morning, but it never really sank in that *the Prince* was real. Only paying attention because of the unwanted attention it could bring Gary and his work. But the news has it wrong, this man is no Prince. He's a monster.

Lauren can't help it. She leans over and recognises macaroni and cheese. It is one of her favourites and her stomach rumbles as the smell reaches her, making her hungrier than ever. Unbidden, tears fill her eyes, and she gets mad at herself. She almost lashes out, to kick the bowl away but Angie watches her as if expecting it and instead she settles back, forcing herself calm. She hugs her legs and hides her face in her knees.

'Are you going to eat that?'

Lauren looks up and Angie is pointing at the untouched bowl of macaroni with her spoon. 'Be my guest.' And tactfully tosses it over.

Angie catches it awkwardly like catching a baby, careful not to fumble and stain her spot further. 'You should eat ya know.'

'I'm not hungry.' Lauren mumbles, muffled by her legs.

'Bullshit. I bet yesterday was the first day in your adult life that you didn't eat. You can go without for a lot longer, but I'd bet you could eat a horse right now.' Angie tucks into her second helping.

Even if Angie had Lauren and Dhanni's share for a month it would probably only get her up to a healthy weight. Both Dhanni and Angie are thin but now Lauren looks properly, both have bags under their eyes, both are underfed.

Angie investigates the taste of the food, as if trying to discern a mystery ingredient. 'I dunno Dhanni, I think it's my turn. I'm not sure. Two out of three is good odds I suppose.' She nods to her two helpings, eating regardless.

Dhanni visibly licks her lips and then spoons another tiny portion into her mouth. Lauren still can't get it through her head. These two women are so calm. Dhanni is obviously living a nightmare but there is no fight in her, totally given up. Angie acts like this is just part of the deal, like this is just her lot now. Lauren almost wishes she had the same attitude. Waiting for that awful screech to herald the Bull, for what he wants to do is more than she can take. And deep-down Lauren considers that sooner or later she may become one of these women. Both have been in here too long and have accepted their fate. Dhanni has retreated into herself, just waiting for the nightmare to be over. Angie has accepted this new ruin of life, believing going with the flow is easier than fighting the current. Lauren considers the mentality of each and doesn't know which is worse. One thing is clear to Lauren though; she needs their help.

'Dhanni?' Lauren asks. None of them should be here and it seems absurd to try small-talk in such a hole but they stand a better chance of making it through together than alone. Dhanni hugs her knees and lays her head sideways, staring straight back at Lauren. Lauren is struck again by her beautiful rare blue eyes. Under the sweat and grime Dhanni really must be stunning. 'Tell me about yourself. Before… this.' Lauren waves at their room, afraid to call their situation what it is. Somehow, saying it out loud will make it worse.

Sadness infects those big crystal eyes and Dhanni turns her head away like her life before is too painful to think about.

Lauren edges closer but Angie stops her. 'I used to be a model.'

Lauren isn't surprised. Angie may be a little older, but she is undeniably attractive. It isn't hard to believe she was gorgeous when she was clean and only a little younger. 'Really? Wow. What for? Fashion, or...?'

Angie finishes Lauren's macaroni, smacking her lips and smiles at the memories. 'I did all sorts. Nothing huge mind, not fame and fortune but I lived in London for four years, made enough to make it there for a bit. I did shoots for wedding magazines and holiday brochures, played an extra in commercials and that. Even did a gig for a sex toy website.'

'Really? No, you're messing with me.' Lauren brushes her hair back, realising her bobble and clips have also been taken away.

'No, really. The resort shoots were good fun, even if half the time we were just lounging around pretending to sunbathe. I was paid to try on new clothes and put my make-up on, it was the best. The wedding shoots were my favourite though. The dresses and the flowers… It was amazing.' She tells like she can't believe she had it so good. 'For the sleazy website, they had us, me, and the rest of the girls, in these li'l lace numbers, hugging and holding these dildos; all matching the colour of our underwear. I'm serious! Like that's how lesbians spend their evenings, ha-ha. The kids in their li'l tail-suits were the cutest. On the wedding shoots, I mean! Not the sex site.' She laughs and Lauren snorts despite herself, even Dhanni's lips turn up. 'It was a lot o' fun.' Angie's smile fades like she has just found out her favourite singer has died, knowing she will never see their like again. She catches herself, making an obvious attempt to smother the melancholy. 'What about you, Blondie? What were you before?'

It is a blow to the stomach. Thoughts of Gary and their life flood her and for a moment she can't talk. Dhanni's reaction to being asked about her own life now makes sense. Thinking about her life as before, as her *old life*, just shines a light on the fact that it has been taken away and might never be returned. Doubt clogs her up. *What if I never get out of here? Am I going to become like Dhanni and Angie, just waiting for the next time that animal comes down those stairs? Losing myself like Dhanni, or becoming someone else like Angie? I just want to go home. I want my Gary.* 'I… I just work in an office.' It is such a simple statement, something that should never make a person's resolve crumble but Lauren bursts into tears. The sheer contrast between her life and the situation she is now trapped in is too far apart. She hides her face in her hands. Nobody speaks. What can they say?

Moments, maybe hours pass by where the only sound in the basement is Lauren sobbing. Her cell-mates let her cry. Eventually the tears dry up and her chest stops heaving, the tightness in her stomach melts away leaving only hunger.

'I was training to be a Doctor.' Dhanni's voice is softer than anything in this place has any right to be.

'What?' Lauren looks up, unsure whether Dhanni actually spoke. 'A Doctor?'

Dhanni absently scratches at the small of her back, her face blank of emotion. 'An intern, at Belleview.'

Lauren wipes her eyes, clears her throat. Dhanni speaking out brings a little strength back to her. 'You always wanted to be a Doctor? That's one of those things people want to be when they're kids, right?'

Dhanni nods but she could be matching to a tune in her head for all she looks to be listening. Those clear blue eyes scrunch tight, like she hasn't blinked in hours and Lauren wonders how she and Angie can sleep. 'Ever since I was little.'

'So, you always wanted to work in an office?' Angie asks, smirking because who dreams of an everyday job like that?

'No, never. I always wanted to get into music. I used to date this guy in college, a singer, did shows up and down the country. We even had a summer in Europe.' It's Lauren's turn to smile at old memories but they soon sour as the memory of how that relationship ended corrupts her train of thought.

Angie doesn't notice or doesn't care. 'What do you play?'

Lauren laughs at herself for how much she thought she was in love, how much she would have done for that piece of shit she followed around for two years. 'I don't. I know, silly, right? No, I guess I was a groupie. Making music never really worked out.'

'I married.' Angie chucks in. 'Twice. First one was to an agent of a friend of mine, another model, used to get her great jobs, who I caught getting 'jobs' *from* my friend as well as *for* her. Daft thing was I knew. Wouldn't have minded so much if they didn't lie to me about it, the shits.'

This woman is so different to Lauren. 'And the second?' She asks.

'He's up there somewhere.' She nods at the ceiling, the barrier that separates them from the outside world and their lives. For the first time, Angie's armour slips fully and she looks like she would pay anything to be out of here; to be with her Husband instead of down here in this filthy prison.

Lauren leaps on the opportunity. 'You can be with him. You can go home. We all can! We just have to find a way to get out of here.'

Angie is already shaking her head; the thought of escape is an impossible fantasy to her. 'No one escapes.'

'But there were others, right? You said so yourself. How many? The news said eleven women... I guess... I make twelve. What happened to them? You think that animal just let them go? It's down to us to get out of here or we never will!' Lauren must find some spark of hope left in these women and bring it back from the brink of going out. Angie's grimace softens a little. Maybe she isn't a lost cause? Maybe through all the 'don't-care-attitude' there is an ember of will to get out of here. Together, they can figure something out. *There must be a way, right?* Lauren leans forward as Angie drops back, like a shark smelling blood. 'I need you to talk to me, Angie. Tell me everything you know about this place. We can find a way!'

'You were right, Angie.' Dhanni drones. 'It's your turn.'

Lauren is confused but then her meaning strikes home. What she took for Angie's resolve joining with her own is actually numbness. Her hands sit lifelessly at her side, her legs are crossed awkwardly as her head slumps sideways onto her shoulder. Her eyes are wide, looking from Lauren to Dhanni, up to the door at the top of the stairs and back again. Her body is completely dead apart from her eyes.

'Oh, God!' Lauren panics, shuffling back as if the paralysis is contagious. 'What do we do? Dhanni?'

Dhanni barely moves; she inches back but then settles, only adjusting her position. The next thing to happen is an inevitability to her; nothing can stop it, and nobody is going to save them.

'Shit. Shit. Shit.' Lauren looks all around the room, from woman to woman, desperately trying to think of something she can do-

The bolt shrieks free and the Bull strides in. The Minotaur wears joggers and instead of their next meal he carries only a strip of thick, black fabric. He kneels beside Angie's limp form and tenderly brushes the hair out of her eyes. Angie's eyes are wide, strained but then they disappear as he blindfolds her.

'Hey…' Lauren's voice cracks but her courage holds. 'Hey! You hear me? Get away from her you bastard!' She pulls forward, tugging at her chain to get to Angie. Her sense of protection for the woman surprises her. There is no real love between them but they are in this together. And she can't watch it again. What happened to Dhanni is burned into the back of her eyes, scorching her brain. More of the same will only fuel that fire. 'Just let us go!'

The Bull slowly turns on his knee and the full face of the Bull seeps the bravery right out of Lauren. She falls back against her wall and collapses in on herself, as if becoming smaller can hide her from this creature. His big hand reaches into his pocket. Lauren cringes back, whimpering but he only pulls out a small ring of keys. He selects a key and unlocks the shackles at Angie's wrists. He lifts the woman up like a sleeping child.

'Hey.' Lauren croaks, her nerve distant and weak but this new development lights a fire in her. 'Hey!' She forces. 'What are you doing with her?'

The Bull ignores her, King of this sick little Kingdom. He carries the paralysed Angie up the stairs and out of sight. A moment later the door slams shut and their prison is made whole again.

'Dhanni? What's going on? Where has he taken her?' Lauren begs her for answers, desperate to know what is happening.

Dhanni, barely moved, like she just witnessed a leaf on the wind and not a woman being carried away, looking like there is more hope in the slop bucket than through the door at the top of the stairs, just hugs her legs. 'Sometimes he takes us upstairs. He'll wash her.'

Lauren is stuck. Her entire world has been reduced to this basement. This smelly, dirty cell has become her everything and she hates it. She wants to escape, to do something to change what is happening but she doesn't know how. She wants to pull free from the chain locking her to the wall. She wants to escape what the Bull will do to her, but she cannot. 'Dhanni, please. Talk to me. What's up there? Have you seen where we are, see a way out?'

'Whenever he takes us upstairs he blindfolds us. I've never seen what's up there.' Dhanni's blue eyes are like glass. It barely looks like she is breathing.

'And he… you know?' Lauren means what he did to Dhanni, but upstairs.

'He puts me on a bed or sofa.' She shrugs, like it could matter where it happens.

Lauren is desperate to make any information useful; anything that can help her, that can help them. There must be something they can do! Lauren's heart bangs like a drum as her mind races. The dynamic of their prison has changed, her understanding turned upside down by Angie being taken away. 'And what about the food? Does he do it every day?'

'Not always. Though, I don't know how much time passes.' She runs her eyes over the dark ceiling as if tracking the Sun. 'I think he feeds us once a day.'

Lauren can believe it. Both Dhanni and Angie are underweight but one meal a day would keep them fed enough not to starve. Another question spills from her lips even though Angie explained before. 'Dhanni, the woman before me. Jo? Did she really starve?'

Dhanni's face scrunches up and she turns away, her darker than black hair falls over her shoulder, hiding her face.

Lauren crawls forward but her chain checks her. 'Please. I need to know.'

'It's like Angie said. There are things worse than the Bull.' Her voice is so devoid of emotion that Lauren can hardly believe it comes from a human being. After a moment Dhanni slowly turns back around. 'Jo was nice.' Light shines in those crystal blues as she remembers her friend, but it is gone in an instant.

'What happened?' Lauren asks again softly.

Her bony shoulders jolt again. 'She had enough. Was here a long time and didn't want to be any more, not after Theresa didn't come back. She stopped eating.' Dhanni shudders and a tear cuts through the grime on her cheek.

Jo chose to starve to death rather than live this nightmare. 'How many others?' Lauren thinks of all the pictures from the news, on her phone, in the papers. Eleven missing but not all of them could have ended up here. The police have said as much in Press releases that the Prince is a creation of the papers. But at least some were brought here, Dhanni and Angie are proof of that.

'I don't know. I knew Jo, Angie and Theresa—'

'Theresa?' Lauren racks her brain remembering if any of the missing women were called Theresa.

Dhanni nods. 'Was next to you. Jo was where you are now.'

A shiver runs through Lauren at sitting in a dead woman's place, like Jo's ghost just placed a hand on her shoulder. She scans the wall but in the gloom it takes her a moment to see it. Above on the wall is another lock-loop, the same as the one above each of them. On the opposite side, next to Angie's spot, Lauren needs to squint to see it, is another. With Dhanni's loop on the end wall there could be a total of five captives down here. 'How long was Theresa here?' It is a stupid question, like Dhanni said, they cannot track the time down here.

'I don't know. Brought in before Jo. They were close.' Her voice is a murmur.

'He took her away? For good? Why?' Lauren jumps on the chance that this might be something they can use but her stomach is a pit of butterflies as to what the Bull might have done with her.

'She fell ill. Bladder infection, I think.' Dhanni explains, her emotion back to being a flat-line on a heart rate monitor. 'I hadn't been here long then and I wasn't thinking properly.'

Lauren can relate. By her guess she has been here a couple of days and every moment so far has been a mix of panic, fear, and disbelief. Only now is she starting to think clearly. 'And he took her? She never came back?'

'Angie says he dropped her at the hospital. That being a murderer is different to… what he is. Angie needs to believe that I think.' She shrugs again. 'Maybe that's why Jo did it, to make him a killer. Show him what he is doing to us.'

Lauren doesn't know what to say to that. Questions swirl through her mind and blend together. It is hard to think and separate them. Her stomach aches. 'How long have you been here, Dhanni? What's the last thing you remember?'

Dhanni is quiet for a moment and Lauren lets her think. 'I was coming out of work to my car. I forgot my parking pass, so I parked around the corner down the road. There are trees on both sides, I didn't see anything. I got knocked down when I went to put my key in. Woke up here.'

Lauren can see it now; Dhanni, in her scrubs, coat wrapped around her, a step away from her car when that animal knocks her out. 'What was the date?'

'December 10th.'

'It's May…' Lauren whispers.

Dhanni's eyes scrunch tight, and hides her face, the truth of how long she has been in this prison is a different pain to what she has been forced to endure.

The thought that Lauren might be here for another hour is almost more than she can take. The possibility she could be here for months is too much. 'Dhanni. We must find a way out of here. There has to be something we can do.'

'Let me know how that goes.' She says dryly and rolls over, facing the wall.

'Dhanni? Come on, we can't just…' It's no use. Dhanni is numb to the possibility of freedom. The girl has been broken. Lauren wants to rage at the world, pull her hair out and scream. She needs to get Dhanni and Angie to work with her but maybe too much damage has been done.

The silence drags out but Lauren can't think of what to say. Dhanni just lays there waiting for her next 'turn' or death, whichever comes first. She tries to pull at the chain again, but she may as well be chained to a tractor for all she can make it move. With her wrists raw and burning, she huffs down, energy drained. She feels sick from her efforts and from hunger.

A groan like an old door, creaks through the basement. Lauren jumps around as if putting the wall at her back can offer protection. Dhanni doesn't even flinch. Preparing herself for the worst, Lauren climbs to her knees before she realises that the noise was her stomach and not the Bull's return. A wave of dizziness rolls over her and she slumps back down, hungrier than she has ever been. Cramp stabs into her side and she curls herself around the pain, hugging her middle. Another need of the body makes itself known and she hammers the floor with her fist in frustration. Despair blankets her, and she cries. With no other choice, she crawls forward and drags the bucket of slop toward her. Every echoed noise, drip, and plunk from using the toilet is like a megaphone in her ear. There is a smell, and the embarrassment layers itself on top of the fear that owns this place. There are no wipes left in the packet, no paper or anything to use except her shirt and underwear but Lauren can't bring herself to use the only clothes left to her. She will not give that animal the satisfaction of taking what little dignity she has left. Lauren tries to shake her hips in a vain attempt to be clean and pulls her underwear up. Her wet misery boils and turns to embers; rage rises in her and it is all she can do not to dash the bucket at the stairs.

Maybe Lauren sleeps. The bolt on the door shrieks alive and Lauren instantly snaps alert, ready. Angie appears but Lauren's eyes hurt looking into the light from beyond the doorway. It must only be a regular household bulb but after so long in the dimness of this pit it is like looking into the Sun. The Bull carries Angie through, limp, and brings her down.

The Bull gently places Angie back in her spot. With something approaching affection, the Bull brushes the hair from her face and replaces the manacles about her wrists. He stands, his powerful form towering over the three women. For a second he just stands there, watching Lauren through the glassy black eyes of the Bull. Then he turns, grabbing the bucket and marches up the stairs. He replaces the empty bucket and drops a fresh pack of wipes beside it. The bolt shrieks and they are alone.

Lauren's breath comes back, and she gets a better look at Angie. She is a completely different woman. Angie's streaked and grimy legs are now smooth and glistening; they look fabulous. The thin shirt she wore before has been replaced with a clean T-shirt. Her underwear is different, clean. The stale sweat that made her arms look like they were mottled in old yellow bruises is gone; wiped away to leave smooth, pale pink. Her hair has been washed. Where it was clumped into dark ropes of greasy knots before, now it is silky and combed. Angie is a beautiful woman; Lauren doesn't doubt she was a professional.

'Hey Angie.' Dhanni drones without turning over.

'Are you OK?' Lauren asks but tuts at herself as Angie cannot respond. Silence becomes the ruling occupier of their prison again. The only sounds that penetrate the aura of silence are the occasional cough or ruffle of fabric as one of them shifts position.

Eventually, Angie stirs. She croaks, throat dry. Her fingers stretch first, then her shoulders, stiff after being dead for so long. Lauren leans forward to see. Although steadfastly resolved not to fall into the same state as these women, she must know the dangers. She must know what could happen should she fail. Slowly, sluggishly, Angie groans over onto her side. Her legs don't move on command but the poor woman drags herself up so she can sit back against the wall. She looks ten years younger without all the muck. Her hair falls forward and she flicks it away, but she is clumsy without full control in her fingers. She tries to shift her legs but winces with the effort. '…ins-zan-needulz…'

'What?' Lauren asks but gets the message. 'Pins and needles?'

Angie nods but her head falls lazily onto her chest.

'Will you be alright?' A voice in Lauren's head is screaming at her to stop asking stupid questions but she can't help it.

Angie, with an effort, raises her arm and forces her thumb up. It wobbles as if a great weight is on it and she is only just strong enough to lift it. Then she falls limp again, to rest.

***

'It feels so much better to be clean.' Angie stretches out from her fingers to her toes; she points her bum up into the air in a yoga position. 'He did a good job on my legs as well, Dhanni, look.' Angie shows off her smooth legs but Dhanni looks like she couldn't care less.

'What did he do?' Lauren asks, unable to look the woman in the eye because it is a question born more out of concern for herself than Angie.

Angie huffs but relents. 'You really wanna know?'

She doesn't but needs to. Lauren nods.

A smirk plays at the corner of Angie's mouth like she is going to tell a horror story in gruesome detail but thinks better of it. 'He had me. He cleaned me up. Then he had me again. Now I am here.'

Lauren is struck again by how nonchalant this woman is about this whole thing. In times of trauma and pain the mind finds a way to deal with it, she guesses. Some people fall into themselves, like Dhanni, others repress it like Angie. Lauren snorts a laugh, not knowing which is worse. Those two options being the only outcomes is dryly funny to her.

'Something funny?' Angie cocks an eyebrow, smirk gone because Lauren seems to be laughing at what happened to her.

'No! No… just something I was thinking. Damned if you do, damned if you don't type thing.' Lauren sighs. Her stomach croaks and she hugs her body as another cramp takes hold, as if she can somehow squeeze the hunger away.

'Must be pretty hungry by now?' Angie asks, looking Lauren up and down, smirk in full effect.

'I'm fine.' Lauren says defiantly.

'Yeah, sounds it.'

'I'm fine!' Her stomach groans again, betraying her lie and Angie smiles triumphantly. Lauren wants to punch her in the mouth.

'You know what, Blondie, I get it.' Angie soothes. 'I had a big ol' war with myself when I was brought here. You think this is what I wanted? I'm here because of the Bull. Just like you. We're here and we can't get out so we may as well make the best of it. Right?' She appeals to Dhanni, still facing the wall. She gives no sign she is listening. Angie motions like the other woman backed up everything she said. 'See!'

'So, what, if you can't beat 'em, join 'em?' Lauren asks, disgusted. She would spit if she could spare some.

Angie stretches her glistening leg up like a cat. 'I'm not joining anybody, Blondie. We've been dealt a bad hand. We'd all like it to be different, got people we care about, but we can't do anything about it right now. So, if it's a choice between living in misery or putting my shit to one side 'til this is over, I know what I'm going to pick.'

Lauren shakes her head and changes position, trying to get comfortable but her ribs are sore. How long can she go without eating or drinking anyway?

'I'm just trying to save you some pain, Blondie. I was a London model in my twenties; I know what it is to be hungry, but listen,' Angie's serious tone makes Lauren look around. 'It's nothing compared to starving. And I mean really starving. Don't do that to yourself.'

Lauren ignores her and focuses on not throwing up.

***

The shriek of the bolt announces the Bull's arrival. All three of them jump at the sound after being in silence for so long. The terrifyingly familiar sight of the Bull enters with a tray with three bowls on it. There is also a pitcher of water. He sets the bowls down, refills the plastic bowls with water. Angie pulls up her meal and starts eating with gusto. Dhanni and Lauren both eye the food, porridge with honey, but Lauren turns away.

The Bull moves towards Lauren and her heart freezes. His powerful hands flex at his sides and the dead eyes of the Bull bore into her, reflecting what little light there is. An eternity passes by and still the Bull stands over her. He points at Lauren's little bowl.

Lauren wants to scream, to fling herself at him and tear the head from his shoulders. But she can hardly move. She is weak from days with no food or water. Her will is iron but she cannot even plead with him to let her go any more. A stab of panic fills her, her heart that was frozen in fear a moment before is now racing at the realisation of a new threat. *What if I'm so weak I can't stop him?* Lauren could barely hold off a toddler the way she is feeling right now. A few days and already her strength has left her. How long can she keep this up before she can't move, can't think? He won't need her to eat his poison for him to do whatever he wants with her. She must find a way out of here, and soon. Desperation lends her new strength, and she screams at her captor. 'Let me go!'

The Bull seems to huff but no sound escapes the beast. He stamps over to Angie and, breaking his boundaries enforced up to this point, leans in close and yanks the porridge out of her hand.

'Hey! What are you taking mine for?' Angie complains.

The Bull takes up Dhanni's bowl, untouched, and storms out of the basement with all three meals. He all but slams the door closed and that awful screech makes Lauren's skin crawl as it is bolted.

'That's great. That is just great, Blondie.' Angie drops back against her wall and pulls absently on her chain, making it whip tight. 'Now we're all going to go hungry just so you can hold on to this stupid notion that you can survive this place as pure as you came in.' There is a snarl to Angie's tirade. Lauren ignores the woman. But guilt and frustration add to the hunger and her insides churn. Angie doesn't let up. 'So, what's the plan, eh? Stay off the food so he doesn't have you? And in a couple days when you can barely lift your head, what then? Hey!' Angie throws her plastic spoon at Lauren, left over from her porridge.

'I don't know! What do you want me to say, huh?! I'm not just going to decide 'Yep, I'm OK with this you freak, rape me! Bring on the next fucking portion!' I'm sorry but I won't. I can't.' Lauren's breath comes ragged and suddenly she is exhausted. She sticks her chin out defiantly, matching Angie's glare but another cramp bites into Lauren's stomach making her keel over.

'You're selfish you know?' Angie says quietly but it is the only sound in the cell. 'We're going to suffer because you think you're better than us. Fuck you, Blondie. Fuck you.'

Lauren's eyes are scrunched tight against the pain in her stomach. *What am I going to do? What can I do?*

8. Inspector Roy Harvey

'How is he getting rid of the bodies?' Nora asks out loud as she stares at the crazy-wall, one of the missing girls' files open in her hands. Her mousey-brown hair is tied back exposing her neck.

Roy forces himself to look away, back to the report in his hands, angry at himself for getting distracted and by Nora of all things. That will hardly help things with Emma and is certainly no good for the missing twelve. 'Bodies?' He must have heard wrong. His sour mood bleeds into his tone and he knows he will sound bitter before he opens his mouth. 'Where has that come from?'

Nora throws her pen down, equally frustrated but by the case. 'I'm thinking big picture here, Roy. Saving some is better than saving none. If we figure out what he does at the end, maybe we can follow a trail back and catch the bastard.'

Roy sees the logic. It makes sense to cover all angles and cast as many nets as possible, but he keeps it from his face. The meeting with the Viper and another night in his car has stained his bones with an acidic mood. 'Why don't you tell me what you think?'

Nora bites down her reply and crosses her arms. 'We've got hard-hats and forensics all over this. If he was killing them we would have turned something up by now. Hair, blood, out of dumb luck one of them would have been found.'

'That's assuming it is one person working alone, and without a clean workshop.' Roy means somebody with a pre-prepared place to do what they are doing. A 'workshop' is the location the abductor takes the abductee after the actual kidnapping. It could be anywhere; a hotel room, a bathroom, behind a bush at the park, wherever the guy takes his victim. A 'clean workshop' is somewhere that nobody would think to look because the guy is supposed to be there. Roy's first breakthrough as a missing person's Inspector came from a miracle solve of a clean workshop case. It quickly became a murder case, but it was Roy that made the find. A local Butcher, Todd Barnett, was grabbing members of opposing darts teams after losses in his team's league. With his Butcher's to cut up and store the bodies it could have been an infamous story with no ending. Especially as he had the presence of mind to mince up recognizable parts, like ears, hands and feet. Roy hasn't been able to eat sausage since. It wasn't until it came to Roy that all the victims had a set of darts at home that he saw the connection. The way his mind can sort through information and link it into an answer has been his key strength, but he cannot rely on it anymore. His skill is abandoning him. The point is, there is nothing out of the ordinary with a clean workshop case. It is damn near impossible to catch the culprit if he is careful, or if there is more than one person to cover each other. Roy hopes the Prince isn't one of those, but the length of this case suggests otherwise.

'There has to be something.' Nora mutters to herself, not letting the possibility of an untraceable crime get in the way of her thinking.

Roy can hear the cogs turning in her head. 'When I was a kid you know, my Brother and I used to steal wine when my Mum was out. Then top it up with water or blackcurrant or whatever matched best. Mum didn't even notice until she came back from work and we were both drunk.

He takes in the wall of information. Nora is thinking about how the guy is moving the bodies post-mortem, but Roy's mind starts to slide into focus. Moving the bodies can be done in plain sight; any car, any van, hell, even a rucksack can transport a body if it is cut right. No, trying to catch the guy at the end opens more doors when right now they need to narrow their choices down.

If we can figure out how he is taking the women, undetected, then we can track him down.

The streets of Berry begin to colour again, flowing in lines across the map as his mind codes what he knows about the case. Areas fill in and flash with addresses and points of interest, they sail passed him as he sorts through the microcosm that is Berry. His mind tingles as it synchronises with the map, dissecting it and finding his way through the fog. The world goes silent and then something occurs to him. 'Maybe he isn't picking the girls?' Roy thinks out loud.

'Eh?' Nora asks, confused.

'Each point of disappearance is a blind spot. Every single one. That's not a coincidence. And each woman seems to be as different from each other as they can be. Different ages, colours, it's like they are random by design but I'm starting to think that isn't it. He doesn't appear to have a type other than they are all pretty, and married. No connection between them other than that. What if he is picking the place and then the woman? Instead of risking himself on a girl he's hung up on, he's picking a place with privacy and then decides on the girl that happens to pass through.' Roy scans the map on the wall, now suddenly still and its regular colours.

'We've been trying to crack this psycho by connecting the victims, to prevent the next.' Nora sets her jaw. 'So, how does he know where to be, and when?'

'Right.' Exhaustion sloughs off his shoulders as they see a new path in this bog of dead ends. Roy stands with new purpose. 'What if our guy is in security? Or works at the Council? He knows the lay of the land, has access to CCTV footage around the city?'

Nora's eyes sparkle as she watches Roy work. 'Roy, this could be *something*.'

Roy is reinvigorated and all thoughts of the Viper evaporate as he sites his orders. 'I want to go over every statement again, find out if anybody has any history in surveillance jobs, landscaping, anything that could give an insight to Berry's surveillance. I want access to every bit of camera footage around each point of abduction. I want footage from their places of work checked, the hospital, supermarkets, car parks, buses, anywhere there is footage I want it checked, all of it. If the same dog walked passed our missing women on camera I want to know about it. We need a new map with all the blind spots in the city. If the Prince knows where we can't see, then we must too. Right now.'

Nora snaps to action quickly, making notes. 'I'll get the guys to bring up a full list of people we've already spoken to. You want to talk to them personally? Between you, me and Joey we could get through the statements inside the week. Faster if we get some more hands on the job. We're going to need court orders for some of the footage. For the places of business and hospital at least. You think the Viper will sign all that off?'

Roy smirks confidently. 'I think she'll help us out this time.'

***

Chief Superintendent Piper signed off on six extra sets of hands and a total of forty-two warrants applied for to Judge Niesbit. New life has been injected into the case. Nora is compiling the details of every person who gave a statement; they will begin again in the morning with a new scent in their noses.

Roy left Nora to it, taking advantage of the tasks keeping her and Joey busy and headed home. To Emma. What was once his favourite possession in the entire world, Roy's car now fills him with spiteful boredom. Night after night spent trying to find a position that doesn't leave him stiff has drained every drop of pride he ever had for his car. Before he would have raced home, pushing the speed limit just to flirt with the power of his vehicle, now he rolls over the tarmac, foot barely on the peddle. A light rain spatters off the wind screen and blurs of red, white, and yellow light zip passed as he is overtaken. Horns scream to life, fog lights flash on and off to make him hurry up. Shaking himself from his lethargy he puts his foot down and leaves them in the distance. He pulls onto his street in a dream like state; his foot floats off the accelerator until the car glides up the road, rolling as if being pushed by the wind. Suddenly he can feel every stitch in the leather of his steering wheel, every house that drifts by is etched in perfect detail but it is as if he has never been here before, like he has never driven this car before. In this dream-place Roy knows he could be happy, that here, now, there is a possibility that when Emma sees him, she won't hate him, that all will be forgiven and they can have their life back. Roy pulls around a black BMW and onto his driveway. As soon as he gets out of the car and looks at his own front door, reality comes crashing down and with it the possibility of failure. Roy hesitates, fear of Emma slamming the door in his face is a hurt compared to the ignorance that he can live with here, hoping all will be well.

Roy tries to summon all ambient willpower from within him even as it leaks away. After taking a huge breath he finally marches up the path to see his Wife. The front door opens suddenly, and Emma stands there, beautiful, the light from the hall makes her dark hair glow. She wears her slim black dress, her diamond earrings; she looks wonderful. She is smiling. Smiling like she did when they were first engaged, when they were everything each of them could ever want. The longing that has pinched at Roy suddenly opens and there is a physical pain in his chest, like pulling a splinter.

Emma sees him and she stops dead, her smile keels, frozen in the doorway. They stare at each other for a moment, Emma with her shock, hand glued to the front door and Roy in his half-real fantasy where everything is perfect, car keys in hand while the drizzle blankets him.

'Emma... it's good to-' Roy takes a step forward.

'What are you doing here, Roy?' She sets her jaw. She was always a beautiful woman, angry or not. She stays firm in the doorway but pulls the front door to so as not to let him in.

'I wanted to see you, have done every minute but I didn't want to rush you. But I can't take it anymore, Em. I want to come home, and fix this.' Roy means every word. He misses his Wife and his home. He knows he betrayed her, that he doesn't deserve her, but they can't let what they had die.

'Now isn't a good time.' Emma is cold, her mind made up. Her expression is so cold Roy wonders how her smile could exist on the same face.

'But Em, I...' Roy's mind suddenly catches up, adding it all together. Emma's black dress, for going out, her earrings, her face is done, she is trying to hide the inside of the house and there is a black BMW parked right by the driveway. Roy slowly looks around at the other car and then back at Emma.

For a second she has the decency to look guilty but then her eyes go hard and she pushes the front door wide open. 'John, wait for me in the car. I'll only be a minute.' Emma stands aside and 'John' steps out.

'You're sure?' John asks, sparing a look at Roy.

'Yes, just a minute.' Emma nods.

Roy isn't the biggest guy in the world but he has 'John' by a few inches and by a stone at least. As soon as 'John' gets out of his doorway Roy steps forward, blocking the way, an inch away from his face, ready to punch his nose in. 'Who are you, 'John'?'

John makes no show of being intimidated even though he must know Roy is a policeman. He is younger than Roy, clean shaven with dark hair oiled back. His suit is pressed and fits like a glove. 'I think you answered your own question there, Roy. Aren't you an Inspector?'

Roy would have kneed him in the balls right there but that would hardly appeal to Emma. 'The black BMW, that yours 'John'?'

'Yes, it is. Gets me from A to B.' He smirks, knowing it is worth more than Roy's Porsche, if not as classic.

Roy's temper flares at the unsaid comparison to his Wife, that she is also just a humble little thing he has in his hands. Roy leans in, nose to nose, and it is everything he can do not to heave the man off his feet and dump him head-first onto his lawn. 'Get the fuck off my property.'

John's smirk doesn't slip and he smoothly slides passed and onto the street.

Roy watches him go and makes sure he is out of ear shot before turning back to his Wife. She cuts him off. 'I'm not doing this, Roy. I'm going out.'

'No shit.' Roy spits. 'Who is this guy?'

Emma ignores him and slams the door shut; stalking passed him.

'Emma.' His voice hardens more than he means.

She stops and stares into him, hard. 'He's a friend of Shay's. She thought it would be good for me to get out. None of your business though, is it.'

Roy grabs his Wife's hand. 'Emma, talk to me. Let's go inside and fix this.'

She pulls her hand away and suddenly there are tears in her eyes. 'You don't get to decide when we fix this, Roy. All these years, the work, the cases, all those times I watched you killing yourself over trying to save whoever, have I ever not been there for you, ever?'

Roy's heart cracks. 'No.'

'All I asked was that we had each other. That's all I wanted. And it was enough for me!' Emma half-pushes half-slaps him in the chest, trying to control herself. 'And you slept with that girl!'

It's all true; it is all Roy's fault. After everything Emma has done, stood by him through the hard cases and the grisly details that Roy must live with knowing, never once did she falter. She listened, saw to him when the cases were pulling him down, was always there for him. She blames herself for not giving them a child but even in that she is strong, knowing that Roy loves her. In his act of betrayal, Roy has ripped away the confidence and security that Emma's life is built on. Roy is all but speechless. 'Em... I...-'

'This won't be fixed, Roy. Do you have any idea how much you have hurt me?' Emma tuts, disgusted with him. She shakes her head and stalks away.

'Emma!' Roy calls after her. 'I'm sorry! It's my fault, OK?'

Emma stops at the end of the path and turns around, storming back up to him. 'You're damn right it is! I hope she was worth it. I loved you Roy but now I don't want to see you again.'

With that she marches back up the path. Roy searches for something he can say that could fix this. But there isn't. He follows her to the end of the path, hoping, desperate for Emma to turn around but John opens the car for her to get in.

'I need things, Emma. For work. I have responsibilities. You know what case I am on.' Roy says knowingly. Emma can hate him all she wants but she won't let innocent people get hurt because of it.

'Why don't you just leave the lady alone?' John pipes up, one hand on the car door, the other in his Wife's, helping her in.

The idea of punching the smug look off his face wins over and Roy storms onto the street. Emma climbs out of the car again, knowing her Husband far too well. 'Take what you need, Roy.' She allows softly.

Her change in tone stops Roy and he's gratified to see that John had taken a step back, putting Emma between them, the coward. 'Thanks, Em. I want to talk-'

'No.' Emma shakes her head, as cold as bitter frost. 'Take what you need and leave. John is taking me out and I don't want you here when we come back.' She doesn't wait for a reply and slides into the car. John smiles as if to say, 'Sorry old chap', skirts around the back of the car and climbs in.

Roy watches them pull away, noting the plate number of the BMW. A hot spike of spite erupts in his mind and he pulls out his phone. 'Nora? I'm sending you a plate number for a black BMW. Belongs to a 'John'. Find out what you can. Thanks… No, I'm fine. Bye.'

The street is quiet now but movement in the window across the street catches Roy's eye. The curtain drops back to normal as if the nosey old bag were never peeking. Roy stares into the window for another few seconds before storming around and entering his own house for the first time in weeks.

***

Roy took the opportunity to shower, shave and collect everything he could fit into his car; clean clothes, razor, phone charger, tools, pictures, movies, all the crisps from the cupboard, the fresh loaf from on the counter, some chosen spitefully. Roy isn't proud of that, but it is done now. He considered sitting outside his house and waiting for them to get back, fold the guy up and put him back in his car too but decided against it.

Roy speeds down the motorway and growls at the passing traffic, to himself at how little power he has over the elements in his life. His Wife could be in that guy's arms tonight, in his bed. Helpless fury winds itself tight inside Roy's chest and he puts his foot down. Faster and faster he rockets up the motorway, reckless and not caring because the love of his life is out with another man. Roy veers around other cars, screeching passed blaring vehicles as they bellow their horns and still he races faster. His Porsche roars with his heart at being released, at the indignation of being held down for so long. Soon, Roy is driving so fast that the slightest movement on the wheel could cause him to veer and crash.

ring *ring* *ring*

Roy's phone cracks the bubble of heedless self-destruction and he instantly comes back to himself. His foot eases off the accelerator and within a mile he slows enough to pull over. He didn't realise how much his heart was racing. It takes a moment for his pulse to slow before he answers the phone. Nora has called but there are also several missed calls from Joey. He calls Nora first.

'Nora? I was driving. What's up?' The thud in his chest is as loud as a drum.

'Joey tried to call; you spoke to him yet?' She sounds flustered.

A knot forms in Roy's stomach. *This can't be good news.* 'No, I called you first. What's going on?'

'Judge Niesbit has only signed off on half the warrants. None of the victims' family's homes have been approved. The Viper's idea apparently. You know it was Niesbit who dealt with her sister's case? She doesn't want the families being dragged any further into this. We got the private CCTV footage and places of work but that's it.'

'Sonovabitch.' Roy barks. The Viper is up his ass trying to get this case squared off and then pulls this? He didn't think he could be more aggravated, but this does it. 'What about the extra hands? Tell me we still have some manpower?'

'Yeah, she's signed off on the six. We meet them day after tomorrow…' She trails away as if deciding whether to say something or not.

'What is it, Nora?'

'It's not everything we asked for, but this is as fresher start as we're going to get, I think. Tomorrow, from tomorrow, I mean, we need to be on this guy 100%. We need to get him before another one is taken.' She is building up to ask him again, Roy knows.

'Nora…' Roy sighs, repeating the same reasons in his mind why he can't go to her, to stay over, even for the good of the case.

'My spare room, Roy. Eat, rest, work. That's it. They need you.' Her logic is irrefutable.

Roy's mouth works into different shapes as his automatic responses war with his wants and needs. His instinct is dragging at him to say no, that he shouldn't stay at Nora's place, that it isn't worth making things with Emma worse. But then the spiteful animal within rears its head and all he can think is that Emma has given up on them, that his belongings are crammed into the boot of his car, that his face is raw from the hasty abuse he shaved into it, that Emma is out with another man which could lead to God-knows-what and tomorrow may result in another woman going missing because he hasn't acted well enough. Rain batters the earth and it sounds like the roof of his car might buckle beneath the assault. His mind shifts. 'I'll be there in 10.'

***

If somebody were to look in on the two of them, sitting at Nora's dining table in her small two-bedroom house in the village, they would think they were friends who had enjoyed a meal. Various files Nora brought home to review are spread out across the table in between plates and wine glasses. To look at them both, a bystander would think nothing amiss or inappropriate is happening between them. But every breath in Roy's chest is filled with anticipation. Every second that goes by he is on guard. Nora's little house is filled to bursting with tension, both Roy and Nora do an expert job of acting natural, but just down the hall by the front door is where they gave in and kissed, the stairs is where they pushed each other, pulling at clothes, and the end bedroom beyond is where they lay together. The tension fills the house like too much air in a balloon.

Nora sighs after going over some of the details of the case for the thousandth time. She swings up out of her chair and clears the plates, leaving two odd gaps in the collage of paperwork that looks more and more like the crazy-wall from the office.

Roy's eyes betray him, and he watches Nora as she drops the dirty plates in the sink. He takes in her legs and her behind, her neck and her bare forearms. She is wearing casual clothes and every line and curve of her is new to him. On duty, she is restricted to sensible shoes, shirt and trouser suit, most of the time. Seeing her in an old baggy gig T-shirt, jeans and her hair tied back in a tail instead of a bun is almost scandalous to Roy. He shakes his head clear before she turns around and catches him looking. He almost laughs to himself; he has had sex with this woman but seeing her in a T-shirt is making him lose focus.

Nora comes back to the table and leans over, looking at the files, one hand on the back of Roy's chair. 'Where does he take them?'

Roy is all too aware of how close Nora is but she is oblivious. He shakes himself and comes back to the picture in his hand. It is a college picture of one of the missing women, Dhanni Sandhu, missing for five months now, last seen leaving her place of work at the hospital. 'He has to know the blind spots, where there are no cameras and little chance of witnesses.'

Together, they go over the reports but instead of focusing on the victims, they focus on the locations. There are never any witnesses, no camera footage and yet, all the places of abduction are public enough that anything Forensics has pulled is useless, be it hair, tyre tracks, fibres, or skin. There is simply too much traffic in those locations, having been used by thousands of people every week. There is too much to narrow down.

'Somehow he knows where the blind spots are. And he's patient.' Roy explains. 'Unless he's a psychic then he can't account for when people are going to be around, so he waits for the perfect moment when his target is alone.'

'What if he works at the Office of Surveillance, or knows someone who does?' Nora ventures. 'He could have access to surveillance areas, or at least know where doesn't have coverage, and then waits for his moment?'

Roy considers the theory. Somebody with that kind of access at the Council would know where was being recorded and where wasn't. It doesn't explain where the women are being taken or exactly what the scumbag is doing with them but it's a lead they can follow. 'That's good, Nora. That's really good.'

Nora blushes at the compliment, a barely controlled smile creeps onto her face. She is beautiful when she smiles.

'We'll go in the morning. We might need another warrant to get the employee details. Unless the Viper wants to poison our lead again, I can't see it being a problem.' Roy hopes Piper sees the logic and the gains they could make by seeing what their enemy does. Nora is still smiling, and Roy knows they should go to bed. Separately, before something happens. His will is iron, until it isn't. 'I should call it a night.'

'Right.' Nora steps away, sheepish at how close she was.

The second of silence grows between them and it feels like an hour. Roy forces the invisible hold to break. 'Right. I'm for bed. Good night.' He turns to leave but his legs are wooden. He wants to stay with her, talk with her, touch her but he can't. He shouldn't. The pain of his meeting with Emma from earlier washes over him but he forces it down, imagining the feeling as a burning energy that forces his legs to move.

She stops him short at the stairs. 'Roy?'

A silky despair runs over Roy as he both dreads and welcomes the words that must surely come next. If she asks or makes a move then Roy will spend the night with her. But she makes no move. She only stands awkwardly against her table like a child needing to ask their parent something she shouldn't.

'We're going to catch this guy, right?' Her soft voice belongs to a soul too young for this kind of work.

Roy forces a confident smile onto his face. 'Of course. We'll get him.' Nora smiles back, convinced and he forces himself away and up the stairs. He meant every word. To Roy, the question of catching this sicko, the Prince, was never in doubt. *Catching him in time to help these women? That's another matter.*

9. Lauren Tanner

Angie is crazy, to be able to settle herself into this nightmare, but say one thing about her; she is a survivor. Lauren lies on her side, with barely strength enough to hold her head up but Angie rotates through various exercises. They have been thrust into this pit against their will but Angie has found a way to stop it eroding her. She practises her exercises, treats Dhanni like a dear friend, somehow this woman has made her peace with this place until she is free. Something tells Lauren Angie's wrath would be something to behold should she ever get out of here, like she can bide her time forever and then unleash hell on this place. Lauren is envious of her attitude; must be easier than the fear.

It feels like a week since the Bull came in and took their food away. But Lauren knows that she would probably be dead if that were the case; it feels like she could pass at any moment. The cramps stopped a little while ago but now an ache like nothing she has ever felt has settled into her stomach, into her hips and her ribs, like a poison is slowly eating at her. Headaches come every few minutes with sharp pains behind her eyes. *Am I dying?*

The helplessness of her situation makes her doubt the point of everything she has been through so far. If she is this weak then how will she get out of here? And she will only get weaker. And if she dies? Then she will never see Gary again. She considers, not for the first time, if she must suffer the Bull and let him have her. Getting out and back to Gary is worth that, isn't it? Lose now to win later? Silent tears run over her face as she realises what she is doing; rationalising letting this place have her so that she can eat, so that she can embrace the hope that one day she will get out and be with her Gary again. But the angry voice in her head, smaller now, is just strong enough to fire up what little resolve she has left. *And that monster will let you go, will he? C'mon, what do you think, he'll just drop you off at home once he's had enough?* No. She can't let herself cave. She must do everything she can while saving who she is. Lauren watches Angie. She is sound of mind, on the outside, but not who she was before this place, surely. Can Angie go back to who she was if she ever gets out? Lauren doesn't think so.

Lauren's joints hurt as she pulls herself across the floor to the jug of water. She is sure a body can survive without food longer than without water. She must drink or she *will* die. And she is sure the Bull doesn't taint their water; none of them has fallen limp from drinking, only after eating. It takes everything she has to whimper over the padded floor to the jug between the three of them. There is only a mouthful left. She needs to lean to get the jug, the chain pulling one arm back as the other reaches.

Angie stares hard at Lauren as she changes position, dropping into and holding a plank on her elbows and toes. Guilt weighs on Lauren like a lead weight but it is nothing compared to the pains of her body. She hasn't even the energy to look ashamed. She upends the pitcher and savours every drop.

'Hey!' Angie pushes up to her knees and bangs on the wall. 'We need more water, you fuck!'

Lauren sluggishly rolls onto her back, her arm still held up by the chain and not caring. She hasn't felt her fingers or toes in hours, longer.

'Hey! You big black bastard!' Angie yells.

'Angie.' Dhanni mutters, her back to the rest of the basement. 'I want to sleep.'

Angie huffs back onto her bum angrily. 'I hope you feel good, Blondie. But I bet you don't.'

Lauren doesn't have the strength to fire back. Her eyes droop...

***

The shriek of the bolt jolts Lauren awake and she scuttles back against the wall, joints screaming. A fresh pitcher of water is in the middle of the room and Angie is wiping her mouth on the back of her arm from taking a drink. There is no sign of the Bull, both other girls are in their place, nothing seems amiss. *Did I miss him? He came in and I didn't even wake up?!*

Angie reads Lauren's mind. 'I told you before, Blondie. I get it. I really do. It is admirable what you're doing, but it is only a matter of time. Save yourself a lot of hurt.' In that moment she could be Lauren's best friend, the concern in her voice is so sincere she would weep if she had the energy. 'But more importantly, we're hungry, so get over yourself and do us all a favour.'

Lauren collapses back and tries to rub her eyes, but her hands shake. She clenches them into fists as hard as she can but still they wobble, her entire body shakes as if she is shivering.

Dhanni watches on. 'You should eat, Lauren. It's only going to get worse.'

'Believe us, we know.' Angie says quietly.

Lauren asks the question without making the decision to ask, her thoughts trip over each other. 'What's going to happen to me?'

A silence stretches out in the basement, long enough that Lauren thinks she never actually asked the question. Dhanni sighs. 'It varies. Depending how much body fat you have, how big you are... Right now, I'd guess your body is stripping itself to keep your nervous system active.' Every shred of emotion in Dhanni's voice has been grated away. She could be talking to a corpse.

'And then?'

'You'll get more and more lethargic. It'll hurt to move. Apathy. You won't care if you drink…' Dhanni pauses. 'Dehydration. Diarrhoea. You'll start to atrophy. Your stomach will bloat. It will hurt to swallow, to blink. Your body will continue to use up what nutrients are left throughout your system. You will fall unconscious. And death.'

Lauren feels sick. 'How long?'

Lauren can't see Dhanni from on her back but she imagines the woman shrugging her little shoulders. 'Maybe a month. A week if you dehydrate.'

Fuck. Lauren knows she can't go on like this. This is no real plan. There is no result to this. She is already finding it hard to think. Her body aches and she can hardly be bothered to roll over and take water. What is she expecting? Carry on like this and hope that somebody comes before it is too late? These women have been here months! And more before that.

Lauren doesn't know what to do. But this isn't going to work. She won't die down here but she can't live here knowing what that means either. Living here means accepting the Bull. Dying means never seeing Gary again. Maybe he'll never find out what happens to her, never know what she has been through? A new wave of sorrow threatens to drown her but she forces it away, some raw determination takes control of her and she jerkily gets onto her hands and knees. She quaffs as much water as she can but after only a mouthful it feels like she has been punched in the stomach. She falls back, gasping.

Angie sighs, frustrated, but she relents. 'Sips, Blondie. Bit at a time, yeah?'

'Do you care?' Lauren asks irritably.

'I won't watch this a second time!' She snaps and turns away.

'What choice do I have?' But Angie won't look at her. 'Dhanni? Do you hate me for this?' The Indian beauty's eyes just drop to the floor. 'There has to be something...' Lauren mutters. She shifts her position; her legs numb but the cramp in her stomach has eased. Whether that is a good sign or not though, she can't guess. 'Angie. Tell me about Jo and Theresa. Who was here with them, before you? Did anybody try anything, know anything?'

She ignores her.

'Angie?!' Lauren wants to scream at her for being difficult, for not helping her but she just can't dredge up the energy. Angie's head dips a little and then Lauren sees it. Her hands are limp in her lap. Slowly, she slides over onto her back, numb from the nose down. 'Angie...?'

Panic rises in Lauren's chest. Her heart beats like a hammer striking a nail inside her chest. She fitfully looks from Angie to the jug of water between them. *Oh no... the water... He put it in the water!*

Lauren tries to shift her legs but they won't move. She tries to pull at the chain in a vain attempt to be free, knowing it is futile, but her fingers won't close. What she took for another symptom in her stomach cramps easing away is just the numbing effect of whatever that animal puts in their food. Her head is heavy. She is wide awake; if her eyes could dig through the walls and carry her to safety then they would. Dhanni looks on with mild disinterest. She looks like she wants to say something to comfort her. But there are no words. Not for what is about to happen. Lauren puts every ounce of strength into lifting her head, every shred she has, just to raise a finger. But it is no use. Her body has betrayed her, seduced by the drug in the water. She screams. But her lips don't move. Her throat groans but it is a pathetic thing. Her heart jolts as the bolt slides free and the Bull enters. Tears flow free like two rivers suddenly released from a dam, precious moisture her body needs.

The Bull appears in her peripheral vision. The beast looks down at her like she is a trespasser in its pen, ready to charge and skewer her against the wall. He is topless again, but he wears joggers to cover his lower half. Lauren can hear the monster's breathing grow heavier and then he is on top of her. He doesn't hang her up like he did with Dhanni, he just uses his vast strength to manhandle her around and beneath him. Lauren has no choice but to look straight up into the face of the Bull. Its eyes bore into her with a certainty that she is now his. Her legs are dead weight, and they thump back down onto the padded floor as the underwear is pulled off her heals. He forces her legs apart but there is no fight in them; a weakling could manipulate her. Her body is a puppet with her trapped inside. She wants to claw his eyes out, she would kick him away and choke him with the chain, would do anything and everything to be rid of this monster. Lauren is screaming *no!* in her own head, screaming so loud her brain could crack but only a diminished squeak escapes her.

The Bull takes off his joggers, discards them on the floor. The monster hesitates, traces a thumb over the little spider tattoo on her hip. Her own little totem, tattooed by her Gary. The beast is slowed, his intent swerved? No, the moment passes and he enters her. There is no affection, no tenderness. Lauren is not ready, she is not wanting or wet, not like with Gary. The Bull forces himself in further and then he is fully on her. She can feel every throb and thrust of him and inside her own head she screams. Fresh tears roll over her cheeks. The Bull grunts, his energy boundless. Lauren rages, she screams like a harpy, except that she doesn't, she can't. She lies there, rocked, shoved, and her body responds. Slowly, it becomes easier as her body becomes wet, and the Bull renews his efforts. He enters as deep as he can go and if Lauren was able she would tear her own throat out. Then she recognises something sewn through the Bull's ear. The rings in each ear have jewels set in them but with fresh horror she sees her wedding ring. A row of wedding bands line each ear and Lauren knows they belong to each of the women he has kidnapped, imprisoned, and raped. The blanket of despair that has wrapped around her to this point flares up to suffocate her.

After a nightmarish eternity, a lifetime of humiliation and torture, the Bull's head arcs up. His heavy breathing peaks, faster and faster until finally he pulls out and ejaculates over her belly. Lauren feels the warmth, the wet as it seeps into her dirty shirt. She feels disgusting, ashamed. But it is a distant sensation compared to the pain in her groin. She aches and wants nothing more than for the animal to leave her be, to let her die and for this reality to be erased forever. But she can't move. She cannot even properly express the anguish that is burning hot in her like a needle.

The Bull glistens with sweat; droplets coat his shoulders and chest. He climbs back to his feet and starts to limp away as if his legs are stiff from his exertions, snatches up his joggers. He stops after only two steps as he sees Angie, sitting awkwardly the way she was. He drops his bottoms instantly, kneels and pulls her straight so he can get at her.

Lauren would call out to the other woman, to help her somehow but it is a half-thought; a whisper in her mind while her own pain drowns out all else. Everything else is consumed by her instinct to curl up and hug herself, to blot out the world and pray that this is just some repulsive nightmare and not real. Still, she can't help but watch from the corner of her eye.

The Bull lays Angie back and brushes the hair out of her face. Then the vile piece of shit pulls Angie's arms above her head and lifts her top. He exposes her breasts and life comes back into his manhood. Lauren can't watch again. She drags her eyes away and stares hard at the ceiling while the Bull mounts his second victim that day. Lauren's eyes are streaming, struggling to blink and a hurt, devouring sorrow eats at her insides.

The Bull finishes the same way, soiling Angie's stomach before stumbling away, clutching up his bottoms and throwing the prison into silence once more.

***

Lauren doesn't know how long she lay there unable to move. It could have been an hour, a day. Eventually, her malnourished body starts to wake up. First, she can move her lips, she presses them closed to let her dry mouth rehydrate but she has no spit to spare. Then, a dull ache, and then a rockslide of pains from her pointless starvation avalanche over her, making her groan onto her side.

'Lauren.' Dhanni acknowledges her revival.

Lauren ignores her, couldn't answer if she wanted to. Her mouth is heavy like trying to chew twenty pieces of gum at once, and dry as a desert. There are no more tears. She can make her hand into a fist, but it is with an effort of will that makes her fear if there are permanent side effects to the Bull's poison. A second later, blood flow makes her cringe as pins-and-needles attack her hands and feet.

'It'll pass.' Dhanni advises softly.

Lauren shudders, tries to lift her head but gives up only an inch off the padding.

'Nnggrrrgh.' Angie groans.

'Hey Angie.' Dhanni doesn't even look up, just rests her head on her knees.

After a few more minutes Lauren can roll over properly and get to her hands and knees. Her groin is in agony, like when she got kicked there by accident during football in school. Absent-mindedly she holds herself, hands clasped over her groin, still naked from the waist down how that freak left her. She inches her way over and retrieves her underwear. Getting them back on is a struggle with clumsy fingers but she won't be left so dishevelled. She would dress herself to cover what happened to her; she feels so stupid.

'Daargg… damn it…' Angie uses the wall to drag herself back into a sitting position but her face is scrunched against the pinching numbness in her limbs. Sluggishly, she manages to get to her knees and pull her top back down. She reaches for the pack of wet-wipes and cleans off her stomach.

'Mmmnn… For… me?' Lauren concentrates, forcing her mouth to obey.

Angie nods and throws the pack over to Lauren. She wipes off her own belly and throws the wipe into the bucket like it could burn her.

'For… what it's worth, Blondie… I'm sorry.' Angie works around the words but she recovers quickly.

Lauren doesn't want to speak. She doesn't want to chat. To do so would give what just happened to her power. To glance over it and do things as if everything is normal will turn her into these women. To let it affect her like it is, for the trauma of this despicable thing to hurt her the way it does, is better. The hurt gives it power also but not as much as the insidious way that she might become a part of this place with nothing left of her from outside of it, like Angie and Dhanni. So, Lauren curls up and faces her wall, hugs her abused body, and lets all the pain, fear and humiliation grow, she lets them fester. *I have been raped.* The thought replays in her mind repeatedly. *Raped. Am I different now, less than what I was?*

Angie puffs out a load of air. 'Jeez, he was rough today…'

'What's new?' Dhanni asks sarcastically but her tone is dead.

Exploited.

Angie chuckles briefly. 'This… isn't going to make me sound good, but… I got more practice than you.'

Abused.

'Your Husband?' Dhanni asks.

'Yeah… my Joe is about… the same as… him. I guess you two are not as used to it as me.' Angie flexes her fingers, trying to force the tingles away.

Damaged.

Silence stretches out for a minute or two. Such a small conversation is about as much as any of them have said to each other down here. It is as if, now Lauren has been reduced and subjected to what they have, an unseen barrier between them has crumbled away; a bridge between two cliffs connecting distant points on the same island where she only needs to walk and join the others. Lauren can't step onto that bridge though, not yet. She wishes she could just burn into ashes, purify her very existence and let the wind carry her away. But she can't do that either. There is no ablution or cleansing after what has been done to her and there is no free wind to carry her away. She weeps dry tears. Lauren tries to keep it in, to stay silent but her sniffles may as well be shouted at the top of her lungs for all any sound is hidden between them.

'I was only with one man before here.' The simple statement from Dhanni breaks the silence and chokes the sobs in Lauren's throat.

'One? Really?' Angie asks lightly.

'Mmm. My Husband. His name is Arnav. Means ocean. My folks are traditional, we were set up to be married years ago, but we met up here and there.' Dhanni takes a sharp breath as if tears threaten her, but it passes. Dhanni doesn't seem capable of crying any more. 'I miss him.'

A familiar voice in Lauren's head urges her to speak up, to convince Dhanni that she can see her Husband again, that she shouldn't give up. But the confident, resilient voice that was so strong before is stripped bare, skinned and raw from what she has suffered. The voice is there but it is a hurt thing, barely a squeak compared to the bellowing resolve it was. *What will Gary say? How can I go to him like this? Broken. Used. He won't want me anymore.*

Angie and Dhanni chat in bursts. Lauren keeps her place on her side facing the wall. Gradually, the ratio changes back, more and more the silence takes over; it suits Lauren fine. Every silent second is filled with images of her freedom; somehow slipping her chain and secretly fleeing back to Gary. Another minute and her visions of escape become more aggressive; she breaks the chain and storms up the stairs, throwing the door wide and racing through the house or whatever is up there, right in front of that animal and away before there is anything he can do. Another stretch of silence and her route to the outside world turns violent; in vivid motion she harms and even kills the Bull as he tries to stop her, beats at him, and fights her way clear to find Gary waiting for her. Each scenario is more and more ridiculous but each one gains weight in her mind. Suddenly, the cold sorrow that wrapped its icy fingers around her heart has thawed and her rage burns. Not a flame but embers; smouldering and ready to ignite the instant kindling is added.

The day when she severed with her college boyfriend, from him and the band; she won't even think his name after what he did, what he was going to do, was the worst day of her life. Now it is a distant second. Everything she would want for her and Gary to have has been taken away, ripped from her grasp in the most despicable way. Lauren can feel the shade of her old self fade within her; like a snake shedding its skin except into a more vulnerable self. The Lauren from before has been cut away by that fiend's rape, the Gary that she knew has been changed for surely she and he can never be the same again. The thought is a glowing brand inside her brain, searing and permanent.

Suddenly, there are no more sobs. Her breathing settles. She isn't alright. She will never be the same again. But the most hurt that animal can do to her has been done, even if he comes back a hundred times, or a thousand. She will bear that hurt because it is nothing to having her Gary taken from her in such a brutal way. This captivity could have cut what she and her Husband have, such a unique and divine connection but she won't let that happen either. Gary may hate her, blame her but he needs her as she needs him. His work; it is more important than she and can help him achieve his greatness. He has given her purpose. She won't be broken and cut off from Gary forever. *He can come back a million times, but I will get out of here. I won't give up.* She will do anything to get out of here. Starving herself, growing weaker and weaker will not make that happen. She must stay strong. She must eat. She sees that now. Lauren cringes against herself because that means the Bull will be back for her, but she forces herself still, controls herself with power she never knew she had. Her hand settles on something light and hard beside her. Slowly she brings the small object up to her chest and clutches it tight as if it were the key to her chain…

A plan blossoms and takes a hold of her soul. She doesn't plan to rip the chain away from the wall or fly away like the half-mad grief-stricken visions from those moments ago. She hugs Angie's plastic spoon to her heart, that she threw before, such a small thing but even small things can do grievous hurt. The Bull will learn to fear the Spider. She will make this small thing a weapon, a shiv, and she will make that animal bleed for everything he has done. Then, Lauren will take the keys from the Bull, undo their chains, and get out of here.

10. Inspector Roy Harvey

'Here you go, Harvey.' The Viper hands over the folder with the warrants in. She could be a hunting bird perched in a tree for all the warmth she shows. Like her, the office is ordered and cold as always, everything in its place, everything relevant; three pens are lined up perfectly next to the reports she is working on, her keyboard is at a level angle to her monitor. Roy would not be surprised if the vertical blinds were measured so they were an exact distance apart.

The only thing out of place is the picture on her desk. It faces away from him, toward the Viper but Roy knows who the picture is of. Sabrina Piper, Lesley's sister. Fourteen years ago, he was assigned to his first missing persons case, to help follow up on witness statements much like Joey has for this current case. Green, enthusiastic, and completely out of his depth, Roy began his career. Sabrina Piper was missing. This was before Lesley was even on the force. Sabrina Piper was found sexually assaulted, murdered, and buried along with two others. Lesley joined the force soon after and rose in record time, like nobody before her, to make sure something like that didn't happen again. Of course, it always does. Roy looks sadly at the back of the photo frame. He had no control on the proceedings of that case but there has always been a noose of barbed wire around both he and the Viper's necks where it is concerned, he was involved in the case that ended with her sister's death; in part Roy failed her. It is a ridiculous notion, there is nothing he could have done but he must be a constant reminder of that terrible event. 'Thank you, Chief.'

The Viper must pick up on Roy's train of thought because she adjusts the picture. 'It wasn't easy to get you a warrant for the Office of Surveillance at the Council. This had better be good. What have you got so far?'

They haven't got anything solid so far, nothing has changed since the last time Roy stood in this office. He absently flicks through the folder. 'I think our guy knows where the CCTV blind spots are. We figure he either works at the Office of Surveillance or has access, maybe working with somebody to get the info. It isn't a coincidence we're blind to all the abductions.'

The Viper nods, impressed with the idea. 'Sounds feasible,' And the cold posture is back. 'But it's still a hunch.'

'We also want to check the surrounding areas covered by CCTV; a camera somewhere will have caught this guy even if from a distance. Nor- Murphy is setting up rotations for the new guys now.' He explains.

'Good. Keep me informed.' The Chief dives back into her report, her pen scratching across the paper as if Roy were never there.

Roy almost leaves but holds still, sensing there is more.

After a moment the Viper sets her pen back down next to the others and sits back. She looks Roy up and down. 'You look better. Are you back home?'

Roy grimaces. 'Not quite. Getting there.' The lie comes easily.

'Well, whatever you're doing, keep getting you're rest. You have been an asset to the department these last few years,' *And not before.* Her thought is left unsaid. 'We stand a better chance of catching this one if you are in good shape. And not the homeless galoot that was here last time.'

It is about as much of a compliment as he is going to get. 'Yes, ma'am.'

She regards the folder in Roy's hand. 'Get it done.' Her pen is back in her hand and Roy dismissed.

Roy doesn't hesitate this time. He leaves without another word.

***

The conference room next to Roy and Nora's office, with the 'crazy-wall', has several tables in rows for when meetings and presentations are held. The new hands that volunteered or were assigned by the Viper come in and Roy offers them all a seat. They chat and mutter amongst themselves, one says something that makes one burly officer chuckle like a chimp. None of them are Inspectors but up and coming beat walkers, two are Sergeants. Volunteering for these extra assignments doesn't give any extra credit to passing the exams for Inspector but if and when they do pass it is all experience they will need. All six are men in their late twenties, early thirties, all tall and eager. Joey sits down with them. Nora is up front and centre in front of the whiteboard.

'We've got a lot of ground to cover so I'm going to skip your intros and learn your names on the way.' Nora speaks confidently. Roy smothers a smile at a 5 foot-something girl talk to them like part-timers. She knows their names and details by heart, but she needs them to hate her a little bit; real respect is born from contempt, it is won. Jones, Watkins, Mathers, Wyatt, Simpson and Davies, to a man, shuffle their positions. 'Any questions before we begin?'

'Yeah,' Wyatt, a balding Officer who can't be any more than thirty asks. 'Why is he called the Prince?'

'Started as a bad joke.' Joey leans in but loud enough for them all to here. 'After the first few rings were found somebody made a joke about the guy using them to pierce his prick. You know, a *Price Albert*? Well, somebody let slip to the papers and they had a name to scare folk with.'

'Who made the joke?' Simpson asks.

'Couldn't tell ya.' Joey shrugs with a twinkle in his eye.

'Rings?' Jones, the biggest of them, asks.

Nora has the projector remote in hand ready. 'I'll get to that.' *click* A picture of a woman in her late twenties with long curly brown hair appears on the board behind her; a photo provided by family. Nora steps aside out of the projectors light. 'This is Sam Somersby. First woman we believe is connected to The Prince, reported missing fifty-one weeks ago. She worked as a self-employed beautician so travelled up and down the country. It was a friend of hers that reported her missing,' Nora checks a list of names on the table next to her. '…A Sandra Hardy. We are going to go over each statement and revisit every person on this list. It is boring. It will suck. But we need you to be focused. Any small detail could be pivotal in catching this guy.'

Mathers, a lean Officer with fiery red hair raises his hand.

'Yes?' Nora invites.

Mathers moves to stand but adjusts his seat instead. 'Leigham Mathers. What do you mean connected?'

'There have been twenty-two missing people reported in the last twelve months, from Berry local, that haven't turned up inside 72 hours, or fit the Prince's pattern. Twelve of those have been in the last fifty-one weeks. You've read the papers, heard about the missing twelve. It may be more. We hope it's less. But a month apart, give or take, a new name is reported and hits our desk. The profile is married women who live in Berry, conventionally attractive.' Nora sighs and lifts the remote again.

click The picture changes from Sam Somersby to a woman in her early twenties with a striped top and mousy brown hair. 'Karly Schwarz. Last seen by her postman, a month after Mrs Somersby.'

click A black woman with an incredible smile appears. 'Beverly Wainwright. Last seen leaving her gym a month later.'

click 'Zoe Knowles.' A blonde, teacher at Alton Primary.

click A white girl appears, a graduation photo. 'Theresa Reynoulds.'

click 'Joanne Hannah,' A woman in her mid-thirties.

click 'Angelia Smith.' On her wedding day.

click 'Dhanni Sandhu.' From a group photo at the hospital where she worked.

click 'Edyta Durak.' On holiday.

click 'Penny Wainright. No relation to Beverly. A month later.'

click 'Gemma Simpson.' Also on her wedding day.

click The final image is of the latest reported missing person. A slim blonde woman, twenty-six years. 'Lauren Tanner. Two weeks ago. Gentlemen, these women, by our psycho's design, have disappeared. They have families, children. Our aim here is to get them home.'

Roy knows the profiles; he knows the information but Nora's presentation hits him like he is seeing it for the first time along with their new recruits.

Nora pauses to let the list of names sink in; the faces, the time spent missing and what that means. Most of these women have been missing from the world for months where absolutely nobody, that doesn't mean them harm, knows where they are. It is a terrifying concept for even these flat-footed officers who deal with domestic violence, robberies, and road accidents every other day. The fact that somebody is taken, who can just vanish into thin air at the manipulation of another isn't, or shouldn't be, an everyday thing. It is good that they are stunned; means they will try harder.

Roy scans the faces of his six new men. They are glued to Nora. They have no words, no more laughter. These women need help and now they could be a factor in whether they come home alive, if at all.

'It seems pretty random but there are some similarities. We believe these women are connected because of the circumstances surrounding their disappearance and because of what our guy leaves behind.' Nora is grimly determined. *click* The projector brings up a blueprint map of the city with highlighted spots across it. 'The green spots here are the locations where our missing women were last seen. The red is where we believe they were taken.'

'Sorry, what do you mean 'what he leaves behind'?' Davies, a black Officer with a shaved head, pipes up.

Nora glances at Roy but it is not for support, more just to acknowledge that this is the big crack in their logic. 'At each scene we have found exactly one item left behind. An engagement ring. All these women are married. The reason these particular women are on our list is because their rings were found at what we believe to be the places of abduction.' She shrugs. 'We think it's a middle finger, to prove he has them. Like keeping score.'

'You're sure it's a *him*?' Mathers, the redhead again.

Roy steps forward and hands Nora the warrants. 'We've got the Surveillance Office.' He mutters and turns back to Joey and the others. 'In these sorts of cases it is almost always a man. Males, generally, maintain dominant traits of superiority. They entertain ideas of taking what they want and to hell with the consequences. They can be more reckless. It is also easier for women to feel apathy when it comes to strangers.' Roy regards the map. 'By all accounts, none of these women have anything in common; they work in different areas, have different friends, most are different race and religion. It seems the only thing they have in common is that they are all between the age of twenty and forty, married and attractive.

'Female kidnappers usually have a specific connection with the victim, usually very personal, unless the victim is a child, ironically. It is likely a male predator is targeting these women because he likes what he sees. He is taking them. After that? We don't know yet. But I'm sure you can guess.' Every man in the room knew about this case, they have all heard about the missing women but to have it explained like this is something new to them, most of the details have thankfully been kept from the papers. Roy hopes these boys can handle it.

'The reason we have brought you on board is because our guy is careful.' Nora steps forward as Roy steps away. 'Every location where we found an engagement ring is out of CCTV coverage. There have been no witnesses. We need to check the CCTV in all the surrounding areas for 24hrs before each woman disappeared. We have warrants,' Nora shakes the folder from the Chief Superintendent. 'To obtain the CCTV from the places of business, street camera's, security from surrounding buildings, the works. We also have warrants for employee records. We will be interviewing anybody we think can help. We also want to go over every statement and revisit those we need to. We do everything and miss nothing.'

It would be a colossal task for twenty let alone the nine of them. Roy grimaces at the thought of the months that Nora, Joey and himself have been struggling through, only receiving extra help for a short time when a new disappearance was identified. *With enough support could we have stopped this guy by now? Maybe. How long will we have these guys for, at least until next month when another woman goes missing?*

'We have a lot of work to do but first we need to go over each missing person. You all need to know the details, inside and out. After that we'll divide up the tasks and get to it. I want to bring these girls home. And bring them home alive. That's what we're about.' Her words make every man in the room nod, jaws set to task. 'Let's start at the beginning… Sam Somersby-' Nora looks each one of the officers in the eye and in that moment Roy is besotted. Nora may be small but she is strong and determined. Roy feels like they can't fail.

The rest of the afternoon is spent going over the specifics of each missing person's case; dates, locations, profile, friends, everything they have without reading each statement and file word for word out loud. It is the first of many long days ahead but they are keen. Each man is assigned a series of cameras, dates, and statements with instruction to report anything of even the smallest value. They set up recognition software that overlaps the CCTV footage added to the program. It should find and catalogue anyone on the ID database that appears in the same frames as the missing women. It is by no means a perfect set up hence why Nora and Roy set the lads to search manually too. After all, there are only so many million identities saved on the system, and it is not 100% accurate. But it could help. They need more equipment, and more help besides, but suspects, familiar vehicles, any detail that repeats itself or links the missing women will do. There must be a common factor and as soon as they find it they will have a link to the bastard behind all this.

***

After three days of meeting with the victim's families again, reviewing statements and getting slapped in the face from Joanne Hannah's Mother, thrown out of the house by Theresa Reynoulds' Husband, for not doing enough, they are still no closer to finding these women than when they started. Roy doesn't blame the families for their anger; their Wives and Mothers have been gone for nearly a year in some cases, and now Roy is asking them the same questions they asked in the beginning. But with each dead end and cold trail Nora's determination doubles. She is bulletproof to the eroding time frame that eats at the possibility of any of these girls coming home alive and well.

At home, at Nora's place, each evening they complete the same ritual. They eat and go over all they can, cross referencing employee records with victim affiliations, anything in statements that might suggest a common factor and then awkwardly say goodnight and go to bed separately for a few hours before starting again at the office. During the day both Roy and Nora are the peak of professional conduct, only rarely does Roy see Nora in that dangerous way where his mind slips. Nora during the day, to her credit, doesn't show any sign that anything ever happened between them. She handles the team with confidence and in all but name is the chief of the squad. If Roy is the tower of experience, then Nora is the searching light on top of the lighthouse. But when they are in the car, alone, when they step through her front door and she can pull off the shell that is Inspector Nora Murphy, and become Nora Murphy, twenty-six-year-old with what seems like an endless amount of old gig T-shirts, she slips and Roy can see her wanting to hold him, to ask him to. But she won't. She said there would be no funny business, that staying with her is for the good of the case, and she won't ruin that. The pressure is on Roy not to give in for he surely feels the same wants, needs, if not more so.

One morning Roy came out of the spare room and Nora stepped out of the bathroom, towel wrapped around her from the shower. By accident or by fate the towel slipped and exposed Nora's wet form. She caught the towel in time to cover her front, holding it against herself with a giggle of embarrassment but Roy took in every line of her hips and curve of her breast before she was able to get the towel back in place. Nora looked at him then, stuck halfway out of the bathroom door, naked and spotted with water apart from the damp towel. He was certain that was it, they were going to give in again. Her hand twitched at the towel as if to tug it away and just let him have her. Roy juddered within himself, caught between his want and his guilt from the last time. The second passed and Nora stepped away and into her room. Maybe she meant for Roy to follow, to make the first move, but he didn't.

***

'Roy! Nora!' Joey calls through from the conference room that has become a hub of action and not just their centre of operations.

Each member of the team has borrowed, stole and blackmailed bits of equipment from whoever they could so that now each of them have a laptop, stationary, portable hard drives, phones and anything else they could carry away. Each of them has recognition software running side by side with CCTV footage whizzing by at 4x regular speed. There is barely enough room to put down a cup of 'coffee' from the machine amongst all the monitors and cables.

Roy and Nora find Joey standing behind one of the laptops, helmed by Sergeant Mathers, the others out following up on statements. 'What is it, Joey?'

'We found something.' Joey nods at the laptop, fan whirring as the old piece of kit struggles to do what they need it to. 'Leigham might have found a suspect.'

Nora looks at Roy and the strength of light in her eyes makes him believe they have caught the guy already. 'Show me.'

'I've been going over the CCTV footage from the surrounding areas of Dhanni Sandhu, Joanne Hannah and Lauren Tanner. From their places of work, car parks, street cam's, everything we've got. Well, look at this.' Leigham speeds through different windows and brings up some stills from various cameras. 'This is a traffic Cam from Sitwell Street near where Joanne Hannah lives…'

He shows them a man in a duffel coat with balding hair, half hidden by the turnoff, seeming to look down Joanne's street. It is hardly excellent quality but good enough for a profile of whoever this guy is. '…and this.' Leigham expands another window showing a hospital wing and presses play on the recording. Dhanni Sandhu is talking with a nurse over a counter, handing over a file of some sort. 'This is where Dhanni Sandhu works at the Belleview. Look there.' He points in the background and waiting on a bench is the same man in the duffel coat and he is staring straight at Mrs Sandhu. She walks away leaving the frame but the man follows her, staying back but matching her pace. 'These two are from a fortnight ago. The recognition software flagged this as a hit. Lauren Tanner's bus as she rides to work. Mrs Tanner is there look.' Leigham points to her on the left side of the screen; she is sat looking at something on her phone. 'And look who is sat next to her.'

Roy leans in and Mr Duffel Coat is beside her. He looks at her and Lauren seems to shuffle uncomfortably. A minute later she gets off the bus and before it can pull away, Mr Duffel Coat gets off too.

'This is from a security camera across the road from her stop, a few minutes from her office. There's Mrs Tanner.' Leigham points her out at the top corner of the monitor. Lauren Tanner pulls her blazer tight about her as if cold and heads into an alley that comes out across from Cavendish & Son's. Mr Duffel Coat waits at the bus stop and watches as Lauren Tanner disappears into the alley. The look on his face is that of a vulture waiting for his food to give up, greying hair wisps around his ears. After a moment he follows Lauren Tanner's steps and disappears into the alley, the same alley where they found her ring.

Nora looks deep into Roy's eyes, asking, searching for something, not permission, but agreement. Roy makes the call. 'Alright people, we have a suspect. Leigham, get the best picture of this guy you can. Trace him back on the footage, find out where he got on that bus. Joey? Same for the hospital. Check their records, see if he signed in or had an appointment. Call the others and have them keep at it. This guy fits the bill and is connected to three of our missing persons, at least. Let's find him. Now.'

The four of them jump into action, Joey and Leigham each taking a station and loading various bits of footage. Nora follows Roy as he marches from the room. 'Mathers? Joey? Send me those files. As soon as we have an address we're going to bring him in. But the Viper will want an update.' He shouts back.

'...Done! Should be with you now.'

'What do you want me to do?' Nora asks.

A scandalous thought bully's its way to the front of Roy's mind involving slamming the door shut on his back office and making sure they have privacy, but he forces the fantasy away. He falls into the role of teacher and friend once more. 'You know what to do, Nora.' He means it too. Nora has been the driving force of this team and she knows exactly what she is about.

'I'll pull the guys back and start going over the footage to see if this guy shows up again. And I'm still going over the employee records from the Council, as soon as we find out who this guy is, I can see if he has any connections there.' Nora runs through a dozen different jobs in her head and sets herself to task.

'I'm going to see the Chief with this footage. I'll need an address before she signs off an entry team.' Roy sends the files to the Viper.

'On it.' Nora grins like a shark and they set out with fresh blood to follow.

***

The footage was more than enough for the Viper to sign off on bringing in Harry Chelby aka Mr Duffel Coat. Fifty-three years of age, widower, served several months, several different times, for breaking restraining orders. It happens to people; they lose the thing in life that keeps them in a civilised structure and go off the rails. It can be a Wife, like in Chelby's case, or a child, a job, anything that grounds a person to living a conventional life. When a man has nothing else, he soon finds something else to rule his life, even if that something isn't his. Harry Chelby has been picked up before for stalking and harassment, seems now he has decided to do the picking up. Chelby has no history of aggression, as per his psychological profile from his time in prison, so Roy has hope that the missing women are alive. Held against their will certainly, but Chelby most likely won't have harmed them beyond how he has them kept.

Roy and Nora are in the back of a hit van. Both are clad in stab vests and fully equipped riot belts. Eight response officers are in the van with them ready to break down Harry Chelby's door, subdue him and secure the victims. Another two vans are behind them with another eight officers in each, scattered with their team and Joey who update the entry teams, with ambulances on standby. The psychological profile may not rule this guy as a violent offender, but they will take every precaution when going into his den. And there could be twelve women who need immediate assistance.

Nora adjusts the Velcro strap under her armpit for the fourth or fifth time, adjusts the pouches on her belt that hold the handcuffs and Taser pistol.

'Nervous?' Roy asks but regrets it instantly in front of the other Officers. None of their heads turn but they hear every word. He shouldn't suggest that she has any shortcomings in front of them.

Nora looks up sharply, eyes hard but she doesn't spit back in front of the others. 'I'm fine.'

Roy rolls his shoulders knowing he made her look weak. He knows it isn't entry or apprehension of Chelby that bothers her but whether or not the missing girls are alive, whether they are too late. 'I'm nervous.' He donates even though outwardly he shows no sign. His stomach always gets twisted up before going in like they are. Admitting it in front of the other Officers is asking for mockery later but Nora has enough of that just from being a female Inspector. Times have changed but there is still an element of prejudice in the Force. Roy was a chief offender when Nora first started on his team but after seeing her work, in solving the Garner case, his opinion quickly changed.

Nora softens, recognising the gesture but she becomes serious instantly, knowing they have a job to do. She takes the lead. 'Jones?' The big Officer, with a laugh like a chimp, leans up. 'You crack the door. Watkins? You have point. The rest of us will follow you in. I want every room secured. Every door, cupboard and hole checked. Remember we have twelve missing women. He could have them anywhere.'

Watkins is in the passenger seat up front. 'Yes, Ma'am. Sixty seconds.'

Every member of the team has already been briefed; each van assigned one of the three houses to secure. Harry Chelby's recorded address is a detached house on Stenson Avenue, but he owns the houses on either side of him. After his Wife died in a car accident her life insurance made him a wealthy man and he bought up the three houses, two to rent out and one to live in. They could find no rental agreements for the properties; it's possible tenants hold private agreements with Chelby but Roy and Nora don't think so. With three houses at his disposal, he has the room to keep twelve women separate and confined. With some soundproofing the neighbours wouldn't hear a thing.

'Everyone clear?' Nora asks. Thumbs go up from every member and she gets an all clear from the vans behind on her radio. They pull up and then the double doors are open. Jones strides forward with the ram and lets out an almighty grunt as he slams it into the door at the lock. The door blows away after a second hit and the way is clear. Jones steps to the side out of the way and drops the ram ready to join the back of the team.

'Police!' Watkins is in and shouting.

Simultaneous bangs echo from each side as the other teams break through the front doors. Three officers stay behind to secure the street. And then Roy is in, Nora a step behind.

The inside of the house is as one might expect from a house on Stenson Avenue; textured wallpaper on the walls, voiles in the windows, carpeted floors, pictures on the shelves, dining table that folds down to save space, fridge-freezer with magnets on the front. All normal. There is shouting and a scuffle from upstairs. Roy directs two officers to the back of the house, reminding them to check every access point, behind sofas, floorboards, anything that may be a compartment or a hidden room. Nora is already halfway up the stairs; Roy takes them two at a time to keep up. It is not an enormous house, two bedrooms, one bathroom only. Watkins and the other officers are on top of Harry Chelby in one of the bedrooms. He is on his front, hands cuffed behind his back with the weight of three men on him. He is dressed only in a pair of underpants.

'I've done nothing!' Chelby croaks out, his voice dripping with panic.

Both Nora and Roy ignore him. The window is half open. Roy guesses Chelby spent precious seconds wondering what the crash of his front door slamming open could be and then decided to escape. Roy checks out the window. Below is the kitchen roof and garden. Where he would have gone from there is anybody's guess, especially in his underwear but it would probably be better than Watkins' knee pinning him to the floor.

'Downstairs clear!'

'Clear up here!'

'Good job!' Roy calls. 'Find the women.'

'What women?' Chelby squeaks.

'Shut the fuck up.' Watkins grunts and proceeds to read him his rights. 'You're under arrest for the kidnapping...'

One wall of the bedroom is covered in photographs. The whole wall is an enormous collage of women; some are whole shots and from a distance, at the supermarket or the train station, obviously taken by him from some vantage point. Others are cut out from the background, added to gaps in the wall to fill every inch. There are a few print-offs from the internet, much more sexually explicit pictures spliced in with the photograph's Chelby has taken of women around Berry. Roy can't help but scan the wall and take it all in. There is close up's of breasts and women on their knees with their tongues out, stills from some porno's. In the corner is a pc and printer. Roy shakes his head clear and turns away from the wall. Nora meets him, her eyes taking in the wall.

'Is this what men really want?' She gestures at the pictures, no doubt meaning the pornographic shots and not the pictures taken about the city.

'Sometimes.' Roy mutters.

'Inspector's?' Jones calls.

'In here.' Roy calls back.

Jones finds them and reports. 'Sir. The other two houses are clear. Lived in. Occupants are probably at work-' Jones reports but trails off at seeing the wall.

'Jones?' Nora prompts, irritated.

'We've not found anybody.' He looks sheepish.

'Chelby?' Roy asks. 'Where are they, Somersby, Wainright, Tanner?'

'I don't who you mean! I've done nothing!' Chelby is turning purple.

'Watkins? Leave off a little.' Roy kneels so he and Chelby are almost face to face. 'This'll go better for you if you just tell us. I want to know where they are, what you have done to them and how you took them. In that order.'

Chelby tries to shake his head in disbelief, but he can't. 'I don't know what you're talking about!'

'Hey...' Jones steps up to the wall, hypnotised by something there, one of his big hands pointing. '...that's Alice... that's my Wife!' Suddenly he is across the room and Watkins is thrown off Chelby. Jones doesn't flip Chelby over to get at him, he just pounds into the back of his skull, bouncing his cheek off the floor. He scores two massive hits before the other Officers pull him off.

'Get him out of here!' Nora orders. Two officers drag the big man out.

Chelby is whining like a pig, his head and cheek no doubt swelling already. Roy leans down again. 'Where are they Chelby?'

Snot, spittle, and a little blood all connect Chelby's face to the carpet. 'I don't have any women!' He spits. 'I just want to be left alone!'

Roy shakes his head in disbelief. 'Get him in the van.'

Watkins hauls their detainee away. Chelby calls for justice and to be let go, his words thick in the air after the beating Jones gave him. Wyatt sets up at Chelby's computer and begins taking it to pieces for seizure and examination.

Nora calls to another Officer on hand. 'Call Forensics, tell them it's clear to come down. Get this place checked over. Double check every nook and cranny of these houses. I want to be sure we haven't missed anything. Last thing I want is for Forensics to open the biscuit tin and find somebody's hand already in it.' Nora steps close to Roy's ear. 'What if they're not here?'

'Then he has them somewhere else. We'll find them.' Roy nods at Wyatt as he bags up Chelby's PC. 'They'll be something we can use even if he doesn't talk.'

***

There is nothing. After six hours of questioning, a few hours respite and then another four hours of talking to Chelby his story hasn't changed. He doesn't know the missing girls. Recognition flared from a couple of the pictures but he didn't know their names, he had just seen them around. Chelby has been known for stalking women, following them, taking their picture but never gone any further than that, never harmed anyone or so much as called them a disrespectful name. He just likes to look; infuriatingly there is little Roy can do to him for that. Worse, his PC is clean. Well, it is filthy. There is a thousand hours' worth of pornographic videos, a few thousand images both explicit and decent, his internet history was deleted but Wyatt was able to recover that and aside from a few dozen dirty sites there is absolutely nothing to tie him to any of the missing women bar a handful of pictures taken from a distance. Worst of all, forensics came up short too, nothing. No evidence other than the few instances of Chelby on CCTV in the vicinity of the missing women to tie him to this case. In short, Chelby is a loner and weirdo, but innocent of everything else. The whole operation is a bust.

Roy and Nora were only home for a few hours before they came back in, a thousand things still need doing; reports, cross examination, following up with forensic results, catching up with witness statements and not to mention continuing the search to find a link between the missing women and how the Prince can abduct them and stay invisible. They are back where they started.

The Viper has left two voicemail messages along with several messages demanding that Roy turns in so he can report directly to her. Joey, Watkins, and Mathers are back searching footage. Jones was sent home to cool off after the Chelby incident and the others are either out chasing statements or at home catching some sleep. All of them give Roy a sympathetic look as if they know he must walk into the snake's lair barefoot. Nora has been summoned too.

There is no point in putting it off so they both find themselves in Piper's office. She permitted they come in, but has yet to even look up, let alone acknowledge them further. The silence stretches out to an unbearable degree when the Viper's pen clatters down on the desk, and she addresses Nora. 'Well, that was a cock-up. What happened, Inspector?'

Nora grimaces but covers it quickly. 'They weren't there.' It's Roy's turn to grimace. The Viper won't like that.

The Chief's eyes harden to glass. 'I don't expect an answer that is obvious, Inspector. Tell me *why* they weren't there. Tell me whose cock-up this is!'

If Nora had a tail it would have tucked itself between her legs. 'Chief, Chelby ticked all the boxes. We had every reason to suspect he was The Prince.'

'The Prince? I don't care what funny little name the papers have given this maniac. I care if we do our jobs. This was your operation, yes? This colossal waste of time is on you.' The Viper licks her lip preparing for an onslaught, like the snake she is named after, rattling her tongue before springing into the attack.

Nora straightens her back, head up, ready. 'Yes Ma'am-'

'It was my call on this one, Lesley.' Roy interrupts.

Nora jolts a questioning look at Roy, part incredulity at using the Chief's first name and part accusing him as if she needs protecting. Roy ignores her and just hopes she keeps her mouth shut and accepts the ticket out of here.

The Viper checks the report in her hand. 'Says here Inspector Murphy directed.'

'That is an error, Ma'am. I headed this one.' Roy can feel the disbelieving eyes of both women burn into him, daring him to slip up; the Viper because there is no way the information she has is incorrect, and Nora because she wants to prove she doesn't need looking after like a rookie.

The Viper's stare drills into Roy for an excruciating second. 'Murphy. Get out.'

Nora dips her head a fraction and leaves without a word.

'You're fucking her, aren't you?' She says it like she's tired of the answer before he has even voiced it.

Roy gives her a hard look. 'No, I'm not.' *Technically true.* He explains further before she can interrupt him. 'She has offered me her spare room for a while until I can sort things out at home. She's a good person.'

'But you want to, yes?'

'What possible relevance would it have if I did?' Roy asks, defensive.

'Answer the question, Roy.' She won't back down.

'She's a brilliant young woman, surely there'd be something wrong with me if I didn't, Lesley?' He stands his ground, refusing to look away.

The Viper chews her reply before standing, straightening her cuffs. Her small heels tip-tap as she comes around her desk and settles on the edge with her arms folded. 'You will call me Ma'am or Chief Superintendent Piper.'

Roy sighs through his nostrils. 'Yes, Ma'am.'

'Good. Now,' she stares right into Roy's mind. 'This business at home, is it because of Inspector Murphy? Have you slept with her?'

It's a gamble to lie. And a sentence to tell the truth. What if it comes back on him? It doesn't matter, the missing twelve stand a better chance of being found with him on the case. 'No.'

'I don't want to hear any different.' Her eyes dig into him.

'You won't. It's just a temporary thing.' Roy puts all his will into keeping eye contact, selling his lies and desperate not to examine the Chief's body. Whether it is the nature of this case, with the attractive twenty to thirty-something's going missing, living with Nora this past week, or seeing all of Chelby's pictures, Roy doesn't know, but he has definitely been feeling more lustful. Even alone with the Viper he must focus. This woman burns his skin but her authority, maybe her derision toward him makes his loins stir and he wonders if he has lost his self-control along with his edge.

The Chief glances out of the window as if pondering her next words. Roy can't stop himself. He glances down and takes in the Chief's body. She could never be called a beautiful woman, but neither is she repulsive. The dislike and bitterness that her name brings out in people is largely due to the way she conducts herself; she is the Viper after all. Her figure is trim despite being behind a desk for most of every week and the buttons running over her chest are taught from a bust too big or a shirt too small. Roy straightens up as she looks back and he knows he was a split second too late. She caught him. The Viper's eyes harden to diamonds and Roy dreads what is about to happen. She stands and closes the gap between them in a step. She is so close that Roy can smell the light perfume he didn't know she wears. 'Find. Those. Women.' Her tone is slate on ice. She whips around and is back in her seat before Roy can blink.

'Yes, Chief.'

'Harvey?' She stops him as he reaches the door. 'If you are distracted then I will put you somewhere where you can't be. If today really was *your* fuck up, then I would get my act together if I were you. You were a liability when we first met, but we were both young, and you proved to be competent in other cases, so I let it drop. I also know it was Murphy that gave you the big break on the Garner case. I would think it would be you leading her what with your experience, not the other way around. Now find something for these women and fast. Get out.'

The words are a slap in the face. Roy slams the door on his way out. The further Roy gets away from the Viper's office the more the simmering rage within him boils up. He charges through the station toward his office. He can't believe himself for getting distracted like that. What is going on with him? It must be his mounting temptation from living with Nora. And then Chelby's place, the nature of his pictures and videos.

Nora catches him as soon as he walks in, her eyes search his for answers. 'What the hell was that Roy? I don't need looking after like that.'

Roy passes her and throws his jacket over his desk. 'You're welcome, Nora.'

'Hey guys, how did it go with the Viper?' Joey asks as he comes in.

'Not now Joey!' Nora barks without taking her eyes off Roy.

'Right you are.' And he spins around on the spot, pulling the office door closed.

'I'm serious, Roy. The noble act won't fly with the Chief, and I can look after myself!' Nora's hands are on her hips as her eyes burn. 'What the hell gives you the right to jump in like that?'

'What do you want me to say, Nora? Why don't you go and tell her it was your operation if you've got such a problem?' Roy isn't mad at Nora and doesn't want to take his frustration out on her; she has been nothing but kind to him, but a rage is on him and it will let itself out, even if it's himself he should be mad at.

'It didn't go our way yesterday. We're a step back, I get it but what the hell is wrong with you? What did the Viper say?' She demands, her chin jutted up defiantly. She knows him well enough to see his mood is a far cry from when she was dismissed.

'There's nothing wrong with me, Nora. I'm doing just great!' Roy barks a corrosive laugh and makes for the door.

Nora catches his elbow and swings him around. He whips his arm away and Nora's eyes aren't burning any more, they are hurt. 'Talk to me.' She pulls at him, distraught at not knowing what is going through his head.

'What do you want me to say?!' Roy is all but shouting now and with an effort he brings his voice under control. It sounds more of a dangerous growl. 'We may as well be back at square one! I am useless to these women. There is a connection here, I know it, but I can't figure it out!'

'We're going to find this guy…' Nora tries to soothe.

'We?! *We've* been at this for months now. We wouldn't know some of these women if their bodies were left out in the street!' He rages, truth fighting its way out and attacking his partner. 'Fat lot of good we've done. I've got nothing on this one Nora and so far you've had fuck all to offer too.'

'Don't do that, Roy. This one is different, you said so; he is careful and he has method. Don't you dare blame me for not finding them?!' Nora is incredulous.

This is just the fight Roy has needed, but it is with the wrong person. He should have had this blow out with Emma when he first told her about Nora. Without all this time for her resentment to fester, maybe they could have taken steps to building something new. But now he is here, Nora is getting both barrels. 'You should thank me. The Viper already hates my guts over what happened to her Sister. With all of your fuck ups she's only adding to the list!'

'You're an arsehole. I don't know what I was thinking.' Nora's eyes turn cold.

'You and me both.' Roy puts as much venom into the words as he can. 'Because of you I can't even get back into my own house! My marriage is over, and this case is a joke. We have nothing and it isn't all on me.'

'Then why take the bullet back there, eh?' Nora accuses. Her eyes shine but she won't let herself cry. 'Are you so desperate to get yourself thrown off this thing? That it? A little bit more self-destruction of Inspector Roy Harvey-?'

'You don't know what you're-'

'No, shut up Roy! It's my turn. You've made mistakes, on this case, in your marriage,' *With me*, she doesn't say the words Roy knows are screaming in her head. 'But it's time to grow up! Take some responsibility you coward! If not for yourself or Emma, or even me,' She almost cracks at the last but her anger is close to boiling point. 'Then for them.' She jabs her finger at the crazy-wall in the other room. Nora opens the door but has one last thing to say. 'Maybe Emma is better off.' And she leaves.

Roy is left raging on the spot, not knowing whether to storm after her or scream the station down. He goes with instinct and charges into the other room of desks, upending the first and sending computer equipment and files flying. Watkins and Mathers back away hastily, pulling their wheely chairs with them in case they are caught in Roy's whirlwind. He takes up another chair and is about to add it to his symphony of fury when he sees a familiar face; the next match on the recognition program on an upturned monitor. Roy drops the chair with a clatter and pulls up the monitor. A dozen hits found. It takes Roy a moment to find the name in his rage-fogged mind, but it shines through and clears his thoughts; Gary Tanner.

'Roy? You OK mate?' Joey leans his head through the door at the other end of the office, no doubt he heard the whole thing. Mathers and Watkins would look more comfortable sat with the Viper for afternoon tea.

'Yes Joey, never better. Do me a favour would you? Get all this cleaned up and keep on the statements. You're in charge until Nor… until either of us is back.'

'Where are you going?' Joey asks.

'I've got a lead to chase up.'

11. Lauren Tanner

Lauren's resolve to escape has hardened to bedrock. Lying there on her side, for hours, days maybe, but each second, she hugs her lifeline, her children's spoon, like her only candle in the dark. She clutches it so tight she absorbs it's hope and strength directly into her body. Distantly, it occurs to her she may be delirious. She needs to eat. A ripple washes over her as to what that means; eventually, today, tomorrow, maybe every day, her body will betray her, ignore her commands, and allow the predator to feast. She will fall victim and that animal will have her again. *But only in body.* That fiend can do what he wants to her body, but he will not have her, not what makes her Gary's. She will get out and be with her Husband again. And it will be good because he loves *her,* not just the skin and meat on the outside but *her.* She will draw the beast into her web and put him where she wants him. She must let the Bull feed, so that she can bite him back. *This spider has teeth.* Lauren grips the spoon tighter.

The Bull comes back. She scampers back, like a caged animal made feral from being tested on. The Bull is topless as normal, with his loose joggers and braces, if the word normal can be applied to anything in this pit. Their next meal is on a tray. He goes through the routine of placing the bowls down where they are in reach, but he isn't. Steam dances into the air from the bowls and the rich smell of spaghetti fills the basement. The Bull leans to collect their waste bucket and Lauren lunges forward. The big man takes half a step back, but it is instinctive; Lauren cannot reach him. Instead, she swipes her bowl and is already back in her place spooning in a mouthful before anyone else can move. Both Angie and Dhanni stare at her in disbelief. The Bull is perfectly still, silhouetted by the light from upstairs. He watches, the dead eyes of the Bull watch, her fellow captives watch and although she wants to rage and burn so hot to engulf this place in fire, she must wait; she must play by this animal's rules. The spell she created by doing the unthinkable, in eating, that holds the cell in silence is broken as Angie takes up her bowl. Dhanni drags hers over and nibbles again, as if the hunger and weakness she must be feeling can be kept at bay by a morsel alone. The Bull replaces the bucket and leaves.

The spaghetti is full of flavour, the sauce is thick and the meat tender, her mouth waters, and her body groans in anticipation but Lauren forces it to be ash in her mouth. She will do what she must to get out of here, but she can't let even one thing bear a positive mark. To let something be good in this place only takes her a step towards becoming Angie. Lauren has another spoonful and watches her cellmate. She respects the woman's ability not to be broken but at the same time feels sorry for her. Angie hasn't let this place destroy who she is by accepting that this is her due; that there will be a release at the end of this sentence. But that has crushed any will she has to get out of here herself.

After only two mouthfuls her stomach cramps and she must stop. She sets the bowl down and leans back, careful to keep her extra spoon hidden under her backside. So long without food has really done a number on her.

So far, the Bull has come down in good time for when his drug kicks in. That can't be coincidence can it? Lauren assumes there must be a camera in here, but she can't see where. The corners of the room are too gloomy to see properly and gaps in the staircase are cloaked in shadow. *Next time he comes in I need to use the light.* If he is watching us, then she must keep her weapon a secret. Her stomach cramps again and she has no choice but to whine through the pain.

'Not to sound ungrateful but take it easy, yeah?' Angie advises through her own chewing. 'Small bites for a few days.'

'Urnngh.' It is all Lauren can manage over the twisting in her guts.

'Water, first, if you can.' Dhanni advises, her voice little more than a whisper.

After a few minutes, the twisting ache eases a little and Lauren can manage a few sips from the jug.

'I'm glad for you, Blondie. You've done a brave thing.' Angie admits.

'What do you mean?' Lauren asks. She is exhausted already. A small thing like a mouthful of food, just chewing, swallowing, and hugging her abused stomach has brought her to ground.

'Deciding to stay alive. It's tough but I'm glad you've turned from the other way.' Angie smiles her gorgeous smile and carries on eating, running the food around her mouth every few bites as if the insidious ingredient will reveal itself.

Lauren eyes the rest of her meal hungrily, but her body cannot take it. She pushes it towards Angie with her foot and lies back down on her side. Facing the wall, she palms her spoon and starts rubbing it against her manacle, slowly so as not to draw attention but with as much force as her sapped strength allows.

***

'Urgh. They're like sandpaper already.' Angie has her back to her wall, but she stretches her leg straight up in front of her like a cat, stroking her skin. 'Why on Earth do we need hair on our legs anyway?'

Dhanni doesn't respond. She rarely does. Lauren figures it is a rhetorical question anyway so doesn't answer back either. It does make her grin though. Outside of this prison Lauren thinks they would be friends.

Four meals. Three or four days, she guesses. Four visits from the Bull. None of them have fallen numb in that time; he just collects their bowls and empties their bucket. Lauren was able to finish her last meal albeit with a crippling ache in her side after. Another few meals, by Lauren's estimate, and she'll be able to stomach a meal without pain. Some way back to normal but nowhere near. Already, she is thinner, she can count her ribs by feel and her skin is dry. She must scrape back as much strength as she can. All the while, between her crossed legs, she scrapes the handle of her stolen spoon against her manacle. After four days she has given one side an angle. Every few minutes she scrapes it again so as not to draw attention. Each time the Bull comes in Lauren tries to see into the corners of the room, using the light from the doorway, but hasn't seen anything. The angles aren't right and after adjusting to the dimness down here the light from the door is blazing bright. The corners above the door and spaces under the stairs are plunged into an even darker veil of shadow. If it were her, she would have a camera in the top corner above the door, out of reach and where she could see the whole room.

'I mean, I know when we were cavemen we needed to stay warm but we hardly live out in the wild, naked to the elements nowadays do we?' Angie folds her leg down and flips over onto her back, legs pointed up the wall. 'What do you think, Lauren? Do away with leg hair, for the sake of women's pride everywhere?'

Lauren considers. 'Some places, women grow it out. Apparently very sexy. Armpits too.' The idea of feeling attractive freezes into a spike of ice in her head but she shatters it as if hitting it with a hammer. She won't let herself get sucked into despair, another kind of escape is at the end of that road.

Angie pulls a face, upside down as she is. 'Oh God no. I think I'd rather have legs like a Labrador than hairy man-pits. Urgh.' She shudders.

Lauren snorts a chuckle. It is the first since being here. Angie laughs too. Any joy down here is like a drug, contagious to the brink of insanity. Compared to the silence that forces its weight on the three of them, small-talk and chit-chat is like the Sun rising after a decade of darkness. Even so, the effects wear off soon. Lauren grasps the light feeling with both hands, even if it is forced. 'What about you, Dhanni? Legs or armpits?'

Dhanni is on her back. She absently traces her arm with the other hand. 'I don't know. Armpits, I guess.'

'Yeah, me too.' Lauren strokes her own hairy legs, missing the smooth skin that she liked to keep so much. 'I've got one. Would you rather shave your head or… ermm… have dreadlocks? Down to your bum.'

Angie twists over onto her front. 'Ooooo ermmm…' She twirls a finger through her hair considering the pros and cons. 'Completely bald, yeah?'

'Yes.' Lauren scrapes the spoon handle against the edge of her manacle.

'Mmm. The bald look can work for some women… but so can dreads. But down to my arse? That is a lot of hair. But you know what; I think I could get on board with that. Dreadlocks, for me.' Angie decides.

'Dhanni?' Lauren asks.

'My parents would disown me in either case.' She mutters.

Lauren thinks of her own parents. She misses them in a distant kind of way. The talks with her Mum and hugs from her Dad; all memories from when she was in school before she left for college. She misses those moments but no memory of her parents hold any warmth for her after that. Her Mum didn't have the same words and her Father was always angry about what she was doing, how they both disapproved. It was worse when she married Gary. They didn't understand and still don't. They don't see the beauty in his work or how Lauren can help him complete it. 'They're very traditional, your parents?'

Dhanni nods, rolling over to face the wall.

'Mine too, sort of. They never approved of my Husband.' Lauren admits. 'I saw my Mum a while ago, but I haven't spoken to them properly in years.'

'What's wrong with your fella?' Angie asks.

'Nothing!' Lauren defends. 'He's an artist. They don't like what he does. They think his work is… bad. They don't understand.'

'He's good then, makes a living? Does he paint?' Angie begins her exercises, fluidly arcing up and then down into another position.

'He paints, he sculpts, photography, even did tapestries years ago, before I met him. He does whatever his inspiration commands. His work can be quite adult though, it's not for everyone.' It is as much defence as she can give her parents. She scrapes another stroke on her restraint. 'He even did this.' And she pulls the elastic of her underwear down an inch, shiv tucked under her, to show the small spider tattoo on her hip.

Angie balances on her fingers and her toes and stretches up, an arc in her back, squinting to see. 'Mr Blondie is a Jack-of-all-trades artist then, eh? Wait, adult? Like raunchy stuff?'

'Sometimes.'

'Mmm, intriguing. I might have to check some of his stuff out.' A mischievous smile plays at the corner of her lips but then it is gone. It could be an awfully long time before she can see Gary's work for herself. For all Angie's calm down here, her armour does have cracks in it.

Lauren takes a chance. 'I'll show you when we get out of here. I'm sure Gary would even do something just for you.'

Angie smiles gratefully, either for the offer or for the possibility of there being an *after* this place. Either way, it is obvious to Lauren that Angie doesn't really believe they will get out of here. 'So' She covers. 'Mr Blondie's name is Gary?'

Lauren smiles at hearing his name out loud. 'Our surname is Tanner.'

'Is he a looker?'

'Mmm. He's tall, handsome, his eyes...' Lauren trails off just thinking of him. 'I love him dearly. I'd do anything for him.'

'Is he white?'

'Yeah. Yours?'

'No, black. His name is Josef. Josef Akoum. I'd do anything for him too.' Angie thinks inward, some memory of her Husband pulls her in.

Akoum? Jerry from work, his last name is Akoum. 'Does he have a Brother?' Lauren asks.

Angie comes back to herself. 'Yeah, why?'

'Is his name Jerry?' Lauren asks seriously, the spoon forgotten between her legs.

'How did you..? You know him?' Angie asks, gobsmacked.

Lauren is dumbstruck. 'Y-yes, he's the security guard at the firm where I work.'

'Small world, eh?' Angie changes her position, thinking no more of it.

Lauren is startled. *What does this mean? Is this a coincidence?* Lauren bats the thought away. It must be a coincidence but this faint connection piques her curiosity. 'Dhanni? Do you know Jerry Akoum, or Josef?'

Dhanni shakes her head. 'No.'

'Come on Dhanni, think! You never met him? Black guy, thin-cut beard, built but chunky... anything?'

'Could be the Bull.' Dhanni says flatly.

It's like a cricket ball to her forehead. Lauren is rocked back against the wall. *Jerry? Could he be...? No, Jerry is a naïve teenager in a man's body. He's sweet; he could never have any part in this. Could he?* Lauren's mind races with questions. How well does she really know Jerry? Casey has been with Jerry, so far as she knows, and has never mentioned anything weird. Lauren thinks back to all the *hello's* and *good morning's*, all the *how are you's*, all the times they spoke, searching for something to add up. It could be him. The mask covers his face. His build is about right, she would have guessed the Bull was leaner, but she has never seen Jerry shirtless, he may well be as muscular underneath that shirt and tie. *Jerry, have you done this to me? Are you the Bull?*

'Did Jo or Theresa know Jerry?' Lauren asks, trying to keep her voice level.

Angie scrunches her face up like it's a silly question. 'I've no idea, why?'

'But you spoke of him, of your Husband?' Lauren urges.

'Yeah, once or twice. Nobody said they knew him. It's not a big deal, Blondie. So, you know my Josef's Brother through work; we haven't seen him in years. Why are you getting upset?' Angie folds down out of her yoga and looks genuinely concerned. 'Here, have a drink.' She offers the jug.

'Yeah... thank you.' Lauren sips and takes some deep breaths. It is possible that Angie and Lauren just happen to know the same guy. It isn't too big of a coincidence. People meet with things in common every day. 'I'm fine, I just... it's nothing.'

Angie isn't convinced but she doesn't force the issue.

The moment grows and silence invades their prison once more. Her stomach rumbles loud enough for all to hear. Lauren and Angie share a look that makes them both laugh. Lauren is a little hysterical, but she gets control of herself at the thought of their next meal. She will eat; the Bull will have her again. Her soul screams but she must endure if she is to be strong enough to escape. She *will* escape. Lauren leans forward on her crossed legs and secretly renews the work on her weapon.

***

The Bull collects their empty bowls and leaves them be. Lauren stares white hot spikes into the Bull's back, hoping he keels over in agony. He doesn't. He ascends the stairs and disappears, the door to their prison locked back in place.

'So, what do want to do in the long run, Dhanni? Nursing, a GP or something?' Lauren asks. Slowly but surely, Lauren has tried a different tact with her roommates. The plea of 'let's escape right now' fell on deaf ears so now she is trying to give life to hope after this place. It is nice to have someone to talk to.

Dhanni is sluggish but not in the 'her turn' kind of way. It is like her brain is digging through mud to find thoughts and memories she has tried to bury. After all, when escape is impossible, memories of happier days can both sustain and cripple you here. 'Doctor. Maternity specialist.'

'Wow. Babies? That's great.' As happy a topic as it is, such an innocent subject drops the three of them into a spiral of thoughts. *What if I fall pregnant here? What will the Bull do if that happens? Has it happened before?* Lauren forces the thoughts away. Anything that hinders her in getting out of here must be left behind. Escape first. Everything else comes second. Even fear. Her heart stammers, betraying her will but she powers through. 'Angie, what about you? You used to model. What about now, before here?'

Angie shrugs as if embarrassed. 'Lady of leisure I'm afraid. Met Josef years ago when I was first married. Ran into each other later when I was divorced and hit it off. He earns a fair bit. I buy and sell stock here and there, a few thousand a month, enough to pay my share.'

'You? On the market?' Lauren asks incredulously.

'Yeah.' She smiles along too like she's also surprised it's something she is involved in. 'My Father talked me into buying stock in coffee… fifteen years ago? After I got my biggest pay check from a shoot. He was always going on about investing so I did it just to shut him up. Anyway, it paid off, I sold and put the money into other stuff. Been doing it ever since. Pays for my wine anyway.' They all laugh. Dhanni barely smiles but it is something.

Lauren leans back. 'Ahhh, I'd kill for a glass of wine.'

'I'd take the hairy legs for a sip.' Angie counters.

Lauren snorts again and that makes them laugh harder. Dhanni barely lets out a breath but her smile is something to behold. It fades quickly, but Lauren finds she wants it to stay. These women are damaged in ways that make Lauren sick, but she wants them to survive this cage. She can see these women for who they are, or at least shades of who they used to be. They have little in common, but they could be friends, Lauren wants them to be. She has never had many friends but this ordeal together has shone a light on the gap in her where they could be. It isn't that they stand a better chance of getting out by working together but leaving them behind is a notion that curdles within. She considers telling them about her plan to kill the Bull and take his key for their chains.

The shriek of the bolt cuts their atmosphere in two. The Bull enters; horns and rings in full glory, the fur oiled and eyes piercing everything and nothing that they see. Lauren can see the readiness on the inside of his trouser leg.

Lauren's breath catches in her throat. *Wait, none of us are paralysed. None of us have dropped. Is he done with that game? Does he want us to fight him off now? Is he here to kill us?* Lauren palms the sharpened spoon behind her back, the little thing reassures her as much as a duvet in the middle of the night. He gets to the bottom of the stairs. His chest is thick, his arms bunched. Lauren looks at Angie; her eyes wide in the face of their captor. Dhanni's head is down. *Oh no...* The Bull descends on Dhanni and it takes everything Lauren has not to throw her shiv at him. She forces herself to look away, not wanting to watch this. Dhanni's chain rattles and the Bull grunts. Skin slaps skin, a shriek like a mouse being snatched up by a hawk drones and fades in Dhanni's throat.

Lauren would cry for the woman, knowing now what she is going through, but she doesn't. It won't help her. Right now, short of bolt-cutters or the key from the Bull's pocket, nothing can help... The Bull's joggers lay only a few feet away, Lauren might be able to reach them. With the beast on top of Dhanni, with Lauren to his back he cannot see her but every limb is submerged in honey. Fear of being caught drowns her. Slowly but as fast as she dares Lauren edges toward the discarded pair of bottoms. Angie watches her, wide-eyed and licks her lips in anticipation. Lauren's chain pulls tight and her outstretched hand is short of the joggers by an inch. She pulls but there is no give; she cannot reach.

Eventually the Bull finishes, his ecstasy echoes around the basement. Lauren drops back, heart in her throat. The Bull staggers up and grabs his bottoms leaving Dhanni on her back. He stops halfway back to the stairs. *What now? Do you want to go again, you fucking animal?* The Bull turns back and kneels over Dhanni, his expression and intent hidden behind the face of his actions. He strokes Dhanni's legs and runs a hand though her hair. Then he takes the key from his pocket and sets Dhanni free from her chain. He blindfolds her with the scarf from his pocket. He lifts her up, the powerful muscles in his back bumped out as he carries her.

Lauren almost cracks. Every emotion she has is at war with one another as Dhanni is taken away, from being so close to having a way out of their chains. 'Wine!' She shouts.

The Bull stops mid step and slowly turns to Lauren. Sweat beads his dark skin. Dhanni hangs loose in his arms, blacker than black hair hanging low.

'We want wine.' Lauren demands but her voice is barely more than a whisper.

The Bull seems like he is about to answer when suddenly he spins on the spot. He takes Dhanni upstairs and they are gone.

Lauren and Angie are left staring at each other, Dhanni's spot a chasm where she was only a moment ago. 'Wine?' Angie asks.

Lauren shrugs but her hands shake. She may have cast her plan to escape in stone within her, but their captor is truly a monster, the sight of him terrifies her. There was nothing she could do to stop him taking Dhanni or save them from what he will do to them. But maybe the Bull would be willing to make their imprisonment more bearable. A tiny voice in her head mocks her for what she told herself about not allowing compromise in this place, but she ignores it. 'Worth a shot.'

***

Lauren tries to count the time that Dhanni is away but she loses the count. It's hours since she was taken upstairs, at least. No sound gets through from whatever is above, she assumes it is a house. Their cell is exactly like her parents' basement from when she was a child. The stairs and door are in the right place, the room is about the same size. She imagines above them is a normal house with sofas and rugs, pictures on the walls and pots in the sink. The gas man could be upstairs taking a reading and not know they were down here even if they were screaming at the top of their lungs. She works on her weapon, knowing nobody is coming to save her, slowly getting the plastic handle to a point. She lies on her side facing the wall and works on it, nurtures it like it is a growing part of her. Exhaustion assaults her. She is stronger but still weak. With every day she becomes stronger. And she must be strong. Setting the shiv against the wall, hidden in the gloom and shielded by her body, she tries to sleep but as tired as she is it just won't come.

She imagines what Gary could be doing now. She hopes he isn't losing his mind with worry. Desolate. Not knowing what to do. *Don't worry, my love, I'll be out of here soon.* The image of after her escape, of catching Gary by surprise as he is working fills her up. It is a fantasy; she doesn't even know where she is; she could be a thousand miles from home for all she knows. But his face and strong arms as he takes her up, so happy to have her back, slowly spreads through her. He kisses her and they embrace. The flood of emotion that flows through her is so strong that tears streak down her face and spot the floor. It is so real in her mind she can feel her Gary's arms around her, the feel of his lips. She misses him so much. She wants him with her, to keep her safe and to make sure nothing ever hurts her again. She imagines kissing him again.

Warmth builds in Lauren and more than anything she wishes Gary were here, that she were away from here too, but she would settle for her man. She checks over her shoulder. Angie is facing her own way against the padded wall, her breathing steady in sleep. Lauren tentatively slips her hand between her legs and lets her imagination transport her back into Gary's arms. He kisses her deeply, one arm holds her close against him and the other hand holds her cheek, strong but with a tenderness that makes her melt in his arms. Impossibly, he draws her in closer, so close, so entwined as to be the same person. She pulls him against her lips so hard that it hurts but he doesn't pull back. Lauren's breath is heavy, and she forces herself to be quiet as she rubs herself. She wishes she could spread out, comfortable and free to move but the chain would make too much noise. She imagines Gary taking her, making her feel like no other and falls into the fantasy. The heat and building tension blossoms within like a balloon. Her eyes are screwed tight. This basement, the bucket, the chain, all of it is forgotten. It takes everything she has to stay silent, clamping a hand over her mouth as she imagines Gary spilling inside of her; she erupts at the same moment, her sex throbbing and making her shake. Desperately she tries to control her breathing, to stay silent. She grips her sex until the pulsing reaches its peak and she slumps. She rolls onto her back and sighs, satisfied, if nothing compared to the real thing. She reaches for the wipes beside the bucket but freezes in the face of Angie, watching her with a tight smile. Heat flushes Lauren's cheeks and she hurriedly takes a wipe. She cleans her hand and wipes her groin and throws the wipe into the bucket. Except she misses and it slaps against the rim. Her face is roasting as she crawls forward, embarrassed. By the time she finally gets the wipe into the bucket and lies back down, facing the wall, her heart is racing, and she wishes the ground would swallow her.

Angie doesn't say a word and neither does Lauren. She is convinced the heat from her cheeks is enough to boil the wall. The intensity of those moments, how much she misses Gary and the embarrassment at being caught roll together and she cracks. She sobs. If Gary could wrap his arms around her now, it would all be fixed. She imagines him laying with her, kissing the back of her neck, telling her everything will be OK. But the cold gap where he should be is too much for her to ignore and she huddles against herself. With Gary in her mind, knowing he doesn't know where she is, she slips into dreams where she is alone. She searches for him, but he is gone.

***

Lauren is woken by the bolt. It doesn't feel like she has slept at all. She remembers last night, if it was night-time, and looks at Angie. She makes no sign of recognising her embarrassment; she shuffles back as the Bull carries Dhanni passed and chains her back to the end wall. He leaves.

Dhanni's hair shines. She has clean underwear and a fresh button up shirt on. Her legs gleam; freshly shaved and oiled.

The Bull reappears with a tray. He sets the food down; toasted sandwiches that fill the air with a scent more delicious than Lauren has ever smelled. He also puts a gym flask on the floor with the jug of water. He leaves, bolting the door.

'No way.' Angie's shocked face is a picture as she smells the flask. She tilts it for a sip and her smile grows and grows until it seems it might split her face. 'Red! And good too!'

'Here?' Lauren reaches for the flask. Angie slaps the spout closed and tosses it over. She doesn't sip it; she drains as much as she can before needing to take a breath. She throws it back. 'Dhanni, you OK?' But of course, she can't respond.

Angie sips at the bottle again, smacking her lips appreciatively. 'I haven't had wine in… I don't know how long.'

The effect of the wine hits Lauren faster than she would believe. Her head becomes foggy in moments and Angie blurs across from her. In her malnourished state the wine is having its way with her after only a few mouthfuls. Angie offers her the bottle back, but she waves it away. She takes one of the sandwiches instead and tears into it.

Dhanni stirs soon after. Angie herself is a little tipsy. 'Hey, Dhanni. Drink?'

Dhanni awkwardly tries to sit up; her limbs are loose, and they drop before she can take her weight. She flexes her fingers and toes, trying to get feeling back.

Lauren takes in the restored Dhanni. Caked in dirt with greasy hair, filthy clothes, and weeks-old stubble on her legs Dhanni was a beauty. Now, she is breath-taking. Her eyes sparkle, even in the dimness of the basement, against the pale caramel of her skin. Her hair is thick and sleek at the same time; Lauren would kill for hair like that. 'Dhanni, you OK?' She asks again.

'Mmm.' The Indian girl grunts, hugging her groin. 'Ss-sore.'

'Have some wine, hon'. You'll feel better.' Angie offers the nearly empty bottle.

'Nnno. I don't drink.' Dhanni manages to say through her thick-feeling tongue.

'Why not start?' Angie jokes.

Dhanni just rolls over, stretching her limbs as her body comes back to herself.

'You look good Dhanni.' Lauren absently scratches at her own stubbly legs.

Dhanni groans in response but Angie jumps in with a smile. 'He'll get round to you, Blondie. Maybe a week, he'll clean you up.'

Lauren's tipsy head clears up. 'That's not what I meant.'

Angie takes another sip, her face straight. 'I know. I'm not as funny as I think.'

It seems this place can ruin any moment, no matter how small. Lauren pushes past it and reaches for the bottle, desperate for any win in this hellhole. 'You like your wine then?'

'Yeah, poison of choice! Bit o' Gin when the mood takes me.' Angie looks over Dhanni. She would reach out to her friend, but the chain won't let her.

Lauren thinks back to whether the three of them would be friends in the outside world. They are all completely different people. But in here they are all they have, and Lauren is grateful for them. Like Casey, a friend doesn't have to be a kindred spirit; they can just be in the right place at the right time for you. Even if the right place is as wrong as this prison.

'I don't drink that often. My Gary likes his Whiskey. My friend Casey likes her wine though.' Lauren says conversationally. She has another gulp from the bottle, but her tummy recoils. She hands it back and takes up the other half of her sandwich hoping the bread will help. She hasn't had bread since that last morning before she was taken. The toast, ham and cheese are delicious.

'My friends were a bit wild. Into all sorts of stuff. Especially the girls from way back. Don't get me wrong I used to do a few pills and powder my nose when it was going but not anymore.' Angie admits.

'The guy I dated in college had pills once but I never took them. He told me to, tried to force it but that's not me. He was furious.' Lauren smiles at the memory. That weasel wasn't worth her spit let alone her health. He bought the pills from a guy in the toilets of a club after all.

'Dhanni?' Angie asks. 'Have you ever gone a bit wild?'

'No.' She says flatly. 'Parents would kill me.'

'Little Miss goody-two-shoes over here.' Angie mocks overly loud but her smile is made of genuine warmth.

Lauren licks her fingers of crumbs. 'I always liked the idea of Scotch. "On the rocks." Like in the films. But it is vile stuff.'

'Yeah my ex-Husband liked Scotch. Horrible stuff.' Angie finishes the rest of the wine. 'But that went down lovely. Thank you, Blondie. Never thought to ask him for anything before.'

'I want my Mum's *Gulab Jamun*.' Dhanni admits.

'Eh?' Angie asks, confused.

'It's a dessert. Little bit like a doughnut but made from milk-solids. My Mum's was the best. She used to put cashews and coconut flakes on them.' Dhanni's voice cracks but she masters herself. Such a small show of instability speaks volumes against the cold and expressionless front she puts up.

'That sounds nice.' Lauren tries to put on a cheery smile. 'I'd like to try that some time. I could come over when we get out of here?'

'Sure.' Her smile is tight-lipped, instantly dismissing the possibility that such a meeting could ever happen.

'I mean it. We are going to get out of here. It might not be today or tomorrow, but it will happen. And when we do I'd like to try your Mum's cooking.' Lauren tries to put as much conviction into her voice as she can, but she needn't try so hard; she means every word. She imagines Dhanni's family, what her Mum's cooking smells like and paints a picture of them around a table. She sees Brothers, Sisters, friends, imagines what her Husband looks like. The image is so vivid that her every word becomes truth.

Dhanni softens a little. 'That would be nice.' But then rolls over.

'What do you want to do after, Angie?' Lauren asks. She wants to set something free in these women's minds. A want, a something more, something to look forward to, to keep the hope alive that someday they will get out of here. When the time comes Lauren is going to need them to move, to act when she tells them to. Ultimately, she has no idea what is upstairs or where they are. Every second could count and if either of them hesitate it could cost them their chance. If hope can come from a small thing like a dessert, then Lauren is going to feed it. But it is more than that. Lauren doesn't want these women to despair, to accept that this is all their lives are now. She truly wants them to get away from this prison, together. Lauren shifts her weight; the spoon underneath has made her bum numb.

'My bed.' Angie says after a second's thought. 'I miss my bed. Miss my duvet…' She wraps her arms around herself imagining being tucked in and warm. She closes her eyes and groans like the thought is the best thing in the world. Between the wine and the thought of her bed Angie could fall asleep any second. 'What about you, Blondie, what do you miss?'

The question catches her off guard but the truth hits her before she can even think about it. How much she misses Gary lands on her like a house. She crumbles beneath it and suddenly she is blubbering. The wine has no doubt made her emotional, but the weight of her feelings is real. She hugs her knees to hide her face. *I am supposed to be getting stronger but look at me! I'm a mess.* She needs to shift her bottom again but her legs are heavy. *Oh no…*

Angie tries to comfort her. 'Hey, don't cry, Blondie. We're here, it's alright.'

It takes every ounce of will she has to lift her head back so that she doesn't fall forward on her face. The sorrow in her heart becomes hard and then barbed like a porcupine's back; it hurts and burns hot in her chest. The hate and contempt boil away the misery in the face of what is about to happen to her again. Angie looks at her, confused, but realisation dawns. Lauren's chest is tight, lips feel thick, but she manages to say the words before Angie does. 'Itz-my… turn…'

12. Inspector Roy Harvey

'I'm sorry to drop in on you like this, Mr Tanner. I wouldn't usually call at such a late hour but I've got some questions for you?' Roy asks but it isn't a question. He is not leaving without answers.

'It's fine.' Gary Tanner is as taught as a bowstring as he lets Roy into the house, just like the first time they met.

'Are you alright, Mr Tanner?' Roy jibes; his temper gets the better of him after the Chelby bust, his meeting with the Viper and the argument with Nora.

'I'm fine.' Tanner leads Roy into the living room and offers a seat. 'What can I help you with?'

'Your Wife's case of course.' Roy just can't figure this guy out. His Wife has been missing nearly three weeks now and he is acting like he's burnt his toast. He should be raging, demanding progress, and asking after his Wife. 'A dozen women have gone missing in similar circumstances to that of Mrs Tanner. I have some pictures for you to look at. I'd like you to tell me if you recognise any of the missing women, might be I can rule a few things out if you do.' If Mr Tanner does have anything to do with these abductions, then he can't have taken that as anything but a threat. If not, he'll jump at the chance to help.

Tanner sits in the same chair as when Roy and Nora first spoke to him. His lip twitches as if to say something but then holds out his hand for Roy's file.

Roy hands it over and waits patiently for him to go over the pictures and details of the twelve missing women. Roy stands and paces the room, taking in every detail he can; the cushions are perfectly placed, the carpet is spotless, the TV doesn't have a speck of dust on it. Gary Tanner is a man that likes to keep a tidy household. Maybe this is Tanner's way of dealing with his Wife's abduction? Everybody reacts differently but never this calmly in Roy's experience.

The painting above the fireplace draws Roy's eye. He tries not to stare but he can't help himself. The predatory look on the blood-winged male, the four arms ending in claws, pinning his prey down, the look on the females face; it is revolting. Roy wonders if his uneasy opinion of Gary Tanner is based on this one painting. He could be as reclusive or eccentric as he likes but that doesn't mean anything, it wouldn't scream warnings in Roy's head like what is happening now. It was this painting. Since he first saw it Gary Tanner hasn't sat right with him. Wildly unfair, Roy realises, but his instinct is telling him to watch this man closely. And he was a hit on the recognition software.

'This woman seems familiar.' *Karly Schwarz.* The picture is from her graduation. Gary Tanner looks harder at the picture. 'I've seen pictures on the news about missing women but I don't know who she is. Maybe she lives around here, and I've seen her before.'

A likely explanation. Miss Schwarz lives less than a mile away and one of the hits that flagged up was Garry Tanner and Karly Schwarz in a supermarket across from her place of work.

'And her.' Gary reads from the attached profile. 'Penny Wainright? Again, familiar but, I don't know her.' He hands the file back. 'What did you mean, similar circumstances?'

Roy never admits to the family of the missing that foul play could be involved unless absolutely necessary. Though it must cross their minds it only panics the loved ones when heard from a Policeman and makes his job harder. And ultimately, despite the clues and coincidences, he doesn't know for sure that

Lauren Tanner, or any of the missing women, are connected by some sick pervert out there. It is possible all twelve women decided to leave home without saying anything, throwing their rings away as they went. It could all just be a coincidence. *But I know it's not, I would stake my career on it.*

Roy never expected Gary Tanner to crack in five minutes and confess to having twelve women, including his own Wife, tied up or thrown in the river. He just wanted to see his reaction. And Roy is unsatisfied. Something is going on with this guy and Roy is going to find out what. 'Thank you, Mr Tanner. All of these women are Berry locals so it's not surprising you may have run into each other.' Roy stands up to leave. 'Oh, I would like to look around if that's alright?'

'No.' Tanner flatly denies.

'Excuse me?' Roy expected resistance but not a straight refusal. 'I'm only looking for something of Mrs Tanner's, photo's, letters? Could be that somebody she knows might be able to help?'

'No. I'll show you out.' Gary Tanner pushes passed to the front door.

After the last couple of days, what with Chelby losing all substance as a suspect, after Emma the other night, after the Viper, after Nora, it takes everything Roy has not to slam Gary Tanner in the back of the head. His fist is clenched so tight his fingertips pinch into his palm. There is so much pressure to find these women, so much is at stake and this idiot won't even let things roll on, and with his own Wife involved. Emma, Nora, Lesley, each of the twelve missing women, all of them depend on him to fix this, to make things right, it is too much for Roy to bear. The disregard this man shows for his beloved is a brand that burns Roy's feelings towards his own Wife. How can a man be so cold? But Roy's frustration gutters out as a cold realisation settles upon him. He hurt Emma in a way that he can only guess at. Is he any better than what he thinks of this man? Emma is missing from his life, and he has done virtually nothing to get her back. Have Gary and Lauren had marital issues, is Gary responsible for Lauren's disappearance, or at least privy to it? Roy thinks so, but that doesn't mean foul play. But still, Roy can't shake his feeling about this asshole. 'Thank you for your time Mr Tanner. I'll be in touch.'

Gary Tanner closes the door as soon as Roy's back foot is clear. He strides back to his car imagining all the things he could have said, wondering if he would have handled that any better. Of course, he could. *Story of my life.* In his car, Roy watches the Tanner place as if some answer will suddenly appear on the brickwork and tell him exactly what is going on. Mr Tanner is hiding something, of that he is sure. Only the private and the guilty hide away like that and either way it means Gary Tanner has something he doesn't want Roy to see.

Mr Tanner suddenly comes out of the front door and Roy shrinks down behind the steering wheel. Tanner strides with purpose to the garage at the side of the house and lifts the door. In the fading light Roy can't see much other than various tools on the inside wall and shelves lined with pots of paint. Tanner pulls the garage closed after him.

Roy would guess the garage is Mr Tanner's workshop, where he creates his 'art'. After meeting the man and his flat refusal to let Roy investigate his property there is no doubt in Roy's mind that there is something else inside that garage that Gary Tanner doesn't want him to see. Roy's phone rings inside his pocket; it is Nora. He stares at the name for a second and then drops it back inside his coat pocket, wanting to *do* something instead of talking.

Roy has been honest and by the book up until this point and what has it got him? A broken marriage and an axe above his head after arresting an innocent deviant. The Viper be damned, Roy takes matters into his own hands and moves his car back to a spot at the end of the road. He needs to see inside the Tanner place, every instinct he has is telling him that Gary Tanner has something to do with this case. The evening dark settles on the world, streetlamps blink on one at a time. His phone rings again but he ignores it. He slips out of his car and works his way around to Tanner's place, popping his head over garden hedges to check there is no sign of movement. A strip of light glows from underneath the garage door. Fast paced rock music filters from the garage. Without trying to look suspicious, Roy treads as lightly as possible up the driveway and to the garage door. He leans in against the large door and groans meet his ears. Scuffles and loud taps join the chorus of deep grunts. Is Tanner working out, hammering a new sculpture? Roy focuses on his task and tests the front door; it is open. Roy enters the house.

***

This is stupid. This is really stupid. The moment the front door closes behind him, doubts and consequences flood his mind. Gary Tanner could come back into the house at any moment. What if he is caught here illegally? What will Gary Tanner do? What will the Viper do? What will Roy do?

Roy almost turns around right there but a photo of the Tanners stares back at him from on the wall; a selfie where Lauren has her arm around Gary, both out in the Sun with sunglasses on. Her smile is stunning, like she has never been happier. Gary in comparison is tight-lipped, he could be stood next to a stranger for all the warmth he shows. The sight of Lauren plants Roy's feet. He must find these women. Lauren is the most recent to disappear and stands the best chance of coming home alive and in one piece. Roy moves further into the lion's den.

Luckily, Gary has left the lights on so that Roy doesn't have to feel his way through a dark house. He checks every door, for any sign to satisfy his distrust of the man. In the kitchen, a small dining table sits in the centre surrounded by counter tops and appliances. Fridge magnets are arrayed on the tower fridge-freezer, mugs hang from small hooks underneath one of the cabinets. The oven, the toaster and kettle are matching chrome. A thick wooden door leads under the stairs where a larder keeps jars of preservatives, tins, and bottled drinks. A conservatory at the back of the house is more lived-in than the living room; a basket of washing sits on a wicker sofa with enormous cushions, a TV is on the wall, an exercise bike in the corner. Through the window Roy can make out the garden, the enormous garage extends right the way back, side by side with the garden until it meets a fence some ten meters back.

Gary Tanner appears from the garage through a side door, throwing a strip of light across the garden, and Roy throws himself on the ground to avoid being seen. Hiding under the windowsill Roy dares to peek over. Gary tosses a clump of metal away onto the grass with a grunt. Dirt streaks his shirt from whatever work he is doing. Thick welding gloves cover his hands and forearms. He storms back into the garage and the garden is dark once more.

With a relieved sigh Roy backs out and goes upstairs. One of the steps is creaky and he freezes on the spot. He breathes a laugh at himself knowing that Gary Tanner could not have heard him from outside in the garage. There are two bedrooms, though one has been converted to an office, and a bathroom.

Bookshelves line one wall of the office, full of titles covering photography, sculpture and various other medium. A laptop sits open but off on the desk. Roy is tempted to take it for Joey and the boys to look over but anything they found wouldn't be admissible as evidence due to how it was obtained. Roy chews his lip but lets it go. He is about to leave when a sculpture behind the door catches him off guard, stopping him mid-step. On closer inspection it is a mask; triangular in face with curling horns growing from the roof of the skull, it is a goat head but larger than any Roy has ever seen. The eyes of the beast seem to drink in the light, glassy but giving nothing back. The maw is open, like it is baying into the night in panic. The teeth inside the mouth are missing. The open mouth-hole leads right into the mask. The fur is short over the snout and face but longer at the base of the neck. When worn Roy imagines the hair would sit over the shoulders. Roy's reaches out for the mask before he catches himself. Whatever the goat mask is supposed to signify it makes Roy feel ill. He backs out of the office and into the bedroom.

The bed is made. The wardrobes have clothes hung in them, drawers have socks and underwear. Roy flicks through them all for anything hidden. A bedside cabinet is on the other side of the bed, on top is a lamp with a paperback book beside it. Roy opens the top drawer and freezes. Inside is a collection of items that could be from a torturer's kit; a knife, lighter, metal wire, black tape and fishing line. In the drawer below are more conventionally private items but are still a daunting sight; several sex toys of varying shapes and sizes, lubricants, oils, blindfolds, a box of tissues, thin velvet gloves and a red lipstick worn down to the nib. Roy shakes himself from the possibilities, of images of the Tanner's together in this room and checks under the bed. There are two suitcases there, side-by-side. They are both packed and ready with neatly folded clothes, toiletries and in each is a plastic wallet with several credit cards and a few thousand euro. *Were they planning a holiday? Or is Mr Tanner planning a quick exit alone? No, there are two cases, and one is full of female attire.*

The front door slams closed and footsteps echo on the stairs. Roy panics and throws himself under the bed. He must shove the suitcases aside in order to fit and none too quietly. Gary Tanner's feet appear in front of Roy's face at the door. He has taken his shoes off. He paces across the room and opens the wardrobe. Roy tries to control his breathing but to him it is a gale. How does Mr Tanner not hear him? His head is leant awkwardly against one of the suitcases, the strain on his back and shoulders in keeping perfectly still is making him sweat. It is suddenly hot; with his work suit and jacket on, cramped under the bed with no air his breathing gets heavier. Realising it doesn't help either. Gary Tanner's T-shirt hits the floor; dirt slashed across it. After a few moments that feel like months, he leaves. Water sounds from the bathroom.

Roy lets his body take the breath it needs. *I can't stay here. This was stupid. This was really stupid.* Careful to be as silent as possible, Roy shimmies out from under the bed, nudging the suitcases back into place. He won't get a better chance to leave so he creeps out of the bedroom and onto the stairs, listening for any sign of Gary Tanner. Each step is as light as a feather, as carefully trod as if he was in a minefield. The sink tap flutters as Tanner washes, he could be done any second. Roy is halfway down the stairs. He must go now but if he hurries, he could alert Mr Tanner. The next step creaks, yawning through the house like a whale's call. Roy completely forgot about it.

The tap is turned off. 'Hello?'

Roy has no choice. He vaults down the stairs and to the front door. He can hear the thud of Gary Tanner's pursuit as he hits the stairs. Luckily the front door is unlocked, and he can get into the fresh air, slamming the door behind him. Instantly, Roy realises that he can't possibly make the end of the driveway before Gary opens the door, raging after him. If he is caught and the Viper finds out then he will be fired and prosecuted. He'll be removed from the case and then the chances Lauren Tanner, Joanne Hannah, Angelina Smith and all the others being found alive will be reduced to zero. He can't let that happen. His first thought is to take Gary Tanner down; knock him out cleanly and then get out of here but if he glimpses Roy then this whole thing will still go sideways along with an assault charge. With no other choice Roy flattens himself against the wall beside the door ready to pounce and hopefully disable Gary Tanner without being recognised. The creaky step whines as Gary Tanner pounds down the stairs.

The garage door is ajar a foot above the ground, held in place by the spring assist. Indecision ricochets around Roy's brain. There is so much that could go wrong, what has he got himself in to? Tanner will appear at any moment. Roy rolls under the garage door as the front door swings open.

The inside of the garage is warm. Or maybe Roy's adrenaline is coursing through him so fast it just feels like it is hot in here. Desperately, as quickly as he can, Roy ducks between cabinets and around a car, behind several display pedestals. It is near pitch dark in here and Roy feels about him to make sure he doesn't knock anything over. No sooner does he stop when the garage door is lifted open. From in-between his cover Roy can make out the silhouette of Gary Tanner against the streetlights. His arm reaches out and flicks a switch. Strip lights above blink on and cast the whole garage into bright artificial light. The garage is much larger than it looks from the outside. The pedestals Roy is crouched behind are painted an ivory white. A car, a Mazda, shields his right. It is a sleek motor, like his own, designed for speed instead of practicality, perfect for a couple with no children. Nothing obstructs its route to the door bar Gary himself. Behind him and the car is a workshop full of half-finished pieces. Most are stacked against the walls like forgotten projects. Roy can only glimpse though as Gary steps forward.

Tanner scans his workshop. His hunter's hand finds a hammer from the shelf to his right and Roy curses for putting himself in such a position. Gary, thankfully, paces around the other side of the car. 'It would be better if you just came out.'

Roy's heart is racing. He needs to move, or risk being caught. The garage is so silent that any movement, any scrape of his foot on the concrete floor could alert the other man. Holding his breath, he crawls forward as carefully as he can. His fingers support his weight, on the balls of his feet, ready to vault. Silently, he thanks God that Tanner didn't close the garage door behind him. He can see the other man's feet underneath the car.

'Come out. I know you're in here.' Gary Tanner stops in his tracks.

Instinct makes Roy bunch up and freeze, as small as he can make himself behind the wheel of the car. Gary Tanner drops down onto the balls of his feet, scanning under the car. It takes everything Roy has to keep his breathing in check. Any sound could tip Tanner off. They circle the car, Roy now at the front of the garage with Gary making his way further in. He could leave right now, could escape with no other sign he was ever here. He is about to bolt when a metallic screech whines from the back of the garage. Roy inches an eye around the car and watches Gary wrench a bolt free from a thick door at the very back of the garage. From his brief glimpse Roy took it for part of the wall. Gary, hammer in hand, descends steps and disappears.

There's a basement, under the garage? A desperate part of him pulls towards the outside world, just a few feet away, and escape but it is like dragging a sled with no tracks; he needs to know what Tanner is hiding. As quietly as before, Roy inches between the car and the pedestals, in between the half-formed shapes of wood, metal and resin. Some would fit in the palm of his hand, the etching so intricate he would need a glass to examine it fully, some stand almost floor to ceiling with pipework and decoration flowing up and out like a totem. Discarded paintings are stacked against one another, dozens, more. The first depicts a lush garden beneath a vibrant pink sky. Amongst the perfect green is a sombre grave at odds with its surroundings. Bar the headstone, the garden could be a slice of paradise.

In the centre of the garage, a piece that must be nearly complete makes him pause. It portrays three naked and hairless figures; one in brass, one in copper and one in steel. Each of the three subjects is swirling around one another as if zeroing as both predator and prey. Each leaves a smooth trail in their wake, like the heroes in comic books when they fly into the air. Their paths twist and spin around each other like birds dancing in the air, passing through and around the other. The figures meet at the top where their flight ends. The copper figure, masculine in appearance, has a face of agony and fear. He reaches up as if trying to catch the others but instead of holding on, his outstretched hand reaches up, fingers inside the feminine steel figure at the groin. The steel figure is buffed to brilliance, a mirror finish, bald like the others, 'her' sex covered by the copper hand. Her face is saddened as she looks down at Copper but shows no other sign that she doesn't want to be lifted away. The brass figure is more muscular than Copper and his pose is that of superiority. There are no facial features, only a smooth flat where eyes and a nose should be. Whether it is unfinished or left blank on purpose, Roy can only guess. Brass flies proud, one arm straight at his side and the other clasped around that of Steel, under the arm and by the breast.

Roy can't fathom what the meaning behind the piece is. He shakes his head clear and tries to listen. For all he knows Gary may well be on the other side of the door. He can hear soft words and movement. With the bolt drawn on this side, Roy could hardly have hidden down there so Gary must be checking on something else; something that needs locking in. Roy reaches the doorway at the back of the garage and listens close.

'It won't be long now. We'll be able to finish soon. Sshhhh…' Gary Tanner's voice comes faintly from within.

Who is he talking to? Does he have somebody down there? Is he mad and talking to himself, his art? Roy risks a look around the doorway, to see what on earth is going on when his phone rings. Panic. Roy fumbles with his jacket pocket but gets tangled with a sculpture covered by a sheet beside him. He flees. The edge of his jacket catches on the sculpture and is pulled over with him, making an enormous racket as it crashes to the floor. A metal skeleton, an aperture of a Bull's head bounces from under the sheet. His jacket is hooked on a horn of metal but Roy kicks it away, tearing his jacket and freeing himself. All stealth is forgotten as he hears the heavy footsteps of Mr Tanner as he charges up the stairs from the mystery room below. In seconds, Roy is at the door, he flicks the lights off and is then out of the garage. He shoves the garage door down, buying him precious seconds to be away. He doesn't slow or stop until he jumps into his car at the end of the street. He slumps down in the driver's seat. His chest burns and every sense is screaming to recognise some sign that Gary Tanner has followed him, but there is nothing. He risks a look over the rim of the door and sees Gary Tanner, hammer in hand, at the end of his driveway, looking this way and that. He seems to look straight at Roy but can't possibly see him, shadowed inside his car. Was he seen? He slowly pulls his key from his pocket and slots it into the ignition, ready to spur his car into life and speed away. Gary Tanner turns and disappears, back onto his driveway. Roy suddenly remembers to breathe, not realising he was holding it. He waits another full minute before starting the car. He tells himself that Tanner could still be watching, and he doesn't want his suspect to recognise his car, but really it is so he can give his heart a chance to slow down.

***

It is pouring with rain as Roy pulls up at Nora's. He runs from the car but is still soaked through by the time he gets to the front door. His phone has been ringing nonstop since he left the Tanner place but he ignored it, not wanting anything to deviate his path home.

Nora comes through from the living room, mobile in hand and a look of worry on her face. 'Where the hell have you been? Why haven't you picked up?' She motions her phone. 'What happened?' She asks, seeing his torn jacket.

Roy pulls his dripping jacket off and runs his hands though his wet hair. Nora is in her pyjamas; an old T-shirt and some chequered bottoms. Her hair is wet too, from the rain or from the shower Roy doesn't know. Doesn't care. After the rush of what he did tonight, and he must admit that it was a rush, Roy's mind and body are alive. The adrenaline and the fear of being caught, acting beyond his usual influence has made him feel younger and more vital than he has since before he and Nora were intimate. After searching Tanner's place and doing so under his nose, Roy feels strong. The subject matter of Gary Tanner's art may be uncomfortable, gross at times, but it is unmistakably sexual. After escaping and by some cosmic joke, just now accepting that Emma does not want him anymore, and that Nora might, Roy is charged up. The last time he and Nora had sex he felt alive like he hadn't in years. Guilt followed, of course, but the act felt good, too good to never feel again.

Roy pulls his tie off with one hand and reaches out to Nora with the other. A question dies on her lips as he pulls her in and kisses her more fiercely than the awkward fumbling that filled their last release together. She resists briefly, probably wanting to know what has gotten into him but then she is pulling at him as hungrily. Nora's tongue dances in his mouth, he lifts her up, legs around his waist and he carries her over to the table. Before he knows it, he has Nora bent over the dining table and is inside her. To his surprise she orgasms before he does. He slows briefly to let her get her breath back but the passion is on him, and he thrusts faster and harder than before. She reaches a hand back to slow him, but he slaps it away. She has no choice but to grip the tabletop and be taken by him. He has never made love like this, never taken control like this. Nora gasps with each thrust and Roy drinks her in as if every breath only invigorates his efforts. He is master of this moment and nothing will stop him. When he is ready he explodes inside, collapsing on top of her, limbs suddenly heavy. His legs shake and he pulls away, falling into the nearest chair.

Nora stares wide-eyed at him, still bent over the table. Her hair is crimped from where he gripped it, her T-shirt ripped from where he pulled it. Her eyes beg a question, but he can't look at her, not as she is. He stalks away, not willing, or able, to explain what came over him.

13. Lauren Tanner

The last week, at least Lauren guesses it to be a week by their meals, has blurred into routine as he has had each of them. The Bull is random in his desires. Maybe he thinks about which one of them he wants but sometimes, like before, he switches their bowls spontaneously as if deciding there and then who he wants. It is sometimes days in between 'turns'. Lauren was bold enough to ask the sick bastard for more food, for the three of them, and they have had more frequent meals, but now her scale of time is off; it was a guess before, now she has no idea how long she has been down here.

Angie has been doing her exercises and Lauren has mirrored her where she can. Although she was fit and worked at her body before this place, it is amazing how quickly her strength left her from her starvation. Even with the relative health she has regained from eating she is a husk of what she was. Most days, Angie is still holding her position when Lauren collapses, muscles burning and heart thumping. Dhanni rarely joins in and only for a few moments. She fairs better than Lauren but has been at her weight for a lot longer.

Each time the Bull comes for her, when it is her turn, Lauren hardens herself against the world. Her estranged body is alien to her in those moments when he has her. Panic attacks her but she forces herself cold, closes her eyes and retreats into her mind where she is with Gary, helping him to complete his work under the garage or alone with him in their room. After each time, her body comes back to itself and it is those moments where she feels the strain beneath her thoughts, can feel the fraying edges of her will. She cries, hates herself, and wishes she were dead, but then she knits herself back together and can focus again. But it is getting harder each time. Her body may be getting stronger but her mind feels like a cocoon, hardening more and more until eventually it cracks. She can't afford to worry about it though, if escape means losing her mind then it will be a price worth paying.

Her shiv has been an anchor to ground her to the present and not get carried away on the waves of failure. It took weeks to finish but now her spoon handle ends in a sharp point. A laughable weapon, but tight in her fist it feels like a sword of the angels. Lauren hugs it against her when she is facing the wall, always against her skin to reassure herself that it is real. Her plan hasn't changed. She will fake being paralysed and when that animal comes for her, she will stab him. Then she will take his key and free herself, Angie and Dhanni. But there is much that can go wrong. What if he realises she is faking? What kind of consequences would she bring about? What if she succeeds and he doesn't have the key on his person? They would all starve to death with no one to bring them food. The weight of her plan, the risk it carries sits on her chest and she can't breathe. She squeezes her shiv tighter.

'Lauren? Are you alright?' Dhanni asks.

Lauren forces a tight-lipped smile on her face. She pokes her weapon back against the wall between the pads. 'Yeah, just thinking about home.' She lies.

'I try not to, but it is all that I see.' Dhanni's focus shifts to something beyond what is front of her, a different place and time.

'We're going to get out of here.' Lauren says, with more belief than that the Sun still rises outside of this place.

Angie rolls her eyes but doesn't chide Lauren for saying it. She spoke about riding this thing out, that the others before them were let go but it is for Dhanni's sake. Neither of their views about escape has changed. Angie believes they will never see their homes again but won't let it cripple her. Lauren can't accept that loss. Not yet and not ever. But their time here has forced a strange bond. They are in this together, and it would be worse without the other.

'What's your house like?' Lauren asks Dhanni.

Dhanni leans back and for once, instead of ignoring the warm thoughts, she lets herself be submerged in them like a hot bath. A tiny smile twitches at her lips as she describes her home. 'I moved back in with my parents after University. My parents were there when I was born; it has always been home to me. University was the only time I moved away. When I took the residency at Belleview, I argued that I should be out on my own again but, really, I wanted to be home. Father didn't want me living anywhere else anyway, where I might be led astray or meet a boy.' The dark irony doesn't fail to strike them, but they don't laugh. 'They live over on Taylor Crescent.' Dhanni explains. Lauren notices that she said where *they live* and not *we live*, to Dhanni, this place is her world, and her home is gone for her. It breaks Lauren's heart. 'My older Brother married and his Wife moved in about a year ago, a year before here anyway. My younger Brother is still there. He is 18 but Mum will have him married soon enough. My Auntie and my Cousin too. Arnav would have us move out as soon as we are able, but I don't mind. It is cramped, and noisy… but… it's home.'

Dhanni's sadness cracks Lauren's armour. She guesses she has the same look when she thinks of Gary. Immediately she conjures up all the things she misses. And the things that hurt to think of aren't the big things she thought she would miss. Gary, of course but it is little things that make her ache to be without. The way he hugs her. The feel of their towels. The sound of the world; traffic, trees rustling in the wind. Their toaster; the way it ticks as it cooks. All everyday things which she took for granted but are completely denied to her now. The only sounds down here are the rustle of their backsides as they move and whatever functions their bodies need to make. It is a complete detachment from how the world should sound. *Sunlight!* She misses the warmth on her skin but she would settle for overcast clouds right now.

Lauren guesses how long she has been here; it feels like every hour is an eternity, but it can't have been more than a month? *Could it?* She doesn't know, between her starvation and the increase in meals she could have been here a lot longer than she is willing to consider. And there it is, that other power of this cage; her sense of time is a splat of paint against the wall, no rhyme or reason to the pattern, only a direction. It *could* be months. Months taken from her, out of her life, without Gary, without happiness. Taken with no hope of repayment.

Angie asks Dhanni something about her family. Lauren barely hears them. She tries to think rationally. When she was starving, she was on the point of passing out, Dhanni said that takes weeks right? But again, her sense of time is off, every hungry hour she spent wasting away felt like a fortnight. Absentmindedly she hugs her knees, strokes a hand down her shin. Her legs are hairier than she has ever known them. She usually shaves her legs every week or so. She can pull at the hair on her leg. *It must be months...* Lauren chokes the sob that threatens to spill out of her throat. She won't let this place take any more from her than it already has.

'…huge garden that I used to sunbathe in. Had tall fences around so I could just lounge around naked, with a cocktail. Jeez, I miss the Sun.' Angie laments.

'Naked?' Lauren asks incredulously, desperate for the distraction.

'Oh yeah, I used to stretch out in the morning when it was nice,' Angie leans back, stretching from her fingers to her toes as if she is out in her garden right now. 'My husband would come home and find me in the same spot. I'd tell him that I had been there all day just to wind him up. I hadn't obviously, I needed another pitcher.'

Lauren laughs despite herself. Dhanni smiles daintily. Lauren vows she will sunbathe just the same way when she gets home. Gary can put up fences or not, regardless she will do it. The sheer freedom in the act is attractive to Lauren as much as the thought of Gary catching her and what would happen next.

The bolt shrieks aside and the fragile dream is chased away. Lauren clutches at the shiv behind her but forces herself calm. Dhanni startles at the sound but otherwise is a statue. The Bull enters, silhouetted against the light. His powerful form is shadowed to total black until he escapes the lights barrier. He pads down the stairs and it is all business from there; he puts down a tray with three plastic plates on. He replaces their bucket and swaps their water bowls. As always, he doesn't say a word, but Lauren can feel his gaze on her through the eyes of the Bull. They are silent until he leaves, the door locked behind him.

The three of them take up their plates. Lauren's mouth waters at the smell, her nose telling her what their meal is before she sees. On the plate is a sandwich of thick bread and bacon. Butter has soaked into the bread, warmed from the hot rashers. Lauren tears into it immediately. The bacon is tender, lightly cooked just how she likes it. In a moment the whole thing is gone. She licks her fingers appreciatively, savouring any crumbs. Angie finishes hers soon after. Dhanni peeks into hers and then pushes her plate away.

'Dhanni, you should eat, hon'.' Angie says motherly.

'I cannot eat pork.' Dhanni says wistfully.

'*Shiva*' will forgive you this thing after everything else.' Angie mocks but there is no malice in it. She would have Dhanni with hot food in her and not without.

'Don't joke. You do not know. And Shiva doesn't forgive.' Dhanni curls up but her eyes don't leave the plate. Her religion may be the only thing left intact within her, but she is hungry.

'Why not just the bread?' Lauren reasons. 'I don't know the rules but surely that is OK? For us?' She doesn't mean it selfishly, so that the young woman can help her escape. She doesn't consider that she needs these women, and they her, when the time comes to act. She wants her to eat because she doesn't want her to hurt, or to be hungry. They have suffered more than anybody can fathom, are still suffering and Lauren is right here with them.

Dhanni fights with herself but then peels the bread away and nibbles at it, handing her rashers of bacon back to Lauren and Angie. Angie takes it without a second thought, taking half and tossing the other to Lauren. A fearful thought occurs to her, that if Dhanni's food has been tampered with this time then it will result in all of them succumbing to the Bull's desires. Lauren shakes the thought away. She is passed worrying about the food. This place is a nightmare but she must eat if she stands a chance of ending it.

After eating, the three of them lay down, hardly full but enough that weariness creeps in and puts down roots. Lauren dozes but jolts awake as she falls.

'Bad dream?' Angie asks.

'I tripped. Didn't even feel myself drift off.' Lauren rubs her eyes.

'Who does?'

Lauren reflects on that for a moment but closes her eyes against the familiar sluggishness in her legs. She resigns herself to what is about to happen. She would warn the others, tell them she is going numb but it can do no good. Angie looks more closely; she knows already. Panic rises in her as she realises that she hasn't pushed her shiv far enough against the wall where the cushions meet to make it invisible. Desperately, Lauren tries to shift and move the sharpened stake of a spoon from underneath her butt. Her fingers are like a bunch of grapes, swaying and moving against whatever they touch, her elbows are like a coat on a hook, hanging uselessly.

Her movements bring Angie up further and mistaking her panic for fear of the Bull, she tries to calm Lauren down. 'Lauren, it's OK. Just calm down, be still.'

Lauren wants to scream as her body shuts down. She can feel the spoon beneath her, but she cannot get her weight up to move it. *What if he finds it? What if I don't get another chance?* Lauren's opportunity is slipping away. With every ounce of control left, she scrapes her weight onto her side, hopefully pushing the spoon from under her and against the wall. Lauren and Angie stare at each other, Lauren now still but her heart is pounding. She cannot feel her weapon of hope beneath her; it is either against the wall and barely concealed or it is for all to see. There is nothing Lauren can do about it now. Her body ignores her, cut off by the Bull's poison.

'It will be alright.' Angie soothes, wanting to calm her.

The Bull enters and Dhanni and Angie shuffle back. Lauren hears him descend the stairs but can't see him until he kneels in front of her. His dark hand digs into his pocket and produces a small ring of keys. He sits her up and she lolls, powerless against gravity.

Wait… is he taking me upstairs? What is going to happen? Lauren has spent virtually every moment, conscious or otherwise, focusing on escaping this basement, on ascending those steps and getting out of here. This was not what she had in mind. The unknown fills her with a fear that bounces around her head like a marble in a jar. Down here at least, with the door locked, she knows what to expect. Upstairs? Lauren doesn't know what awaits her.

The Bull unlocks Laurens's wrists, but she can't express the relief she feels there. The manacles have a thin layer of worn leather between her skin and the metal, she hasn't felt air there since before waking up here. A strip of black fabric is wrapped around her head to blindfold her and then she is lifted at the knees and armpits. The Bull carries her with the ease. She can't see a thing. The world is now pitch-black and the Bulls breathing. She feels the Bull turn to get her through the door without banging her head. He probably thinks he is doing her a favour, the bastard. He carries her forward and her hand grazes something. *Was that wood, a chair or something?* Her senses are alive. Every shift in the Bull's step tips off a direction in Lauren's mind, telling her they have turned left or right. Every scrape, every sound clues her in as to what is around her. First, his feet clap lightly as if on tiles, then a soft thud like carpet. Lauren logs it all trying to build a picture in her mind as to what is outside of their cell. She may be blindfolded and unable to move but every other sense is pushed to their limit by necessity. Suddenly she is lowered, placed gently onto a bed, maybe a sofa. She is stuck there as his steps die away. After a few seconds she hears the familiar scrape of the bolt hitting home as the Bull locks their prison door. Lauren counts how long it takes for him to get back. *10 seconds...*

The Bull is close, she can hear his breathing. Lauren is as vulnerable as she possibly can be, unable to see, speak or move but also feels that other vulnerability that comes from being watched. A muffled click pierces the silence and then the Bull grunts in relief but clearer than Lauren has ever heard him. A thump on what must be a nearby table confirms the Bull has taken off his mask; the face that makes the monster is removed and the one that looks like a man is in place. It occurs to Lauren she could have met him. Nobody knows what happens behind closed doors after all. The man takes a few relieved breaths and the sofa dips as he sits next to her. It must be quite restrictive in the mask, and hot but Lauren has no sympathy for him; she hopes he burns.

A touch at her forehead makes her scream but no more than a timid release of breath escapes, like a kitten's wail. The Bull brushes the dirty hair off her forehead. '…beautiful…' His voice makes her soul shudder. When the Bull was a monster he was something to fear, to hate. To hear words from him and in a voice so ordinary makes Lauren shudder inside her paralysed shell. A man shouldn't be capable of these things, which makes him capable of anything, and that is terrifying. Angie's and Dhanni's telling of their previous cellmates come to Lauren; Theresa and Jo. *Jo died but what happened to Theresa? What did the Bull do with her after she fell ill? Were there others before them?* The news said there were eleven missing women, have all of them been in his clutches and now done away with? Lauren's mind swirls.

Without warning the Bull is on her, forcing her legs apart with the smallest push. Her legs fall apart, one leg aside and hanging toward the floor, limp and lifeless and pulls her underwear away. He rips her shirt open and then he is pressing to get inside her.

Lauren evacuates to the very centre of her armour; a bubble within her mind where she and Gary are together. She can feel her body being ravaged and used but it is a distant thing like a bright light being shone against her closed eyes; the light is there, bright but if her eyes are closed then it cannot blind her, cannot hurt her. Gary takes her hand, and they walk through a beautiful garden barefoot. Their own slice of paradise. The grass is crisp and itches at the sides of her feet, but it is a glorious feeling. Flower beds line the edge of the garden making the place sing with colour. No matter how many steps they take the edge of the garden never gets any nearer. This place is infinite for them. The sky is pink as the Sun slowly disappears over the horizon, making this world of hers a dream. The pink is too perfect, the grass too green, too vibrant, even Gary couldn't paint the world this well. Clouds streak the sky but the air is relieved, as if the day has been scorched by the Sun all day and only now thrown into shade. The air makes her skin tingle. Gary's hand is warm against hers and she revels in the touch. For a moment he has the visage of his demon, the four-armed devil with gushing wings flooding the grass, eyes blazing with dark light, but then he is back. His hair hangs at his temples and he flicks his head to shift it from his eyes, the way she has seen him do a million times. It falls back into place exactly where it was, but he doesn't mind. They stop and watch the receding Sun in the distance. It is bright but it cannot hurt her here, nothing can. Tears stream down Lauren's face but it is not all born of despair, she knows this place is made up, that her Gary is not really here, she knows what is really happening to her, but the beauty of this place hits her, grateful she can choose ignorance over reality. The edges of the garden crack and skip in spurts as if it could break apart at any moment. Lauren brushes her tears away roughly with her free hand, desperate to stay strong with her not-Gary.

'We can live here one day.' Gary offers. 'We'll find it and stay forever.'

Lauren hugs Gary's arm, pressing against his shoulder. 'I wish we were here.'

'We are here, L. Together. Look.' He tenderly frames her face with his hands.

She closes her eyes against his touch as if it is the only thing in the world. His touch is so fulfilling that the garden gains some strength back against what is really happening to her. She kisses his palm and holds on as if she can stop him from disappearing. Her cheeks are patchy and wet as tears run free again. Gary wipes them away. The pink sky shines back in his eyes. 'We'll find this place, L. One day we will, I promise.'

The edge of the garden flickers again as her armour breaks down. Harsh light shines through the cracks in the garden as if a great pressure is pushing from the outside of their bubble.

Lauren weeps. 'I don't want to go!' And she throws her arms around Gary.

He hugs her back as fiercely as her heart demands. 'We'll come back. We'll find it. I promise!'

Lauren holds on to her Husband for dear life but the very fabric of this place starts to thin. Gary's touch becomes cooler, the grass under her feet doesn't itch, the cracks in the sky widen. Grunts echo from outside, from through the cracks. Laurens's belly feels warm as if a dog has drooled on her.

'Just don't tip the bucket and you'll find me…' Gary smiles but the cracks in her bubble of paradise split over and through him. He is still smiling as their world splits apart. 'Don't tip the bucket…' He echoes from nothingness.

And then Lauren is back. Her groin is on fire, she would keel over and hug it if she could, and her belly is warm from the Bull's seed. He pants beside her, a hand on her leg, his passion spent, for now at least.

He gets up and leaves. She is left there, all but naked, for minutes on end. Her skin bumps without clothes or a blanket. The fluid on her stomach cools and dries on her skin. Lauren desperately tries to move, she puts every ounce of hate into moving her fingers, to make a fist but her body is foreign to her. The Bull's drug is beyond her power, completely separating movement from command. He returns and lifts her up. With purpose he carries her upstairs. Lauren can hear running water. Her heart hammers in her chest as a vision of being thrown in a bath and drowning while she is paralysed fills her. But he only lowers her into the water. It is steaming hot and she would scramble out but for her inability to move an inch. Her skin tightens against the heat. She imagines looking like a prawn as her skin turns pink. She is cradled by some sort of plastic seat so her head lolls back above the water. She is left there for a minute and every second that passes eases her muscles. Even with the effects of the Bull's poison, weeks of not being able to sleep normally has left her body in sore shape; no pillows to lay her head, no way to sit so that her back is properly straight, her legs are sore some days just from sitting cross-legged for too long. The hot water makes her skin tingle, but it is a balm to her aches.

She jolts in her head as the Bull suddenly takes her rag of a shirt and cuts at it with a sharp *snip* of scissors. He pulls the dirty shirt away, grabs her ankle and starts scrubbing. The sponge tickles her foot but she wouldn't laugh even if she could. She would gouge his eyes out. The Bull scours her hairy legs and her sex, working his way up. He cleans her all over, tipping water over her body and scrubbing again in places where she must be particularly grimy. He wedges a hand under her back and lifts her up with one powerful arm to do her back and bottom before lowering her back down into the water.

He washes her hair. Twice. He undoes the blindfold but leaves it in place over her eyes as he massages shampoo into her hair. Beautiful smelling conditioner is added and is left to soak while he lathers her legs and arms in foam and carefully shaves them. It is the most bizarre feeling to be pampered while in utter terror. The sheer tenderness in his touch pulls at the threads of her hate, unravelling core parts and soon she is glad of the treatment, thankful even. She scratches and bites at the insidious thoughts, pulls and tears at them until they feel like offal in the back of her psyche. Those thoughts, of gratitude and soft things are what turn her into Angie. They will wear away at her resolve to escape and make her accept what is happening to her. If the Bull set her free now, with every dream she ever had come true, then it would not be enough. It wouldn't scrub away what he has done as easy as the dirt now. She cannot let herself be broken down. She must stay strong and get out of here before she loses herself. She knows that this is the start. If one positive thought, one single happy attachment sets root in her brain then that seed will bloom and kill everything she is. She must stay angry to escape this monster, this psychopath, kidnaper, rapist, thief. She conjures every name for him that she can, fanning the flames of her disgust. She can't let him become anything more to her, even if that could make it easier to survive here. Surviving here isn't what she wants, to live away from here is.

Lauren can feel the eyes of the Bull on her naked form. She expects him to pull her from the bath, but he resists, wiping her down one more time, washing the conditioner from her hair. After, he pulls her from the bath and carries her through to another room, putting her on what can only be a bed. He towels her dry and rubs rich-smelling oils onto her skin. He blow-dries her hair and brushes it with care, navigating around the blind fold. Her head is in his lap as he gently picks at the knots and makes sure her hair is untangled after her time in the basement. He strokes her head, tenderly flattening the hair behind her ear and rubbing her temples. Lauren would scream. She is a whirlwind trapped in her head. The delight the Bull is giving her body is worse than the rape. It is sinister in its form. Her body responds to it, and she is turned on by the gentle nature of this fiend. She screams in her head, hating herself.

His manhood grows beneath her. She despairs. He flips her over on the bed, wet towels beneath her, and he has her from behind, all tenderness gone, replaced by the animal. He pushes into her and she would kick and claw away. But she can't. With each pull he grunts. With each thrust she fears for what is about to happen. And then she feels it. Pleasure. Her mind, her will, is disconnected from her body, she cannot control herself. She screams at him to stop but the sound is only in her head. Soon, she would have it be never, but all too soon she is on the verge of erupting. He speeds up as he nears his finish, and she orgasms. The smallest sound murmurs from her throat. He keeps pushing and pushing, her groin throbs and begs for release until it feels like she might explode. Then he pulls out of her and he cries out in ecstasy as he splatters her rear with his shot.

Tears run down Lauren's nose and into the towels. She wishes she were dead.

The Bull catches his breath and wipes her off. He leaves for a moment, and then dresses her. T-shirt and knickers only. Probably old clothes, maybe they were Dhanni's or Angie's when they were first brought here. He carries her downstairs and she is placed on the sofa from earlier. The all too familiar shriek of the bolt reaches her. There is a buffered difference in the Bull's breathing; he has donned the Bull's head to take her back down. He lifts her up and takes her downstairs. The temperature shifts to the warmer air of her prison, and she is greeted by its stale smell. She is placed on her back, the blindfold removed and wrists chained again to her wall. The Bull leaves and locks the door.

'Hey, Lauren.' Dhanni says softly.

Angie crawls forward as far as her chain will let her. 'You look great, hon'. You're beautiful.'

If Lauren could answer, she wouldn't. If she could move she would scramble up and hang herself with her chain. But even that isn't high enough. Lauren hates this place, she hates what it has done to her, what it is doing to her. She can't go through that again, not and stay disconnected enough to fight, she won't last. *Lauren* won't survive it. She must get out of here before she is changed, diluted, and made into someone that can't escape.

By chance, her hand has fallen against the wall, glancing her shiv. She tries to close her fingers around it but only the tip of her middle finger curls a fraction. *Soon.* She thinks. *Next time. I am going to do it. I don't care if I kill him.*

***

Angie stretches and shows Dhanni some other yoga positions. They chat sparingly as each conversation soon dies as silence strangles its way back on top. Lauren's body slowly comes back to herself and as soon as she is able she claws her way up to sitting.

'Hey, there she is.' Angie smiles.

'Lauren?' Dhanni asks.

Lauren hasn't slept a minute. She closed her eyes after a while, but sleep would not come. Her limbs may have been frozen in place, deaf to her commands but inside she is raging; her heart has been pumping adrenaline through her system in anticipation for what she is going to do. It may be hours away, tomorrow even, but the desperation she has known has been nothing compared to her need to escape now. Having the Bull force himself on her in such a way makes her feel pathetic, without a fight, to be tainted and shamed, how everyone must surely think of her, is a pain she never thought she could endure, thought that it would kill her. But it hasn't. It has changed her but there is a strength inside that keeps her fighting. But the fire inside will burn out, she can feel it. Her hope is guttering away. It is a nightmare, every waking second living with dread of when the door will squeal open and that animal will come for her, or one of the others. Now though, she faces something much more terrible; this place will change her so she won't want to fight anymore, she will wear out and this prison will have her. She must do everything in her power to stop that from happening. Even becoming a killer again; safe and sharing her life with Gary she never thought she would have to turn her hands red again but she has no other choice.

Hours pass and Lauren says nothing. Dhanni and Angie make half-hearted attempts to make conversation, but Lauren just strokes her gleaming legs, twirls the soft hair between her fingers. With each stroke, she lets her plan grow. The only unknown left to her is when to act. Should she eat her next meal, whenever it comes? She'll have to pretend either way, but the gamble will be whether she should actually eat it. If she eats and it is 'her turn' then she will have no choice but to wait, be taken and wait for her next opportunity. If it isn't her turn then she will have a last meal to fill her stomach, to give her vital strength. When the Bull is close enough she will burst into action and stab the monster. If she doesn't eat and it isn't her turn then she will be one meal hungrier, and the Bull might see that she hasn't eaten. Lauren weighs up each choice, knowing that there is so much that could go wrong.

Angie and Dhanni leave Lauren to her thoughts, no doubt through experience after the first time they were taken upstairs and cleaned up. She is grateful for the quiet. The consequences run through Lauren's mind again. What if she kills him and he doesn't have the keys on him? She would condemn them all to starvation. *Surely that is better than this.* Lauren frowns and watches her two cellmates, her friends in hell. She hasn't had many in her life and finds she doesn't want them to suffer and die because of her. Casey is colour in a black and white job, always has been, even at school, but Lauren has never been able to trust her with everything. She would never understand how Lauren helps Gary. Angie and Dhanni probably wouldn't either, but they have lived this torture together and that makes them real friends, right? Lauren considers bringing them in on the plan, on what she is going to do but what would they say? Would they agree, say it's too risky? They wouldn't warn the Bull and couldn't physically stop her from going through with it, but their disapproval sits awkwardly with her. She shakes the indecision away. They'll thank her when they are free and in the Sun again. *Gary, I'll be with you soon.*

***

Lauren waits and waits; it is an eternity before the Bull returns. Her heart is turned around, so used to dreading his arrival now she impatiently anticipates the fiend. But eventually the bolt is drawn free. He carries the usual tray with three plates on, sets it down and replaces their bucket. He leaves. *This is it.* Lauren takes up her bowl as calmly as she can but her hands shake. Each of them sits back against their wall and tuck in. Dhanni still picks at hers as if unable to commit to taking a full bite; Lauren doesn't blame her.

'Hmmmm... We haven't had Bolognese in at least a month. Must be a month, eh?' Angie says wistfully with a full mouth.

Lauren chews her own thinking on that. The first meal she ever had here was Bolognese. *A month...* Her resolve hardens, burns cold like ice and she hopes it isn't her turn, so that she is able to hurt the Bull before it shatters and she sinks. She savours every mouthful, knowing they could be her last if she fails.

'We should ask him for wine again. Or cold beer. Was never my thing but that sounds nice right now. Ooh, no! Ice cream!' Angie points her plastic spoon at the roof. 'You hear me, you fucker? We want ice cream!'

Dhanni's face releases her beautiful smile and Angie chuckles at her own outburst. These women don't deserve to be here. Lauren must act. For all of them, she must.

They finish their meals, even Dhanni for once. Angie needs to use the bucket. A few minutes after so does Dhanni. The mortifying noises that echo from the act have long since lost their effect between them. Lauren once cried while she did her business, out of embarrassment, but now it is just part of this prison, just something that happens. Lauren vows to burn this place to the ground.

Lauren tries to pinpoint each feeling inside her body. Inwardly, she feels her heartbeat, her insides begin to process her meal as a tiny burp builds in her chest. She flexes her fingers to test for numbness, crosses her legs the other way so they don't imitate the poison's sluggishness, but everything feels normal.

'Is it you?' Dhanni asks, noticing Lauren test her limbs.

Lauren can't be sure but she feels fine. Either way, she must make it look like it's her turn. 'I... I think so.'

'Unngh...' Angie groans. Her head is on her shoulder, her eyes staring straight at Lauren. She slowly sinks to the side until she is flat on her back.

Lauren matches her, making a show of sliding over and laying still. The show isn't for the other two women; Lauren suspects the Bull watches them through a camera in one of the dark corners, so he knows when to don his disgusting totem and come for them. Lauren palms her sharpened spoon and waits.

It isn't long before the shriek of the bolt heralds the Bull's return. He thuds down the stairs and stops before his prey, looking from Angie to Lauren and back again. Lauren can hear his thoughts now; *did I drug two of them? Did they share the food? It must be my lucky day!* But in his arms is a woman, dark skinned and unconscious. Laurens breath catches in her throat. *Oh no...* The monster has stolen another from their life. And added another to the weight of possible failure from Lauren's plan. If the Bull doesn't have the key then another will starve and die with the rest of them. But then he places the new girl down beside Lauren, produces a new chain and seals the woman's fate by locking it about her wrists, with the keys.

Lauren forces herself still, the want to grin at her deception is almost too great. She watches the Bull stand over her, looking to Angie and back again. He visibly shrugs. He strips his joggers off and discards them. They land beside Lauren's foot.

'Urgh...' The new girl stirs. Lauren feels for her. Lauren woke to Angie and Dhanni ready to explain things to her. This woman wakes to the Bull in the act.

The Bull kneels over Lauren and pulls her top up, roughly exposing her boobs. Her legs tense but she forces herself limp. She won't fail at this; she will make him pay and get the four of them out of here. He takes Lauren's chest in both hands, treating himself to a feel. It is all Lauren can do not to leap up and stab him. She grinds her teeth together, desperate not to move or give any indication that she is still in control of her body. He doesn't seem to notice, his attention fixed on what is in his hands. Her grip on the shiv is tight but on one knee he is too high for her to strike anything but his leg. She must wait. His rod is upright, ready. He nudges her legs apart. He closes and takes his member in hand, dropping his weight on his knees and sitting on his feet, ready to pull her knickers aside. It is all she can bear. With a cry she swings her fist over as close to the neck as she can get. He jolts up in surprise and the shiv sinks into his shoulder. He cries out inside the mask but with the muffled roar the Bull comes alive, baying and bucking away from her. Lauren wraps her legs around him, locking onto his waist and stabs again and again. He protects his body where he can, blocking her with his thick arms. The shiv does bloody work, puncturing his forearms wherever it lands but he manages to get leverage on one of her legs and forces himself loose. Dhanni is wailing behind her. Angie can only look on in horrified numbness. The new girl is wide-eyed, a scream trapped in her chest as she is spotted with blood. Lauren won't let him get away. She vaults forward and stabs at him again. He is ready for her as he gets to his feet and catches her wrist in a blood-slick but powerful grip. He pushes her back, slamming her against the padded wall like he is throwing open a door. She is unhurt but dizzy from the effort. She hasn't moved like this in months, and it is obvious she is weaker than she thought. He thumps her wrist against the wall, arm held in a grip too strong. He bangs her wrist again and again. The shiv punches holes into the padding with each slam, the Bull's horns tear gashes in it. Lauren refuses to let go. He strikes her in the face, and she almost passes out. Her face is red hot from the hit, her nose and cheeks feeling too big for her head. He twists her arm around and forces her to her knees. He has the leverage and the strength. He pries the shiv from her fingers.

Lauren screams out. 'Nooooo!'

The padded walls is in tatters, the Bull's body is slick with blood that could be oil in the gloom making him more a monster than ever. Lauren is slick too, her arms and front dark with blood. She cradles her twisted arm but lunges for his joggers and the key. Too fast, he whips them away from her. He backs off, groaning and hurt. He takes one look back, cradling his wounds, and flees.

'Oh my God. Oh my God. Oh my God…' The woman on Laurens left rocks back against the wall, desperately trying to scratch away the blood that greeted her into this prison.

'Lauren, what did you do?' Dhanni asks, looking at Lauren as if she is rabid.

Lauren collapses back. Her adrenaline runs dry and in the face of her failure she breaks down. She pulls her top back down and screams at the doorway above. Her scream would rock the heavens but they cannot hear her down here. She bangs her head back against the padded wall. Fabric wobbles and stuffing is knocked free after the battle with the monster. He was too strong and she too weak. Now she has no weapon in which to hurt him and no idea what to do next. She collapses on her side, heart pounding like a drum. Her veins could burst from the blood raging through her. She wails into her hands. She hurt the Bull, made the monster bleed, but it wasn't enough. And who knows what he will do now.

14. Inspector Roy Harvey

The security offices that run CCTV for Berry main, local areas, street watch, speed cameras, council security feeds and some local security is all monitored in the same building. Thousands of cameras dot the city covering high profile companies, public transport, monitored establishments such as schools, hospitals, car parks, supermarkets, and leisure centres, not to mention road camera's, all that cover most every place in Berry's city centre. Thousands of cameras and, forgetting all the parks, fields, and back alleys, still only covers about 25% of the city proper. It is a higher rate than most cities for CCTV coverage but somehow the Prince has avoided every one of them when he makes his move. Every wedding ring is found outside of coverage, some only feet away from capture. Roy doesn't believe it a coincidence. Their guy must know where he can act without being caught.

Roy looks at Nora beside him in the back of the squad car. Joey is driving, Leigham in the passenger seat. Nora has her hair up, in trouser suit, her work attire but Roy keeps catching himself staring at her. He has caught Nora looking at him a few times too. They have spent every night together since he got out of the Tanner place. He instinctively slides his hand over the seat to take hers but comes to himself, realising that Joey or Mathers might see. He trusts them both but if the Viper finds out about their affair it can only serve them to be ignorant.

Nora must sense his desire and turns to him, gifting a smile that makes his loins ache. The other night, he was more dominant, more forceful than he has ever been with a woman. Nora seemed to enjoy it and has let him do whatever he wants since but this change in him, that man is not usually Roy. With Emma he was always gentle and conservative in the bedroom, not through lack of inspiration but he thought he was happy that way and Emma only ever complied, seemingly happy too. After the rush of escaping Gary Tanner it is like a new man has awoken within him and Roy isn't sure he likes it. Maybe after so many years of working on these cases it has left a lasting effect. After sleeping with her last night, Nora read what was really on his mind. She told him he isn't becoming like some of the sick bastards they catch, that he is an important man, and he can take what he wants, with her anyway. Of course, that sparked him into action instantly, barely giving Nora chance to catch her breath but the fear of his change hasn't left his thoughts. She moves her hand closer but pulls back, also wary.

Roy shakes his head clear as they enter the Council Security block, showing their ID badges and following directions from the officer on the gate to where they can park. They need to be on the other side of the site but there is a 5mph limit. Joey flirts with the powers that be and averages 7mph. They pass various offices, suited employees pass by with folders in hand, ID lanyards swing around every neck.

Nora breaks the silence. 'What do you think then, Mathers? Is the life of an Inspector everything you thought it would be?'

Joey smirks at Roy in the rear-view mirror.

'Yeah, we're making progress.' Mathers says flatly.

'It's alright Leigham, the Viper isn't up my ass right now. You can speak freely.' Roy reassures the man.

Mathers considers a minute. 'I thought it would be faster.'

'What d'you mean?' Joey asks.

'There's a lot of digging. Don't get me wrong, I know the job, but the footage, the follow up statements, there is so much to get through and we haven't got anywhere. When Chelby came up I thought we'd cracked it. Is it always like this?' He asks no one in particular.

Nora and Joey look at Roy expecting him to make the guy feel better. 'Sometimes.' Roy admits. 'The careful ones are slow. Our guy is careful, so we need to be too.'

The car is silent for a moment. Mathers shifts in his seat, working his way up to a question. 'We're not going to find them all, are we?'

Nora and Joey actively look away this time. They both know the likelihood of finding the missing women let alone bringing them all home alive and well. 'Mathers, you'd better prepare-'

'I know boss. I'll deal with it. It's just a bitter pill, you know?' Mathers puts on his best poker face and looks out the window as if nothing in the world is amiss.

'Yeah, I know.' Roy whispers. Right now, he would pay anything to hold Nora's hand, to have contact with someone. Everybody looks to him as if he has a handle on the situation, like they are just waiting for him to click his fingers and solve this mystery. Sometimes, he would just like to be the one taken care of. Emma appears in his mind, several memories wrapped up in one. They are arm in arm on a walk, he can't remember exactly where. Then, they are in bed together, white sheets flow behind Emma making her hair wisp and flow as if caught in a breeze. Then, she is stood in their kitchen beside him as they dice peppers for a meal, laughing as Roy accidentally gets some in his eye. The memories blur together, desperate to make something more out of them, to make something real. But they *are* real and Emma *was* always there for him.

She told him everything he needed to hear and now she is gone and it's all his fault. Guilt washes over him but it is a familiar acquaintance now.

He pulls out his phone and calls Emma's mobile. Too late he realises he has no idea what he is going to say, and in front of Nora? Are they an item now? A secret to all apart from themselves? A male voice answers. 'Hello?'

Roy recognises the voice but he asks anyway. 'Who the hell is this?'

'Oh hi Roy, it's John. Emma is in the shower.' John Dockhorn, Emma's date from that night. *In my house.*

'What are you doing in my house?' Roy asks angrily. The other occupants of the car shuffle uncomfortably with no choice but to listen. Roy really didn't think this through, should have waited until he got out of the car. 'Joey, pull up.' Joey breaks and Roy gets out, striding across into the shade of the nearest office building. 'I said, what are you doing in my house?'

John responds calmly, Roy can see his smug little face now. 'I'm not in your house. Emma is in my shower.'

Roy's blood runs cold. His Wife is naked in another man's house. If he were there he would be on top of 'John' beating the hell out of him. 'Tell her to call me back.' Roy hears John take half a breath to form his reply but doesn't give him chance; he hangs up. The car window hums as it is lowered down. 'I know, Joey. I'm coming.'

'We're here, boss, by the looks of it.' Joey points to the next building over.

Roy waves for Joey to carry on. He could use a minute for the fire in his belly to die down. Nora gets out of the car and lets Joey park up. 'You OK?' She asks.

'Fine. I just want something to go on. I want to find this guy.' It isn't a lie but that is obviously not what Nora was referring to.

'We can talk about it later if you want? I'm not sure what we are right now Roy, but I can't expect it to trump your marriage. Even if I want it to.' Nora is really trying, he can see. She wants to be able to have him fully, all to herself. A part of Roy wants that too but he can't just forget about Emma, can't just move on without so much as a proper conversation. Nora is letting him make the decision and in his own time. It is more than he deserves.

'Let's just do this. We can talk at home.' *Home.* Nora's place is home now? Roy leads off into the surveillance office, Mathers and Joey a step behind.

***

David Leach, head of security for the Council Office of Surveillance, offers his meaty hand. 'Nice to meet you, Inspectors. I understand we may be able to help with something.' He is a big man, gone grey, well over six feet with a bulk to match. Although age has made him large in the stomach his broad shoulders and back show he was once a force to be reckoned with. He was a soldier twenty or so years ago; a career man but even soldiers settle down sooner or later.

Roy shakes his hand. 'Mr Leach? Thank you for having us.'

'This way.' He leads the four of them through the office building, passing several rooms until they reach a set of double doors. He enters a pin code on the wall and a buzzer signals the door is now unlocked. He holds the door open as the four of them squeeze passed his stomach and into his department.

The Office of Surveillance is split up into dozens of different cubicles, each with an employee. A room sits open at the back with enormous tower servers humming away in cages. Everyone is in shirts and ties, typing away or going from cubicle to cubicle with folders on whatever. Roy's first impression is that they are understaffed and under budgeted to do their job properly, considering the scale of their responsibility. Much like his own department, but then Roy wonders if he is being generous considering nearly half of his entire staff are stood next to him. With more hands, more access, they could do so much more. If they had the recognition software from day one then maybe they would have the Prince behind bars by now. Roy silently curses the Viper.

'So, what is it we can do for you?' Leach asks, arms folded on his gut.

'I'm sure you've heard about the Prince, and the missing women about town? We have reason to suspect that the man responsible may have extensive knowledge of the surveillance layout across the city. I need employee records for your department for the last three years, at least.'

'Employee records? You think somebody here is involved?' Leach is defensive straight away. Roy was told he used to be a squaddie so his sense of loyalty towards those he works with is understandable. He probably holds his judge of character in high regard; the idea that someone he knows could be something other than what he thinks must be ridiculous to him.

Nora promptly jumps in. 'We don't know yet Mr Leach. It could be somebody from years ago, likely an associate of someone here, that has no idea. We could be barking up the wrong tree. We need to make sure.'

Leach thinks it over but relents. 'It will take some time to get all the details together. I'll get one of my guys on it.'

'Thank you Mr Leach.' Roy steps back to give him more room.

Roy is grateful but with the warrant in Joey's bag Leach really doesn't have a choice. Leach marches off and calls to two different employees, giving them their instructions and sending them into the office in the corner. He picks up the phone and directs something else to make this happen.

'He seems cooperative.' Nora murmurs beside him.

'Why wouldn't he be?' Roy asks, looking around the office.

Nora considers. 'Military man. Can't become head of security without proving you have good instincts. I thought he might fight the process, against the affront to his experience. I mean, what if someone he knows is involved?'

'Frankly, I'd rather his pride is hurt than another girl goes missing.' Roy leans into Joey and Mathers. 'Have a walk around, have a chat. See if we can get the footage faster than we are.'

'Aye.' They say together and then casually stroll off striking up conversation with the first person they meet.

'You think someone here is holding back?' Nora guesses.

'Maybe. If somebody here is involved then they might be able to slow us down, even tamper with footage. You never know what somebody might be up to.' Roy is thinking about Emma and that ass John Dockhorn, about how you never really know what someone is doing, no matter how well you know them. *How could she just do something like that? And what is she doing showering at his house?* The fire grows within and he knows he needs to cool it. They could be on the verge of breakthrough information here; he must keep a level head. He douses his anger and jealousy with a full bucket of cold truth; he did this, he failed Emma and now she is… what, getting her own back? Moving on? *No, she's wrong. What happened between Nora and I is completely different.* Roy made a mistake, yes, but it wasn't to hurt Emma, or because he wanted to leave. It just… happened. *And it just happened every night this week.* The snide voice in his head makes a mockery of him and he looks about for something to punch. Leach comes back and Roy forces the simmering emotions within him under control. For now, at least.

'I'm having the employee files put onto a secured drive for you. It will just take a little while.' Leach eyes Joey and Leigham now sat with two different employees suspiciously. 'What else can we do?'

Nora begins to shake her head to decline as their request has been met but Roy jumps in. 'I need footage of this address for the last 12 hours, if any. And a private room.' Roy jots down John Dockhorn's address that Nora pulled up for him last week, and hands it over.

Nora see's the address before Leach can grab it and looks at Roy incredulously. She knows as well as he that this is not something the Viper should hear about. Leach nods and marches off to a cubicle, handing off the task.

'Roy, what are you doing?' Nora whispers.

'Dockhorn answered Emma's phone. Said that they were at his place. I want to know for sure.' He doesn't want to go into more detail with her. She deserves more, so does Emma, but Roy can't help who he is and right now he needs to know if his Wife is in another man's house.

Leach returns with a laptop and leads Roy to a private office at the back, big enough for a small desk and chair only. He logs onto the laptop and offers the chair. 'Perry is compiling a file with the footage now and sending it. Just double click the file when you see it.'

'Thank you Mr Leach.' Nora closes the door after him before storming around on Roy. 'What *are* you doing? What will it change if she is there?'

'I don't know.' Roy says flatly, refusing to look at her.

'Roy, aside from being unethical, this isn't going to do anybody any good.' She says softly, understanding, trying to stop Roy from hurting himself, but her voice is a barb in Roy's side. He is mad and she is his only outlet.

'You mean it won't do *you* any good?' He bites. The file pops up in the corner as received. Roy opens it to view.

'Excuse me? Why don't you just say what you want to, Roy?' Nora crosses her arms expectantly, guard up and ready for a fight.

She knows what he is going to say, Roy can see it in her eyes. He knows he shouldn't say it but his mouth is already forming the words. 'You don't want me to fix things with Emma! You've got what you want, right? I'm under your roof, just like you've wanted from the start. I hope it's really what you're after because it won't get you any legroom with the Chief.' It isn't fair, it isn't what he thinks of her, but he is hurt, and he would fight his own Mother right now.

Nora's mouth curls in anger. 'You think I'm using you to get a promotion? How fucking dare you?!' She leans forward. Roy pushes his chair back to meet her, but she grabs the arms, making him sit down again and holding it in place so that their noses are an inch away from each other. 'I've looked up to you Roy. I like you a lot. Maybe more than that. If you think, even for one minute, that I am manipulating you then that's an insult to both of us.'

Roy won't look into those perfect crystal eyes. The rage will die if he does and right now it makes him feel better. 'I guess we'll see.'

Nora grabs his crotch. He jolts but she has got a grip on him as if she is hanging off the edge of a cliff. 'I've learned a lot from you, Roy; your old cases, with the Funder case, and then Garner. But we both know the Garner case was all me. And I've been the driving force on this case! You think *I* need *you* to get ahead?' She eases her grip slightly and massages him.

Roy moves to pull her off his package but she grips tighter briefly as a warning. He spreads his hands, submitting. She rubs him and it doesn't take long for the blood to find its way, he begins to harden.

She leans in to kiss him but then stops, lets him go and he can do nothing but look into her eyes. 'Maybe it isn't *me* that's using *you*.' She shoves his chair back and storms out of the office.

Roy blows out a breath knowing he was acting like a prick, regretting what he said as soon as he said it. The cursor hovers over the play button but he can't decide whether to press it, to find out if his Wife is at another man's house or not. John answered Emma's phone but that doesn't mean they are where he said they are. Like Nora said, what difference does it make? What if he and Emma have just moved on? No, he knows Emma, better than anyone and she is just trying to get back at him. But if not this 'John' guy, then it will only be somebody else. Unless Roy can fix things and get her back. His finger rests over the mouse. *Does I want to fix things?* Roy looks out to the department floor, through the office door window. Nora is talking with Mathers, pointedly not looking back at Roy. His finger rests on the mouse, all but shaking to play the video footage and skip through to when Dockhorn and his Wife arrive. Maybe they'll be tipsy after a day out or laden down with shopping bags from him treating her. Maybe they'll make love on the front doorstep and the universe can really kick him when he's down. *Is that what I want?* Roy considers that maybe he wants Emma to be as unfaithful as he is so that he can have Nora without feeling so guilty. Maybe, deep down, he does want a different life to what he had with Emma, and he is using Nora to make that happen.

Roy pushes away from the desk. The thumbnail for the video is a street camera. No house front is visible, only the road from the elevated angle. He wouldn't be able to see much anyway. He closes the link and leaves.

'We've got the list.' Joey says, lifting a memory stick.

'Did you find what you were looking for?' Leach asks.

Joey, Mathers and Leach look at him expectantly. Nora too but there is another layer to the question for her. Roy can't fix things with Emma just like that. He can't turn back the clock and make things better. But maybe now isn't the time, another day, another dawn maybe they still have a future but it won't be built today. Maybe he and Emma can't be mended, and it is better if they seek the things each of them needs elsewhere. He has Nora and she deserves more than his guilty spite. So, he chooses Nora, as hard as that may be on all involved. Nora is everything he could want and she is here, now. Roy only has eyes for her. 'I didn't watch it.' He says with gravity. 'It was the wrong address, my mistake.' He covers for Leach.

Nora smiles and they share a private moment. Leach is oblivious and extends further help if in his power. He leads them out through the double security doors, Mathers and Joey behind him, Roy and Nora bring up the rear.

'Thank you.' Roy says only for her.

'You were being a prick.' She says, eyes forward.

'Yeah.' He almost flirts something like *I'll make it up to you later* or some such, but the guys are only a few feet ahead and he daren't risk being overheard.

Nora seems to read his mind and she lets him have one of her gorgeous smiles. She becomes serious as Leach escorts them outside. 'I want to catch this guy, Roy. Whoever he is, The Prince, it isn't personal like it was for Garner, and he won't stop unless someone stops him. *We* have to stop him.'

Joey holds up the memory stick as he unlocks the car. 'There are hundreds of files on here. We're due a break, I bet he's on here. Right, Roy?'

'I'd stake my career on it.' *Which the Viper has all but said.* 'But even if he isn't, we'll get him.' The clock is still ticking for all twelve missing women and every day that goes by is another decrease in their chances of coming back home, not to mention more names being added to their list. 'They need us to.'

***

Back at the office Roy is ready to spring into action, but Nora beats him to it. She takes control and realigns their operation, she assigns Roy, Simpson and Davies to cross referencing the Council employee files with known affiliates of the missing women. Even with the list there are still hundreds of potential connections to make; it could be the employee, or anybody close to them, are any of them in debt, have past offenses, a history of violence or ties with the missing women in any way? It's a new mountain of work and they haven't even finished the follow-up reports and witness statements. She separates the statements alphabetically, taking whatever is left of A-G, Wyatt takes H-O and Watkins gets P-Z, leaving immediately.

She is right in what she said, she doesn't need to use anybody to get where she wants to go. She is a force to be reckoned with and if anybody can catch their guy then it is her.

The rest of them set to their tasks. Roy takes up one desk with a sheaf of pages from the list of Council employees. Each name has limited additional information; what positions were held and how long for, disciplinary procedures and even training reports, none of which are in great detail but Roy will take anything at this point. He reads for hours, well into the afternoon before he comes up for air. The rest of the boys work as tirelessly as he, hoping to stumble onto something useful. Roy pinches the bridge of his nose. Unfortunately, this is a large part of detective work. There is a lot of digging, it is mind numbing and 99% of the time it doesn't lead anywhere. After reading through what must be five hundred names and histories Roy decides to get a steaming cup of crap from the coffee machine. He leaves Davies and Jones to it while he stretches his legs. Joey, Mathers and Jones are glued to their monitors, three or four each and each running a different stream of footage; CCTV, home movies from old camcorders or mobile phones, videos volunteered by friends and family of the missing, weddings, birthday parties, anything and everything pertaining to the missing women. Their faces are grey and slack after watching such un-interactive video for so long. Roy decides to get a round of coffees in to keep them awake, not that they'll thank him for it. The names on his list buzz around his head, swapping details with each other and overlapping like bugs in a hive. He can't even remember the last name he read. The coffee machine whirs and processes his order and he pinches his nose again, wishing for a breakthrough much like he has every day since he was assigned the Prince. He tries to conjure his skill and let the pieces fall into place and reveal the real picture but it doesn't come. 'Anything substantial?' He asks as he rounds back into the office and hands out the plastic cups.

Mathers leans back and rubs his eyes under his glasses. 'Thanks.' He sips his coffee, grimacing. 'A couple of matches but nothing out of the ordinary. No suspicious activity from what we can see, watching it back.'

Roy sighs again. One laptop shows CCTV from a supermarket with Dhanni Sandhu waiting in line with a basket of shopping, another shows Karly Schwarz on holiday in a hotel room being filmed by her partner as they watch the Sun set, the next is Angelina Smiths wedding, all ivory white with the men in tuxedoes, Edyta Durak signs in to work at her security office and on and on and on. Thousands of hours of mostly useless footage, viewed with the small hope that between them and the recognition software they find a new link. Roy shakes his head and sips his coffee. *Even if we had fifty guys checking this stuff around the clock...* A familiar face on one of the monitors catches Roy mid-thought and his head whirls. Names and dates spin through each other. Meetings with the victims nearest and dearest play out from every angle inside his brain, all at once. The video on Simpson's monitor is from Angelina Smith's wedding. Second wedding, Roy corrects himself. Mrs Smith is gorgeous in a white dress with lace sleeves, the gown flows back behind her in a traditional style. The footage is an amateur shot, taken by some member of the congregation. Stood at the front, waiting for the bride is a line-up of groomsmen. The second man in line, perhaps the best-man is the security guard at Lauren Tanner's firm. Roy's mind reels in on itself trying to remember the man's name. *Jerry... Akoum!*

Slamming his coffee down on the desk, almost collapsing the flimsy cup, Roy races to his own cluttered table and rifles through the list of Council employees he spent the day digging through. Joey and the others all slowly edge forwards, sensing something important is about to be revealed. 'What is it boss?' Joey asks. Roy ignores him. His eyes and hands are a blur as he scans page after page, searching for what his gut knows is true. He didn't add it up before, his mind was too full of different names to pick up on one he had heard before but there he is. Jerry Akoum, worked at the Council Office of Surveillance two years ago. 'Jerry Akoum. I need an address right now!' Roy hands the paperwork over to Mathers. 'We've got another match. Akoum is linked to at least two of our missing persons, he knows Angelina Smith and he works at the same office as Lauren Tanner, and his history at the Council means he could have inside knowledge about camera placement around Berry.'

Mathers is furiously typing away, pulling up all the information they have on Jerry Akoum, but it is Jones that holds a sheet up. 'I have the address here.'

'What?' Mathers can't believe the big guy could have beaten him to it.

'How did you do that?' Roy asks the Officer; he isn't even next to a computer.

'Akoum is one of the names on Inspector Murphy's list. Of catch-ups. She'll be meeting him now.' Jones explains.

Nora... Roy grabs his jacket. If Akoum is their guy and Nora has gone over there alone then she could be in danger. 'Keep on it! Joey and I are going after her, call a squad in to that address!' Roy shouts as they rush into action.

15. Lauren Tanner

Lauren's stomach rumbles. She doesn't know how long it has been since the Bull stumbled from their cage, but he has missed one meal, at least. *God, what if I killed him?* Her, Dhanni, Angie and the new girl will die. Lauren's arm is sore, nothing permanent, her wrist is bruised but it is nothing compared to the disappointment in her failure. She came so close, but he was too strong. *Is there anything else I could have done, anything different?*

'Do you know what you could have done?!' Angie rages at Lauren again. 'You could have killed him!'

Lauren lets the words wash over her. They are nothing she hasn't considered herself and not the first tirade from Angie since the effects of the Bull's poison wore off. She clawed her way up and demanded answers from Lauren as soon as she was able. 'I can't believe it. He's hurt… What if he's dead? You could have killed us all!' Angie is restless. For the first time Lauren sees her pulling at her chains, itching to be free.

Lauren feels for her. In Angie's mind she had a safe bubble in which she lived, not there by choice but with consequences she forced herself to accept. To her, what the Bull is doing to them is better than the alternative. And now that security is gone. She has seen what starvation does to a person and the pinprick fingers of fear have pierced Angie's armour to scratch at her terrors.

Dhanni by comparison has said little but looks at Lauren like she has never seen such a creature before. The Bull is everything a monster should be; he hurts them, takes away what can't be replaced, and is able to appear as soon as they are helpless. In making the monster bleed, Lauren has shown he is just a man; a man capable of monstrous things, but a fallible, very human man. The look that Dhanni gives Lauren isn't of fear or rage like in Angie's case, it is respect.

Their new cellmate hasn't said a word. She is younger than Lauren, her fluffy black hair nearly as gorgeous as Dhanni's. She has cried, pulled at her chain, picks at the dried blood but hasn't spoken yet. Lauren wonders how long the effects of shock can last. This woman woke to a bloodbath and locked to a wall surrounded by strangers. Angie's raging at Lauren is the only context she has been given. She must be terrified. Lauren would speak to her but failure chokes the motivation to make anybody else feel better.

Lauren's element of surprise is now gone. If the Bull lives then who knows what he will do. Maybe he'll let Lauren starve. He won't trust her with cutlery again, that's for sure. Maybe he'll only serve her mushy meals, that she must eat directly out of the bowl. Lauren laughs to herself at the image.

'What's so funny?' Angie demands.

'Nothing…' Lauren smiles at the image of the Bull, scared to give her a spoon. 'Just thinking, bet I'll have to eat with my fingers after this. If he comes back?'

'This isn't fucking funny!' Angie pulls at her chain so it goes taught, knuckles white around it. If she could reach over and slap her, Lauren is sure she would. 'What if he's dead? Oh God, what if he's *dead*?'

'It's less than he deserves.' Lauren says flatly.

'And what about what we deserve? Eh?!' Angie spits. 'Did you think about us when you… when you planned to stab your way out of here?'

Lauren did. She thought about every option left to her, every scenario, every consequence she could. Except one where the Bull is still breathing and they are still chained up in this hole. Saying it so simply does make it sound like a stupid plan. Angie shakes her head, disgusted. The look on the older woman's face sparks the fire in Lauren's belly she thought had guttered out. 'I *was* thinking of us! I was thinking if you had the choice to leave then you would.'

Angie's mouth works into a retort but Lauren ploughs ahead. 'You have no idea what happened to the women before us. He is keeping us in a fucking dungeon! He rapes us! He is not going to just let us go one day. One way or another, this cell is the last place we're going to see unless we get out of here.' Tears build in Lauren's eyes but they are not the desperate tears of the helpless anymore. Lauren is desperate, sure, but now she is angry. She hurt the Bull but it is nothing compared to what he has taken from them. 'We are not *his*.'

The simple words stun both Angie and Dhanni. The new girl blubbers. Lauren leans back against the wall not realising she had inched forward. Covered in patches of blood, on her clothes, in her hair, stained on her hands, she must look feral. The padded floor is sticky with it, black like oil in the low light. The girl beside her shakes, cracking, but Lauren has only silent sympathy for her. She can spare nothing else. The woman may think she is afraid but real fear hasn't wrapped its shards of ice around her throat yet.

'I don't want to be here.'

The words are so quiet that Lauren could have imagined them. 'What?'

Dhanni is shaking, holding back sobs. 'I don't want to be here anymore. I never did but… I feared dying, of being hurt. So, I didn't try. I just stayed here and let him…' Her lips shake around each word.

'Dhanni…' Angie begins softly.

'I don't want to be his!' Dhanni screams, shocking her cellmates. 'I'd rather die than let that man touch me again.'

Lauren's heart could burst. Dhanni, her friend, has overcome herself, her fears and decided; to be free or die. Whatever her motivation, be it love for another like Lauren or born of primal survival to escape this prison, Lauren's heart would join with Dhanni's if it could, knowing the need to be free. 'We're going to get out of here Dhanni. I promise.'

'What are we going to do?' Dhanni asks, wiping her cheeks with the back of her hand, determined but not knowing where to start.

Lauren, dirty with the Bull's blood, hungry and fresh out of secretly made weapons, locks Dhanni's eyes to her own. 'I don't know yet. But one way or another we are going to get out of here.'

The Indian girl nods, her will set.

'You're both insane.' Angie scoffs. 'Show me a way out. Hell, *tell* me how and I'm on board! But you can't. There's no way out of here. You're just setting yourselves up for disappointment. Hope kills you down here. You know that Dhanni!' Angie pleads.

'I'm sorry Angie. I won't be here anymore. Even if I starve. He's not taking any more of me.' Dhanni says gently but with a force that bellies Angie's appeal.

Angie throws her hands up making the chain rattle, and sits back.

'Lauren, what do we do?' Dhanni asks, her eyes as big as ever.

Angie looks to Lauren too; she expects there to be no plan whereas Dhanni is hoping for the perfect one. One of them is right. 'I don't know yet Dhanni. I wanted to get the key but…' She rattles her chain, fingers stained with the Bull's blood. '…we'll think of something.'

Angie snorts, knowing Lauren had nothing. Dhanni looks grim but she nods her head, determined to escape. The courage of the girl makes Lauren's soul ache. She has watched somebody die slowly and has made a choice to face that if that's what it takes.

What are *we going to do?* Now that Lauren has an ally her hope is restored but the reality of the situation hits her like a brick. They are back where they started.

***

The bolt on the door squeals and they all jump despite themselves. Every eye is on the Bull as he ducks through the doorway; he lives. As much as Lauren wants the bastard dead she is glad she hasn't sentenced them all to starvation. The Bull's fur is as black as can be, eyes glistening as bright as the rings in his ears. His upper body is patched and striped in bandages. The linen runs under the mask over his shoulders and down and around his thick chest, beneath his armpit. One forearm is wrapped from where her shiv found him, but the other arm is dotted with plasters. Lauren doesn't remember every detail of her attack but she must have dug at him with her nails as much as the shiv. An animal from deep within led her in that moment, controlled her. The Bull sets four plastic plates onto the floor; sandwiches.

No cutlery. Lauren wears the evillest smile she can conjure. It may be a coincidence that he made them sandwiches which require no cutlery to eat but it pleases Lauren that maybe she set a small fear in the monster. Chained to the wall as she is she could be no more threat to him, surely, but Lauren glows, at how dangerous she might appear to him and loving the power it gives her. He may watch her through that dead thing on his shoulders, but she grins wider, hoping she looks as shotgun-mad as she needs to be to get through this. He hesitates, takes half a step forward, raising his hand to strike her. Lauren juts her chin out, daring him to come closer. His hand drops and he leaves.

Angie reaches for her sandwich the moment the door starts to close. She takes half the sandwich in one bite. 'Mmmm… Christ, I'm starving.'

Dhanni and Lauren look at each other, the same question on each other's mind and seeing it they both know their answer. Lauren leans over, picks up her plate and Frisbee's it across the room toward the stairs. It clatters and the sandwich explodes sending salad and whatever meat was in it all over the place.

'Hey!' Angie looks perplexed. 'What are you doing?'

Dhanni leans over for her plate, but Angie beats her to it, snatching it up. 'Ahhh no you don't. If you two want to play that game then that's fine but I'm not going to suffer.'

Dhanni looks a little disappointed but then holds out her hand. 'Plate please.'

Angie puts both sandwiches in her lap and hands over the plate suspiciously.

Dhanni nods her thanks and then flings it away, just like Lauren. Her smile is gorgeous, a real smile, borne of a moment truly unhindered by the rest of the world. It is infectious and Laurens's cheeks hurt from joining her.

'So that's it? You two are just going to stop eating? Great fucking plan. So, what? You two are just going to starve and I have to watch that shit-show again? Well, that ain't fucking fair! Not what I signed up for you selfish bitches!' Angie takes up one of her sandwiches in a clamp grip. 'And when you give in? You're going to be weaker than before and no better than when you started. You're going to go through all that pain for… what? He'll just have you anyway.' She noisily chews down on her meal, tutting and turning away.

Lauren needs to pee. She pulls down her knickers and squats on the bucket. Her water echoes from her seat. 'I'm sorry Angie. But we can't stay here.'

Angie tuts, refusing to look at her. She eats her sandwich as aggressively as possible, huffing and smacking her lips.

The new girl watches Lauren relieve herself on the bucket. There is pity in her eyes but it is a small reflection of her own disbelief. She is in the same situation but can't believe what is happening to her. Was Lauren so detached, so haughty about Angie and Dhanni when she saw them, to show such disdain and refuse to be anything like them? Of course she was, without meaning offence but pitying them all the same. At least this girl isn't screaming at them like Lauren did.

'What's your name?' Lauren asks her. The woman shakes her head and edges away as if Lauren's question can trap her. Lauren wipes herself without taking her eyes from the new girl. 'I'm Lauren. This is Angie, and Dhanni.' But the girl puts her hands over her ears and starts rocking back and forth as if ignoring the world can save her from it. Lauren feels for her but there is nothing she can say that will bring her around. Lauren has little motivation to try. Angie has a good point though; they need a new plan or they will fade away.

Facing her wall from on top of the bucket, at the extent of her chains range, Lauren takes in her wall that has been her home for God-knows-how-long now. The papers said the Prince struck every month; with the introduction of another it must be at least a month Lauren has been here now. The floor is blotted with the Bull's blood, the wall is scored with cuts from his horns and Lauren's wild strikes, and her stretch of floor is dipped from where she has been sat. Something in the wall catches her eye. In the din she can't make it out. Lauren pulls up her underwear and then inspects where the wall took the brunt of the damage. The tacky fabric is torn and the foam underneath disembowelled. Lauren digs her fingers into a tear and merely an inch into her investigation is stopped by a wooden panel. But there is a seam. From a very specific angle, for a fraction of a milometer, Lauren can see light. At a point where the wooden panels don't quite meet Lauren can glimpse a spec of the outside world. It is too small for any detail, for anything but light to get through but Lauren has just found out how close they are to the rest of the world.

'Lauren, what is it?' Dhanni asks.

Lauren barks a hysterical laugh. 'I see daylight!' An alarmed voice in her head screams at her to shut up, the Bull could be listening, watching them right now. But this find is too exciting for her to keep silent. 'We're in a basement, right?'

'So?' Angie spits but her eyes are on the wall as well.

'So, I think my side is where the street is. The drain-grate-thing must be right here!' Lauren explains.

'What? You can see outside?' Angie presses.

'No... It's just a spec of light, there's a backboard to the soundproofing.' Lauren shrugs. 'But still! If I can get the board away maybe we can get out.'

'Eerrmm... hello!' Angie shakes her wrist and makes her chain rattle.

Lauren grips her own chain. *We must get free of the chains. But how?* She has no idea. She sinks back down onto her butt and desperately tries to think of a way out of their bonds. The Bull will be on guard now; he will never let her, or maybe the others, have tools to use against him. *How do we get the chains off?* Lauren examines her wrists. She could force it, probably break her hand in the process but she isn't sure she could pry the board away with two hands let alone one. Any way she can think to break the manacle or the lock would injure her. *Think Lauren, think!*

'Without the key, I don't know.' Dhanni says softly, inspecting her own chain for perhaps the first time in months.

'There has to be a way… Angie?' Lauren watches Angie's head dip, her shoulders shake as she tries to keep herself upright.

'Sorry, Angie.' Dhanni mutters.

Angie slumps over onto her face, shirt ruffled and legs splayed awkwardly. The next minutes are spent in helpless silence. Both Dhanni and Lauren would reach out to their friend, hold her close, but they can't. All too soon, the door whines open and the Bull enters, naked apart from his totem and the bandages across his torso. New Girl screams. He pads down the stairs and descends on Angie.

***

New Girl is dead. Lauren considered hanging herself before but thought the loop of the chain not high enough to do the job. She was wrong. The poor girl wrapped her chain around her throat to remove the slack and dropped. Her bum is only inches from the padding. Lauren woke to the chain clinking and New Girls heels scraping the panels but the girl kept her resolve to leave here without putting her feet back underneath her. After Lauren's fight with the Bull and then seeing him take Angie it must have been too much. She fell limp as Lauren realised what was happening. Angie stares at the girl, cried for her but is numb to it now. She rolled over and hasn't spoken since. Dhanni shakes but faces the sight of her body with bravery, knowing their decision to rebel against the Bull will surely end the same way, if not slower. Guilt weighs on Lauren, was there something she could have said, done to give the girl strength? No, the woman had more strength than the three of them. Lauren wonders how long the Bull will leave her there. If there is a camera he must surely see. Maybe it's the middle of the night and he is sleeping. Lauren checks her microscopic gap in the backboard but the spec of light could easily be a streetlamp. Maybe he leaves her hanging as a warning. Not for the first time she wishes the Bull dead.

***

The Bull took the body down what felt like a day later. She had started to go grey and it seemed like the Bull was tired of it all. With no care, like the woman was a rubbish bag to be thrown outside, he dragged her up the stairs by her shackles, her feet bumping the steps. He slammed the door shut in a rare show of violence. Lauren would revel in the face of his frustration but she could not. A woman died beside her and this place is darker, colder than before. If nothing else, Lauren vows to kill the monster. If she has a chance to escape or kill the bastard she will make sure she ends him.

Lauren's gut cramps again and she crumples in on herself, hugging her middle. She has had the presence of mind this time to count the meals as they are brought in. Angie has been eating like a Queen while Lauren and Dhanni starve but of course every day the Bull has been taking her. Four days now. Four days without food or water and they are all suffering. Lauren and Dhanni have barely said a word in the last day, every ounce of energy needed to rest and fight the cramps attacking them. They have taken to stretching themselves out as far as they can, legs toward each other so that their feet touch when they can get to sleep. It is a small comfort but they both relish the contact. When they do sleep it is fitful and light, waking more exhausted than when they closed their eyes, or they are dead to the world as if it has been four hundred days and not just four.

Lauren jolts awake, her heart pounds like her chest is paper thin. She searches the room but all is quiet, Angie and Dhanni are asleep. Remnant shards of her dream stroke her memory before drifting away. She tries to hold onto them, the sounds, the smell, whatever it was, wherever she was… Gary was there, she's sure. But it's gone. Lauren rolls over and tries to get comfy but it's like every inch of her, every joint, is bruised. Her body is starting to eat itself again. She was barely back to strength from her starvation before and her body has slid back faster than she feared. Her skin is itchy, her hair like straw, even after the Bull's attention to it. A scuffle makes her look up and it is only then she realises the basement door at the top of the stairs is open. It takes a moment but she finds the outline of the Bull sat at the bottom of the stairs. She almost screams but masters herself, breath caught in her dry throat.

'I'll bury you.' His voice is muffled from inside the mask but in the silent basement it may as well be whispered directly into her ear. 'Like the others.'

Lauren is stunned, she can't get her words out. He spoke before, when she was upstairs but that was when it was the man speaking. This is the Bull in his pen.

'You're strong.' His deep, muffled voice slurs as if he has been drinking. 'But not strong enough. You'll lose and I'll bury you. Is that what you want?' His voice increases in volume but he catches himself, wary of waking the others.

Fear has Lauren by the throat but her inner fire builds and burns away its icy fingers. *So, Theresa did die.* The fact should terrify her but that mad smile creeps into creation on her face. *To be down here like this, he must be worried, scared even. He doesn't want more blood on his hands, he just wants to fuck us and for us to be happy about it.* 'Go to hell.'

The Bull's head shakes slightly as if the man inside is shaking his head, unable to fathom why Lauren is fighting like she is. He retreats up the stairs. Lauren screams after him. 'Go to hell!'

Dhanni and Angie wake up, their eyes dart around searching for an answer for the commotion. Dhanni is slower to rise than Angie, but she is alert. Angie rubs her eyes. 'What is it? What's happening?'

Lauren burns holes in the door with her stare but the Bull is long gone, their cell bubbled in silence once more as if he were never even here. 'He was here.'

'What? Just now?' Angie asks.

'Yeah, he wants us to give up, for us to let him have us.' Lauren explains.

'I didn't hear the bolt.' Angie dismisses, adjusting her seat to go back to sleep.

Neither did I. Lauren didn't hear the bolt as he left either. *Was he here? Did I imagine that?* Lauren rubs her temples and scrunches her eyes shut. *No, he was here, he wants me to give in.*

'Lauren? Just sleep, OK?' Dhanni asks gently.

Lauren wants to scream that she isn't crazy, but she knows she is just irritable from hunger and hurt. 'Yeah.'

The bolt shrieks and the Bull enters with three fresh meals. Dhanni and Lauren simultaneously turn away as if nothing could be more mundane than his arrival with food. The Bull descends and places the contents of his tray on the floor between them. Lauren watches him out of the corner of her eye, refusing to consider she may be losing her mind. He has a fresh jug of water but their bowl is still half full. Their meals from the first day have been left to rot underneath the stairs. He stands there for a moment as if deciding what to do. He turns to each of the women in turn as if an answer will appear; something to satisfy his frustration and make them play along with his nightmare. Suddenly, his muscles bunch and he slams the jug of water down sending up a splash of water. The three women jump. Dhanni cringes away, terrified he will fly into a rage. Angie stares wide-eyed at their captor. The Bull storms away and slams the door so loud that Lauren is sure the padding couldn't cover the sound.

'I don't know what he's going to do.' Angie says, reaching for her bowl of porridge. There are no spoons in the bowls. 'You're making him unpredictable, angry. And that's dangerous.' Neither Lauren nor Dhanni say a word. They have made up their mind. This time there is no going back. Angie blows her porridge. Without a spoon she cannot cool it spoonful at a time; she'll have to wait until she can drink it from the bowl without burning herself. 'You know you two are selfish, right? What choice has he got but to use me now?' Again, neither Lauren nor Dhanni say a word. 'Hey! Don't you dare ignore me. If you two are going to leave me here then the least you can do is talk to me.' Angie spits, she almost throws her bowl but relents, leaning back to stare at her porridge. The heat be damned, she gulps at her porridge to spite Lauren and Dhanni's efforts.

'What do you want us to say, Angie? What should we do?' Lauren asks calmly.

'Live!' Angie rages. 'I want you to live! You think dying, and on your terms is the better choice? Well, it isn't. When you're dead you're just dead. You're not his, that's what this is, right? You don't want to be his? Well, when you're dead you're not his. Or yours or anybody else's, you're just dead.'

'I don't believe that Angie.' Dhanni says softly.

'Well, you should know better. You've seen it!' Angie spits.

'But I don't believe that. Maybe we'll be dead but I don't believe that we are not ours then. We will live a new life when we are born again, different but still us. The only thing here that is his is our bodies. Soon, he won't even have that.' Dhanni's words are as calm as can be. A strength that had long since fled has taken up her spirit. Her force of will invigorates Lauren's own.

Angie sets her porridge aside. 'I'm sorry Dhanni, but that's crap. You're here now. And that's it! You may as well make the most out of it coz there is nothing after.' The words are like a whip on Dhanni's back and for a heart-breaking second the Indian girl stumbles within herself. Angie gulps her porridge down.

'Don't you dare tell her how it is!' Lauren's voice is hoarse and dry, barely carrying the conviction she feels. She struggles to her feet, anger rising. 'You don't know anything do you? You think you have this place figured out, but you don't know what happened... He said he buried them.'

'What?' Dhanni asks, shocked.

'What, how do you know that? When did he say?' Angie asks, a look of mortification in her eyes.

'Before. When he was here.' Lauren leans back against the wall, dizzy. A wave of sickness washes over her just from standing. It takes all her concentration not to pitch over onto her face. 'He didn't let Theresa go...'

'Blondie, he wasn't here. You're seeing things...' Angie steadies herself even though she is sat down.

'He was!' She yells but everything is muffled as if Lauren is underwater. She can see Dhanni calling to her, worry plastered over her face, but she blurs. Lauren can see the shape of Angie slide over onto her side, limp and helpless from her porridge. Lauren matches her as the floor rushes up to meet her. The padded floor is a soft kiss on her face. Darkness takes her.

***

Lauren opens her eyes and Gary brushes the hair from her brow, tracing her face with a tender finger. She is on her back, soft grass beneath her, feeling like the silky coat of her childhood dog. She thinks the grass should itch but Gary envelopes her. He glows with the pink sky behind him. The clouds swirls in hypnotising patterns like milk has been massaged into strawberry syrup.

'How're you holding up, L?' Gary's voice is the only sound in this place. She pulls him tight and for a moment it is all she can do not to collapse into a broken, crying mess. 'Hey, hey, it's alright. I'm here.' Gary holds her close, his touch is a healing balm that covers her and soothes her body's aches. For one endless moment they just lay there on the grass beneath her pink sky. But of course, it does end, it has to. Gary leans up onto one elbow and strokes the hair from her face again. 'You need to wake up, L.' He whispers softly.

'No, I don't want to.' She scrunches herself against the truth. A part of her knows what this place is; a dream, an unreality inside of her head to keep her safe while reality has its way with her life. Lauren knows but saying it out loud, even thinking it coherently could bring it all crashing apart. She remembers the cracks in their garden the last time she was here. The flowers have grown taller, the grass longer, but everything seems paler, stretched, like it is worn out. But it is theirs all the same. Lauren wonders if she is dead.

'You're not dead.' Gary strokes her hair again. 'But you need to wake up. Just don't tip the bucket, OK?'

The sky above them swirls faster and Lauren pulls Gary against her. 'Just find me. Please. I'm fighting but I can't win. Find me.'

Gary smiles sadly. He would do exactly as she says but he can't. That tiny voice in the back of her mind almost admits he isn't really here. 'You can do this, L. Just don't tip the bucket.'

'Why do you keep saying that-?' The garden explodes in a wash of white light.

***

A cold slap hits Lauren in the face and she shoots up into a sitting position, gasping against the water in her nose. Her whole face, hair and front are soaking. She blows her nose into her hand and tries to clear her eyes, desperate to know what is happening. Her fingers run red as the dried blood from her fight with the Bull is rinsed from her hair. Grunts and movement echo around her. Finally she can see and Dhanni is as close to her as her chain will allow, her water jug empty in her hands.

'I'm sorry! Didn't know what else to do!' Her impossibly big eyes are apologetic but then she watches Angie, horrified.

Lauren licks her lips, desperate for hydration. The fact that the water could be drugged hits her a second later and she spits. On the other side of the room the Bull is taking Angie rougher than Lauren has ever seen. She is face down, arms awkward at her sides. Angie is powerless against the onslaught as the Bull all but throws her forwards with each thrust. Sharp claps cut the air as the Bull's hips slap against Angie's rear. Lauren would help, but can do nothing without being free of her chain. The movement shakes Angie's hair away from her face; tears stream into the padding. The poor woman can do nothing but hope the fiend finishes soon. Lauren pulls at her manacle but the chain is strong and she is weak. 'Angie!' Her wrist feels like it might snap but Lauren doesn't give up. She pulls and pulls, trying to get to her friend. 'Angie!'

Suddenly, the Bull arcs his back and his bark of pleasure is total within the basement. He holds Angie against him, as deep as he can possibly be and climaxes within her. He groans endless seconds before pulling out and leaving her where she slumps. Lauren and Dhanni stare in horror as the Bull stands, his wet and ready manhood threatening them with its menace, and stares at them both. He nudges a bowl of porridge toward Lauren. The message is clear. *Eat, and this won't happen again.*

Angie's wide eyes are still on Lauren as she takes up her bowl. And flings it at the Bull. He steps aside from her feeble throw and the bowl clatters from the wall sending porridge everywhere. Lauren's heart is pounding so hard in her chest, the blood so loud in her ears she could pass out again. The Bull steps forward and unleashes a roar that would belly the proudest lion. His arms and chest bunch, his veins fatten. At any moment he will discard whatever perverted rule he has and take Lauren in his hands, to hurt her, to kill her. Instead, he returns to Angie. He is erect faster than thought and inside Angie.

Dhanni collapses back, hands over her ears and eyes scrunched tight. She is saying something. Some prayer, some mantra, Lauren doesn't know. All Lauren can do is sit back, helpless. After a lifetime, an eternity, the Bull finishes inside Angie and stumbles away. Lauren barely notices. No sound, no feeling, no thought is part of her being, only the sight of Angie after her ordeal. Dhanni rocks back and forth, eyes and ears closed, blocking her senses from the world. Lauren distantly hears the squeal of the bolt as the Bull locks them away.

'I'm sorry, Angie…' Lauren mumbles but the words are dust on the wind, so small that they may as well have never existed for all the good they will do. Lauren watches Angie for hours. When Angie does stir it is her face that scrunches up first. 'Angie? Pins and needles?' Lauren offers, hoping beyond hope that somehow, she can make this alright. She scorns herself. *How can you make this alright?* 'Angie?' She wants to be here for her but there is no comfort that can equal what has been done. Lauren's rage at the unfairness is dowsed in ice-water. None of this is her fault, it is the Bull's! But she feels responsible. Angie could be pregnant now and what does that mean? Will Angie be taken away, disappear and be buried like the others?

When she is able, Angie gets to her hands and knees, joints shaking and breath ragged. She stretches but it is obvious she is hurt. She locks Lauren's eyes to her own and her breathing becomes calm. Her look is disgust. 'S-selfish.'

Lauren lurches to say something else, anything to try to comfort her but Angie turns away. She reaches for the wipes and gently wipes at her privates. She soon gives up, too tender to touch. She collapses onto her side facing the wall, exhausted and not wanting anything to do with her cell mates.

16. Inspector Roy Harvey

Joey's fingers are white on the dash as Roy speeds toward Jerry Akoum's residence. They took Roy's car as he knows his baby like no other, knows how fast she can go and how she handles. Some of the unmarked police interceptor vehicles could outstrip Roy's car on the flat but in his hands? Roy takes corners at 60mph and doesn't bat an eyelid. The cherry light on the roof whines and glares in all directions. Traffic has a split second to swerve out of his way, pulling over with only inches to spare.

'Just slow down a bit, eh, Roy?' Joey asks nervously as he struggles to stay upright in his seat as they skid through the next junction to get onto Radley St.

Roy ignores him, every fibre is focused on getting to Jerry Akoum's address as fast as possible before Nora becomes the next name on his list. 'Try her again.'

Joey hesitantly pries the fingers of one hand from the dash and pulls out his phone. He calls Nora. After a few seconds he shakes his head; no answer.

'Damn it!' Roy hits the steering wheel with his palm. The Akoum address is only a few minutes away. 'C'mon… c'mon…'

Joey's phone rings. 'Hello? Joey here… yeah, good. See you there.' He hangs up and drops his phone into his lap, gripping the dash again. 'Back up is on the way. Mathers has jumped in with them. They're five minutes behind us.'

'That might be too late. We're going straight in.' Roy switches the light and the siren off and makes a hard turn off Radley and onto Chambers St where Jerry Akoum is listed. Chambers is a long street, half a mile at least, and Roy opens his baby up like he has never done before. When Roy finally slams on the breaks it takes them a solid five seconds to screech to a halt in the middle of the road. Roy's door is open before the car has stopped. Joey is pale from the journey but only a second behind him.

In the boot is Roy's spare belt with stab vest, Taser, spray, cuffs and old night stick. He rips the Taser from the holster and leaves the rest for Joey. With redundant stealth, as half the street would have heard either the siren or Roy's screaming tyres, Roy flattens himself against the wall outside Jerry Akoum's terraced house. Joey throws his back against the wall beside him having strapped on the protective vest and belt.

From inside, Roy can hear a woman's raised voice; sharp and in pain. With a quick nod to Joey, Roy steps away from the wall and delivers a kick to the sweet spot of the door just underneath the lock. The door explodes inwards, the broken lock tooth bounces away as Roy and Joey rush in. 'Police!'

The door leads them directly into the front room but nobody is here. The female screams echo around them, upstairs, Roy guesses. Loud music booms from somewhere. Roy charges through each room trusting his senses to warn him of any danger and with Joey at his back. The kitchen diner is also empty but dirty plates and wine glasses litter the small counter-top. Stairs lead off in the corner and Roy takes them two at a time without a thought for anything apart from Nora. *Just be ok. Don't be you...* The music is bass heavy and thumps against the walls. The woman's screams become clearer and less like pain and somewhat joyful. Roy is moving as fast as he can as he throws his shoulder into the door at the top of the stairs and crashes through it to find Casey Williams' face turn to shock as he and Joey pile into the bedroom. She is naked, her curly red hair loose and wild as she half-climbs half-jumps from the man beneath her. She falls off the other side of the bed dragging a blanket with her. She lands awkwardly as a dark-skinned man with a bull head roars off the bed and confronts whoever has just invaded his house.

Roy pulls the trigger on his Taser and the pins explode from the box-loader to stab into the black man's thick chest. He tenses up as Roy gives him the full voltage. For a second he keeps his feet but then falls back, limbs stiff as if made of clay, and shakes as the Taser racks his body. Joey pulls his handcuffs and Roy lets go of the trigger, allowing him to cuff their suspect.

Miss Williams is upright again and screaming, hands clutching at the blanket to cover herself. 'Oh my God! What are you doing!' Miss Williams lets loose another scream and Roy holds up a hand for her to be quiet. He may as well blow into the wind for all the good it does as she wails again in shock.

'Miss Williams! Quiet! On your front, hands behind your back!' Roy orders.

She doesn't hear him over her wailing, eyes only for her partner so Roy ejects the wire box from his Taser and forces her down, pulling his own cuffs. In seconds, both are restrained and quiet. Joey checks out the other rooms as Roy throws a sheet over them to cover their nudity. Siren's grow louder and a moment later two cruisers pull up outside full of flatfoots, Mathers among them. Roy turns off the music from the computer in the corner.

'Clear!' Joey calls downstairs. 'Up here! Two perps, under control.'

Roy leans over the bed and pulls the full-head bull mask from the shoulders of their guy; Jerry Akoum. The head mask is heavy, as if real. The fur certainly feels real enough but there are pieces missing. There are no ears, the eyes are visibly sewn on instead of seamless like the fur and horns, like his mask is unfinished. Roy hefts the head onto a dresser at the side by the horns, the idea of making love in such a thing makes his lip curl. Roy has seen it's like before; from back at the Tanner place, in the garage. His torn coat is evidence of it. Roy logs the connection for later. 'Mr Akoum, you are under arrest for the kidnapping of Sam Somersby, Karly Schwarz-'

'Fuck you, I didn't do it!' Jerry Akoum's breathing is laboured, and he has spittle at the corners of his mouth, from the Taser, or his efforts with Miss Williams, Roy doesn't know or care.

'Joey, read him the rest.' Roy discards Jerry Akoum and directs the team of Officers as they spread through the house. 'Check every nook and cranny, every cupboard, the loft, basement, back garden, everything, right now!'

'Yessir.'

'Where's Inspector Murphy?' Roy turns back to Akoum. 'If you have hurt her then I'll personally make sure you never see the light of day again.'

Akoum tries to sit up but Joey holds him down with a shove. 'I ain't hurt nobody! I've done nothing, let me go!'

'Where's Nora?!' Roy screams down at him.

'I'm here.'

Roy spins around and standing in the bedroom doorway is Nora Murphy. Roy steps toward her but he catches himself before he embraces her. He is so relieved that for a moment he cannot speak. 'Where have you been? Why didn't you answer your phone?' He demands.

She looks like she might snuff him but she remains professional despite his tone. 'I was with a colleague of Karly Schwarz; she lives at the other end of the street. I checked my phone the second I got out and saw what was going on. Mathers messaged me.' She takes in the room. 'Can we get them some clothes?'

Roy chews his cheek, feeling foolish rushing across the city like he did. It would be appropriate to find the missing women but they didn't occur to him on his race over here; he just wanted Nora to be safe. 'Mmm. Get them up.'

Nora steps passed and pulls up a pair of skinny jeans obviously belonging to Miss Williams. 'Yours?' She asks. Casey Williams nods, tears streaked down her cheeks, blotchy and red. 'I'll hold them out, just step in, OK? Miss Williams let me be clear, if you try anything then this man will Taser you.' Nora explains calmly, motioning to an Officer to Roy's side. 'Do you understand?'

Miss Williams nods jerkily, wide eyed at the Officer with his hand on the Taser at his belt. Nora helps Casey up and lets her face the wall. She kneels and opens the trousers for her to step into. Roy and Joey look at each other just to look elsewhere. In seconds Nora has Miss Williams in her jeans and a sheet wrapped around her top half.

'And him?' Joey asks Roy, nodding at the prone Mr Akoum.

Roy winces and nods. 'Same deal Mr Akoum. Move nice and slow, behave or we will stun you again. Understand?'

Jerry Akoum's face is less than happy about any of this, but he nods. Joey pulls him up to his feet by the elbow. Nora blushes a little but turns away, her grip on Casey Williams' arm. As soon as Akoum is on his feet he charges forward and slams headfirst into Roy's stomach knocking the wind out of him. Several officers are on him in a flash but he is a big man and even with his hands restrained behind his back he shoulders them away. Joey is quick behind him and delivers a sharp strike with his baton to the back of the security guard's knees, dropping him. Three men jump in and hold him on his front. He is cursing and struggling to get free even as two officers put their whole weight on him to keep him down.

'I didn't do anything! Let me up!' He roars.

Roy coughs a breath out and a wheezing breath in as his insides try to recover from the blow. 'You… assault a Police Officer… when your innocent, do you?'

'Fuck you! I haven't got anything to do with those women!' He argues and struggles beneath the two hard-hats like a fish on the deck of a boat.

'Get some trousers on him and get him in the van.' Roy instructs.

'C'mon lad.' The Officer's haul up their captive and escort him downstairs, hands on his arms and shoulders to keep him in line the whole way.

'You alright?' Nora asks, still holding Miss Williams' arm.

'I'm fine.' Roy is just glad that Nora is safe. 'I thought that…' He looks hard into Nora's eyes hoping that she can finish the rest of his sentence without needing to hear it.

She smiles curtly and a little colour even comes to her cheeks. 'I know.' Their moment is soon over but it is enough. Nora escorts Miss Williams into one of the cars outside.

'Alright people, check this place over! Check everything twice, the loft, floorboards, under the bed, everything! There are twelve missing women. I want them found right now! Joey? Get Forensics down here.'

'Yes, boss.' Joey nods.

'Let's get these back. I want answers.' Roy says, daring the universe to scupper this new lead and follows Jerry Akoum downstairs.

***

'How long have you been seeing Jerry Akoum?' Roy asks with a tone that suggests no answer Casey Williams can give will be believed.

Nora had the presence of mind to grab her top and shoes from Akoum's bedroom floor and now she sits fully clothed in interrogation room 5. It is cold and dull with grey painted walls on all sides. Nora gifted Casey a too-large sweater from lost-and-found.

Rooms 3-6 don't have two-way glass but rooms 1-2 do. Jerry Akoum is a few doors down in 2 with Nora; Joey will be watching through the glass as Akoum rocks in his chair. Time is of the essence; every minute could be life and death for the missing women but if they go in too hard then Akoum will know how desperate they are and start playing games. They can't afford for that to happen. But they are *that* desperate; initial findings at the Akoum residence show nothing. No bodies, no sign of any wrongdoing other than having Casey in his bed whilst his Wife is away visiting her Sister in the South.

Casey Williams is blotchy and shaken from the whole thing and has stuck to her story each time; Nora and Joey have already spoken with her. 'I told the others all this already!'

'Miss Williams.' Roy prompts.

She sighs and slumps back in her chair. 'A few months.'

'Do you love him?'

'What?'

'Do you love him?' Roy likes to throw in a personal question to throw off the interviewee. It seems like it has nothing to do with what they are about here but of course it has everything to do with it; if she loves him then she may lie for him and if she lies then she risks getting caught up in something she may well have nothing to do with.

'…Well, no. It's just… you know, it's been fun.' Casey squirms in her seat but not because she's lying. Nobody likes having their affairs laid out so simply.

Roy is sure in her head Casey's meetings with Jerry have been exciting but admitting that their affair is nothing more than that must make her feel cheap. 'Has Jerry ever mentioned Angelina Smith?'

'I told Inspector Murphy before, no! He's never mentioned any of the girls that are missing, except Lauren.' She pulls her feet up on to the chair and hugs her knees. Nora took her cuffs off, confident that Miss Williams isn't about to launch an attack in the middle of the station.

'And what did he say?'

'We were talking a couple weeks ago. I said that I missed Lauren, and that I couldn't believe how long it has been since anyone has seen her.' She explains.

'And what did *he* say, Miss Williams?' Roy prompts again.

'The same! He said he hopes she's alright and that she turns up safe. He works with her too, you know! Alright?!' Casey sniffles, blows her nose on an already sodden bit of tissue. 'I've been struggling with this, OK? Lauren is my best friend, and I don't know what's happened to her. You should be out there trying to find her, not here with us! Jerry has been there for me these last few weeks.'

'I'm sure he has.' Roy pulls out some stills taken from the footage at Angelina Smith's wedding. 'This is Angelina Smith, she'd be thirty… six now, a former model and one of the missing women. You recognise him?' Roy points to Jerry Akoum standing off to the side. He doesn't wait for an answer; he pulls out another photo. This one from a singles bar on the East side of town, security footage that clearly shows Jerry talking to a young woman in a black dress; Theresa Reynoulds. This instance was found by the boys while Roy and Joey raced over to Akoum's house. 'This is Mrs Reynoulds, another one of the Twelve. We know Jerry knew Lauren through work, of course, so that ties him to 3 of the missing women. So far. He also had access to the security feeds at the Council where he used to work, he has the knowledge to avoid all the areas covered by the cameras, it just so happens that the women were kidnapped in those areas.' Roy lets the information sink in.

Casey looks over the stills, her mouth working into questions that her mind can't focus into words. 'He wouldn't… he can't have…'

Roy changes tack. 'Look, Casey, I don't think your apart of this. The people that do these things are expert liars, they spend every waking moment fooling the world, no one will blame you for not knowing. But Lauren and the others are still missing. Out there somewhere. If there is anything you know, a small detail, something he might have said, anything, I need to know.'

Casey's face is frozen in shock, stunned by the gravity of the situation as she realises it. A tear breaks and runs over her cheek. 'I can't think of anything.'

Roy believes her, genuinely thinks she has nothing to do with this but he has to be sure. 'Alright Miss Williams, I'll be back. Just hang tight.' Roy gathers up his documents but leaves the photo of Jerry Akoum in the bar and a home picture of Lauren Tanner.

'How long do I need to stay here?' Casey asks as Roy opens the door.

'As long as it takes.' And he leaves. 'Get her a drink would you?' He asks one of the flat-foots on watch by the door and heads down to interrogation room 2 to check on Akoum. Roy steps into the viewing room adjacent to watch the interview through the two-way glass. Mathers and Watkins make to stand when he enters but he waves them down. 'How's it going?'

Mathers blows a chest-full of air out, dropping his pen on the desk. 'He's denied everything. Over and over. Waiting for his lawyer.'

'He coming?' Roy asks, checking his watch.

'*She*, apparently. And yeah, on the way. We going to get shit-canned for questioning him without his lawyer?' Mathers asks.

'*I* might. But I don't care. We can't wait for his lawyer.' They should wait, the Viper will have his head but this case has gone on long enough.

Roy pings the intercom to let Nora and Joey know that they should come out. They gather up and leave, joining Roy in the observation room. 'Anything else from Casey Williams?' Nora asks.

Roy shakes his head. 'No, nothing. They were just seeing each other on the side, don't think she knows about anything else. I've left her in 5.'

'She doesn't strike me as the type. But who knows, right?' Nora asks, looking at Jerry Akoum. 'He's stuck to his guns so far. He's called his lawyer but he's answering our questions readily enough. Usually, they shut up quick on their lawyers say so but… apart from denying any involvement he is cooperating.'

'We can't wait anymore.' Roy takes off his jacket. 'I'm going in.'

'I'll support. Good cop, yeah?' Nora smirks, making a joke of the clichéd good-cop bad-cop routine.

'Fine.' Roy leads them out and through into room 2.

Jerry Akoum sits up straight in his chair as they enter; he is restrained to the lock-loop in the centre of the desk. Nora also arranged for a sweater to be given to Jerry but this one is snug on his big frame.

'Jerry! How are you doing?' Roy asks sarcastically.

'I'm good. How's your gut?' He barbs but he *tssks* straight away, not wanting to get into anything else.

'Oh, I'll live. Why did you assault me?' Roy and Nora sit down, Roy leans forward aggressively and Nora daintily at the side crossing one leg on the other.

'I want my lawyer.' Jerry says flatly.

Nora leans in too. 'I know this is frustrating Jerry. Roy, back off.' Roy makes a show of being chastised and sits back. Nora goes on. 'Inspector Harvey wants to check some details, if you recognise any of the missing women, OK?'

'I've already told you...'

'I know. I know, Jerry. Please.' Nora asks as nice as can be.

Roy doesn't wait for Akoum to say no, he pulls out various photos from his file and spreads them out across the table. He lists the names of the missing women, pointing to each one in turn. 'All we want to do is bring them home. That's it.'

'I don't know where they are.' Flat and way too quick.

Yeah you know where they are you sonovabitch. The extent of this case pulls at the inside of Roy's brain. It has cost him his marriage and his home, could cost him his job as well as his reputation. They have gone down every avenue to find these women and Jerry Akoum, who blatantly has connections with at least three of the victims, is sitting here like sooner or later everyone is going to realise that Roy has it wrong. 'What have you done with them, Akoum?' Roy asks as if he's tired of this game. It's not an act.

'Roy.' Nora warns.

'I don't know where they are.' Akoum says again flatly.

'Bullshit. Where are they? What have you done to them?' Roy raises his voice.

'Roy.' Nora scolds.

'I don't know where they are.' Akoum simmers.

'You been fucking them in that sick bull mask too?' Roy bates him. It works.

'I don't know where they are!' Akoum's eyes bulge.

'Miss Williams only fancy you from the neck down, is that it?' Roy spits.

'Shut your mouth!' Jerry pulls at his handcuffs chained to the loop on the desk. He doesn't lunge forward but tries to pull himself free in a rage.

Roy knows how much room he has if Akoum decides to lunge forward. He feels Nora's sense of anxiety beside him but this has already gone too far; Roy may as well see it through. 'You used the network of coverage from the Council, right? That's how you knew where to take them?'

'Shut up!' Akoum's hands turn purple as he pulls at his cuffs.

'How did you do it? Throw on that shitty mask and attack them, kill them?' Roy is all but shouting. He thinks of the similarity to the one he saw in Gary Tanner's garage and it strikes him as too much of a coincidence. It's obviously an exposed point for Jerry. 'Where are they, Jerry?'

'I don't know where they are!' Jerry pounds the table but it is bolted to the floor, it doesn't even jolt despite Akoum's strength.

'You should get your money back on that two-bit bull mask. Could probably get something better online. Cheap bids, am I right?' Roy prods.

'Shut up! You don't know about the Bull!' This time Jerry lunges forward.

Roy leans back despite himself. The big man's reach ends abruptly, cut off by his bonds to the table. Nora looks back at the glass, about to call an end to this but she doesn't. Roy smirks, hoping to really tip Akoum over the edge. 'Like a bit of roleplay, do we? Want to be a *breeding bull*?' Roy snorts a laugh as if the sheer idea is nonsense.

'Take these fucking cuffs off and I'll show you what I want!' Akoum rages.

'You threatening me, Akoum?' Roy sparks.

Jerry suddenly gives up on pulling at his cuffs and slumps down, but he laughs. 'The Bull isn't afraid. Threaten? He can do more than that you fucking pig. You have no idea what is about to happen.'

'Sure sounds like threats to me. But tell me, what is *the Bull* going to do, eh? Roy rolls his eyes, daring Akoum to tell him more.

'Just wait… he knows all about you, Harvey.' Akoum grins like a man with winning lottery numbers, sweat beads down his forehead from his efforts. He chuckles staring at Roy's left hand.

Nora leans in, like a Mother soothing her baby. 'Jerry, who is the Bull?'

Jerry's focus seems a little sluggish, it takes him a second to realise that Nora is even there. He looks her up and down as if admiring a piece of meat in a butcher's shop. 'He'd like you ya know.'

Nora isn't fazed. 'Who is the Bull, Jerry? Are you the Bull?'

That glassy look stays in Akoum's eye. 'No… not yet. One day.'

Nora and Roy share a brief look. Roy tries to reign this back in before it gets even weirder. 'How do you know Angelina Smith?' Roy shuffles through to the still from Angelina Smith's wedding. 'You work with Lauren Tanner. The club owner has corroborated that you go there to pick up women so that's what you were doing with Theresa Reynoulds. But you were at Mrs Smith's wedding, you *know* her. How? Do you know her Husband?'

Focus comes back to Jerry's eyes and he clams up again. 'I'm not saying anything until I speak to my lawyer.'

Nora presses on heedless. 'Are you the Bull when you wear the mask?'

'You wouldn't understand.' Akoum mutters.

'Help me to?' The way she asks she could be after the world and would get it.

Akoum argues within himself, licks his lip as he looks on Nora.

'Where did you get it?' Nora changes the subject to something easier for him to answer, pulling out a photo of his mask. A masterful switch, Roy is impressed.

'It's not finished… he finished the first one, but Tanner backed out-!' Akoum's eyes are alive with rage as soon as he mistakenly says the name.

'Tanner? Gary Tanner?' Roy bids. *I knew it!*

'Stupid. Stupid!' Jerry tugs at his cuffs again, shaking his head.

'Tanner made masks for you, there's more than one?' Roy pushes.

Akoum grits his teeth and clams up, staring at the ceiling like he's begging for forgiveness from some unknowable entity.

'You're the Bull when you wear the mask, aren't you Jerry?' Nora asks softly. Akoum starts to cry but he is grinning through the tears like only a desperate man can do. 'And there's more isn't there? How many masks did Tanner make, Jerry?' Nora's tone could massage blood out of a stone.

Jerry laughs, his teeth a brilliant white against his dark skin. 'He was supposed to do us one each... He did a mock-up... the one I have. But the first, the finished one, is beautiful...'

Roy thinks back to the Goat's head in Gary Tanner's office. It was unlike anything he had ever seen but beautiful is not how he would describe it. The bull head in Tanner's garage must be the other, unfinished, piece.

'Tanner wanted more money.' Akoum sniffs a wad of phlegm back up his nose, calmer now. 'He broke the deal. Wouldn't give us the other mask. My Brother took the first one-!' He realises he has let something slip again and drops his head onto his chest as sobs attack him, ashamed of himself.

Jerry Akoum obviously has some serious mental problems but it is disconcerting to see such a big man break down like this. But Roy has no time to worry about his psychological state, they are finally on the cusp of getting somewhere. 'Your Brother? He has a mask? Did you target Lauren Tanner because of her Husband?'

Jerry starts laughing again, tears streaming over his cheeks. Roy asks again but Jerry is beside himself. Nora leans in to try and get some sense from him but the intercom beeps and a moment later the door bursts open. Jerry Akoum's lawyer is here and the interview is over.

17. Lauren Tanner

There are few moments now where Lauren can think lucidly. More and more she jolts awake from seeing Gary in their morphing garden only to writhe and shake as her body drags her back into reality. It hurts to move, to talk, the waves of dry pain across her body last longer and longer. In another day or two Lauren fears she won't be able to move at all. She doesn't know how long it has been; she lost count of Angie's meals, was unconscious for some of them anyway.

Angie hasn't said another word. The Bull has been back for Angie each time, sometimes only hours apart. He takes her upstairs and doesn't even clean her up, he just uses her and brings her back, for his comfort, she guesses. Lauren wishes with all her heart there is something she can do to make all this better, to fix this, to save them but she just can't see a way out of here; not in these chains and not with that door locked.

Angie throws her plastic bowl away. She hasn't even finished the meal. She lets it spill onto the floor, completely uncaring that this place is becoming more and more disgusting by the day. Lauren's nose wrinkled at the waste bucket but now there is rotten food in the corner from where they have thrown their meals away. The Bull hasn't bothered to tidy up throughout their rebellion. Before, he showed some impatient attention to keeping this place at least liveable, having them wipe up any mess and changing their clothes but now it's like he has given up on them, only appearing to satisfy his needs. When he takes Angie away he doesn't always bolt the door until he brings her back. His structure has broken down and Lauren can still do nothing to take advantage of it. Angie has given up too; given up arguing or trying to get them to see sense, she eats a little but doesn't indulge every bite like before, as if she will cling to life but cannot live in ignorance anymore. Angie's façade, her show of strength, for it to be gone is a blow that Lauren didn't think this place could inflict.

Angie could be pregnant. The thought makes Lauren shudder and a yawning pain in her chest builds that has nothing to do with starvation. After all, the Bull doesn't use protection. He may well finish on their bellies and backs but that is far from a fool-proof plan to prevent conception. Lauren's hands shake as this place continues to heap one thing after another on top of her resolve, relentlessly trying to make her fold like too much weight on a rope bridge. Eventually, she will snap and nothing will be able to fix her.

'Ungg, I... I can't do this...' Dhanni whimpers. 'I-I'm not strong enough.'

'I know, Dhanni... Just hang on. You're... you're stronger than me, look how long you've been here and you're still fighting.' Lauren must bolster Dhanni's resolve. They will collapse without the other to hold them up.

Angie nudges one of the other bowls toward Dhanni with her foot. She doesn't say a word, doesn't even look up.

Dhanni looks at the bowl like it's the poison that it is, but Lauren knows what she is thinking. *'Just a bite.' 'Just a little bit, it can't be that bad.'* But Dhanni ate the smallest mouthfuls before and the Bull's drug still took control of her, as hard as it did Lauren. Dhanni's lips tremble as she wars with herself, but her resolve wins out, taking up the bowl and flinging it away. 'No!'

Angie tuts, angry.

'It's alright Dhanni. I know it hurts but we're getting out of here... we just need to think...' Lauren tries to sound reassuring, for conviction to coat her words but they are shaky. Lauren's vision blurs and she drops her head into her hands as headaches spike across the back of her skull. 'I promise, Dhanni... Dhanni?'

The Indian girl is silent, unmoving. Lauren looks up; Dhanni is on her side and for a moment Lauren's breath catches as it doesn't look like she is breathing. It takes every ounce of will Lauren has to roll onto her hands and knees, teeth gritted against the ache in her joints, her gums hurt, her eyelids feel like sandpaper. But then Dhanni's eyes flutter in her sleep and Lauren is overcome with relief. She just passed out, the effort of throwing the bowl even too much. Lauren doesn't want Dhanni to die, not any of them. She wants them all out of here. Angie shouldn't have to make peace with this place like she has, shouldn't have to be put through this trial. All of them should be safe at home with their Husbands, safe and warded against the terrors that this world can harbour. Angie mumbles and Lauren can only watch as she slumps, head down on her chest. Instinctively she looks at Angie's discarded bowl. *He'll be back soon.*

Lauren tears at herself inside her own head. *Just laying here and waiting to die isn't going to fix anything is it? Get up!* Every hour that goes by, every minute makes her weaker. There must be a way! The spec of sunlight reinvigorates her. Such a small thing but she is drawn to it like a Sunflower. She frames the gouge in the padding with her hands as if it is a flame that needs protecting from the wind. Lauren digs her fingernails into the padding, tearing, pulling at the fabric and the foam underneath. Her knuckles feel bruised, every grip and pull makes her wince but her blood is on fire. She will do everything she can before she passes out again. Her fingers are swollen, her toes are numb like she never had feeling in them to begin with. Her skin burns. Soon, the gouge from the Bull's horn or her shiv, whatever caused it, is nearly a foot wide. Scraps of soundproofing foam and tacky fabric litter the floor at her feet.

Angie mumble's something behind her but without her muscles and lips to force the words it is just a low note from her throat. Lauren uses it as fuel to force her body on. The spot of sunlight peeks through between the seams of two wooden back boards. Lauren tries to get some leverage, digs her fingernails into it but the boards are tight. She throws her shoulder into it but her strength is pitiful. For all she knows the boards are bracketed directly against the wall, if so she doesn't stand a chance, even if she had tools. The chain is so heavy on her wrist she drops back down, more tired than ever. Frustrated, she pulls at her manacle. She pulls until it bites into her skin, would pull more but she is hit with wave of dizziness that makes her keel over. For a second she is back in her garden, her beautiful, impossible garden with Gary, flowers at her feet. Gary's touch is so comforting she wishes she could stay forever but she knows she can't. Is she losing her mind, or if this is a vision of the afterlife? Gary is speaking but Lauren can't hear him. Then she is back in the basement, she jolts, catching herself before she falls. Lauren takes a deep breath, to calm herself and stay awake. A part of her wants to just give up and live in her garden with non-Gary forever but that would mean letting the Bull win, would mean dying and never seeing the real Gary again. *He would forgive me, wouldn't he? If I just lay down and never got back up? After everything I've been through, surely I can be selfish and let the Gary in my garden look after me?* But then the real Gary would be alone, maybe never knowing what happened to her. She makes up her mind. Gary is more important. He won't be able to complete his work without her. And Lauren is an integral part, working with the others in their own secret basement. Nobody understands, everybody would judge but Lauren understands his work and she must help him to finish it.

In her mind's eye, Gary holds her up. Her headache builds in pressure until she is sure her head is going to burst but the image of Gary is clear. He's speaking but she can't hear him, she knows what he is saying though, the same words he has been telling her since she first retreated to their garden. *'Don't tip the bucket...'* An idea strikes Lauren like a physical slap to the face. *The bucket...* Lauren had always taken Gary's words as the phrase, to make sure she didn't die, but maybe she should have taken it literally. Lauren crawls over as far as her chain will allow and reaches for the slop bucket. It is closer to Angie on her side of the dark basement. She must pull and stretch to get her feet around the metal bucket. Her wrist is in agony, close to dislocating when she finally gets enough of a grip to tug it toward her. Desperate not to let it spill everywhere she carefully drags it toward her until she can hold it without fear. It reeks. The Bull hasn't cleaned it out in days. Angie's waste fills the bucket. It makes her wretch. Acid-hot bile rises in her throat and she winces as she forces it down, the act of swallowing making the muscles in her throat hurt. *Oh God, I hope this works...* Lauren plunges her hand into the bucket so that the contents soak her arm halfway up to the elbow. She gags and tries not to think about how her skin is raw around the manacle. Infection is something she can worry about later. She rips her hand out letting the excess drip back into the bucket in thick globules. The smell doubles in potency as if the bucket is angered at being disturbed. Bile rises again. Swallowing the acid and her revulsion Lauren tries to slip the lubricated manacle. It is as tight as before and her arms scream at the punishment of being pulled so much. Lauren's thumb is so far against her palm as she forces her hand she fears breaking something. With an almighty scream, like some animal has taken hold of her for one moment of aid, the manacle comes away. Her wrist is bloody and her hand swollen and throbbing, but it is free of the chain. She laughs erratically as if this can't be. She flexes her fingers and waves her arm about as if it is new. Her other arm is still bound but without the weight of the chain her free arm is lighter than air. With new energy, Lauren attacks the wall, tearing and pulling at the padding, making her way further up. She follows the seam, minute after minute, knowing that the Bull could be here any minute for Angie. She claws at the foam and like a woman gone mad, like a wild cat, scratches fistfuls away with each swipe until suddenly a full spot of sunlight hits her in the face.

At the seam, inches above her head, is a semicircle missing in the wood where a knot once was. When the boarding was cut it must have come away. It is only a couple of inches wide but she can fit her index and middle fingers through, soaked in brown as they are. The light warms her skin and she giggles like a child shown a magic trick. She hooks her fingers in the gap and gives it a pull. It shifts, barely, and bounces itself back into place. The wood is pliable. It isn't bolted. *This could be it!*

'Dhanni! This is it! We're getting out of here! Just hold on!' Lauren tries to get through to Dhanni as she gives the board another pull but then the bolt shrieks open and the Bull enters. 'No!'

The Bull strides in looking like a monster from hell. Another woman is in his arms. He freezes at the top of the stairs, seeing how close Lauren could be to being free from the cage he built for them. He drops the poor woman like a rucksack and then he is moving.

'No!' Lauren screams and flings herself at him.

She is weak and he bats her aside easily. He spins her around and heaves her off the ground, arms around her. She kicks and fights but she may as well press against the earth to make it move. He manhandles her against the wall and cuffs her in the head. The blow would have stunned her but her forehead bounces off the exposed boarding and she slumps down, head spinning. Everything is muffled for a moment, like there is a pillow over her ears.

'…Lauren? What's… happening?' Dhanni asks from somewhere. Lauren opens her mouth to talk but all that comes out is the bile that threatened earlier, warming her lap. 'Lauren?' Dhanni asks, panic in her voice.

The Bull thumps back beside Lauren and then a deafening mechanical thunk makes her jolt. Beside her, the Bull holds a new board in place with one hand while he shoots nails into the corners with a nail gun in the other. Over and over he pulls the trigger and with each nail sentences her escape attempts to death.

'No…' Lauren murmurs, her legs jelly.

In seconds the Bull has completely covered the exposed area, banishing the sunlight and any hope Lauren had of getting through the grate or whatever is on the other side of this wall. The Bull is heaving, surely not from effort although the nail gun must be heavy; no, he is scared at what almost happened, at what Lauren almost managed to do.

He brings the new woman down and places her next to Angie, hastily locking a new chain about her wrists. The woman has dark hair but Lauren's vision spins. It occurs to her that it has only been a few days since New Girl was here, it can't have been another month yet, can it? Maybe the animal is tired of his game and is now taking whoever and whenever he wants.

With the new woman safely locked up the Bull takes up the other end of Lauren's chain, adding up what she did. The Bull stares at her for a second and then snaps, tossing the manacle aside. He takes Lauren's free arm at the wrist and slams it against the exposed board, his ragged breath audible through the bull head. The nose of the Bull is an inch away from Lauren's and she stares back, donning her evil smile despite the pain in her arm. He takes the nail gun and presses it against her palm.

'No!' Dhanni screams.

The Bull pulls the trigger.

18. Inspector Roy Harvey

Another woman is missing. Jody Maru, black, twenty-five, Berry local, recently married. It was three days before she was reported missing but they added her name to the list this morning. She was supposed to attend a course, staying overnight, and 'she' had text her Husband in reply. Her Husband didn't think anything to it until she dodged his calls the next day. They followed her route and sure enough found her engagement ring. Roy thinks the Prince texted in her place to waste precious time and give him an unnecessary head start. Jody Maru's number has since gone dead. They were desperate before Jerry Akoum, without him Roy might be beating people in the street for leads.

'Thank you for coming down, Mr Tanner.' Roy leads Gary Tanner through the station toward the holding rooms. 'I need you to confirm a few things for me. And that in turn may mean I have some questions.'

'It's fine. Anything I can do to help find Lauren. After all, you've been in my house, least I can do is come into yours.' Tanner says in a low tone.

Roy's heart stops dead. *What? Was I seen?* 'Excuse me?'

Tanner motions around him as if all this is a novelty, but his lip curls as if there is a bad smell. 'I've never been in a police station. You've come to my house before, now I can see yours.'

'Right...' Roy leads off, unsure if Tanner means anything by that. Does he mean he knows Roy infiltrated his residence that night, or just when he has visited? Roy shakes the worry away; it is done now, Tanner either knows or he doesn't, until Tanner outright confirms it there is no way Roy is going to play into it. 'We've detained two people. A Casey Williams and Jerry Akoum-'

'Akoum?' Tanner asks immediately.

'Yes, you know him?' Roy asks but he knows he does.

'Barely. We met twice. He wanted me to do some work, a series of masks but he couldn't pay. What has he got to do with Lauren? Wait, did you say Casey?' Tanner asks, more concerned now he knows Jerry Akoum is involved.

Roy doesn't answer until he stops at a door in the next corridor. 'I need you to take a look and confirm you definitely know our suspect.'

'Suspect? Akoum has something to do with my Lauren?' Tanner's fists bunch together but he masters himself quickly, loosening up.

Roy watches him for a second before swiping the pass at his belt to get into observation room no.2. They both enter and join Joey who quickly pulls his feet from on top of the desk. 'Boss?' Joey nods sheepishly.

'You remember Gary Tanner? I've asked him in to tell us what he knows about Jerry Akoum and Casey Williams.' Roy sits beside Joey, scraping the only remaining chair out from under the desk, leaving Tanner to stand.

Gary Tanner is silent, looking through the two-way glass at Jerry Akoum. 'What makes you think he has anything to do with Lauren?' He asks, not taking his eyes off Akoum.

'He has affiliations with three of our missing women-'

'Five.' Joey hands over new sheets. 'Software came up with Edyta Durak and Joanne Hannah too.' The printout shows Jerry Akoum conversing with Mrs Durak in a night club and Mrs Hannah on the street.

'Five, so far. From various footage we know he also knows Angelina Smith, Theresa Reynoulds and your Wife-' Roy explains.

'How does he know her?' Tanner's voice is calm but his hands are fists again.

'You don't know?' Roy jabs. 'He works at Cavendish with Lauren. Security guard on the front desk.'

'I didn't know.' Tanner says quietly.

'What about Miss Williams?' Roy prompts.

Tanner shrugs. 'Lauren and Casey were friends in school. What has she got to do with him?' His eyes haven't left Akoum.

'They have been seeing each other… privately.' Joey says tactfully.

'How did you meet? You and Akoum, I mean.' Roy asks.

Tanner finally breaks his lock on Akoum and leans against the wall beside the glass as if not wanting to be seen in return. 'He contacted me through my website. Wanted to commission a series of masks. Bull masks, specifically. He's local. Shipping can be a hassle, so I took on the job. I made a test piece, to make sure I had the size right…-'

'This?' Roy pulls out a photo of the mask that Jerry Akoum was wearing when he and Joey burst in on him and Miss Williams.

Tanner spares it a glance and nods. 'I completed the first mask after this initial piece, he wanted it ASAP so collected straight away. Almost finished the second one but we had a dispute over the price. The other one is still in my workshop.' Tanner looks Roy dead in the eyes as he says it. *He does know.*

'What was the dispute?' Joey asks.

'I quoted per mask. He thought it was for the lot.' Tanner snorts.

'How much?' Roy and Joey ask together.

'Fifteen thousand. Each.' Tanner shrugs as if it is what he makes on a weekend. Joey whistles at the amount. 'He paid me 15k in cash when he collected the first completed piece. Wanted me to let him know when the last one was ready. I said about a week,' Tanner shrugs. 'And that cash again would be fine.'

'And that's when you had a dispute?' Roy guesses.

Tanner nods. 'He refused to pay more and I don't work for free. He stormed off with the mask he paid for, angry and threatening me. I let the test piece go,' He glances at the photo of Jerry Akoum's mask. 'It is rough work and not worth fighting for. Anyway, he said I'd be sorry. I'm pretty sure he broke into my house last week. I have no evidence but there was somebody in my house and in my workshop. I think he came back to steal the other mask.'

Roy's heart lurches in his chest but he affects the best poker face he can. 'It's possible. We will look into it.'

Tanner looks like he knows every word out of Roy's mouth is bullshit but Joey is oblivious. 'Mr Tanner, do you know who the other mask was for? Or were they both for Mr Akoum?'

'I have no idea. I asked him myself because the masks were to be made to fit. He mentioned a Brother but no names. Just gave me a list of measurements to work to.' Tanner recalls. Roy and Joey share a look. 'Why?' Tanner asks.

Roy takes a breath. 'We have reason to believe that they are responsible for the disappearance of some, if not all the missing women on our list, including your Wife. It's likely she was targeted to get back at you over the commission. We're trying to find his Brother now.' Roy explains.

'Let me in there.' Tanner says calmly but his threat is unmistakeable.

The sight of him with hammer in hand as he searched for Roy flashes through his mind. 'I can't do that Mr Tanner. You have been an enormous help, if you wouldn't mind following Joey down the hall you can get a cup of coffee while we sort out a few more-'

'I'm not going anywhere. If he knows then I'm going to find out what's happened to Lauren.' Tanner stands straight, the authority in his voice is total.

'Mr Tanner...' Roy stands to his full height ready to jump into action if need be but leaves his palms showing, applying for peace. The observation room door opens at that moment and Nora appears. Her appearance cuts the atmosphere in half. 'Inspector Murphy?' Roy jumps on the opportunity to swerve the situation.

'I've just sent Miss Williams home.' She stops in the doorway, acknowledging Gary Tanner. 'Told her to stay home next to her phone in case we need her. Mathers is showing her out now-'

Hurried footsteps echo from outside the door and then Casey Williams bursts into the room almost knocking Nora aside. 'You can't keep him here! He's not done anything!'

Mathers appears at the doorway a second later, out of breath. 'Sorry... she pulled back... as the door closed on me.'

'It's alright, Mathers. Miss Williams? You can't be in here.' Nora takes Casey's elbow to direct her out, but she flings her arm away.

'No! He hasn't done anything. Just let him go... Gary?' She sees Tanner for the first time, stood beside the viewing window.

'Casey. They think he has Lauren. What do you know about this?' Tanner asks.

'This isn't the time or place-' Roy begins.

'Gary, he wouldn't! He has nothing to do with this! I'd bet my-' Casey is shouting but Tanner cuts her off with a look.

'Casey, where did you get those earrings?' Tanner asks seriously.

Every eye in the room looks to Miss Williams' ears and the white gold earrings with small blue stones in the centre. She consciously shrinks, now the centre of everyone's attention. 'It-it was a gift. From Jerry.' She says nervously.

'They're Lauren's.' Tanner explodes passed Casey, snagging Nora's lanyard from around her neck, slamming the door behind him.

'Stop him!' Roy shouts as he tries to get by Casey as she wails in shock.

Tanner uses Nora's cardkey to get into the interrogation room and is on Jerry Akoum before Roy gets out of the door. It takes Roy a second to fumble his own cardkey from his belt and open the door.

Gary Tanner is beating the hell out of Jerry, fists rising and falling with Akoum's own hands still restrained to the table. 'Where is she?! Where is she?!'

Akoum's lawyer flattens herself against the wall, wide-eyed shock plastered across her face. Roy hugs Tanner, holding his arms down but the man's strength is surprising. He shoves Roy away and hits Akoum another two times before Roy, Mathers, and Joey pile on top to drag him away, feet still planted. Akoum is bloody and all but senseless, limp in his chair, defenceless against the barrage of blows that Tanner dealt him. Tanner surges but is off balance, falling forwards on top of Akoum. The five of them topple over tearing a link in Akoum's cuffs so they all go down. In a flurry of limbs they manage to restrain Tanner, facedown with all their weight on his back. The strength goes out of him and he lies still now he has been stopped. Joey gets handcuffs on him.

'Nora! Kit!' Roy shouts at the viewing glass.

Nora appears with a first aid kit, calling down the hall for help. She kneels beside Akoum and takes some gauze from the box to clean up their suspects face. Faster than Nora can protect herself Akoum is on his feet and has his arm tight around her throat. He pulls her back and around the table as he edges back toward the door. Blood and sweat run freely down his face. Wide-eyed, the whites are a stark contrast against his skin and blood, he looks crazed.

'Akoum. Let her go.' Roy warns. He shifts his weight and Joey grunts letting him know they have Tanner under control so he can stand. 'This can only go sideways from here.'

Nora digs her fingers into Akoum's forearm but there is no give. Her face gathers colour as she struggles for breath.

'I'm getting out of here, *Roy*! I'm leaving and she's coming with me.' Akoum's face begins to swell but his eyes are bright. He spits blood as he speaks.

'You're in the middle of a police station! You're not going anywhere. How do you think this is going to go?' Roy matches Akoum's pace, keeping equal distance between them as he retreats.

'With this little thing in my hands?' He shakes Nora by the grip he has on her. Her eyes are watering as she chokes. 'Yeah, you'll let me out or this one will hurt. Or maybe I'll give her to the Bull…' Akoum threatens wistfully. He smells Nora's hair but doesn't break eye contact with Roy as if he knows she is his. 'Just like your other bitch.'

'What do you mean?' Roy's hand glides to the pocket with his spray in.

'I told you. The Bull knows all about you, Harvey.' Akoum shakes Nora in his grip again, like a child playing with his favourite teddy bear. It won't be long before she passes out. 'You'll like the Bull, I know he'll like you-'

crack

Akoum drops along with shattered pieces of plastic as Casey Williams grips the other half of the laptop she hit him with. Nora drops onto her knees, coughing and holding her throat.

Roy gathers her up to look at the damage. 'Are you alright?'

'I'm fine.' She rasps. 'See to them.'

Roy smiles because even in this moment she is professional to a fault. 'Get him in cuffs. And let *him* up.' Roy waves at Tanner. Mathers puts another set of cuffs on the unconscious Akoum and Joey stands Tanner up. Roy takes the key from Joey and sets Tanners hands free. His look asks why, sceptical after what he did. Roy tosses Joey his cuffs and key back. 'He's not going anywhere and we're finding his Brother, whatever his name is. Lauren is going to need you when we find her.' Roy doesn't like the man, something about him, ever since their first meeting, has been off. But he isn't apparently behind their missing women so he lets the unsaid words shine through; *don't make me lock you up.*

Casey Williams is crying silently as she pulls Lauren's earrings from her ears and hands them to Tanner. 'I didn't know, Gary. I swear. Piece of shit!' She kicks Akoum but she may as well kick a mountain for all he moves. She takes Roy's hand gently. 'Find her.'

Roy tactfully takes his hand back and leads her out into the hall. 'We will. We're going to find them all. As soon as we have his Brother.'

Davies appears at the door, taking in the full interrogation room, unconscious suspect and broken laptop. 'Roy?'

'What is it Davies?' Something in his tone turns Roy's stomach. Another name can't be added to the list, it has only been days since the last.

'There's a John Dockhorn here to see you. I would have taken a message but he says it's about your Wife. She's missing.' Davies explains.

Roy is speechless, locking onto Nora like she can click her fingers and call off this prank. But every set of eyes is on Roy. Jerry Akoum is awake and chuckles as his blood tip-taps onto the floor where Casey hit him. Roy grips the front of his jumper, desperate for answers. 'Where is she?'

Akoum spits blood. 'The Bull has her now.' And he starts chuckling again, winking at his lawyer making her cringe.

***

Their resident first-aider patched up Akoum and they got him back in a chair, swollen, cheek split and a lump on his head but talking. His lawyer advised him to talk as, after assaulting one policeman and taking another hostage along with the undeniable possibility of him being involved in the kidnappings, and God knows what else, of now fourteen women, there is little she can do for him as it is. After explaining the likelihood of expected prison time to be served against what to expect if he cooperates, he is more accommodating. Roy leaves the others to it and follows Davies to a waiting room on the other side of the station.

Dockhorn all but leaps out of his chair as Roy storms in. He opens his mouth but Roy shuts him up, pushing him back into the chair. 'Tell me everything.'

He looks to get up again but thinks better of it. 'We were supposed to meet for dinner last night but she didn't show. And her phone has gone through to voicemail since. It isn't like her.'

Roy would punch his nose in but controls himself with Davies present. He pulls a pen from his pocket. 'Times. Last known location. Where, when, who with, everything. Everything you know. I find you have left anything out I will have you cuffed and thrown in the river.'

Dockhorn turns pale but takes the pen. Roy eyeballs him for a second and then leaves telling Davies not to let him out of his sight. His mind swirls as he marches through the station. *Emma is missing?* But he forces his mind to focus. Just because she stood 'John' up doesn't mean Akoum's claims are true. He tries Emma's mobile but it doesn't connect. 'Fuck.' He joins the others in the observation room feeling disconnected from it all. They are so close but the stakes have been raised. *I should have been there for her. To protect her.*

Nora comes to him immediately. 'What do we know?' She rasps, from Akoum's hold. She takes his hand but Roy can't take joy in it.

'Dockhorn is making a statement now. Her phone is dead.' He explains with as much enthusiasm as if reading from a phone book.

Nora turns his face to look down into hers. 'If he has her, we'll find her. We are so close, Roy. Don't buckle on me now.' She pleads. It is all Roy can do to nod.

'I know areas around the city that aren't covered by security feeds, from my time at the Council. We were able to plan where to grab the girls.' Akoum explains in monotone to Joey and Mathers. He cried again, like a child caught stealing from the biscuit tin but as soon as he started talking his emotions flat-lined, like nothing matters anymore.

'I knew it.' Roy mutters, watching through the glass. He would normally conduct this interview himself but time is of the essence and he had to see Dockhorn, to see the guilt in his face from losing his Wife. But the guilt is Roy's. *If I hadn't slept with Nora then Emma would never have been in danger.*

Nora clears her sore throat. 'You were right. But we can sort all this later, we need to know *where* he has them.'

'We pick the women because they deserve it. Living the lives they do, bedding the men they do, they deserve better.' Akoum drones but he perks up as he explains. 'That's what the Bull gives them. They keep liars and crooks in their lives, like Gary Tanner-' Akoum spits the name as if backing out of their deal for the masks is the most heinous thing he has ever known. '-how can they be fulfilled? So, we give them to the Bull. To show them what they could have.'

'You choose married women because you think their Husbands aren't worthy of them? And when you wear the mask, you become the Bull?' Joey asks. Mathers looks pale as he takes notes. 'You abduct and rape them, for their benefit?'

Akoum's lawyer looks like she would rather be sat in a frying pan than next to her client but she keeps a straight face. Akoum looks up at Joey. 'Rape? You don't ask a dog for permission before you give it a shot. You do it because it is best for the dog.'

Joey presses. 'Jesus. And what about your Wife? Is she really out of town or do you have her locked up somewhere? Where are they, where is your Brother?'

Akoum affects not to hear. 'I thought Casey might recognise Lauren's earrings, but she didn't.' Akoum laughs to himself. 'Wanted to give her to the Bull too, but he said she didn't deserve him. But she's a sweet girl, I couldn't resist. He always was stronger than me. It's good that he has the first totem.'

'Totem? The first mask?' Joey asks but looks at the viewing window, at Roy and Nora though he can only see the reflection of the room. He knows they need to find Akoum's brother and where they are keeping the women, and fast. 'Where are they, Akoum? Are they alive?'

Akoum's head seems to sway as if there is a song in his head. 'Some of them couldn't handle what the Bull gave them. But some are stronger. Like Lauren Tanner. I had a go on her myself, and the others when he let me.'

'Christ.' Roy curses.

'Do we tell Gary Tanner?' Nora asks quietly beside him.

Roy has Gary Tanner waiting in an interrogation room down the hall under guard. He hasn't been arrested but Roy has made it clear he is to stay put; he might be able to help yet. Despite having the whole team searching for Jerry's Brother they have been able to turn up very little. 'Not until we find her.'

'Help us out here, Akoum. We need to know where you have them?' Joey is more assertive.

Akoum's lawyer leans in to offer council in his ear but it is clear she doesn't want to be in the same room as him let alone close enough to whisper. He listens for a moment but recoils. 'How can I tell them?!' He shouts, making his lawyer jump but then he is laughing. 'Josef made me promise not to tell. Told me I was almost ready to join him. To become the Bull alongside him…'

'Josef? Josef Akoum?' Joey asks and looks at the window again.

'Call Watkins, tell him.' Roy orders urgently.

Nora already has her phone and is confirming the name to narrow down the search. Even with the surname, finding anything on the Akoum's has been hard work, like everything is under a different name.

'He even let me on Angie a few times. He's a good Brother to me, he is.' Akoum says reverently.

'Angie? Angelina Smith?' Joey asks, checking the list of missing women.

'Yeah... She's a good one, she is.' Akoum speaks as if he is scoring a prize pig. Then he chuckles through tears as if it is the funniest thing he has ever said. His lawyer shudders so slightly you could blink and miss it. Roy wonders how much longer she will last before she calls in a colleague to take over.

Watkins and Wyatt burst into the observation room making both Roy and Nora jump. Both are out of breath having obviously run from their office all the way down here. Watkins gets his breath back first. 'We... know what... Akoum... was doing... at Angelina Smith's wedding!'

'Well, how does Jerry Akoum know her?' Roy asks, impatient.

'He's her Bother-in-law.'

'What?' Nora and Roy ask together.

'We contacted all the relatives and friends we could find numbers for. Anyone who knows Angelina Smith. After the wedding she just kind of fell off the radar, nobody knew where she went until her Mother reported her missing, right? Her wedding ring was found outside her house? So, she was added to the list. But Smith is her maiden name; she kept it after she married Josef Akoum. She's married to his Brother.' Watkin's nods at Akoum.

'The wedding... the video. Jerry was at Angelina Smith's wedding but she kept her name, how did we miss that?' Roy asks incredulously. 'Wait, Angelina Smith has been kidnapped by her own Husband?!'

Nora comes to her senses and puts the phone down with Watkins stood right here and quite obviously not on the other end anymore. 'But why? This is crazy.' She shakes her head, unable to conceive the motivation.

It is crazy. A pair of Brothers take women against their will and rape them in an animal mask because they think it is best for them. Roy keeps his focus. 'The *what's* and *why's* can come later, we need *where*. Do we have an address?'

Watkins shakes his head. 'Not yet. We can't find anything on them. They could have a place under a different name, or squatting? There's a lot of ways to make sure there's no paper trail.'

'Damn it. We need to find out where they are!' Roy rages. Jerry Akoum is still laughing through his swollen lip as if he has heard everything they just said.

'On it.' Both Watkins and Wyatt rush off.

Joey raises his voice to get through to Akoum as he chuckles away. 'Was Angelina Smith still alive when you last saw her, when was this?'

'She's a good one, Angie is. A good woman for a good man. What Brother do you have that would let you on his Wife, eh? He's a good Brother, he is. And she loves the Bull and what he can do. It was her idea to start keeping them.' Akoum leans back, eyes distant, as if remembering a good day.

A chill goes through Roy. 'Her idea...?' He looks at Nora incredulously. 'Get Watkins back on the phone. Check for Smith. Link any addresses, online shopping, bills, anything that gives us an address in the city. We'll check 'em all if we have to.' Nora relays his instruction as he pulls out his own phone, trying Emma again. 'C'mon...' But the line is dead.

19. Lauren Tanner

Lauren can't move her hand. The nail went through her palm, the padding, and into the backboard. The head of the nail is tight against her ravaged hand, pinning it above her head. Blood runs in a thick rope down her arm and soaks into her already stained shirt. It stings but doesn't hurt as much as she thinks it should. Dehydration and blood loss have thankfully robbed her of sensation.

'Lauren...?' Dhanni asks, not for the first time and so far has nothing to follow.

Lauren doesn't know how long it has been since the Bull stuck her to the wall and took Angie away. Time seems to have slowed down for Lauren; it could be minutes or hours since that animal left with her. She fears for her friend, with each visit the Bull has been rougher and more frustrated that Lauren and Dhanni have set their course away from him. Who knows what that monster is doing to Angie now? 'Dhanni?' Lauren's voice is a whisper.

'Y-Yes Lauren, I'm here.' Dhanni says positively through cracked lips, trying to be as supportive as she can but her own voice is dry, unrecognisable. She lays on her back as still as can be, too weak to sit up anymore.

Lauren struggles to raise her head, it weighs twice as much as it used to. 'I've changed my mind. I don't like this plan.' Despite the weariness and weakness in both women they wheeze a laugh. Dhanni is wracked by a violent fit of coughs, too weak even to roll onto her side.

'Urngh.' The woman on the other side of the room, next to Angie's spot, begins to stir. She is in the same state as any that are brought here; hair ruffled from clips taken away, shoes and jewellery taken, left only in a loose dress. Her chain clinks as she reaches to her head, eyes growing wide as she takes in this hellhole and Lauren nailed to the wall. 'My God.'

Lauren would wave but the effort is too much. 'Please don't scream. I have a headache.'

The woman's breath is erratic as a thousand questions and fears fight to the surface, but she calms herself, squinting at Lauren. 'You're Lauren Tanner.'

Lauren snorts a laugh but it makes her cough. 'I'm famous?'

'I saw your picture on the news. And Dhanni Sandhu? So, the Prince is real.' The woman sinks within herself for a second, accepting the gravity of her situation but then is up examining her lock-loop and chain. She has more presence of mind then when Lauren woke here. 'What happens here? What did the Prince do to you?'

'He's no Prince…' Lauren mutters. 'He's called the Bull…' Lauren's thoughts are foggy but wonders how much she should tell their new addition. Being honest will scare her, perhaps saying nothing is a mercy. 'What's your name?'

The woman leans against her wall, testing her manacles with a probing finger. 'Emma Harvey. My Husband is the leading Inspector for the Prince case. He's been trying to find you, Lauren.' She tries not to look but her gaze darts up to Lauren's hand every few seconds.

Blood tip-taps from her elbow onto the floor. 'Tell him to pull his finger out.' Lauren snorts again but it dies in her throat. 'We could use a little help here.'

'What is this place? Where are we?' Emma asks lightly but desperation is laced in every word. She does a great job of covering it but her mind is racing.

'It's exactly what you think. He rapes us.' Lauren would like to spare her but there is no hiding from it down here. Emma closes her eyes fortifying herself against this new reality. 'He has Angie upstairs now…' Lauren scrunches her eyes shut, her head throbbing, and picks at gunk in the corners of her eyes.

'Angie? Smith?' She gulps, making Lauren look up again. She drinks from the water jug. 'There is only three of you. What about the other missing women, the paper said there was another only a few days ago, Jody Maru?'

'No…' Lauren warns Emma but it is too late now. The Bull has either drugged their water or he hasn't.

'What?' Emma puts the jug down, oblivious. 'Jody Maru isn't here?'

'Jody? She died, I think.' Lauren thinks of New Girl, never knowing her name, and hates this place more that a woman can die down here and nobody even know about it. She vows to bring every brick and board of it down. She snorts again at the idea she can do anything but add to the pool of red collecting under her bum. She must look insane in her state and laughing to herself.

Emma flexes her fingers but ignores the strange sensation. 'Lauren? I need you to tell me everything you can, OK? You're hurt but we can figure this out… We need… w-what's happening?' Emma looks at her hands, analysing within herself and what her body is doing without her consent. She tries to grip the wall and stay upright but it is not up to her anymore.

Exhaustion hits Lauren in a wave and she finds she cannot even explain to Emma what is happening, what the Bull will do to her. She has failed. For the first time Lauren knows she is going to die down here. But it is not fear that strangles her, but regret that she hasn't been able to help her friends like she promised. Finally she has made some real friends and she cannot save them. 'Dhanni? I want to say… Thank you. I hope you're right about being reborn.

Maybe we'll meet again next time too.' Lauren looks over, every joint feels like she is swimming through thorns. 'Dhanni?' The Indian girl is still and silent. 'Dhanni!' Lauren's voice is a croak. She leans to try and see her friend better, to see if she is breathing but the shift in her posture awakens her arm. Her shoulder screams and the hole in her hand burns as if the nail is white hot. She screams but all that comes out is a whimper; it is all her weakened body can spare. *Dhanni?* Lauren can't reach her, can't help her, or Angie or stop the Bull or any of it! 'Dhanni?' She rasps, barely a voice at all, more like claws scratching on wood than a human noise. 'Please… please don't die…'

'What are you doing, L?' Gary asks, kneeling beside her.

Lauren can barely shift her head to look at her Gary. For a brief moment he is the winged devil from his painting, eyes burning as his claws reach to her. Then he is what the world sees again. He takes her cheeks in his hands and lifts her head for her. There is no garden this time, but soft grass beneath his feet, inside the Bull's cage with her. For a moment she convinces herself he is actually here. Every inch of him is immaculate, his hair is silky yet fluffy, his eyes are dark and brooding yet bright as if she herself is shining. He doesn't have a spec of blood, waste or shame on him; he is too clean for this place. 'I'm losing my mind…' She barks a half-cough half-laugh.

'You're not doing great.' Gary's smile somehow takes an edge off her pains. He lowers himself down next to her with a satisfied sigh as if they are relaxing on a warm day. Too-colourful grass erupts from the puddle of blood beneath him as he sits, a breeze moves his hair but the air in here is stale. 'Don't give up, L.'

'I don't know what else I can do…' It has been weeks without food or water. Her body is abandoning her. Her mutilated hand is covered in waste from the bucket. No doubt she has a fever as an infection grips her, not that she can tell. Hot and cold are a distant memory; her limbs are numb, her body a dry shell.

'There's not much further to go.' Gary whispers softly in Laurens's ear. 'I know it's hard, but you can do it–'

'Gary…' She weeps. '…I can't, I can't do anymore…'

'Yes you can! You must. I need you. And so do they.' He points at Dhanni, maybe dead on the floor and Emma paralysed opposite. 'I've never seen you give up, L. Never known you to. Even when that scumbag boyfriend of yours tried to pass you around to his friends to pay his debts, what did you do?'

Lauren never told anyone about that. Not even Gary. Her old *sweetheart* had been her world, he had been into drugs but he was a musical genius; she had devoted herself to him and when he couldn't pay his dealers he had given her over to them. In the middle of four of them in a sleazy hotel room they had held her down, her boyfriend included. She saw a knife on one of their belts and grabbed it. Bruised and shook up, she walked away from that room; she doesn't know if any of them did. She cut everything in reach and left silence behind her. She never told anyone. The smallest hope that this Gary is real flickers out at the mention of that night. She answers him anyway. 'I got away.'

'You fought.' Gary gets back up to his knees and frames her face, holding her glassy gaze. The grass disappears from under him and grows from where his knees touch the floor. 'I need you to fight again. Fight, and come back to me.' The conviction in his voice, the belief he has in her fills her lungs with new air but even such a small shift wakens her body to its raw state. 'Fight, L. You're not *his*.' Whether he means her ex or the Bull, the guttered fire within her cracks and sparks, desperate to burn again. 'You're mine. Now fight. Fight!'

Lauren puts every ounce of will she has left into her arm and presses. Her skin tears, her fingers shake as her tendons are shifted and cut, pain lances down her arm until she is sure her arm will come off before her hand is free. She screams, a feral thing but then, with a wet grating sound, her hand comes free of the nail and she collapses onto her side. She hugs her devastated hand as spikes of feeling razor their way through her body. Each breath is a gasp of agony. Her throat is sandpaper, her arm feels three times its regular size, but it is just skin and bone. She dares a look at her hand; a diamond-shaped hole is in the centre, she can see right through it. Gagging, she scrunches her eyes closed and tucks it under her armpit, unable to look at it anymore. 'Gary? I did it. See?' But she is alone. He is gone. 'Gary?' She looks about for him, for some sign that he is still with her, a patch of grass from their garden, a beam of pink light from their sky, something, but there is nothing. He is with her, she knows, but from this point on she will have to rely on her own strength, what little left there is.

Lauren takes a reinforcing breath and forces her failing body into action. She crawls over, broken hand hugged tight under her arm and drags the bucket close. Once she would have gagged, recoiled at the act but there is no squeamishness left in her now. This place has wrung her out and left only a raw need to survive. She dips her hand into the waste bucket and lets the cold slop soak between her wrist and the manacle. She can't use her other hand the way it is, she uses her feet, presses against the cuff so hard she is sure her toes or wrist will break but the manacle slips and she is flung onto her back from the movement. Her body screams, begging at her to stop but she cannot, if she does she won't be able to start again. 'Dhanni?' Lauren crawls over to her.

The girl hasn't moved. Her eyes are closed and her chest is still.

Even on the cushioned panels Lauren's knees whine at the contact, every joint stiff and weak. 'Dhanni?' She checks her pulse. It is there but it is faint. 'Dhanni, don't… don't fucking die, alright?' Lauren grabs the jug of water and tilts it to Dhanni's lips. It is tainted by the Bull's poison but without it, Dhanni will die. Dhanni can't swallow so Lauren just lets a few drops into her mouth. There is nothing else she can do; just hopes it is enough for Dhanni to hold on.

Her life has been confined to the few feet around her wall, her world only as wide as the manacles allowed; it feels strange to be even these few steps away from her spot. Punctured hand under her arm, legs wobbling, she climbs the stairs toward the door, the gateway that announces the Bull with its awful shrieking bolt. The low-light bulb above the door has been their Sun, their only source of light for months. She fixes her gaze on that light as her destination, forces her body on. At the top of the stairs she cracks, not from relief that her climb is over, or some hysteric happiness to make it this far. The Bull, in his fury after nailing Lauren to the wall, in leaving with Angie, has swung the door behind him but not bolted it.

Lauren takes one last look into her prison, one last look at Dhanni, unconscious against the far wall, and vows to see her again, not in this place but outside, free, and happy in the Sun. Maybe in the next life. One way or another, Lauren knows she will never be here again. She will escape or die. Lauren pushes the door open and leaves this nightmare.

***

Lauren is struck blind. After so long in the gloom of the basement, her eyes can't process real light. The glare makes her recoil but she refuses to step back into the basement after going through so much to get out. She flails and catches a wall with her good hand. It seems an eternity before she can make out the fingers in front of her face. She is dizzy and needs to hold on or risk toppling over. Inch by inch her range of vision expands and she can make out her surroundings. Standalone shelving is in front of her, stacked with tins and packet goods; noodles, beans, pasta; a pantry. Her body groans at the sight of it all. She traces the shelving, following it around. There are only a few feet between the basement door and the first shelf, hiding their dungeon from view. She remembers hitting her hand on something when the Bull brought her up to be washed. Her hand mirrors the memory and she strokes the shelving unit, knowing it is the one. The entrance to the pantry is closed by a curtain.

She passes a shelf with a crate of bottled water. She rips one free. She thirstily chugs at the water but coughs half of it back up. She steps back, deeper into the pantry for fear that she will be heard and the Bull will throw her back downstairs. She sips at the water but after only a mouthful her belly is bloated. She sways back toward the curtain, leaving the bottle on a nearby shelf. Every second she spends is one Angie loses to that bastard.

At the edge of her hearing she recognises the Bull's grunting and movement as he builds to his passion. The sound is kindling to the fire within, and she sets her destination in mind- Her foot catches something heavy and she almost trips. At her feet is the nail gun, leant against spare boards. She takes up the gun but her legs buckle from the weight. Her grip is so weak she needs to rest it against her hip and brace her mangled hand underneath the barrel. Ready, she limps toward her target.

Through the curtain the light assaults her again. It is not even direct sunlight that scorches her, just ambient light through a window but she must squint or go blind. She enters a dining room with a fold away table against the wall. An archway leads into a kitchen and Lauren spies several colourful plastic dishes on the drainer beside the sink; their bowls. On the counter top is a monitor showing their prison in bright green and black from an infra-red camera hidden in the basement. *I knew it...* Beside the monitor is a large Tupperware tub filled with beige powder. Lauren takes a step back knowing it is the Bull's drug. Whatever it is she will never fall under its influence again. Out of the window a small garden is laid out with perfect grass and furniture on the patio. The grass is too green, too perfect. Lauren suspects it must be fake; stuff you can buy in a roll but her senses are inside-out having seen nothing but the dank of their basement for so long. Maybe seeing such a rich colour as green grass has become something she can't fathom as real. Her hand seeks out the daylight, having been denied it for so long, convinced she had made it up and never knew it to begin with. Her skin is dashed with muck, stained, but the warmth of the Sun makes her heart ache. She believed she would never see it again.

Angie screams and Lauren shudders back against the wall, hugging the heavy gun close. A hundred possibilities run through her head. *He's hurting her, killing her?* Lauren is sure he left them to die, sure they won't survive much longer in their state. The Bull didn't lock the door because he thought they weren't going anywhere. And if Emma is the Inspector's Wife maybe she was chosen because of him? Lauren thinks to the Bull mask Gary made last year, he does so many commissions she never paid particular attention to it. Is it the same one? Was she chosen because Gary knows about the mask? What about Dhanni, Angie, the others before them, does the Bull have some connection to them too?

Her grip is slippery with blood and body waste, but Lauren hugs the gun tight like a lifeline as she follows the Bull's passions. The sounds echo from a room at the end of the hall. There are pictures on the walls, holiday snaps of a built black man with a bald head and his friends on holiday, all in Hawaiian coloured shirts and holding cocktails. Lauren sees the real face of the Bull, who must be the Bull underneath the mask. His face, his smile, this house, everything is so normal but for the basement and the deeds that happen here. If Lauren didn't know and visited this place she would have no idea what was going on beneath it all. The pictures, the carpet under her feet, it is all a mask to hide what it truly is. Each picture shows more of the mask, what he shows the rest of the world to hide what he really is. With each step her grip on the trigger gets tighter.

Lauren comes face to face with what must be the living room and the source of all the noise. A staircase leads off to her right, the front door and freedom to her left, the Bull and Angie ahead of her. She could leave, right now; the key is in the door. She could leave and be away from this place forever, and Dhanni needs help. But the Bull has Angie. Leaving saves Dhanni precious time but leaves Angie in the Bull's clutches. Every touch, every stroke from that man fuels the fire within her and it is all she can do not to scream her fury into the Earth so that it cracks opens and swallows this place whole. The brutality of their treatment, the tenderness in his pampering of them; it is all insidious and it has to end. *Hold on a little more, Dhanni.*

Lauren nudges the living room door open with the nail-gun, thinking of Angie. Poor Angie, taking the Bull's desires over and over while she and Dhanni tried to starve, to escape in their self-defeating way. Angie deserves more than what she has been dealt. She has tried to survive in this place and look what it has gotten her. Lauren and Dhanni are free of the Bull, now it is time for Angie to be rid of him too. Lauren hefts the nail gun in her hands and strides into the living room. It is wide with high ceilings. What could be brand new carpet is fluffy beneath Lauren's soiled and smeared toes. In the centre of the room is a glass-top coffee-table with a two-seater sofa on one side and a three-seater on the other. On top of the three-seater is the Bull but not as Lauren would usually know him. His mask, his totem, is sat upon the coffee table, looking straight at Lauren, daring her to act, to raise the gun in her hands and shoot it between the eyes. But she must hurt the man beneath the horns, like he has never been hurt before. He is naked on top of Angie, pounding away like she is a steak that needs tendering, his hips slap into her over and over. Lauren raises the nail gun, aiming square into the Bull's muscular back. Her finger tightens on the trigger when suddenly he flips them around and Angie is on top, hands pressed on his chest as her hips grind away at him. *What...?* Angie lets go a wail of pleasure as she rides the Bull, glistening with sweat. She leans back, takes his hands to her breasts, then leans down and kisses the man that has abused and tortured them. Lauren can't understand what she is seeing. Angie isn't paralysed? She is in complete control and loving every second. While Lauren and Dhanni are suffering, dying downstairs, Angie is enjoying herself like nothing else matters in the world? '…Angie?' Lauren voice is a cracked husk, her strength suddenly gone. The gun slumps in her arms and it takes everything she has just to stay on her feet. The lovers don't hear her in their passions. None of this makes sense! How can this be happening…? Lauren wonders at how broken her mind is.

Lauren's gaze is pulled to a large picture across the room, over Angie and the Bull grinding, on the chimney breast. The Bull, the man, is dressed in a black tuxedo, flower on his lapel, and an enormous grin on his face. Beside him is his bride, dressed in lace and wearing beautiful jewellery; Angie. *Angie is married to the monster.* The tide of emotion that rips its way through Lauren robs her of her senses. She steps forward, gun forgotten in her arms, to tear at the pair of them, until no trace is left. She would demand answers for the hurt and shame she has had to endure. A war of memory, every conversation, each word shared between them is replayed in her mind. Every one of them is a lie.

Angie and her Husband suddenly climax together. Angie lets loose a wail of pleasure and the Bull groans. They are taught, holding each other in place until they collapse. They laugh, kiss and mutter sweet nothings to each other. Angie climbs off her man and sits on the edge of the sofa, naked, clean, her hair still wet from the shower, and free. She pulls a bowl of cereal from across the coffee table and tosses a couple of flakes into her mouth. 'You animal, you didn't even let me finish my breakfast.'

The Bull pulls her back and tickles her, play fighting until she shoo's him off and can pick up her spoon. 'Did you record the next episode, by the way?' She asks, mouthful of cereal and reaching for the TV remote.

The Bull doesn't answer. His eyes are wide at the sight of Lauren in the doorway, frozen in time. Lauren's rage builds in her chest, her heart pounds but she only has eyes for Angie, her friend, who lived a nightmare with her and made it a little bit better. But all that was a lie. Angie knew the nightmare and kept Lauren asleep.

'Joe?' Angie prompts but then twists around to see what he is staring at. Shock strikes her dumb. Her mouth falls open and the spoon falls to the floor. Both stare wide-eyed at Lauren, bloody and shit-stained with the nail-gun cradled in her arms. She must look like a demon crawled from its pit.

'Angie!' Lauren finally accuses. Her cracked voice bellows with new strength.

Angie is thrown aside as the Bull leaps up to confront Lauren. She would have been shaken to the core, but her rage burns the terror away at the root. Too late he gets to his feet. She squeezes the trigger and a four-inch nail punches into his throat, dropping him with his hands clutched around his neck, coughing. There is virtually no recoil but in her state the gun makes her take a step back. She pulls the trigger again and this time the bolt goes into his elbow at the joint. He gargles a scream as he falls back, glugs of red ruin the carpet.

'No!' Angie screams and launches herself at Lauren.

Lauren is crying as she fires nail after nail into the Bull. He is hit in the belly and chest. Lauren is so intent on her punishment of the Bull that she is defenceless against Angie as she crashes into her, tackling her to the ground and knocking the heavy gun from her hands. She is struck with a barrage that leaves her dizzy, her own strikes feeble against Angie's healthy and well-fed strength.

Angie rolls Lauren over and grabs her by the hair, slamming her head against the floor until Lauren's only defence is a nauseous groan. The house spins and it is all she can do not to throw up and pass out in her own vomit.

'Holy shit!' Angie steps back and pulls a pillowcase from one of the sofa cushions and tends it to her Husband's neck. 'Just be still Joe, hold this here, I'll call help! Don't move.' Angie, still naked, leaps over the sofa and grabs the house phone, dialling quickly.

Lauren tries to push up onto her elbows but her body has given in. Her head is throbbing like there is a water pump inside her skull. The sickening hole in her hand has been pulled wider. Every joint screams like a tooth ache, robbing her of what resolve she has left. Her body has been pushed too far.

'Pick up Jerry!' Angie screams into the landline.

Josef Akoum gurgles what he can, a bubble of blood popping out of his lips. 'Arres... arrested.'

'Fuck!' Angie slams the phone down and pulls on a shirt and some jeans. 'Don't move, hon. I'm going to get the car keys. Just stay still!' The affection in her voice is so alien that Lauren is convinced she has lost her mind. The light jingle of car keys reminds Lauren of Christmas bells.

Lauren can only stare at this woman, head pounding and body groaning with every movement. Below, Angie was an ally, someone who shared in her ordeal and helped her cope; a friend. Up here, all that is upside down. Angie is a part of this place and Lauren's heart, along with the rest of her, is broken. Angie steps over Lauren as if she isn't there, intent on saving her Husband.

'C'mon, we have to get to the hospital... Shh. Don't talk, lean on me, that's it.' Angie struggles with the weight of the Bull but they limp out of the room. 'I'll see to her, don't worry, just wait in the car, try not to move…' Her voice dies away when the front door opens.

Lauren tries to move but a wave of nausea attacks and she vomits; putrid acid that makes her retch. The room spins and she crawls a step away.

Angie is back all too soon and kicks Lauren in the ribs turning the air to fire. 'Bitch! You couldn't just leave well enough alone, could you, eh? You could have killed him!' She kicks her again. Angie grabs Lauren by the hair and starts dragging her out of the room and down the hall. Lauren can't breathe and the pressure on her hair is immense. In her starved state it is like every piece of her is extra sensitive; each hair is a nail being pulled. She would scream if she had the air. 'No, you have to fuck everything up. We had a good thing, Blondie! I tried to tell you, didn't I? I tried to tell you that you were better off just letting it happen. But no, you had to fight!' She drags Lauren back into the dining room beside the pantry. She means to throw Lauren back into the basement. Lauren pries at the fingers clutching her hair but she is too weak. She hooks a foot on the leg of the table making Angie stumble to a halt. 'Oh, for Christ's sake!' Angie lets go of Lauren's hair and drops to a knee beside her. She punches and hammers at Lauren's leg until she loses feeling in it, her skin-and-bone leg bruising instantly. 'You're going back in. Josef needs this! He becomes something so much more when he takes us, Lauren. You don't see it but he is more than a man in those moments. And doesn't it feel good?' Angie's face is bright like a nine-year-old showing her best friend her favourite flower.

Lauren is finally able to grind a breath in and out. Her voice is a hideous thing. 'Dhanni… dying…'

Angie's glee dies on her face and an angry snarl grows. 'And whose fault is that? She was eating, she was taking the Bull and becoming more! She was fine before you came in!'

'I never wanted this...' Lauren spits. 'We trusted you. Why the lie, why be down there at all?' Lauren needs to know, to keep her talking.

Angie pushes Lauren down and paces the dining room as if it has been on her mind since the dawn of time. She sighs. 'Theresa was first. We had her downstairs, out of the way, Josef would visit her, blindfold her, and I would watch. Then we had Joanne. It was good.' She explains like it is the most understandable thing in the world. 'But Theresa got sick. And bad. We agreed I would join them. "I'd be a poor kidnapped girl."' She affects a mock innocent voice. 'I could keep an eye on everybody, make sure we had our bases covered. And then my bitch Mother reported me missing. Was a month before we saw the news about the *Prince*. Wasn't like I could nip to the shops anymore. It would only invite investigation if somebody recognised me. So I did what any Wife should; committed to what my man needed from me.

'But Theresa got worse. We couldn't take her to a hospital so... she died.' Angie recalls it with genuine grief. She glances through the window to the garden with the fake grass. 'I never lied about what happened after, Lauren. Joanne was alright for a while. But when Josef brought Dhanni in... I guess she didn't see an end. She starved. And I won't watch that again. So, you and Dhanni can do what you like but it *will* be down there, and I *won't* be there to see it. Not again.' Angie moves on Lauren again, grabbing her by the throat and under one arm, dragging her toward the pantry and the prison below.

I won't go down there again... not after coming so far... 'No!' Lauren tears at Angie's hands, desperate to stop herself from going back down there.

'Stop it! This is happening!' Angie thumps at Lauren like beating a stray dog.

Lauren accepts the blows, too weak to guard against them. 'No! I won't!'

'You just don't understand! Putting yourself below another like I have with Josef… it's what real love is! He is more than the sum of what we are, when he is the Bull he is so much more. Didn't you feel it? And I'm the one he's sharing it with.' Angie has her hand around Lauren's throat but it is to pin her in place, not to choke her. She wants Lauren to understand, harbours some hope that Lauren may still be a part of this.

Lauren grates against her words, believing the same of Gary. Lauren has given up many things in idolising her Husband, in helping him reach his potential. She feels it as adamantly as Angie does about her rapist-monster-Husband but that doesn't mean Lauren is as deluded, does it? No, Gary may not be conventional in his methods, some don't see the beauty in what he creates, but Lauren does, and she will never give up on him. Her own conviction is reflected in Angie's face but she cannot crumble beneath it, she would rather die than let the Bull have her again.

'Josef and Jerry used to kill them before.' Angie admits. 'I never cared who they fucked so long as Josef didn't lie to me about it. But the killing? I tried… I tried to accept it, Blondie. But I couldn't let them keep on like that, seeing those women in the papers everyday…' Angie's eyes dart about, searching her feelings. 'So, I suggested we keep some. The Bull could act whenever he wanted then. It was such a good plan! If only Theresa didn't get sick.' Angie's face darkens and her grip tightens around Lauren's throat. 'And if you won't behave? Then you'll go in the garden too! And we'll find others!' Angie spits and drags Lauren along. She means to throw Lauren back into the cage with Dhanni and Emma, for the Bull or death.

'Angie… I came to save you…' Lauren gasps, gripping Angie's wrist.

'I don't need saving, Blondie.' Angie softens but the fire in her eyes burns.

'...and to kill *him*.' Lauren's evil smile blooms, like Gary's demon it is a grin to rattle the brave, hoping against all else she has kept Angie busy long enough for the Bull to bleed out like the wretched shit he is.

Angie realises what Lauren has done, taking precious seconds away from her getting help, her eyes grow wide as she fears for her man out in the car. 'You...!' She tears and pulls at Lauren, frantically trying to throw her down into the basement so she can lock her away forever. Lauren locks her fingers in the woman's hair, wraps her legs around her body. Angie falls in a tumble, trying to right herself but Lauren clings on. Her sides and head are assaulted by fists, elbows, Angie scratches at her face but Lauren won't let go. 'Josef!' Angie screams but Lauren sticks her fingers into her mouth; bloody and caked in faeces. Angie gags, desperate to be away, to save her Husband.

From deep below, Lauren summons that animal kept hidden within and attacks Angie. From that night at the hotel when she made her ex and his dealers pay, from when she attacked the Bull with her shiv, she gathers her ferocity. From every visit from the Bull, every indignity, every humiliation, every hour spent chained to that wall, Lauren collects her strength. From every lie and false smile that Angie gave her, every minute spent believing they were friends, it stacks up within her and feeds her ragged body the rage it needs. Lauren fights her way on top of Angie. Her body is weak and battered, she is cut from Angie's nails and bruised from her blows, her hand is a ruin and clumps of her hair are wrapped around Angie's fingers but she is in control. She hammers down on the woman with her right hand, complete as it is. Angie fends off what she can but for each she defends another one hits her. Lauren is a shade of what she once was but she doesn't stop. After an age, bones ready to shatter, muscles thin and torn, Angie slumps, bloody and out cold. One of Angie's teeth is stuck in her knuckle.

Lauren collapses sideways and drags herself away. Her fist is numb, her other hand cannot close. With difficulty Lauren stands, using the table for support and looks down at the woman she called friend, pulling the tooth from her flesh. She is alive but her nose is broken, eyes closed in forced sleep. Lauren's heart beats so hard it might punch its way out of her chest. She leaves Angie and limps down the hall and into the living room to retrieve the nail gun from beside the coffee-table. If the Bull isn't dead than she is going to make damn sure he will be. The gun weighs three times as much as it did a few minutes ago and the weight of it nearly pulls her over. She hugs it against herself but a blow to the head drops her to her knees and it clatters from her grasp.

Angie is up again with a broken picture frame in her hands. Glass tinkles onto the carpet and red warmth drips from the top of Lauren's head. Angie takes up a shard and threatens it against Lauren's dazed face. 'You don't understand, Blondie! Compared to him, you don't matter! I'll do whatever it takes for my Bull! I'll kill you and we'll find others. Is that what you want?!' Her words are thick through her fat lips and broken nose.

Despite the acute pain riddling her body Lauren climbs to her knees using the coffee table as support. 'No Angie… I do understand. But I don't care about your piece of shit Husband…' Angie's anger doubles and she readies the shard of glass in her fist. '…you can take the Bull and go fuck yourself.'

Angie stabs forward with all her weight. It is all Lauren can do just to fall aside, limp as a doll. Angie cuts Lauren but her momentum carries her soaring over, tripping and on top of the Bull's mask. The glass coffee table explodes underneath her. The Bull's horns puncture her high in the shoulders and erupts out of her back, snapping them off and sending the animal head rolling.

Lauren untangles herself from Angie's legs and takes precious seconds to gather herself. The glass scored a deep cut across her side; blood burns white hot as it leaks down her side and into the no longer perfect carpet. Lauren is dying, she is sure. Angie lays on her side, impaled by the Bull's horns and prickled with glass from the table. She may be dead but Lauren couldn't care less. There is another she needs to see dead first. The nail gun is just too heavy so she scrapes up a shard of glass instead and forces herself on.

In the light of day she must look like an extra in a zombie movie. She would shield her eyes from the light of day but her arms are dead weight. An estate car is on the drive, Josef Akoum sat in the passenger seat. Her steps are short and irregular after her trials. She edges around the side of the car and confronts the Bull, knife of glass ready to end him. His front is painted red, torn pillowcase loose in limp fingers on his lap. Blood runs over the leather seat and pools at his bare feet. Nails stick out of his flesh like tent pegs as he stares blankly ahead. He is quite dead.

Lauren looks about the normal street and recognises where she is. *Nightingale Road?* She laughs hysterically, part relief in the face of the Bull, but mostly because her house is only a few minutes away. She has been a stone's throw away from her own front door this whole time.

Inside, Lauren uses the landline in the living room to call Gary; the only number she knows by heart. Gary answers. 'Hello?' Lauren breaks down, hurting, but so happy to hear his voice it is more than she can take. It isn't the Gary in her head, from their garden; he is real. 'Lauren?' He asks, disbelieving.

Her breath is broken and the sobs make her words unintelligible but he knows it is Lauren before she is able to speak clearly. 'It's me, Gary. It's me. I love you!'

'L, I love you too! Where are you?' He tells her that he is with the police so they can come to her, but his will be the first face she sees. Standing there, near starved to death, bloody and hurt, all she wants is to be looked after, for Gary to take her up and keep her safe. With Angie at her feet, unconscious and bleeding into her ruined carpet, she has another idea.

'Gary, are you alone now?' She asks seriously, swaying on her feet, gambling with not only her life but Dhanni's too.

'I'm at the Station but I can be. Lauren, what is it? Where are you?' He asks.

Angie is unmoving at her feet and Lauren decides. 'Send the models home. Bring your clean-up kit. I'm on Nightingale Road, number 9, but come alone. And hurry. I need you to help me with something before the police get here.'

20. Inspector Roy Harvey

'Has Akoum said anything else?' Chief Superintendent Piper asks, eyes downcast at the report from Jerry Akoum's testimony and the warrants for Josef Akoum and the Tanner place. Roy heard somebody else in that garage and is willing to bet that Gary Tanner doesn't want them known about. And Emma's ring was found outside Roy's house. The Prince has her.

'No. He's clammed up after his last outburst.' Roy says coldly. He is no mood for the Viper's condescension. If she had let him have the original warrants for family members in the first place they could have been here a month ago and Emma wouldn't be on his list.

'What's his lawyer saying? Insanity?' She asks, signing the Akoum Warrant with the address blank; a rare disregard of procedure from her but considering Jerry Akoum's confession it can hardly backfire on her.

'She's not talking to us either. Keeping closed council so far but I expect so. With his confession there isn't much more she can do for him. She'll be glad to be rid, I imagine.' Roy speculates.

'Where are we on this address?' She taps the Akoum report; waiting on the answer with an expression that says even if they had the address five minutes ago it still wouldn't be quick enough.

'We're working on it.' Roy says bluntly.

'Have a team ready to go. You have my authority to use any means necessary to bring this man in.' Piper says righteously.

'It's done.' Roy steals the wind out of her sails. 'Soon as we get the where.'

The Viper looks into his eyes like the animal she is named for. She could strike at any moment but Roy is beyond caring. This case has cost him more than he ever thought a case could, but it could cost more still. His career, his reputation may be in her hands, and circling the toilet in the Viper's eyes, but Roy will be damned before he lets her take charge of this case when he is so close to finishing it. There is too much at stake. 'You don't like me, Harvey.' She sits back, pen down and in perfect line with the others. 'You think I throw red tape at everything to hinder you and the other Inspector's when I could just let you run riot on your hunches. I frustrate you because I make you jump through hoops just to get one step ahead. You think I blame you for not doing more with my Sisters case? Well, grow up.'

Roy is stunned. He recovers quickly and is about to reply with something that will probably cost him his job but she isn't finished.

'I don't blame you for the result of that case as a junior Inspector. You were to support, not direct. Don't ever think me to act so personally in regard to my work.' She leans forward, fingers interlaced and on the attack. 'That being said, I don't like you either. You are a sub-par Inspector who bumbles through his cases, only succeeding because of the junior Officers he keeps under his wing. Inspector Murphy is twice the detective you are and if I could spare the budget I would give her command of her own team.'

Roy is speechless. *Spare the budget?* Meaning if he were fired then Nora would get his job. In any other situation he would just call the colleague talking to him like this the C-word and walk away. But the laser focus in the Viper's hard eyes keep him in place.

'Now, with that in mind, *Inspector*. Why do you want to search Tanner's property?' She asks pointedly. 'I understand your Wife is missing but I won't let you harass victims of the same case as the one you are neck-deep in.'

There is no way around it without looking like a fool. Roy either admits he entered Gary Tanner's residence illegally, without due cause or he says it is a hunch and confirm everything about him she just described. Roy considers; she already thinks him a bungling chimp so why add maverick to her list of judgments? Either way, he needs to find out what is happening at the back of Tanner's garage; it could lead him to Josef Akoum and Emma. 'I've got a feeling about the man. He's hiding something.'

Piper cocks an eyebrow, waiting for his respectful finish. Roy clears his throat like it is a pill too bitter to swallow. He manages it. '…Ma'am.'

The Viper's mouth twitches in what must be the closest thing to a smile she will allow herself. She looks out the window, considering. 'Another hunch?'

Roy shrugs. 'Inspector Murphy agrees with me if that makes you feel better.'

'Alright.' She says expectantly but her gaze is cold, calculating. She signs the sheet and puts it with the Akoum report to be sent to Judge Niesbit. 'You may be an ape but you have solved every case you have been assigned. You've never asked for permission twice before so this feeling about Gary Tanner must be eating at you. I'll trust that feeling.'

'Thank you, Ma'am.' Roy doesn't know what else to say. He can never get a read on this woman. One minute she is chewing him up to spit him out and the next gifting him what he needs. 'I'd like to leave as soon as-' A series of thumps approach, running feet, and a second later Joey bursts in with phone in hand. 'Joey…?' Roy asks, expecting the Viper to give him a lashing for barging in like this. Joey hangs on the door with an excited smile. 'What is it?' Roy asks. The Viper stands expectantly knowing Joey wouldn't have come in like this unless it was something big.

'Lauren Tanner just called in.' Joey explains. 'And she's got Josef Akoum.'

'What?' Roy can't believe it. 'Survivor? Jesus, what the hell happened?'

'She called a few minutes ago. Dhanni Sandhu is alive too. And Emma is there, alive. Murphy has sent ambulances ahead and left already.' Joey explains. Roy's soul catches, hearing Emma is alive fills his heart.

'I guess we won't need these anymore?' The Chief folds up the warrants and drops them to one side..

'Ma'am, with your permission?' Roy asks to be excused. He wouldn't usually ask but in front of Joey she would like him to.

'By all means. Bring them home.' She waves them off.

Outside Roy questions Joey about Lauren Tanner's contact. 'She's all shook up. Says she fought *the Bull*. Says she didn't mean to kill him.' Joey recounts as they race to the car.

'Josef Akoum is dead?' Roy asks.

'So she said.' Joey shrugs.

'Has anyone told Mr Tanner?' Roy asks, wanting to be on the scene before him.

'He rushed off an hour ago. Watkins went after him but lost him on the way.' Joey winces apologetically. They climb into Roy's car and race over to Josef Akoum's place and his Wife.

***

Nightingale Road is swarming with emergency service vehicles. Half the road is already cordoned off in yellow police tape. Neighbours and Press gather at different points trying to get a closer look at the house in question and confirm the rumour that the Prince has been caught and/or killed. Ambulance and police lights flash, casting the scene into flickers even though it is the middle of the day. Ambulance personnel rush by with gurneys with bright red medical bags slung over their shoulders. Flat-foots stand guard around the house, silently holding back reporters and family of the missing. Eight-foot white screens hide the driveway and entrance to the house from view. Nora set all this up in the time it took Roy to get out from the Viper's coils. Roy spots Mather's who points across, Roy follows his direction passed a screen, an ambulance and finds Nora examining a black male, naked, in the passenger seat of a navy-blue estate. He is dead with what looks like nails in his throat and chest.

'What do we have?' Roy asks. 'Is Emma here?'

Nora leans out of the car. 'They're bringing her out now.' She says uncertainly, making Roy wonder if Emma has been hurt but Nora avoids his eye. 'She is drugged but otherwise unharmed. Better than the others.' She nods behind him.

Sat in the ambulance is none other than Lauren Tanner. One of her hands is bandaged heavily so it looks like she is wearing a boxing glove. Her head is wrapped also. A female paramedic checks a cut on her side but Lauren clings a blanket tight around her shoulders as if the brisk air is worse than her wounds. She is filthy and a lot thinner than her file picture but unmistakably alive. 'Goddamn, we were due a win, right?'

'Absolutely.' She agrees coldly, pulling off her rubber gloves.

'Josef Akoum?' Roy asks, nodding at the deceased man in the passenger seat.

'Yes. We checked his driving license inside the house. It's him.' Nora's mouth twists into a funny shape at seeing the body. 'You should see inside Roy. He had them locked up in their own filth down there.'

'I will.' Roy by no means looks forward to the task but finding survivors after so long is a better result than he could have hoped for. Roy looks back at Mrs Tanner and wonders what hell she has gone through to get here. 'One's going home, Nora. I can't believe it. Joey mentioned Dhanni Sandhu?'

'Here she comes…' Nora closes the car door and steps aside as another team of paramedics wheels out a gurney with Dhanni Sandhu on it. She is unconscious and horribly thin but also alive. A re-breather is on her face and a drip connected to her arm already. A sweaty Paramedic follows with a pair of bolt-cutters. 'Must be a record. Been a long time since she went missing.'

As soon as Lauren Tanner sees Mrs Sandhu she scrambles out of the ambulance to join her. 'Will she be OK? Is it too late?' Her voice is cracked and hysterical.

'We don't know yet. We'll take care of her.' The lead paramedic assures and then directs through the foot traffic to another ambulance.

'Lauren Tanner? I'm Inspector Roy Harvey. We've been trying to find you but it looks like you found yourself.' Roy says with a smile. 'What happened here?'

If Lauren's eyes could cut flesh then Josef Akoum would be in shreds. 'He had us downstairs. He would come down and… sometimes he'd bring us up and…' Lauren's voice sounds barely human. Dark bags shade the skin under her eyes making her look a ghost, her hair could be made of straw and she sways on her feet. 'I got out. Slipped my chain and found him upstairs. I… shot him. He knocked me down and got out.' Her eyes are shards of glass as she looks over Akoum. 'I didn't mean to kill him… but I'm glad I did.'

'It's alright.' Nora puts an arm around Lauren but she tenses up at the contact. 'It's OK. First thing is we get you checked over. We will have questions. But they come after. Sit, let them see to you.'

Lauren mumbles and nods, staggering toward Dhanni as she is loaded into the back of the ambulance. 'Can I go with her?'

Roy gets a nod from the paramedic. 'Sure.' Roy offers his hand.

'Lauren?' The three of them turn and stood in front of Watkins and Mathers is Gary Tanner. He immediately forces his way through to get to his Wife.

Lauren flings the blanket from her shoulders and collapses into her Husband's arms. She breaks down into sobs and lets Gary wrap her up and carry her to the floor where they reconcile. He is holding her as tight as a man can do, brushing at her hair and whispering to her, telling her everything is going to be alright.

Nora steps up beside Roy and lets her hand brush Roy's. 'Look at that.'

'Roy?' Emma's groggy voice calls.

Roy turns on the spot and Emma is stumbling toward him, a paramedic trying and failing to help her as she pushes him away. Stubborn, strong, hates him, but his Wife all the same, she falls into his arms. Roy grips her like a safety blanket in the night. Emma sobs daintily into his shoulder, squeezing him back as hard. These last months without her, missing from his life, and then missing from the world has shone a light on what he did to her, what she means to him. Roy doesn't know if he can fix things but he isn't ready to let her go. *Nora...* He lets his Wife go and Nora stands there stuck, discarded and awkward. She cannot leave, neither can he but it is like she must. She deserves better.

'Mrs Harvey...' Nora starts, somehow looking strong and ashamed at the same time. 'Please let them see to you. Excuse me.' She waves in a paramedic and takes her leave, unable to bear anymore.

'Nora.' Emma stops her. For a second Roy thinks Emma will scream at his partner, expose them in front of everyone, but she softens. 'Never mind.' And lets the paramedic lead her away.

Nora finally looks at Roy and it breaks his heart. For a second her gaze is longing, pleading with him not to abandon her. But then it is gone and *Inspector Murphy* takes control. Her eyes harden and she is nothing but a professional, their intimacy forced aside. 'You should see to her.' And she pulls on her gloves, leaning back into the car and their target.

Roy has no words for her. Emma is one way and Nora another. At least one of them is going to hurt more come the end of this. Cursing his failings he returns to Lauren Tanner. Despite Roy's distrust of Gary Tanner and what he is sure he heard in the man's garage he can't deny that the sight of the Tanner's reunification is a touching one. He drops his jacket around Lauren's shoulders.

'Thank you Inspector…' Gary pulls the coat tighter around Lauren but something makes him freeze. The tear in Roy's jacket; that left a shred of fabric in Tanner's workshop. He looks up and they share a moment of understanding.

Roy casually drops his hands into his pockets, trying to keep the smile on his face as he grips the cuffs there, ready to restrain Tanner if need be. Mr Tanner only smiles though. *He knows.* Roy tells himself he doesn't care but something about Gary Tanner is wrong. But now is not the time, not with Lauren Tanner found. They aren't finished with each other, that's for sure.

'Again, thank you for everything, Inspectors. I'll ride with Lauren to the hospital.' Tanner helps Lauren into the back of Mrs Sandhu's ambulance.

Roy turns for the house and the thousand-and-one jobs that need completing to clear this whole thing up.

'Oh, Inspector?' Lauren calls from the back of the ambulance.

'Yes, Mrs Tanner?' Roy moves to her.

'There were others... they didn't... *He* spoke about them... I think he buried them.' She looks passed Roy toward the rear garden.

'Alright Mrs Tanner. We'll check it out and take a full statement after you have been looked at. Now you get on. You deserve it.' Roy puts on his best smile despite the cold hope of finding the other missing women alive inside.

'What if Dhanni Sandhu and Lauren Tanner are the only ones left? Alive, I mean.' Nora asks gravely when Lauren Tanner's ambulance pulls away.

Roy doesn't want to think about it but this job rarely involves what he wants. 'We have to know for sure. We need to search the premises, dig up the garden, pull the place apart brick for brick if we need to.' Roy thinks of their list, shorter now but still too long. 'Part of me hopes we do find them out back.'

Nora looks sharply at Roy, wanting to reassure him but her professional armour slides into place, not letting her open up. 'My first question is what happened to Angelina Smith? She's married to this guy. Well, where is she? Was she in on this like Jerry Akoum said?'

'Inspectors?' Joey is hanging out of the front door of the house. 'Nobody else inside. Blood and signs of a struggle match what Mrs Tanner told us so far.'

'OK. Let's get to it.' Roy offers the way to Nora. 'You ready for this?'

'Absolutely.' Nora pulls her rubber gloves tight.

'You take the lead on this one.' Roy offers. 'After this you might get your own team anyway.' The Viper's words about his and Nora's ability echo through his head. Some of what she said struck a chord. Some of it she can stick up her arse. But she was right about Nora being ready to lead.

Nora shoots Roy a questioning look. 'What do you mean? Has Piper said something?' Her ambition betrays her as she considers leading her own squad.

'No.' Roy lies. 'But I wouldn't be surprised. After all, you're the brains here.'

'It's true.' Joey and Mathers chime in together as they share out evidence bags.

Nora shows a tight-lipped smile. 'I guess we'll see what happens then.'

'I guess we will.' Roy glances back and finds Emma through the emergency personnel, looking for him back. Nora is cold beside him. Roy wishes he could change his world and reward both women for their faith in him but he can't. 'Let's go, we've got a lot to do.'

But Nora has already gone.

21. Lauren Tanner

In her own kitchen, at her table, her own clothes on her back, with Gary making the toast, Lauren can almost believe what happened didn't happen. Her hand is still heavily bandaged, the twenty-four stitches across her side pull at every movement but the specialist said she will heal. Her ribs show, her clothes hang on her as if several sizes too big but soon that will change too.

The Inspector's, Harvey and Murphy, have visited a few times to check in on her. But they always have more questions. Lauren likes Nora, she seems genuinely concerned and motivated to find out what happened to the missing women before they started abducting them but Lauren knows they are dead. Angie said as much. Jerry is the only person who can answer the question of what they did with the bodies at the start of their campaign but Inspector Murphy said he is no longer making sense. The other Inspector, Roy, is on edge and Lauren can't help but think his mind is elsewhere when he is here. Lauren plays with her wedding bands, now reunited after the police removed her ring from the Bull's ear. She shivers and pulls the blanket closer about her.

Gary has the radio on his phone while he spreads jam on her toast. She is hungry enough to eat a banquet but she cannot take it. Small steps, her doctor said. A news segment comes on reporting a car crash and some scandal involving a MP. Lauren tunes it out, wondering at the alien feeling her rings give her after just a few months without them, but then she hears her name.

"...Tanner and Mrs Dhanni Sandhu returned home this week after being cleared by hospital personnel. It is still unknown how many women were involved in the kidnapping and sexual assaults by the Akoum Brothers. Previously known as The Prince-"

Gary switches off the phone. He has been as supportive as he can, has done everything she has asked but they are hardly back to normal. How can they be? Free and home again but still the Bull holds part of her hostage. She was gone for thirteen weeks, they tell her, and in that time she was abused and broken. Inspector Murphy said she should revel in what she did; not the killing of Josef Akoum, for surely she saved lives ridding the world of him but for fighting the way she did. In causing Akoum the trouble she did, only two other woman were abducted by him during her imprisonment, and one of those was in response to Jerry's arrest. The Prince, the Bull as few people know him, kept a monthly schedule and Lauren interrupted that. Lauren is just sorry she wasn't able to act before Jody Maru killed herself.

Gary has been attentive but there is a horrible distance between them. They may never be able to go back to what they were but Lauren won't give up trying. Lauren wishes Gary would just have her, to get it over and done with. As much as she is dreading it she knows the first time with him will be the worst, but after that it will be better won't it? She wants him but won't ask first, and neither will he. They will be alright, she's sure; it will just take time. Lauren thinks to the room under the workshop outside. *Maybe it's time to start the healing process? Show him how much he means to me?* 'Gary?' Lauren asks.

'Yeah, L.' He acknowledges expectantly.

Lauren can tell he wants to ask what happened down there in the Bull's cage, he wants to ask all the questions that no good can come from knowing the answers to, but he won't, not yet. Gary has always been a dominant man, has always been her King, her religion, but now it's like the roles have been reversed. It has taken being submitted and violated to forge a new Lauren in place of the old. She thought she had seen the worst in her world after her college boyfriend but now her eyes are wide open. If the choice is between waiting for the worst to find her again, or being the worst, she knows what she will pick. She is different after her ordeal for sure, harder if not any stronger. She'll be damned if she is going to let what happened to her destroy the rest of her life. And Gary did exactly as she asked after she phoned him, he came to her and acted without hesitation. Gary is her King, but Lauren is also his Queen, and he has proven he will do anything for her. 'Come with me?' Lauren slides her hand into Gary's and pulls her blanket tighter, leads him out the back door to his workshop. She is still unsteady on her feet and soon needs Gary to lean on. She guides him outside and into the garage through the side door, passed his tools and unfinished pieces. The unfinished second Bull mask, the one Jerry would have owned, has been stripped down and hammered into an ugly shell. At Lauren's request she watched Gary hammer the thing into a formless lump to rot. She doesn't spare it a second glance. He is her instrument in her revenge but it cannot just be for her. In order for them to heal Gary must find peace in what happened. Like destroying the Bull head, Gary needed to unleash his rage as much as Lauren needed to see it. She unlocks the door at the back of the workshop where he takes his inspiration. Gary carries her downstairs.

The idea of freely entering their chamber so alike to the Bull's filled her with dread and left her shaking, but after acquiring Gary's new subject the place fills her with strength. She felt a power she had never felt before and is excited to see Gary work, to be her instrument. This is her lair now, her web, and her catch will never escape. Gary sets her down into a broad backed chair with thick cushions to support her ravaged body.

'Love? I want you to do it, and it's OK. I want this. For both of us.' She explains, pulling him to her, grasping him too tight as if he might fly away.

'You're sure?' He asks, searching her eyes for how she might really feel. 'I can wait. I only need you.'

Lauren pulls him down to her and kisses him deeply. He is more tender than she has ever known him but she needs him to be forceful. Not because she wants him to be but because in a way she feels like she has failed him and wants him to be selfish, to not blame her. Tears streak her cheeks as she forces the kiss, hurting her teeth she pulls so hard, but she is smiling when she lets him go. 'I- we need this. I want you to do it. Just let me watch, OK?'

'OK, love.' Gary turns back toward the stage where he has his models pose. He takes off his shirt and slips off his trousers. The content of his work is explicit and the actors and students that perform are happy to follow his instruction for their pay. They act out what her Husband needs, be it covered in red paint or laying with each other while he sketches them. Most wives wouldn't accept live sex and the kind of debauched scenes that Gary has them act out for his work, but Lauren is not most wives. Lauren has modelled for him and adores how Gary would look at her, knowing that he has never gotten involved with his models and betrayed her in such a way; she is his Goddess. That's what people don't understand about their love, it is above everything else, they are each other's everything, no matter what that means giving up. She would do anything for her Gary and this is the next step. He whips the sheet away, revealing his next project and Lauren's prey.

'Wait.' Lauren orders Gary. He stops, muscles bunched and ready to follow her command. Lauren struggles up, weak after her ordeal but she has never felt more powerful. 'Angie?'

The woman is hogtied on a felt pedestal, hands and feet tied together behind her back, wearing nothing but her wedding ring. She is gagged and a head band is tight about her forehead, tied to the knots around her wrists, holding her head up. She struggles in her bonds but she has no range of motion. Her upper chest, back and shoulders are bandaged from where the Bull's horns pierced her, her nose is still broken. In this position she must be in an awesome amount of pain.

Lauren kneels and frames her old cell mate's face in both hands. 'I know what you're thinking. *This can't be happening! I don't deserve this!*' Lauren mocks in a high voice just as Angie did. 'Well, it is happening. And you do deserve it. You deserve it a hundred times over. So, we'll do this a hundred times and then see if we've settled up.' She nods to Gary. He positions himself and takes hold of his member to use in Lauren's name. He only has eyes for Lauren and he is hard in seconds. She smiles, proud he can do this thing for her. 'Nobody will ask questions, Angie. The police think you missing, maybe you went on the run after helping the Akoum's, or might be as dead as your shitbag Husband.' Lauren creaks over Angie's shaking form and kisses her man. 'This will be inspiration for your best work yet, love.'

'I love you, L.' Gary whispers back and begins his work.

Lauren lowers herself back into the chair, ready to watch with a light heart.

Printed in Great Britain
by Amazon